Resilient Transitions

Sec Guardians

By *Terry Charles*

Preface

More than a century ago our Sun was hit by a shooting neutron star.

The impact created a solar magnetic super flare a billion times greater than any coronal mass ejection or solar flare previously seen. The super flare, filled with radiation, sent a shock wave out into our solar system hitting the Earth killing billions of people, demolished cities and swept away the satellites that allowed us to communicate across the globe.

Once again those that survived did so with a resilient transition into today's world.

The oceans, protected for the most part by its reflective surface, have become the main source of food.

The Earth's rotation now spins at a slower rate than before causing the days to be longer and gravity to be weaker.

Governments fell leaving what few surviving private companies to forge ahead.

What was left of the policing agencies and armed forces transitioned into the new societies created and built by corporations that survived the financial hardships, rebuilding a handful of cities where laws were now enforced by the Sec Guardians.

Chapter 1

Another day, another L-mail, Torian thought as he opened his eyes.

His Comp's musical alarm slowly increased in volume to wake him up gently.

Through the sheers surrounding his bed he could see that the room was also getting brighter, as part of the Comp's attempt to raise him from his restful slumber.

"Shut up!" he groaned.

The music stopped instantly and the room fell into darkness. He closed his eyes with a slight smirk on his face in the hopes of drifting back to sleep; forgetting this was only a mild reprieve.

The Comp, not quite finished with its task, began to play music that sounded like a large orchestra with the volume loud enough to wake the dead. The lights in the room began flickering like a strobe light.

"All right, all right, I'm getting up!" he said admitting defeat.

The music lowered itself to a more tolerable level as the lights steadied to a dim morning light.

Torian heard what sounded like several young kids giggling coming from the Comp.

The Computer was an older model, about five years older than the one he used at the Lib, but with the two Comps integrated there was no need to replace it.

As he rolled out of bed, he could feel the warmth from the floor tiles that the Comp had turned on hearing the phrase: "I'm getting up."

He walked to the cleansing room where the wash and dry turned on automatically.

The warm water gave him a slight shivering sensation as he stepped in. The water changed to a soapy liquid after a minute or so, just long enough for him to scrub up and shampoo his hair then back to water. When he was ready he pushed the drying sequence that sent down a blast of warm air to dry him off.

He stepped out looking into the mirror so he could comb his brown hair. He noticed a few gray hairs and thought it made him look somewhat distinguished. The mustache and goatee helped give him a younger appearance then his age would hold him accountable too.

"Don't want to scare the younger crowd away," he thought to himself.

After shaving the old fashioned way (with an electric razor instead of the usual Laser Razor) he ambled over to the closet where he selected a simple brown pin-striped suit.

Before putting on his pants he replaced the inner lining with a fresh-scented innerwear.

A study had been conducted and determined that constant use of the same undergarments carried harmful bacteria to their wearer. Someone came up with the idea to just attach some innerwear inside the pants and put it on all at once. That way when you wanted to change you discarded the old innerwear and put in a new one. The same thing went for the innerwear in shoes.

Torian believed a man named Shorts invented the idea, "Go figure."

Anyway, it saved on time and they were biodegradable.

As he headed for the front door it slid open, "Later Comp" he said as he took his overcoat from the hook next to the door and exited his dwelling.

He could hear the sound of trumpets playing as he exited.

Torian headed down the lift to the Transport station stopping at the Info-stand to select an info-paper and a Coksi to drink on his way to work.

He swiped his Lib card then sat down to wait for the Tram to arrive.

People living within the city limits worked for one of the companies under the main corporation in charge of that city. Each employee had access to their company's funds. Anything that you needed to purchase you would just use your company wage card.

Of course depending on your position and the days per week you worked determined your wage limit.

As Torian opened the Coksi, he remembered reading an old article on his Comp at the Lib about the two soda companies fighting it out, both trying to do a hostile takeover of the other. Finally they merged and became the corporation to finance and control the city of Angeles.

Companies that had survived the disaster due to their having diversified their money throughout the world and being able to retrieve the funds from the institutions that still existed; merged with other companies to form corporations. They had the financial backing to rebuild and govern any city that they resurrected as it were. It was the way civilization had continued after the Devil's Tail.

"The Devil's Tail," Torian thought to himself.

More than a century ago our Sun was hit by a shooting neutron star.

The impact created a solar magnetic super flare a billion times greater than any coronal mass ejection previously seen. The super flare, filled with radiation, sent a shock wave out into our solar system hitting the Earth killing billions of people and demolished cities around the globe. It also swept away any and all aircraft out into orbit or smashed them to the ground; including satellites that were used to communicate around the world.

To this day debris floating around Earth's atmosphere still falls from the sky when least expected.

Animals on the surface of the planet suffered as well.

The surface of the oceans reflected the radiation protecting our main source of food.

The Earth's rotation now spinning at a slower rate than before caused the days to be longer and gravity to be weaker.

People grew taller, ran faster and were able to jump higher.

The neutron star was consumed becoming a new source of fuel for the Sun.

On Earth, those who survived continued on despite the harsher environmental conditions produced by the Earth's axis changing from the then twenty-three and half degrees to the now twenty-five.

Winters were colder and summers were increasingly hotter.

Civilization as it was once known had changed dramatically; leaving part of the world savage and the other half civilized.

"Maybe it wasn't that much different after all," Torian thought to himself, knowing a little something of Earth's history.

The star was believed to have come through the galaxy known as "Alpha Zen Tory."

The exact cause was of course unknown, but Torian believed that a hyper nova creating a neutron star close enough to a preexisting black hole generated a gamma ray burst sending the star through the hole and into our universe.

Although the Big Bang theory of how our universe was created had merit, Torian didn't believe it happened here.

While he did agree that the planets, stars, asteroids etcetera all came from a single point. Torian's hypothesis was that they came out the end of a black hole from another Universe.

The simplest description would be a boat caught in a whirlpool being sucked down into the vortex and the wreckage coming out the bottom.

We are the remnants from another universe, which doesn't sit well with our egos, since we like to think of ourselves as the beginnings of all existence.

Astronomers of the time named the shooting star the Devil's Tail due to the trail of dust, ice and debris streaming off of it for millions of miles before it impacted the Sun.

Torian continued to peruse the newest net sites in the paper to see where he could find last night's score from the Shield game.

He had a bet with Torian Mariah down in Diego that the Coksi team would beat the Magnasonics.

Just then he heard a man's voice some distance away getting louder, the voice seemed to be quite agitated.

Torian looked over and saw a man wearing a bright yellow suit, with hat and shoes to match. He could see that he was talking to a very provocatively dressed woman who reminded Torian of the Kers that walked the streets of Under-town. She was wearing a short black dress and red halter-top.

The man was pointing to a Sec Guardian standing near the entryway to the Tram.

Sec Guardians enforced the law within city limits and the Riffs patrolled the surrounding areas outside.

Police and military organizations had collapsed around the world along with the governments. The few that survived clashed before transitioning into the corporations that now controlled the cities.

Crimes, disputes or legal disagreements were judged by the Supremes and executed by the Sec Guardians.

The man in the yellow suit walked over to the Guardian.

Although the man was well dressed, Torian surmised that the man in the yellow suit was from Under-town as well.

The Guardian by the entry was wearing a dark red elastic suit that covered his body. Around his waist was a short black skirt, sort of like Hercules from Greek mythology had worn, but with black boots and gloves to match. This was the normal uniform of the Guardians.

The Guardian reminded Torian of one of the superheroes in an old comic book his mentor Chen had shown him when he was younger.

Though most superheroes had some part of their face covered to protect their true identity, the Sec Guardians face was completely covered by a monitor screen with a black hood over the top of their heads.

Communication was displayed on the screen for the viewer to read in any language necessary to communicate.

Torian could see the bright green makeshift eyes on the monitor screen even from where he was sitting that gave the Guardian some semblance of a face.

The man in yellow walked up to the Guardian and started shouting something about his brother being innocent of any charges brought against him by another Sec Guardian in Under-town.

"You're all a bunch of robots!" he yelled. "I'd like to catch you off duty sometime and kick your ass!"

At this the glowing eyes of the Guardian turned yellow and began to blink.

Torian could see the monitor screen was scrolling a message to the man in yellow but was too far away to read what it said.

The Tram had arrived in the Transport station.

Others, who had been observing the commotion as well, seemed relieved at the arrival of the Tram and walked quickly inside.

Torian got up and headed toward the Tram as well, but angled toward the confrontation.

As he walked he could see the young man was about six-one in height with broad shoulders and very lean, but paled in comparison to the Guardian who was the usual six foot ten and well-muscled.

As Torian got closer he could see that the words being displayed on the screen were in English.

At one point the young man raised his right hand and poked the Guardian in the abdomen while still complaining about the Guardians in general.

The Guardians blinking yellow eyes went to a steady red glow.

Torian was close enough now to see the screen displaying the words: "Ruling determined; Approved."

Using only his left hand, the Guardian grabbed the man's right wrist and shoved the man's index finger (the one he had poked the

Guardian with) up the man's own nose. The man fell to his knees as his eyes filled with tears.

The Ker who had been talking to the man prior to the incident said, "See what you get you idiot." She walked over to a public Comp, probably to call a Med-priest to assist the man in removing his finger from his nose.   Torian stepped onboard the Tram and sat down near the door to peer out a small window.   The Ker hopped on board right behind Torian just as the doors of the Tram slowly closed and sat down across from him in a huff, evidently not waiting with the "Idiot" for the Med-priest.   As Torian looked back through the window he could see the eyes on the Guardian's screen had gone back to green and the words: "Judgment Applied," displayed underneath.

Chapter 2

Mel Jenson walked into the Riff station heading for the locker room. She was still in her street clothes and needed to change into her uniformed fatigues.

As she got undressed Katelin Jones walked over to the locker next to hers.

KJ had come from the cleansing room with water still streaming down her ebony skin as she dried off.

KJ opened up her locker so that she could suit up for work as well.

"Hey Mel, how was your weekend?" KJ asked.

"Great! And how was yours KJ?"

"Not bad, I went into Angeles to a new nightclub they have there," KJ said. "It's called the Fish Bowl."

"I think I've heard about it," Mel replied.

Daniel Thompson came around the corner and saw the two female Riffs getting dressed. He took note of both Riffs being in good physical condition and having down right hot bodies.

KJ had short black hair and Mel had medium length blonde hair. Both were tall and part of Daniel's Riff unit.

Thompson snapped a towel at Mel's butt as he walked by.

"Nice assets you got Mel," Thompson said.

Mel straightened up quickly from the snap and said, "Go buy yourself a Ker Daniel, but she'll never be as good as me!"

Thompson laughed as he left the locker room.

KJ laughed too and said, "He's always horny. Get him a jar of peanut butter and put it in his locker. That will keep him busy for a day or two."

Mel smiled. She knew Thompson was only playing. He acted like a jerk sometimes but on more than one occasion she had trusted him with her life. Besides she had already picked out her mate for when she retired.

His name was Trent and even though he lived in the city they got to see each other several times a quarter. Occasionally they even got to work together on an investigation. That was how they had originally met.

The disaster had created a "New World blended with Old World charm" Trent would say to Mel. Luckily love and family were more important than ever before in order to repopulate the world as it now existed. Trent was the one Mel wanted to help with this process.

Mel finished zipping up the tan fatigues the Riffs wore, grabbed her weapons harness, and headed into briefing.

Captain Harding was at the podium getting ready to give out the optical data bulletins they would use in the UCV (Urban Command Vehicle).

Mel walked over and sat down next to O'Doul.

Jimmy O'Doul (the unit's leader) was sitting at the head of the table going over some paper work. His hair had a little gray in it and he stood about six feet tall, but carried with him an air of confidence and experience that made him a natural leader.

Thompson was sitting on the edge of one of the other tables chatting with Summer, one of the female Riffs from another unit. Thompson was about six-foot two and stocky like an ex-shield guard. He brought a sense of humor to the unit.

Thompson looked up at Captain Harding who had an impatient look on his face, so he went and sat down next to Jones, who had come in just after Mel.

The Captain looked around the room then started to give the morning briefing.

"We still don't know who the hackers are or how they have been ripping off the corporate big wigs. We think that maybe somehow their splicing into the conduits outside the city limits running from the power junctions into the city, but we're not sure. They could also be getting inside the city somehow and stealing software right out from under the corporation's noses. That's more the Sec Guardians responsibility, but outside the city is ours. So let's find out who is up to this and put a stop to it."

Captain Harding started handing out the data discs.

"There are a few outstanding warrants on these particular marauders to be brought before a Sec Guardian, so if you see-em, hook-em and book-em."

The Captain left the room and the Riffs got up and headed outside to their assigned UCV's.

Knowing they would be out for the next few days, the unit double-checked their equipment and made sure they had enough provisions.

The UCV was the

size of what used to be known as a recreational vehicle or RV.

Trent had told Mel once that people would travel in RV's for pleasure. They would go to places so they could camp in luxury, almost as if they hadn't even left home, except the scenery was different.

How weird, Mel thought at the time. She was aware of people living in trailers that size as a matter of necessity or survival not luxury. With wild animals roaming free and the ever present raids from wandering marauders, these thin aluminum or steel trailers were all people had to provide some semblance of safety. Very few buildings if any were ever rebuilt outside the restored city limits. There weren't enough people on Earth to use the dilapidated structures anyway.

If there were enough trailers together the outlanders would align them in circles for protection. These settlements were strewn throughout the surrounding areas and some became permanent.

Despite the danger, people that choose this lifestyle claimed they needed their space or more freedom without the weight of corporations dictating their lives.

The Riffs falling under the supervision of the Supremes were allowed the leeway of making decisions in the field when dealing with the protection of the outer boundaries of each city. Not being in direct contact with the Supremes though meant that their decision could be questioned at a later date.

Mel climbed into the UCV and sat in the front right passenger seat.

Jones was already in her seat behind Mel and looking at her Comp plotting their course for the day.

KJ put in the disc that Captain Harding had given her as O'Doul came in and sat in the driver's seat. Thompson came in last as usual.

"Are we there yet?" Thompson said as he sat down on the bench seat behind O'Doul.

O'Doul, who hadn't spoken a word during the briefing, replied to Thompson's inquiry.

"Almost, we're just this side short of finding the rainbow that will take us all to our pot of gold."

Chapter 3

Torian sitting next to the small window watched the walls rushing by as the Tram moved through the subterranean tunnels.

Every now and again he could see some message that a tunnel tagger had put along the wall for onlookers to try and read, but once the Tram got up to speed it was all just a blur.

He slid his Lib card through the microreader in the arm of the seat pulling down the Comp that was embedded into the seat in front of him, so that it would drop just above his knees. He flipped up the top and the screen came on showing the time, date and approximate year.

Torian typed in his CIN (Corporate Identification Number) to access the Outernet and connect securely to the Comp at the Lib.

He entered one of the net sites that he had found in the paper and up popped the site on the screen.

He saw that the Angeles Coksi team had indeed won against the Diego Magnasonics, but only by ten points. The point spread wasn't what he had predicted, but his team had won and it would be fun to L-mail Mariah and razz her a little.

The Shield games were played on a hundred-yard field set up in five-yard increments.

There was an offense and a defense. All the players were dressed in padded uniforms and helmets to protect them from falls or being hit in the head with the ball. The pitcher and all eligible receivers had catching mitts on.

When the center delivered the ball from the line of scrimmage to the pitcher he could either underhand toss the ball to a half or full back or throw it to one of his receivers running down field. If a receiver caught the ball he would head for the end zone.

In the end zone there was a hoop hanging down between two poles about twenty feet up in the air. The object was to throw the ball through the hoop without being tackled.

There was a shield guard on the defensive team that had a shield the size of a trashcan lid that he would toss up in the air to block the offenses attempt to throw the ball through the hoop and score. Hence the name Shield games.

Chen had been the Torian in Angeles before him and was his mentor.

Chen had told him that the Shield game was a cross between two games that had been played a long, long time ago.

Chen took Torian to the Shield games when he was younger and talked about all sorts of things that had existed prior to the Devil's Tail. Most of the time Torian would be so intent on listening to Chen that he would miss most of the game.

The Tram pulled into the downtown Transport station.

Torian got up and walked out, noticing the Ker exiting the Tram as well. He watched her walk to the lift that would take her to Under-town.   For some reason she glanced over her shoulder at him as she stepped onto the lift.   He headed to a separate lift that would take him up to the fiftieth floor where he would take the wind tube to the building connected to it a block away and then down to street level to the Lib next to it.

On the fiftieth floor of most buildings downtown, there were tubes that connected to other buildings in the city. Most buildings were seventy stories high or taller.

You could take the people conveyer at street level to other buildings along the street, but that would take him longer to get to the Lib.

The lighter gravity made it easier to lift heavy materials and rebuild cities taller than they were before.

Initially after the Devil's Tail had collided with the Sun, getting around was done on foot. Vehicles such as trains, planes and automobiles were on the surface disintegrating creating the need for new transportation systems underground.

Many of the subways that had been beneath the surface had survived and were now extended throughout the UCA (United Corporations of America). They had been retrofitted with monorails for less maintenance and faster speeds. They extended across the UCA to connect with other cities.

There were even Transport tunnels laid across the bottom of the oceans to get to other continents or you could ride in zeppelins.

As Torian exited the lift he walked over to the wind tube. He stepped inside and felt weightless as a strong cushion of air swept under him in the direction of the building he was going too. This allowed him too semi-float through the tube.

As he reached the end of the tube he felt the cushion of air subside as he gently stepped out of the tube and onto the floor. He then took the lift down to the first floor of the building and then outside to the Lib located next door.

As Torian entered the outer office he couldn't help but notice the low cut V-neck dress that his assistant was wearing.

It was a light shade of blue and fit snuggly around her. It also offered a nice view of her cleavage. Bonnie feeling a presence behind her turned around and smiled at her boss.

"Good morning!"

"Good morning," he replied looking into her blue eyes then peeking down at the matching cleavage in front.

"See anything you'd like? To read that is," Bonnie said holding up some books and smiling.

"Not yet. I have to go through my L-mails first. But thanks for the offer. I'll keep you--I mean them--I mean the books in mind," Torian added with a playful grin.

"I'll bet you will," she laughed and turned back around to continue her filing.

Torian continued on into his own office and sat down at his desk to start the mundane task of reading L-mail.

Chapter 4

O'Doul had headed east through the rubble of what used to be several cities along the foothills of the Dino Mountains. Nothing much lived in or around this area so he headed north toward V-Ville.

O'Doul wanted to check some of the unmanned Outernet power junctions to make sure there hadn't been any vandalism.

The power junction he was heading too contained conduits that ran from Angeles through V-Ville and on to Vegas.

After a couple of hours on the road O'Doul drove the UCV up next to the power junction he had come to check out.

Mel got up out of her seat pushing a button on the dashboard and stepped outside to take a look around.

The building was at one time a house that had been converted into the power junction.

It held a few generators that were connected to windmills that had been set up in the area to supply energy from the wind to the junction.

Mel walked over to the door pulling out her access card but noticed what looked like pry marks on the door jam. With her gloves on she pulled on the door handle to see if it was open. Sure enough it was. She went inside and could tell that someone had been in there recently due to the footprints on the dusty floor. The room was barely lit and smelled of the dust that filtered in from the surrounding dessert. The desk with the Comps' on it was also dusty. Except for smudge marks on the table next to the Comp that routed info from Vegas to Angeles.

Mel looked around the room a little more then went back outside looking down at the ground around the building. She noticed tire tracks next to the opposite side of the station that they had stopped at.

With the wind constantly blowing in the dessert, sand usually covers any types of tracks within a day or so. The imprints in the ground that the tire tracks had made were still fresh.

Mel followed the tracks for about twenty feet and saw that they were heading north.

She walked back to the UCV and told O'Doul what she had observed.

O'Doul told Mel to "Get in" and he put the UCV in motion following the tracks.

The Riffs were heading along an old highway toward an area called Red Mountain when Jones said, "I think we've got some movement on radar, but I'm having trouble locking on to it."

"Check the GPO for our position to try and verify the distance between the object and us," O'Doul told her.

Jones looked at the Global Positioning Outernet.

The GPO system combined a receiver with a microprocessor that measured the differential between a GPO dish signal being sent and received and then calculated the distance from the Outernet dish back to the GPO. Using three separate signals it then triangulated the latitude and longitude of the GPO in the UCV and any other object added to the program.

GPO dishes had been placed atop mountains disguised as trees.

Jones checked her monitor, "I think the object has stopped."

Mel got up and looked over KJ's shoulder at the screen while Thompson kicked back in his seat with his head bouncing up and down to music coming from his headset.

O'Doul pulled off the highway they had been on and headed down a dirt road in the direction of the object Jones had seen on radar.

"It's still sitting there, I think?" Jones said with some frustration. "There is some interference or maybe they're using some type of jamming device, but something is there."   Mel went back up to the front and sat in the chair next to O'Doul pushing another button on the dash for the forward telescope to turn on distorting a small portion of the windshield so that it magnified and focused in on the area were the object was. Mel turned a knob to zoom in the telescoping lens as she looked at the windshield display.

"I see what looks like a dune buggy sitting next to that outcropping of rocks."

O'Doul headed in the direction Mel was pointing and as they got closer he could see the outline of the rocks and buggy.

He pulled the UCV over to the side of the road approximately fifty feet from the buggy and hit the button for the door to open so he could step outside.

Mel followed behind him.

Jones took Mel's seat looking at the display, using a joystick on the console to scan the area and yelled out, "No movement around the buggy that I can see. I'll try the P.A." (Public Address)

Jones picked up the Microphone hoping anyone within earshot

might get spooked into revealing themselves.

"We are from the Riff's station! Step out into view for inspection!"

Two men came out from behind the rocks and made a dash for the buggy.

"Now where do you think they are going in such a hurry?" O'Doul asked.

"Not sure," Mel replied. "Do you think we should ask them?"

"Yes, but politely."

"You got it," Mel said with a smile.

As the two men started up the buggy it kicked up dirt as it sped off.

Mel pulled out her combat G-club from her harness and extended it, then took out one of her short range Mag-balls and placed it on the ground.

O'Doul took out a small pair of binoculars, "I'd say they're about fifty yards or so now."

Mel already in her stance swayed her hips, as she looked in the direction of the speeding buggy and then down at the Mag-ball. She then lifted the club back and took a swing. She hit the Mag-ball with a fairly straight arc toward the escaping buggy.

The hit had activated the device inside the Mag-ball so that it would home in on the metal buggy and attached itself to part of the frame. Once the ball made contact Mel pushed a button on her belt that sent a signal to the ball emitting a high voltage current through the frame of the buggy and shorting out the engine. The Mag-ball continued to emit a current through the metal frame of the buggy preventing the two from exiting the vehicle.

"Was that polite enough?" Mel asked.

"I do believe they've decided to wait for us after all." O'Doul laughed heading toward the rocks where the two men had come from.

Chapter 5

The screen on Torian's Comp lit up as if aware of his presence.

He entered in his password, "Melanie," and as he hit the enter key with his left hand he placed the fingertips of his right hand at his chin and opened his hand as he made a counterclockwise circle around his face.

The Comp accepted both the password typed in and the gesture that meant beautiful in sign language.

There were several L-mails from other Torians' from around the world including one from the Torian in Diego. He moved the cursor to that one first and clicked it. It began with an optical video of last night's Shield game. A commentator was narrating the scene: "The Magnasonics have the ball. The pitcher is going back to throw. He throws. Oh no! Interception by the Coksi team! Number forty-three, Wilkerson, has it. He's heading for the Magnasonics end zone. Ten yards out and Wilkerson throws the ball. Number sixty-five, Timmons the Magnasonics Shield guard, tosses up the shield. He misses the block! Wilkerson makes it through the hoop. He scores! Coksi team wins thirty-six to twenty-six."

The playback flickered and was replaced with the face of his childhood friend Mariah.

"Okay you win. Next time you're down this way you can pick out one of the artifacts in the basement as your prize. Talk to you later," Mariah had said.

The L-mail ended and the screen went blank.

L-mail was of course laser light frequencies sent through optical lines in conduits underground. The use of radio frequencies from Outernet dishes in nearby mountains was also used as a form of communication, but not as reliable.

Before the Devil's Tail, electronic mail was sent over the Internet through telephone lines or satellites in orbit around the Earth. Afterwards phone lines had come apart and satellites having been swept away created a need for a way to communicate.

The Outernet was designed with optical laser mail and graphics providing instant images of either the sender or the information they included in their L-mail.

The next L-mail he looked at was from the Torian in Toyo.

"*Moshi moshi* Torian-san. (Hello Torian)" "*Ogenki desu ka*? (How are you?)" "Ohisashiburi desu (It's been a long time)," the recorded voice of Hara came through the speakers. "I have something to show you."

A black and white recording of an old 8mm movie with several B-29 prop planes flying past Mount Fuji (circa 1945) appeared as an optical image on the screen.

Hara continued to speak. "I have heard some rumors that one of the *kaisha no juyaku* (company executives) had some industrial espionage within his company in Vegas. This is no good for international ties between corporations. If you hear any news of this or have information please let me know. *Sayonara*. (Goodbye)" Hara's voice ended.

Hara had been one of Torian's first contacts as he was learning the ropes as it were to becoming a Torian. Hara was also a good friend of Chen, Torian's mentor.

It was not like him to be so brief in an L-mail. Usually he talked about the weather or what he had taught his grandchildren that day, so Torian knew something was bothering him.

Torian pressed a button on the desk. The door to his office opened and in walked Bonnie.

"Yes dear, I mean sir.

"Close the door if you would Bonnie."

Her smile now turned to an expression of concern as she closed the door and sat down in the chair by the side of the desk.

"I received a message from Hara," Torian said. "He was very short and to the point." Bonnie's eyebrows lifted a bit. "You believe he is worried?" she asked.

"Yes, but why? I don't suppose you've heard anything amongst the other assistants?"

"No! But I'll make some inquiries."

"Thanks Bonnie." She got up and headed for the door. "By the way, they match very nicely." Bonnie turned and looked down the front of her dress. "You're blue earrings and your eyes." Torian said sincerely. Bonnie smiled but the concern was still there. "Thanks for noticing you old smoothie." She walked back out to her desk closing the door behind her.

He was curious about the image that Hara had sent him so he

pulled up some old newspaper clippings that the Lib kept on disc from that time period.

After some time he found what he was looking for. He found an article by Strebig, James J. "Super fortresses Ranged Far to Become Key War Tool Against Japs," from _The Montana Standard, 14_ Aug. 1945.

There was a picture on the front of the article that matched the old 8mm movie that Hara had sent in his L-mail.

The article talked about the use of B-29 bomber planes used against the Japanese during World War II and how the Wright engine known as the Cyclone 18 was made and put into the B-29's to travel the distance from the then United States.

Knowing Hara, he was trying to tell Torian something with the movie he had sent, but how this was connected to the espionage he had mentioned Torian wasn't quite sure.

Chapter 6

As the UCV closed the distance to the disabled dune buggy; Mel could see the two men inside looking back over their shoulders. Their gloved hands raised slightly above their heads with the palms facing the back of the vehicle to show that they had no weapons in them.

"They've done this before," Thompson said looking out the window.

"Seems that way," Mel replied.

Thompson had driven the UCV from where they had originally stopped the buggy while O'Doul checked out the area around the rock outcropping.

"Fresh Meat," Thompson said with a devilish grin.

He drove the UCV up to about ten yards behind the buggy and stopped, waiting for Jones to report.

"No other contacts in the surrounding area," Jones said looking at the monitor in front of her.

Thompson reached over pushing the door button and headed outside toward the two men. Mel stepped out as well.

About three yards away from the buggy, Thompson yelled out, "License, registration, and proof of insurance." He always liked saying that even though people didn't need a license or permits to drive.

The driver looked back over his shoulder.

"Sorry mate, just having a bit of a look about that's all. Just having a look at your fine country, right mate?" the driver said, looking over at the passenger in the seat next to him as if the question were more of a signal.

At this, the two men hopped out of the buggy and headed toward the Riffs.

The gloves they had on were made of rubber that protected them from the electric current that was still going through the frame of the buggy. They had been waiting for the Riffs to get closer before making their move.

The driver headed for Thompson. Using his right hand he pulled out a six-inch knife from a sheath on his belt loop and was pointing it in Thompson's direction.

The passenger had grabbed a crowbar in his right hand and was heading for Mel.

"You want to play?" Thompson said to the driver with a playful look.

"That's right mate, just a bit of mumble peg with your face is all."

The driver made several slashing motions with the knife. He got within three feet of Thompson and drew back his hand thrusting forward with the knife.

Thompson waited until the knife came within inches of his face then sidestepped to his left grabbing the driver's right wrist and kicking him in the midsection with his right boot. The driver distracted from the kick allowed Thompson to step in underneath the driver's right elbow with his left shoulder and while still holding the driver's wrist, yanked down on the driver's arm. The drivers elbow made a cracking sound and the knife fell from his hand. The driver let out a yelp and tried to pull away but Thompson was already ducking under the man's arm yanking it up behind him. The driver let out another gasp of pain as Thompson took out a pair of handcuffs.

"You have the right to tell me everything you know; from the first girl's blouse you put your hand up to the last time you took a dump. You have the right to be taken before a Sec Guardian. Anything you say, can and will be used against you. You have the right to confess now or later. Now, having these rights in mind, would you care to share your life's story with me? If so, you can start by telling me what the hell you were thinking when you came at me with that oversized toothpick!"

After the cuffs were on the driver, Thompson looked over to see if Mel needed any help. She was standing over the passenger who was lying face down on the ground with his hands cuffed behind his back. Her right foot was placed in the small of his back as he squirmed from side to side. "What took you so long?" Mel asked Thompson with a big grin. "Just getting my morning calisthenics in," Thompson replied.

Back at the outcropping of rocks O'Doul had started looking around at several rocks that seemed to have been dragged through the dirt and placed in a pile.

He walked up to take a closer look and noticed something shiny underneath. He moved some of the rocks and could see a plastic container of some sort. He moved a few more rocks then lifted up the lid of the container where he could see a portable Comp and a stack of microchips inside.

"Well now, I do believe I've found me pot of gold after all."

He picked up what looked like an access card from inside the container and put it in his vest pocket, then picked up the container heading in the direction of his unit.

Chapter 7

As the day went by; Torian continued to receive L-mails from other Torians'.

"Hola, senor Torian," came from the Comp's speaker as Torian viewed the next L-mail. The voice was that of the Torian from Mex City.

"Cuanto mas amigos, mas claros? (Let there be, no secrets between friends?) *Vio con Dios* (Go with God)." The picture ended as abruptly as it started.

"This is getting weird," he thought to himself. Something is definitely going on and everyone has gotten wind of it but him.

Just then there was a tap on the door as it opened.

"Yes?"

Bonnie came in and handed him an envelope.

"This came for you special delivery."

"Thanks Bonnie."   "You're more than welcome. Also the chitchat is that one of the corporations outside Angeles has put a hit out on whoever is hijacking some of their technology. Apparently they're not going to let this go by way of the Guardians. I'll let you know if I get anything more significant."

                              "That sounds pretty significant to me," Torian replied.   "I'm going to get a bite to eat. Want me to bring you back a little something?" Bonnie asked as she ran her hand down the side of her dress.

                              Torian smiled, "If I get hungry for dessert, I'll give you a ring." "Make it a diamond and I'm yours forever. Oh heck, I'm yours anyway. See-ya!" Bonnie replied with a smile.   "Bye Bonnie."

He opened the envelope and inside was an invitation from the CEO (Chief Executive Officer) of Kofu Electronics Corporation.

Mail or letters were a thing of the past. But for privacy sake couriers would sometimes deliver messages from one place to another.

Kofu was one of the major distributors of microchips in the UCA.

Torian had been invited to a dinner party in Vegas. He wondered why the CEO of Kofu had invited him to dinner. Then it dawned on him.

The L-mail that Hara had sent him with Mount Fuji in the background was a clue to the company executive Hara had mentioned.

Fuji was one of the companies' combined to form Kofu.

The dinner was to be held on Saturday night at Kofu's corporate office in Vegas.

If he decided to go he would invite Melanie to go with him. That way if the party was boring the two of them could check out a casino or two.

He put the envelope in the trash and laid the invitation on top of the Comp. That way he would remember to ask Melanie if she was interested in going next time they corresponded.

The creaking sound of a door opening came from his Comp. He saw that Chen had just logged on to the Outernet.

A window popped up on his screen asking if he cared to chat. He clicked on the reply button to accept the live feed and the face of his mentor came into view on his screen.

"*Ni hao* (Hello)," Chen said. "How is my favorite student?"

"*Hen hao, xiexie, Ni ne*? (Very well, thanks, and you?)" Torian replied.

The face of his mentor Chen was that of a little old Chinese man with white hair, mustache and long goatee. The kind of face that had centuries of wisdom all over it.

"I am concerned for your wellbeing, my *xuesheng* (student)."

"You know something I do not yet know? My laoshi (mentor)," Torian replied.

"*Wo xiang qu kan qiusai!* (I'd like to see a ballgame!)"

"*Wo dong* (I understand)," Torian replied.

Chen winked and then said, "*Zai jian, xuesheng.*"

"Goodbye," Torian said to Chen as the sound of a door slamming shut came through the speaker.

Although Chen had retired many years ago he stayed in contact with other Torians' around the world. This was Torian's opportunity to find out what the heck was going on. Maybe even turn it around and start sending some L-mails himself.

Chapter 8

The driver and passenger were now sitting on the ground with their backs up against the UCV.

Thompson was standing in front of them with an electronic notepad taking notes and then pictures to run through the SCIS (Supreme Criminal Identification System) while Mel was searching the dune buggy. She had already turned off the Mag-ball and retrieved it.

"Looks like some fancy equipment in here for a couple of local marauders," Mel yelled out loud. "Not sure what this thing does?" she said noticing a box on the floorboard that had a cable running to a small dish on the dash.

"We'd better have Jones look at this." Mel said looking back over at Thompson then saw O'Doul walking over to Thompson with some sort of a container.

"Look what I found," O'Doul said.

"Looks like that pot of something you're always talking about," Thompson replied.

Just then Jones yelled out from the UCV. "We've got Company."

"What direction?" O'Doul yelled back.

"From the north and northwest," KJ replied.

O'Doul and Mel both looked northwards as Mel back stepped toward the UCV.

Several vehicles were approaching that were bigger than the dune buggy, about the size of small trucks. They were black with tinted windows and had shiny chrome grills in front.

"Not something you normally see this far out," Mel said.

"Maybe they brought lunch?" Thompson chimed in.

"Just as long as we aren't the main course," O'Doul added.

The trucks came to a stop about five yards in front of the dune buggy in a semi-circle in front of the Riffs. There were four trucks in all with two men stepping out from each truck. Each of the men was dressed in black fatigues and wearing sunglasses.

"You're all under arrest!" Thompson yelled to the men in black. "Unless of course you brought pizza and beer." he added.

One of the men walked over to O'Doul.

"*Konnichiwa* (Good afternoon). I believe you have retrieved something that belongs to us."

The man in black pointed to the plastic container that O'Doul had set down on the ground in front of him.

"What this? O'Doul said tapping the container with his boot. "No, this belongs to those fellows over there," O'Doul said pointing to the men in cuffs.

"By the way, did you know you were interfering with a Riff investigation?" he said becoming more serious.

"*So to wa, omoimasen*. I don't think so, O'Doul-san," he repeated in English.

"See they did bring beer. He's so drunk you can't even understand him," Thompson said making fun of the accent.

"You know my name, but I don't know yours?" O'Doul said to the man in black.

"I am *Ichi Ban*."

"I believe that means Number One in Japanese," Mel clarified.

The other men from the trucks were moving closer to the Riffs.

"Ah shit, clones! You know I hate clones," Thompson said as he got a better look at the men in black. The men approaching all looked exactly alike.

"I thank you for finding these men and the items they have taken from us," Number One continued. "We do not wish to press charges, as you would say. You may simply leave them with us and we will show them the error of their ways."

The driver of the dune buggy spoke up. "Bloody hell, you can break my other arm if you wish. Just don't leave us with those slant-eyed Dobie's."

"Enough of this crap," Thompson said as he walked toward one of the clones nearest him.

"I don't know which number you are, but you look like the number two I wiped off my boot this morning." Thompson took another step toward the man in front of him. The man immediately stepped back in a fighting stance.

"That's right, bring it on with your bad self," Thompson said as he also took a fighting stance.

"*Mada desu* (Not yet)," Ichi Ban said to the other clone.

"Stand down," O'Doul ordered Thompson.

"Ah shucks dad, you never let me have any fun." Thompson said kicking the dirt and stepping back over by the UCV.

O'Doul made a hand gesture toward the container. "It's all yours."

"*Hai* (Yes)." Number One stepped forward and bent over to pick up the container.

O'Doul pulled his nine-millimeter handgun smoothly from his holster and rested the barrel on top of Number One's head.

"Well, as you can plainly see I am not in the habit of handing over recovered property or releasing criminals to criminals."

The rest of the clones reached behind their backs each pulling out small sub-machine guns and pointing them at the Riffs.

Mel withdrew her 9mm from her holster and pointed it toward the nearest clone.

Thompson standing next to the UCV hit a panel that exposed an M-16 with an M-203 grenade launcher mounted under the barrel. He took it from the panel and slid the action on it pointing it toward the clone he called Number Two.

A sound of hydraulics came from the top of the UCV as a platform raised up with Jones sitting behind a pair of M-60 machine guns mounted on a swivel turret. She drew back the lever and pivoted it toward the rest of the men in black.

"Your turn," O'Doul said to Number One.

But before Number One could respond a loud beeping sound came from the trucks and the UCV simultaneously. Some of the clones looked skyward as the audible alarm continued.

Ichi Ban backed up slowly saying, "*Oitoma shimasu*? I must go, for now?" he repeated in English.

"Yes, it is getting late, isn't it," O'Doul replied.

Number One turned and headed for the black truck that he had arrived in.

The rest of the clones retreated as well with their guns still out and pointing in the Riffs direction.

As the trucks started to drive away, Mel holstered her weapon and took out her G-club. Dropping a tracking Mag-ball on the ground, she nonchalantly extended the club and hit the ball toward the truck that Number One had gotten in.

As it rolled underneath it hopped up from the ground and attached itself to the underside of the truck's frame.

"Thought we'd keep an eye on our friend *One*," Mel said to O'Doul.

"I agree," O'Doul replied.

As the trucks drove away the Riffs started looking skyward as well.

From out of the sky a Cessna prop plane dropped down where one of the black trucks had been parked. Except for the now smashed undercarriage the plane looked almost new. The paint had been scorched and there was steam coming from the hot metal of the engine, almost as if it had just landed with some engine problems. The reality was that the plane had been floating around in the atmosphere before it finally fell back to earth.

"I think that's what you call a one point landing," Thompson said looking at the fallen plane and then in the air for anything else that might come falling down.

The beeping sound that had come from the UCV and trucks was an alarm notifying them that some sort of debris was falling from the sky in there vicinity.

Chapter 9

As the day came to an end and after putting in his usual ten hours at the office, Torian started getting ready to leave. He thought about how the day went quickly while working at the Lib.   Since the Earth's revolution had slowed the days were longer and counted by thirty hours instead of twenty-four. People working a ten-hour day made it easier to schedule rotations in three work shifts. Although he was the only Torian for Angeles there were other people to help visitors that came to the Lib.   The down side to the longer days meant that people's life expectancy was shorter, which is why most people retired when they were around thirty five years old.   They could start a family if their reproductive genes were safe to do so.

                    Population growth was important and raising children without having to leave for work or put a child in a care facility as it had been so long ago was the way families now existed.   The up side (if you could call it that) was that around sixty-five years old people would pass away not having suffered from the ailments such as poor health, Alzheimer's and most internal cancers. Their lives would be full of accomplishments coupled with being an intricate part of their children's lives as well.   Although some people used modern technology to replace damaged body parts, you didn't find to many people over sixty-five. Some people even worked online from home while raising their family, usually when another family was mentoring their kids for a week or so. That way they were still a resource to the company they had worked for.

                    Then when their children were old enough, they could go back to work if they choose to, or just continue to enjoy their retirement.   Chen once told Torian that the human race had caught up in "dog years" whatever that meant. Chen had been a good contact for Torian's father, so much so, that they had become the best of friends.   Chen seeing the potential in Torian at a very young age, offered to help with his education. Not only did this bring fun and amusement to Torian but prepared him for his becoming a Torian. Maybe that's what his father and Chen had planned all along.

                    Chen had quite a collection of old artifacts in his private collection as well as at the Lib. Chen also carried with him the knowledge that went with each, which is why he made such a good

Torian to begin with.

"History is the one thing you can always count on," Chen would tell him. "Learn of it and it shall guide your future."

I guess that is why every city had a <u>Lib</u>-rary and at least one his-<u>Torian</u> to manage it.   Also fewer inhabitants on the earth now meant our present knowledge came from studying our past.   The corporations all contributed to the Libs' of course so that in return the current Torian would research any information or past documentation that was requested.   Some inquiries even came from other continents when Torians' there did not have that specific information.   After he decided that being a Torian would be awesome, he began learning different languages that would come to good use when communicating with the world around him.   It also was a very prestigious position and held in high regard amongst corporations, which may be why he had been invited to the party at Kofu Electronics.   Occasionally a CEO would invite him to attend gatherings or parties as a pretense to asking him to personally research something for that corporation, confidentially of course.

Torian faced his Comp and placing the palm of the right open hand in front of his face he moved it down to chin level bringing the fingers together. This signaled his Comp to go into sleep mode.

Torian got up and headed for the door.

Outside Bonnie was also preparing to leave.

"Thanks for your help today, Bonnie."

"You're welcome honey--I mean boss."

"Are you going out tonight?" he asked.

"Yes. I hear there's a new nightclub called the Fish Bowl. I plan on going around 25:00. Maybe I'll see you there?" she said with a hopeful glint in her eye.

"I'll probably just get some dinner and then head home. I didn't hear from Melanie today. It isn't like her not to take the time to try and contact me or leave a message on the Comp. Unless of course she is involved in something that demands her imitate attention."

"She's a very lucky girl to have a hunk of man such as you. I keep hoping she'll dump you so I can have dibs on you myself." she said with a wink.

"Good night Bonnie," he said with a slightly embarrassed look on his face.

"It could be?" she replied raising her eyebrow and lifting her right shoulder (in a follow me) sort of way. She turned and sashayed out the door.

Chapter 10

The Riffs had put their prisoners in holding cells on board the UCV.

Jones had used a can of "Quick Cast Foam Spray," on the driver's arm, to keep it immobile until a Med-priest could look at it. Then she sat down at her monitor to keep an eye on Number One's truck, courtesy of Mel's tracking Mag-ball.

"We're not going to make it back to the Riff station before nightfall, are we?" Mel asked already knowing the answer.

"No. I'm heading further north toward a place we can camp for the night." O'Doul said. "I'm heading for an old naval station near China Lake."

"They aren't following us. The trucks drove about a mile then stopped. I think they wanted to know for sure which way we were going," Jones said still keeping an eye on Number One's dot on the radar screen.

The Riffs traveled for about an hour or so before reaching the old base.

"Looks like the main gate up ahead." O'Doul said as they approached the base. "Not much left but a lot of rusted fencing surrounding it."

"See anything up ahead of us?" O'Doul asked Jones.

"No, nothing outside, but I can't be sure about inside the buildings this far away," she replied.

Daylight was fading away as Mel sat down in the front seat next to O'Doul and turned on the front night scope. She used the FLIR (Field Laser Infrared) to detect any heat signatures being emitted from the buildings as they got closer.

"Not showing any signs of anything in or around the buildings," Mel said.

"I'm heading for one of the old airplane hangars where we can park inside for the night," O'Doul said as he drove into a building big enough to hold several UCVs'.

Thompson hit the button for the door and headed out to have a look around while Mel went back to check on the prisoners.

O'Doul also went out but to check on the dune buggy that they had towed behind the UCV. He unhitched the buggy and backed it up a ways, just in case they needed to leave quickly.

Jameson, the driver of the dune buggy, was checking out the splint that Jones had put on his right arm. He looked up at Mel through the clear holding cell door.

"Well now, if it isn't one of the she-la's come to kiss me goodbye. I'll be out of here in a bit. Will you miss me?" Jameson asked Mel.

"What makes you think you're leaving so soon?" Mel replied.

"Well you see, me mates are out looking for the two of us by now. They come from a long line of trackers and could follow the tracks left by this old barge blindfolded." He hit the wall behind him with his good arm referring to the UCV as he spoke.

"Well, I hope you don't mind company then," Mel said, "we only have two cells and some of you will have to share." She turned and walked back up front.

"Still nothing," Jones said as Mel walked behind her, referring to the area around them still being clear.

O'Doul had looked around the front entrance to the hangar and was headed back toward the UCV.

"Have you seen Thompson?" O'Doul asked Mel.

"No, I just came out," she replied.

"Thompson, you read?" O'Doul said into his Microphone. "Daniel, do you copy?" O'Doul asked again.

"Jones, do you have a fix on Thompson?" O'Doul said into his Mic.

Jones checked the FLIR to see if she could get a fix on Thompson's location.   "No, he's not on the scope;" Jones radioed back to O'Doul.   "Damn, what is he getting into now," Mel said. "I'll look around back."

Mel headed toward the rear of the hangar and out a back door. As she was walking away from the door Mel noticed some movement out of the corner of her eye over by a big pile of rubbish. She headed for the pile and when she came within five feet of it she heard a growling noise.

"Daniel? That better be your stomach making that noise?" From behind the rubbish pile a dog the size of a bullmastiff came out. His eyes bloodshot and was drooling from the mouth.   Mel started backing up slowly.

"Nice puppy dog, nice doggy."

The dog stepped toward her, its growl increasing to a snapping bark.

"The way you're acting you must have an upset tummy. Did you eat Thompson? Did yah boy?"

Mel continued backing up. She began to reach for her handgun very slowly, when another dog, about six feet to her right started growling. The dog to her right had two heads, one barking at her, while the other looked at the bullmastiff as if waiting for instructions.

Mel spoke into her Mic. "I could use some help back here," she said with a nervous laugh.

Just then another dog showed up to her left.

"Shit. Will someone get back here? And bring a bazooka with you," Mel said into her Mic.

The dogs stopped growling, their attention now focused behind them and to the left. They took off in retreat up the hill behind the rubbish pile.

Mel stopped and looked to her right wondering what was scarier than three and a half dogs. Thompson was running full speed toward Mel with his M-16 in his hands.

He slowed up as he got closer to Mel and said with a huff, "If you're looking to pet something, I'm available," Thompson said with a grin.

"Where the heck have you been?" Mel asked.

Thompson lifted his left hand and made a follow me gesture with his forefinger just as O'Doul came running around the backside of the hanger. Both Thompson and Mel raised their weapons in O'Doul's direction then pointed the weapons downward.

O'Doul slowed up and said, "Hey, I'm on your side," as he lowered his handgun.

"Now what have you two been up to?" O'Doul asked.

Again, Thompson made the gesture to follow him and they walked toward a bunker in the side of the hill where Thompson had come from. It had two big steel double doors with the one on the right open. The left one had an old rusted sign on it that read, "Area 48."

Chapter 11

Torian floated along inside the wind tube to the building down the street. It held a Modern Food Theater where he could choose from a variety of cuisines.

There were two boys sitting near the end of the wind tube hoping to catch a glimpse up some unsuspecting ladies dress that had taken the wind tube by mistake.

Their faces showed disappointment as Torian exited. Guess he wasn't exactly whom they were hoping for and couldn't help but laugh to himself.

He couldn't decide whether to get cooked fish or Sushi, so he opted for some breaded shrimp. He then took a seat near a window to look out at the Pacific Ocean.

Torian had seen a picture in the Lib's achieves of Angeles and how far it used to be from the ocean. But now it was about a mile or so from the city.

Something caught his attention outside so he looked up and could see what looked like a man falling. It was one of the Sec Guardians gliding through the air.

The Guardian was riding what looked like an old-fashioned snowboard. His arms were out to his sides and Torian could see the stretch of material that was between the Guardian's arms providing lift and giving him a controlled descent. Sort of like wings under the arms of a bat.

He seemed to guide himself using the board and the makeshift wings to land on a slide extending out and into an opening that was set on the side of the building across the street.

These openings were designed for the Guardians to get from one building to another in a hurry. Catching the right wind current the Guardians could jump from the top of one building and practically fly to another building several blocks away.

Torian thought about the incident that had happened earlier that day between the man in the yellow suit and the Sec Guardian and how the Guardians had evolved.

Part of the aftermath of the Devil's Tail was that the Earth had lost a majority of the population. Corporations used their own personnel for security to protect them. Also since they had control over major cities it stood to reason that they would use their security there as well. The problem was that even companies owned by a parent corporation argued boundary lines and on what punishment would be given to criminal behavior. The different security guards would argue or fight when coming into contact with each other.

That's when the Supremes resurfaced.

Descendants of the governing body that once wrote the laws in the USA were given authority over the newly formed UCA, who had come to an agreement to relinquish judicial power to the Supremes.

The Supremes already had control over what was left of the US military after the collapse of the US government. For this reason the Supremes placed military advisors in charge of all security forces within the cities, now under Supreme authority.

Around a decade after that the guards were replaced with Sec Guardians.

The last of the corporate security forces were transitioned into the Riffs with only a select handful left to protect corporate big wigs as personal protectors.

The Supremes originally governed the Guardians from the East Coast of the UCA as they had done in the past. Later they moved their base of operations to an undisclosed location.

Connected to the Outernet and with the use of radio signals the Supremes were able to see everything the Sec Guardians saw through the monitors in place on the Guardians.

From this the Supremes made their judgments on the spot and relayed their decision directly to the Sec Guardian to carry out their verdicts. Punishment was swift and justice served quickly. The Supremes decisions were final.

The Guardians faces' were covered to keep anyone from retaliating against them as individuals, or at least that's what most people thought.

Guardians did have identification numbers on their suits if you felt you needed to L-mail the Supremes with a complaint.

Inside the cities seemed to be very organized and controlled, but outside the city was a different story. The land between cities was wild and untamed.

The Riffs, a mixture of colloquial law enforcement, security guards from the corporations and some mercenaries were used to patrol these outer areas.

The Riffs kept bands of marauders from maintaining any type of strong hold or building up any type of force that would endanger a city.

Mountains and hills caused interference with visual transmissions from the Guardians to the Supremes so the Guardians stayed in the cities for the most part.

Torian's train of thought switched to that of Melanie. He hoped that she wasn't in any kind of trouble, at least any that she hadn't started herself.

He left and headed for his dwelling for the night.

Chapter 12

"What's down there?" O'Doul asked Thompson as they stood at

the entrance to the bunker.

"A room about ten feet squared with a secret door behind some shelves," Thompson said. "I was trying to open it when I heard Mel playing with the puppies."

"The dogs were probably down there when we first arrived," Mel said. "That's why we didn't see them on FLIR or why we didn't see Thompson when we were looking for him."

"It's getting late. We can check out the rest of the bunker in the morning. Right now I want to make sure we are prepared in case we have any visitors during the night. Let's get back to the UCV," O'Doul told them.

Thompson shut the door on the bunker and wrapped some wire around it so that the dogs wouldn't be able to get back in. Then they went back to the UCV.

"Still nothing around close enough to be a pest," Jones said as the rest of the unit came back on board.

O'Doul told them all to get some rest and that he would take the first watch.

Thompson was walking by the holding cell when Jameson hit the clear cell door.

"Hey mate, how about letting me out for a bit of a cleansing? It's a mite rancid in here, if you know what I mean," Jameson complained.

Thompson took a sniff from the air holes in the plastic and looked over toward the cell. He reached over and pushed a button on the wall next to the cell door.

Jameson had a grin on his face as if his wish was about to be granted but instead a spray of water came showering down on top of him.

"There, that ought to clean things up a bit, *mate*," Thompson said mimicking Jameson.

"What about you?" Thompson said looking over at the passenger in the other cell.

"Not me. I'm fine thanks." The passenger said with his hands up in front of him.

Thompson walked away with a satisfied look and hopped up into his bunk.

"If you ladies get cold during the night just hop up here with me," Thompson said to KJ and Mel patting the thin mattress with his hand.

"I'd rather go sleep with those dogs." Mel said. "Fewer paws to worry about if you know what I mean. By the way, thanks Daniel." Mel said to Thompson referring to the dog incident.   "Don't mention it," Thompson said rolling over in his bunk.

Chapter 13

He woke up to the Comp's musical rendition of an old song; "Up, up and get away, with my wonderful--my wonderful, zeppelin."

He hadn't slept very well last night. Rehashing yesterday's events over and over in his mind.

He got up and went to the cleansing room while the Comp continued to play the song it had started.

After he finished getting dressed and was about ready to leave he asked the Comp if there were any messages from Melanie. The Comp turned the volume down on the music and displayed some L-mails that had been sent during the night, connecting to the Lib Comp as well. None were from her.

Torian headed for the door and said, "Later" to the Comp.

The music faded away and the lights in the room dimmed. The front door slid open and as he stepped out he almost walked right into a Sec Guardian standing just outside the door.

Torian came to an abrupt halt and stepped back looking up. "Yes?" he asked.

The screen on the Guardian's faceplate lit up and Torian read the message.

"I have been assigned to accompany you," was displayed on the screen.

The eyes on the face monitor were green so Torian wasn't worried about having his finger shoved up his nose.

"By whom may I ask?"

"Supremes," was displayed on the screen.

"Huh!" Torian said out loud.

The Sec Guardian backed up from the door to allow him to pass. Torian saw that the number on the Guardian's suit was 5000 and said, "Comp, Sec Guardian 5000," and continued on his way out the door.

The Comp began the process of connecting to the Supremes to verify the Sec Guardians story. The Comp would notify Torian if something were amiss.

They took the lift down to the Transport level.

"I'm not going straight to work this morning," he told the Guardian. He had planned on meeting Chen at the ballpark to chat with him.

"I'm going to a Shield game. If you care to meet me at the Lib, I'll be there after the game."

The green eyes flashed for a second: "I am to accompany you," was displayed.

"Huh." Torian sighed.

"Okay," Torian said. "But you're buying your own hotdog."

When they arrived at the Shield Dome, where the Shield games where held in Angeles, Torian slid his Lib card at the gate.

The Guardian walked around to a separate entrance that was manned by another Sec Guardian.

Torian walked over to a food dispenser and bought two, foot-and-a-half longs and two Coksies.   As he entered the stadium he got funny looks from people who noticed the Sec Guardian following about five feet behind him.   Torian went down the stairs to the fifty-yard line and saw that Chen was waiting for him in his usual seat.

His mentor was wearing a silk blue shirt with long sleeves and matching silk pants.

"*Ni hao* (Hello)," he said to Chen.

"*Ni hao*," Chen replied. "*Qing wen*?" (May I ask you a question?)

"*Shi de* (Yes)," Torian replied.

"*Na shi shenme*? (What's that?)" Chen asked pointing at the Sec Guardian.

Torian looked over his shoulder then back at Chen.

"I knew I shouldn't have fed it, now it's following me."

Chen waved the back of his hand at the Guardian with a go away gesture.

The Guardian turned and walked back up the flight of stairs to wait.

"How did you get him to do that?" Torian asked Chen in dismay.

"Come, sit, and let's enjoy the game." Chen said as he took one of the hotdogs from Torian.

Chapter 14

Mel woke up and saw that Jones was already up sitting at her station, monitoring radio traffic and checking her monitor.

The unit hadn't sent any messages yesterday because of the prisoners and still being a long ways away from the Riff station. They didn't want to give away their location to any undesirable elements.

O'Doul was stirring but Thompson was still sleeping. Each had taken a four-hour watch during the night. The two prisoners were also still asleep, leaning with their heads propped up against the side of the back of their cells.

Mel hopped out of her bunk and walked over to Jones. "See anything KJ?" "No," she replied. "Where is Number One this morning?" O'Doul asked Jones as he joined them up front. "He's about a mile southwest of us. Right between the Riff station and us," Jones replied. "Well, no hurry then. We've got time to check out Thompson's little hideaway before we try and head back." O'Doul hit the button for the door to open. "Should we wake Thompson?" Jones asked. "Let him sleep," O'Doul replied.

Jones set the monitors audible alarm so that if anything came closer it would wake Thompson up.

O'Doul, Jones and Mel headed for the bunker that Thompson had wandered into yesterday. The doors were still wired shut the way Thompson had left it as they opened them and walked down a flight of steps inside the bunker. It appeared to have been used as a storage room for old engine parts at one time.

Jones found the secret door behind the shelves that Thompson had mentioned and started looking for a panel that might open it up.

"Here you are," she said finding a metal panel and opened it up.

Inside the panel it looked like some type of microreader that you would insert an access card into. Jones took out her own special card that had a wire running from it to a palm-sized Comp, inserted the card, and then hit a few buttons on the Comp.

The rack that held the shelves moved forward and the secret door behind it slid open. Mel and O'Doul raised their guns toward the entrance.

"Kind of dark in there, isn't it?" Jones said with a nervous laugh. "Maybe we should wake up Thompson and let him go first."

O'Doul turned on his Mini-light and walked in.

Mel followed with her light on as well.

They were about five feet in when the lights above them came on. With a startled look they turned around and saw Jones standing next to a wall switch. "Now doesn't that cheer the place up a bit," Jones said with a smile.

The room widened to about twenty by forty feet. No other doors were visible.

There were several cages on the right side of the room varying in size.

On the left side was a long table that had several glass vials and jars, some in small racks. Rubber tubes ran from some of the glass jars to Comp size machines.

"Looks like a laboratory," Jones said.

There was a Comp at a desk near the front of the long table.

Behind it were several tall cabinets that had what looked like spinning reels of some sort.

"I think that's what a computer mainframe looked like about a hundred and fifty years ago," Jones said walking toward the desk and looking at the cabinets.

"If the lights work do you think you can get that Comp to work?" O'Doul asked.

"I'll have a look see," Jones replied.

Mel was checking the walls to make sure there weren't any other hidden doors or panels. She sensed a presence and looked back at the doorway. Thompson was standing there. "We've got Company coming," he said.

The Riffs ran back to the UCV leaving the bunker secured the way Thompson had left it the night before.

Jones sat down at her monitors and saw multiple incoming dots on the screen.

"Number One?" O'Doul asked.

"No, he's still to the southwest. There is one dot coming up behind us fast but the others are coming from north of us.

"Jones radioed a message to the Riff station notifying them of their position and as much info as they had gathered thus far.

"Here or out there?" Mel asked O'Doul, wondering if they should make a run for it or take a stand.

"Here for now," O'Doul replied, and then headed back out the door.

Jameson and his passenger were awake asking what was going on and complaining about being hungry.

Mel pushed a couple of buttons next to each cell, which opened up a panel inside the cells. The prisoners each reached inside taking out a Coksi and a peanut butter sandwich.

"Bloody hell," Jameson said as Mel waved and went past him leaving the UCV as well.

Mel saw O'Doul climbing a ladder that looked like it went to the roof of the hangar. She went over to one of the windows by the north wall stacking some wooden crates up and around it. Then she checked her M-16 and extra magazine clips.

O'Doul had opened the roof hatch and was now on the roof checking out the surrounding area with his binoculars.

Several dune buggies and trucks were coming from the north heading their way.

O'Doul radioed his team, "Looks like three buggies, two trucks and a couple of cycles heading our way."

Mel looked out the window and could see the dust in the air behind the hill as the newcomers got closer.

Jones was sending the info to the Riff station about the prisoners and the bunker with the name "Area 48," they had found at the base. She had also mentioned the encounter with Number One and that they had incoming targets from the north heading in their direction.

The Riff station acknowledged receiving the info and asked if assistance was required. Jones told the station that any other units nearby were welcome to join the party. She also requested a Med-priest and that he should bring plenty of toe-tags with him just in case.

Chapter 15

It was half time, the score tied at twenty-four all.

The Coksi team had come out strong against the McDon No

Clowns, but the Clowns had a great defensive team and were able to get a few interceptions that kept them in the game.

While they sat watching the game, Torian told Chen about the L-mail from Hara and about the other L-mails that he had received.

Chen informed Torian that the stolen technology might have to do with a possible moon base and the type of rockets that were being used on the Metronome.

Torian knew the UCA had established a space station in orbit around the Earth called the Metronome, but he didn't know the UCA had plans for the moon.

Chen philosophized that the moon was (but a stepping stone to the universe) and with the invention of rocket engines back in the 1920's made landing there plausible.

Just then the Sec Guardian came down to where Torian and Chen were sitting.

His screen had a message: "From Riff station #10, Request Angeles Torian research relevant info on abandoned China Lake Naval station. Area 48 discovered there."

Torian looked over at Chen. "*Qing, duibuqi* (Please, excuse me)."

"*Wo dong* (I understand)," Chen replied.

Torian knew that if the Guardian was delivering this message instead of him getting it in an L-mail at the Lib, that the Supremes must think it rather urgent.

So Torian left the game with the Guardian in tow and headed for the Lib.

In the office Bonnie was wearing a green dress. Her earrings made of jade, matched her now green eyes. She saw the Guardian behind Torian and asked, "Did you hire someone new? I like the skirt he's wearing but the boots have to go," she said placing her hands on her hips.

"I received a message from Riff station ten, or, *he* did anyway," Torian said using his thumb to point over his shoulder without looking.

"They want me to look up some info," Torian said as he went into his office and closed the door.

The Sec Guardian walking behind tried to follow but came to a dead stop when Bonnie stepped in front of him with her arms across her chest blocking his path.

"So tell me handsome, what's your name?" she said to the

Guardian with the blinking green eyes.

Chapter 16

The trucks came to a stop on the other side of the hill behind the hangar.

The dune buggies circled around to the front of the hangar while the cycles kept circling around the outside.

O'Doul could see several men jumping out of the back of the trucks and running up over the hill toward the hangar. He radioed (using his <u>Microphone</u>) that three men with Ak-47s had placed themselves by the rubbish pile. Four more had run to the northeast side and took cover behind some crates and barrels. Several other men were heading to the northwest side carrying lever action-rifles.

O'Doul pulled back the bolt on the CAR-15, placing the first of thirty rounds of ammo into the chamber. Looking through the scope mounted on his rifle he picked out a headshot of one of the men by the crates.

Jones was transmitting simultaneously over the Mic and the P.A. system from the UCV. She announced that they were Riffs and any intruders interfering with a pending investigation would be held accountable for their actions and be brought before a Sec Guardian or God, whichever came first.

A voice came back over the radio. "You have two of our men inside. Release them and any possessions that you have confiscated and you may leave unharmed."

Jones again warned the marauders that if they interfered they would be arrested and taken to the nearest Riff station for evaluation before a Sec Guardian.

One of the cyclists that had been circling the hangar revved his engine and aimed for the entrance to the hangar. The rider not wearing a helmet was reaching for a grenade on his web belt as he reached the entrance to the hangar.

Just as the rider passed through the main door, he was knocked off the bike by a four-foot lead pipe that Thompson had in his hands.

"That's why you're supposed to wear a helmet," Thompson said to the fallen rider.

Sounds of gunfire were heard around the outside of the hanger and began to echo inside.

Mel saw two men running toward the hangar on her side of the building.

She flipped a switch on the stock of her gun to fire a three round burst at one of the invaders running toward the building. She then pulled the trigger for another salvo at the other man. Both men were hit and fell backwards with their feet going up in the air in front of them.

O'Doul took a headshot at the dummy with his head sticking up above the crates.

The head snapped back. No more dummy.

O'Doul heard screams coming from the rubbish pile. The dogs that had been there last night were attacking the three men that had hidden behind the rubbish pile, making it easy for O'Doul to take out each one with a shot from his rifle. The dogs took off after the intruders fell down in silence.

There came an explosion on the eastside of the hanger making a gap big enough for a dune buggy to come driving in.

Two men sitting in the front seat of a buggy, drove through the hole in the wall. A third man was firing a mounted machine-gun on the back of the buggy.

The shots were ricocheting off the side of the UCV.

The turret popped up on top of the UCV with Jones in it firing the M-60's at the approaching buggy. The buggy being shredded with bullets careened toward several rusted barrels out of control and flipped over as it hit the barrels, sliding off to the side.

Jones rotated the guns toward the entrance where another buggy was coming toward the front of the hangar. She let off another burst and the buggy turned sharply to the left and rolled off to the side of the hangar opening.

O'Doul saw that several more trucks were arriving behind the hill with more men getting out of them.

"Blast! There are more trucks arriving," he said into his Mic.

"I've never seen this many marauders at one time before," Mel said into her Mic.

The incoming shots around the building stopped.

The marauders were moving around the hangar taking up positions, but not attempting to gain access.

"They're thinking about it," O'Doul said over the Mic.

Mel saw one of the men run for some trashcans over by the bunker. She double tapped the trigger of her rifle and the guy fell headfirst into the cans.

"They'd better think harder," Mel said over the Mic.

Chapter 17

Torian got on the Comp and was looking through the Lib's info list of discs from over a century ago. He was looking for any information that correlated to the info requested by the Riffs.

As he searched the term, "Area 48," it reminded him of a place he had read about once known as "Area 51." Torian typed in the information on the Comp.

There were several articles in the Lib's data files about a secret military base (which everyone seemed to know about) around a place called Groom Lake.

It had been located in what was once known as Nevada.

Torian had to enter in his CIN to open up the declassified information.

Area 51 was established around 1955 so that the military could work on secret projects such as Oxcart.

Oxcart was the codename for innovative jet planes tested there, like the U-2 and SR-71 blackbirds.

Also it was rumored that aliens from another planet had allegedly crashed near an area once known as New Mexico and the military supposedly took the alien bodies to Area 51 to be analyzed.

Funny that no one seemed to think about the fact that if there was an Area 51 there might be another fifty areas that had come before that. "Could Area 48 be one of these?"

The door to Torian's office opened and in stepped his newly acquired friend.

The eyes were blinking green with the Guardian standing just inside the doorway.

Bonnie was right behind trying to squeeze past him.

Torian placed his hands in his pockets just in case, remembering the incident at the Transport station with the guy in yellow.   "I had him confused for a while when I told him I was born twins and our parents decided to sew my sister and me together back to back." Bonnie said twisting from side to side showing off both bust lines.

"It sure got his lights blinking and gyros turning," Bonnie said with a laugh.

A message on the Guardian's screen was displayed: "Request you go to China Lake to personally search Area 48."

Torian gestured to the Comp to log off and got up.

He was more than willing to go since the request came from Riff station ten.

He might even run into Melanie.

"I'm not sure how long I'll be gone Bonnie."

"I'll keep a candle burning in my window so you can find your way home," Bonnie told him.

The Sec Guardian turned to the side to allow Torian to pass by as he approached him.

"These automatic doors are getting slower and slower," Torian said referring to the door sized Guardian as he passed by.

The two walked to the lift and went up to the fiftieth floor.

The Torian stepped into the wind tube. The Sec Guardian did as well but his weight and size allowed him to walk the wind tube rather than float.

In the wind tube Torian was moving quicker and was way ahead of the Guardian by the time he reached the end. Torian was able to get to the lift before the Guardian.

The lift door closed as the Guardian was walking up to it. Torian waved a simple goodbye.

When Torian got to the Transport station he went over to the waiting area for the Tram that would take him to the Riff station.

He sat down crossing his legs and began to put his hands up behind the back of his head when he felt his elbow brush up against something solid. Torian looked over and up.   "What took you so long? I thought you lost your ticket or something back there," he said to a pair of blinking green eyes.

The Guardian's screen displayed a message: "We are not going to the Riff station. Follow me." The Guardian turned and walked away.

"Huh?" Torian thought out loud.

He got up and followed the Guardian down a hallway.

The Guardian stopped in front of a door that opened up and then walked in.

Torian walked in behind the Guardian and saw that this was an entry to another Tram area that Torian had never seen before.

They both walked over to a Tram waiting there and stepped in. The Guardian went to the front and sat down at the controls.

Torian sat down in a very comfortable chair and said to no one in particular, "Do you still get peanuts in first class?"

Chapter 18

A cycle pulled up next to one of the trucks behind the hill.

A man with a red bandana was yelling something to the rider and pointed north, the direction they had come from.

"That's not a good sign," O'Doul thought.

The cycle kicked up dirt as it took off.

O'Doul was placing the rider in the middle of the cross hairs on his rifle when he heard a "Swak" sound behind him.

O'Doul turned and saw that Mel had come up to the roof and used her combat G-club to hit a long range Mag-ball in the rider's direction. It was a good hundred and fifty yards between the hangar and the rider before the Mag-ball homed in on the metal frame of the cycle and attached itself to the frame.

Mel pushed a button on her belt and an explosion could be heard from where the rider was last seen.

"Oops, I must have pushed the wrong button," Mel said.

"He was going for reinforcements," O'Doul said.

"More marauders?" Mel asked no one in particular. "Something is definitely wrong."

"I think we're going to need some help down here," Jones said over the Mic.

Mel headed back down the ladder she had used to climb to the roof.

As she was coming down she could see a truck driving toward the front of the entrance to the hangar. It had a very heavy metal plate shield on the front.

Mel let go of the ladder and jumped the last fifteen feet to the ground landing on her feet and running back to the crates she had been behind earlier.

Jones fired the twin M-60s at the truck but the ammo did not penetrate the makeshift shield.

Just then several smoke grenades were thrown through windows around the hangar and also thrown through the gap in the eastside of the hangar.

Smoke filled up the hangar and about a dozen men came through the gap wearing facemasks. They were about thirty feet from the UCV when music blasted from the UCV.

Rock and Roll music was heard coming from the P.A.

Thompson had turned on the music not only to distract the oncoming marauders but also because he liked the upbeat tempo. He stepped out in front of the UCV with a SAW haltered around his front and pointed it at the incoming invaders.

The M-249 or SAW (Squad Automatic Weapon) fires seven

hundred rounds of ammo per minute.

Thompson's entire body shook as he unleashed the rain of death onto the incoming marauders. They flew backwards like flies being sprayed with bug repellant.

"Next time try knocking first!" Thompson yelled out at the fallen marauders.

The truck at the front entrance had stopped just inside of the hangar with several men shooting from behind it.

Mel was shooting from the makeshift barricade she had built with the crates.

Jones was giving it her best but having trouble with the M-60's penetrating the thick metal shield on the truck.

Thompson had incoming fire from outside the gap and was keeping that end covered, but things weren't looking to good until some of the marauders that were standing behind the truck with the shield started falling down.

O'Doul clicked the send button on his Mic, "I think we're getting some help out there."

The truck started to back up and the sounds of bullets hitting it from behind were heard.

Mel jogged over to the entrance to look out front.

One of the trucks exploded while another truck turned and headed back behind the hill where it had come from.

Marauders were falling to the ground left and right from gunfire.

Thompson walked up to the front entrance next to Mel. "Ho-rah," Thompson yelled.

What was left of the marauding band was high tailing it out of there.

From the roof, O'Doul could see the man with the red bandana seemingly shaking his fist at O'Doul from the truck he sat in as it turned and sped away.

O'Doul came down the ladder and jogged over to the front entrance where Mel and Thompson were standing as several black trucks pulled up in front of the hangar and out stepped Number One.

"Shit," Thompson said as he raised his SAW in Number One's direction.

O'Doul pushed the multi-barreled weapon toward the ground. "They're the ones that helped us."

Ichi Ban walked over to the Riffs. *Konnichiwa* (Good afternoon)," he said bowing slightly to O'Doul not taking his eyes off him.

"I believe we owe you a debt of thanks," O'Doul responded.

"Lie, do itashimashite. You're welcome," Ichi Ban repeated in English.

"I'm afraid we may still have a problem," O'Doul told Ichi Ban. "I still can't let you have what you came for."

"A, naruhodo, Oh, I see," Ichi Ban replied in Japanese and English.

Several clones were gathering behind Ichi Ban as he was speaking with O'Doul. Each carrying an Uzi sub-machine gun and pointing it in the Riffs direction.

Suddenly they heard the sound of a rotary engine above them. They all looked up and could see a helicopter hovering above. It started its descent and landed vertically to the rear of the black trucks that the clones had arrived in.

The helicopter door on the driver side opened up and a Sec Guardian climbed out of the copter slightly bent forward due to the propeller blades still in motion.

"Ooo you're in trouble now," Jones said to the clones as she joined the group.

The Sec Guardian was walking toward them and someone else was getting out of the other side of the copter. The person behind the Guardian had to jog to catch up and as he got closer took off his helmet.

"Trent!" Mel yelled.

"Well hello. Say, did you leave your phone off the hook on purpose?" Torian yelled back at Melanie with a playful grin.

"As you can see I just flew in and boy are my arms tired," Torian said flapping his elbows up and down.

Chapter 19

The Sec Guardian walked past the men in black ignoring them stopping in front of O'Doul.

Trent following behind the Guardian looked around at the cloned men and nearly collided with the wall that had just stopped in front of him.

Trent sidestepped the Guardian putting out his hand to Jimmy O'Doul.

"Top of the evening everyone," Trent said looking around at the Riffs while shaking hands with Jimmy.

"See, he knows how to talk without pulling out a translation book," Thompson said to Jones pointing at Trent.

Jimmy shook hands and said, "It's nice to see you again Torian."

"I hate to interrupt this pleasant reunion, but we may still have a little problem," O'Doul said nodding toward the clones.

Trent turned to the nearest clone "*Konbanwa* (Good evening)" bowing slightly, but his eyes remaining on the clone in front of him.

The clone returned the gesture "*Ome ni kakarete ureshii desu, Torian-san* (Pleased to meet you Torian)."

"He seems to know everyone he meets," Jimmy said from behind.

"*Domo* (thanks)," Trent said in return.

"Shit, I spoke to soon;" Thompson said shaking his head referring to Torian as he replied in Japanese.

"I believe you are here for the microchips," Trent said to the clone.

"*Hai* (yes)" he replied.

"Jimmy, if you wouldn't mind giving this gentleman his property so we can go on with our business," Torian said to O'Doul without taking his eyes of the clone.

"What the H E double G-clubs?" Thompson said out loud.

"Knock it off." O'Doul told Thompson.

O'Doul took a step closer to Torian.

"Excuse me Torian, but we have recovered stolen property and sort of planned on taking it back to the station, along with the marauders that we caught leaving the power junction."

The Sec Guardian still facing the Riffs screen lit up. "You are to follow the Torian's direction."

O'Doul read the display and said, "Jones, can you get the plastic container we found and give it to the nice people with the Uzi's."

Melanie walked over and stood next to Trent who was still facing the clone.

"Why?" she asked him.

"Because I believe the information it contains belongs to them," Trent replied not taking his eyes of the clone.

Jones came back with the container and gave it to one of the other clones that stepped forward to receive it.

The Sec Guardian turned to Ichi Ban; "Take the microchips and go" was displayed in Japanese across his screen.

"*Sumimasen ga...* (Pardon me, but...)," Ichi Ban started to say to the Guardian but stopped when he saw the Guardian's eyes blinking yellow.

"The last fellow I saw make a Guardian mad can only breathe out one of his nostrils right now," Torian said to the clone in front of him.

Ichi Ban looked at Torian and gave a curt nod of the head then turned and walked away.

"Don't forget to write," Thompson yelled as he waved goodbye.

Trent turned and started walking toward the UCV.

"Well now, it's getting late and I'm starving. Whose turn is it to cook?" he asked out loud, reaching for Melanie's hand and drawing her gently alongside him.

Chapter 20

It was getting dark by the time they had finished eating.

Jimmy O'Doul was full of questions but didn't want to ask them too quickly. Instead he introduced Torian to the two members of his unit Torian hadn't met before.

"This is Daniel Thompson and Katelin Jones."

Thompson was sitting back with his feet up over the armrest of the bench seat chewing on a bite of sandwich. He was cleaning his gun as he waved in the Torian's direction.

Jones was taking a drink of her Coksi and watching her monitor, but stood up to shake hands with Torian.

"You can call me KJ if you like," she said.

"And you can call me Trent," he replied.

Melanie was sitting next to Trent waiting for an explanation about what was going on.

The Sec Guardian was in the back of the UCV interrogating the prisoners.

Trent explained that he and the Guardian had contacted station ten on the flight there and were briefed on the information KJ had transmitted.

A few minutes later the prisoners were released from their cells.

Jameson, the driver, said, "Later mates. It has been a pleasure."

Thompson stuck his foot up across the driver's path. Jameson stopped as his partner bumped into him.

The Guardian approached them from behind. The display on the Guardians screen said; "They are to be let go."

Thompson put his foot down with a scowl.

Jameson and his partner smiled as they walked to the front and out the UCV.

"All right, someone please tell me why we just killed over twenty people today, and it better be good?" O'Doul asked.

"Someone is organizing the marauders," Trent said, "They are using them to help transport stolen tech-info taken from the corporations. The batch of microchips you found came from Kofu Electronics Corporation and the clones in black were assigned to retrieve the chips and if necessary kill the ones who took it. How am I doing so far?"

"Keep going," O'Doul replied.

"The two you had in custody were probably only mules used to transport the goods. They only had limited information so the Sec Guardian let them go. Is that correct SG?" Trent asked the Guardian.

"Correct," was displayed on the screen.

"I don't suppose you would provide KJ here with the transmitter codes from the tracking devices put on the dune buggy and Jameson?” Trent asked the Guardian.

The green eyes blinked for a few seconds. Probably wondering how Torian had guessed about the tracking devices, but the Guardian walked over to Jones and gave her the codes.

“I'm sure we’ll catch up to those two a little later, but in the meantime you’ve discovered something that needs our attention and without any prying eyes.”

“The bunker,” Melanie said.

“Area 48, yes,” Trent said as he looked at her with a warm smile.

“I’d like to see it if I may?” he said now looking at Jimmy.

O’Doul got up and headed outside but with a slightly exasperated expression.

As they left the UCV, KJ told them that it looked clear for a couple of miles or so. She could clearly see that the tracking devices were working on the dune buggy and Jameson. They were heading north following the path of the other marauders from earlier. Ichi Ban was heading west toward Vegas. The Riffs walked to the back of the hangar the way O’Doul and Mel had gone the day before. It was getting dark outside. As they got closer to the bunker, O’Doul stopped and shined his light over by the rubbish pile where he had shot some of the marauders. Only their guns lay on the ground. There appeared to be some blood in the dirt but it had been smeared as if something had dragged the bodies away. “Mel’s puppies must have gotten hungry,” Thompson said. “You bought a dog?” Trent asked curiously. “I was going to ask you if I could bring one home. They’re so cute and cuddly,” Melanie said with a makeshift shiver.

They went down the flight of stairs to the first room. Jones opened the secret door.

“Very interesting,” Trent said watching the door open.

They all walked into the room except the Sec Guardian who had stopped at the bottom of the stairs.

“This is pretty much the way we found it this morning when we came down here,” Jimmy said. “Of course we were interrupted before we could really give the room a good search.”

“I started to try the Comp, but that’s when Thompson came in and invited us to his party," Jones laughed.

"Some party," Melanie said.

"Would you mind trying again?" Trent asked KJ.

She sat down at the old-style computer and started pushing buttons on the monitor and keyboard. "Nothing," Jones said looking on both sides of the Comp to see if it was plugged in.

Trent walked over to the cabinets against the wall. He opened one of the cabinet doors and pulled a red handle. Lights started flickering in the different cabinets and the reels started to turn. A green light on the monitor came on and a dim green glow came to the screen.

"Try it now KJ."

Jones tried the keyboard again and got a curser in the top left corner of the screen, but it just kept blinking as she typed.

"I imagine it needs something to boot it up," KJ said.

KJ looked in the drawers in the table that the computer was sitting on but there was nothing in them.

"Huh. Try looking under the desk," Trent said to KJ pointing underneath.

Jones pushed her chair back and looked underneath the desk. "I don't see anything," she said.

"Try pulling the drawer open and then look up underneath," Trent told her.

She dropped down on one knee and pulled the drawer open and looked up.

"I'll be damned." She reached up and peeled off some sort of diskette that had been taped underneath. "How did you know?" Jones asked.

"My father used to hide his optical imaging disc of Playman's Hunnies under his desk the same way."

"To hide it from your mom?" Thompson asked. "No. He thought he was hiding it from me. Actually my mom would get him a new disc once a quarter and put it up there to surprise him. She always ended up with a new pair of shoes or dress around the same time. I guess they thought it was their little secret." "Now that's my kind of woman," Thompson said with a big grin. "When are you going to sneak some shots of you on my Comp KJ?" Thompson said brushing her shoulder with the back of his hand.

"Oh brother," Jones replied as she rolled her eyes around pulling the tape off the disk that had held it in place.

The disk was about five and a quarter inch squared.

"What kind of disk is this?" Jones wondered aloud.

"I believe they called it a floppy disk," Trent replied.

"Try to put it into the side of the hard drive. See where the monitor is sitting on top of it."

KJ slid it in and then hit the enter key. The screen blinked and displayed a warning: "Government Software. N A S A personnel only. Please enter Password: _"

Chapter 21

"This could take a while," Jones said.

Thompson walked over by the table with the vials and test tubes on it while O'Doul was standing off to the right side of the desk looking at the middle of the room.

Melanie stood next to Trent as KJ entered random passwords into the computer.

"I can probably use my palm Comp and hook it up to the hard drive in order to run a series of numbers and words that might work," KJ said. "Even still it's going to take some time." She got out her palm Comp and started messing with the wires.

"Funny how the middle of the room is empty with all the cages on one side and the big table up against the wall on the other," O'Doul said out loud as he continued looking around the room.

Melanie noticed some pictures on the wall in between the cabinets and the big table and walked over to them. Blowing off the dust, one picture was of a white-haired man shaking hands with another person. "Dr. John Strode welcomes new addition to staff. Mr. Dennis Hansen from Wright Industries comes to us with a great deal of experience after working on the B-29," Melanie read out loud. There was a newspaper clipping of some planes flying past a big mountain with snow on it and an article beneath the picture. But several of the words in the article had been cut out.

"What did you just say?" Trent asked Melanie.

Melanie read the article again, skipping the spaces where the cut out words were missing.

"Did you say Wright?"

"Yes why?"

"Wright--Wright?" Trent closed his eyes for a second seeing the article he had read on the B-29's in his mind.

"KJ, before you take that disk out, type in Cyclone 18." Jones looked up at him then back at the computer typing it in.

"Project Metamorphosis," was displayed on the screen and a humming sound came from the center of the room.

O'Doul standing in the middle of the room with his hand on his chin was looking around the room when the middle of the floor started to descend like a ramp.

"Hey what the heck," O'Doul said jumping to the side of the floor that was still level.

Thompson, with his back toward the middle of the room, turned and levered the action on his M-16 pointing it down into the hole now appearing in the floor.

The screen on the monitor displayed another message: "Access approved."

"Again, how did you know?" KJ inquired.

"The B-29 airplanes used the Wright engine when they bombed Japan back in1945. The name of the engine used in the bombers was the Cyclone 18. It is one of the words missing in the article Melanie just read. I've read that article before.

O'Doul walked around to the front of the square hole that had appeared underneath him looking down the ramp. He started to walk down with Thompson right behind him both looking from side to side as they descended into the open void.

Melanie walked over to where the two had gone down and asked Trent to wait until they had a chance to look around.

"No problem," he told her.

There was a slight smell of ammonia as they reached the bottom of the ramp. The lights were flickering trying to come on.

O'Doul could see what looked like large glass cylinders on the right side of the room, big enough for a person to fit in.

Thompson was checking around the room for other doors or cracks in the walls and stomping on the floor as if it would drop down like the one they had just entered.   Melanie looked at the table on the left side of the room. It had several jars filled with dead animals of some sort. The jars were filled with ammonia to preserve the specimens inside.   There was a larger glass jar at the end of the table that held what looked like a dead monkey inside; minus the ears.

Jones had succeeded in pulling up the information on the disk and tried opening several of the files but they kept coming up corrupt.

"This disk is old. It's lost most of its memory." KJ said as she clicked on one file named GATC.

Up came a picture of what looked like a rope ladder that had been twisted all the way down. Letters appeared on each of the rungs of the ladder. The letters that repeated themselves were g, a, t and c and along the rope part of the ladder going down were the letters s and p.

"Human DNA," Trent said out loud.

Chapter 22

"Unusual that they would go to such lengths to hide DNA research," Trent thought to himself. "This kind of information is readily available and taught to students that want to become Med-priests." Trent thought it was also taught in schools of the past.

Schools had been built and designed so that while parents went to work, teachers provided education to children attending, instead of parents teaching their own kids the things they wanted them to learn. Parents' even complained about what their kids learned or who was teaching them but most continued with the status quo.

Today parents taught their own kids, allowing others to mentor or teach things that the parents themselves did not have an expertise in. Often parents learned side by side with their children.

"Seems like most of the files have the same diagrams with different letters in them," Jones said, bringing Trent's attention back to the task at hand.

"The diagram is called a Helix," Trent told KJ.

He looked down to see that KJ had opened another file titled Meiosis.

It showed another Helix diagram but much thicker. It also had some notes printed next to the diagram.

Notation: Acceptable amounts of N and Ar tolerable.

Notation: Using sperm with the contrived mutant gene before being introduced into the ovum created the desired mutation during the meiosis phase.

Notation: Raised pH levels necessary to maintain blood count passed infancy stage.

Melanie walked back up the ramp to where KJ and Trent were.

"There's another lab down here with different kinds of dead animals preserved in jars.

Trent asked KJ if she could access the Outernet with her palm Comp.   "No, for some reason when we're down here there's interference keeping us from communicating with anyone outside the bunker. We couldn't reach Thompson when he was down here yesterday on our radios or see him with the infrared," KJ replied.

Trent walked down the ramp to take a look at the lab below.

"You coming, SG?" he asked the Guardian in the other room.

The lights just blinked a light shade of green.

"He hasn't moved away from the stairs?" Melanie said.   "I think that whatever is blocking the communications down here is affecting his receiving signals from the Supremes," Trent told her.

He continued down the ramp and looked around the room.

Thompson was on his way up mumbling something about having

the munchies.

O'Doul was looking at some of the dead animals in the jars.

"I've never seen some of these species of animal before," O'Doul said.

Melanie walked over to O'Doul "Me either," she said.

Trent looked around the room noticing the large empty cylinders and then walked along the table looking carefully at each of the jars until he got closer to the end and saw the fetus in the last jar.

"What kind of monkey is that Trent?" Melanie asked.

"It's not a monkey," he replied.

O'Doul looked back over at the jar. "What is it then?" he asked.

It's a fetus of some kind, but of what I'm not sure. The skin color is very unusual."

Thompson yelled down into the hole that the Med-priest had arrived with other Riffs and a clean-up crew.

Trent picked up the jar with the fetus and brought it up the ramp with him.

Seeing the jar in his hands KJ made a sour face and pinched her nose as he walked past her.

"If you would bring the floppy disk with you I think we've done all that we can here," Trent said to KJ.

They went back up to the surface and Thompson secured the bunker.

The Sec Guardian had advised O'Doul and his unit not to discuss the information that they had retrieved from the disk and only to report the activities that had occurred in and around the hanger.

O'Doul had a problem with that, but when he saw another Sec Guardian was with the Riffs that had arrived, he decided to follow the Guardians directions.

They walked back toward the hangar and could see the generator lights that the clean-up crews had set up in order to check the surrounding bodies and confiscate weapons lying on the ground.

The Med-priest was wearing the usual white coat and white collar with a red cross in the center of it.

A Med-priest was a doctor with medical training who had gone through religious training as well.

Back in the twentieth century a handful of priests had come under scrutiny for engaging in unlawful or immoral practices. These incidents had been reported in the news creating such uproar that religious organizations feared losing their hold as spiritual leaders. Rather than see religion fade away and to regain some sort of credibility the wealthier religions decided to mix the two professions together hoping to appease the public. Besides, it only made sense to heal body, mind and *soul* all at once.

Torian approached the Med-priest and asked him if he would perform an autopsy.

"Sure!" he responded. "On which one of these guys did you need it done?" the Med-priest asked looking around at the bodies being gathered.

"This one," Torian said handing him the glass jar.

Chapter 23

O'Doul was reporting to the Captain who had accompanied the newly arrived Riffs along with both Sec Guardians.   Jones and Thompson had gone back into the UCV while Melanie and Trent walked up the hill that was behind the hangar.

The stars were plentiful and the moon was close enough to want to reach up and touch it.

"That's the Dragon in-between the Big Dipper and the Little Dipper," Trent said pointing up at the stars.

Then he looked at Melanie holding her hand.

"I'm glad to see you're all right," Trent told her now that they were alone.

"You know what I do," she said.

"Yes--I know--and I'm proud of you for it. But that doesn't mean I don't get to worry about you once in a while, does it?"

"You'd better. Of course that must mean you sort of like me, right?" Melanie said as she sashayed her shoulders back and forth, putting her finger to the corner of her mouth and gently biting down on her fingernail.

"I'll be happy to show you how much once I get you home and into something a little less combat-butch," Trent told her as he pulled her close to kiss her.

"Hate to interrupt, but the Sec Guardian wants the Torian to accompany him back to Angeles," Gunner, one of the other Riffs said climbing up the hill toward them.

"Figures, just when things were really getting interesting," Trent said.

Melanie laughed.

"Don't worry. You'll get your chance." Melanie told him giving him a quick peck on the cheek.

They walked back to where all the activity was.

Melanie let go of his hand and went back inside the UCV as O'Doul and the two Sec Guardians were coming toward Trent.

"Sec Guardian 5000 is taking you back to Angeles; the other one is going with the Med-priest to keep an eye on your monkey," O'Doul said.

"We have to report back to the station and log everything, I mean almost everything in," O'Doul said looking over his shoulder at the two Guardians.

O'Doul walked part of the way with Torian back to the helicopter.

Torian asked Jimmy if his latest additions to the unit worked well together.

Jimmy knew what Torian was getting at and told him that Mel could handle almost any situation just fine, but that yes they had become a very cohesive team.

Jimmy then took out the access card he had taken from the container with the microchips in it and handed it to Torian.

"This was with the microchips. No sense in it getting lost in an evidence locker somewhere," O'Doul told Torian.

Torian took the card and shook Jimmy's hand firmly, then walked off toward the copter. Torian had asked the Med-priest to send him the info from the autopsy to the Lib. He also asked him to check the number of chromosomes in the fetus as well. He had a hunch but didn't want to say anything at this point.

The Med-priest had told Torian to be that specific he would have to take the jar into the city, but would send him the info as soon as possible.

As Torian approached the copter he could see that SG had the floppy disk from the underground bunker in his hand as he climbed into the pilot seat.

It had been quite an exciting ride. Only Sec Guardians were allowed to fly aircraft like planes or helicopters.

As the cities were being rebuilt, corporations were reminded of an incident that happened on Sept.11 in the year 2001 and allowing civilians to fly wasn't something corporations wanted in and around their towers. So they opted to allow blimps and zeppelins for use by the general public.

Torian glanced back at the UCV then climbed up into the copter next to the Guardian. Mel stepped out of the UCV and watched the copter as it hovered above the ground then flew away.

"So you kind of like that guy?" Thompson said standing behind her.

"Yes, a great deal," she replied not taking her eyes off the departing copter.

Thompson came up and put his arm up on her shoulder. "Good. I was having a hell of a time fitting you into my schedule anyway."

Mel laughed and they both walked back to the UCV.

Chapter 24

Torian woke up around ten in the morning. He told the Comp when he came in at midnight (30:00) not to wake him up early allowing him to sleep in.

His date yesterday with SG had ended when the Guardian walked Torian to his doorstep then left without so much as a hug or kiss goodnight. "Typical Guardian," Torian said whimsically.

He was glad that he had been with Melanie even if it was for a short time yesterday and was still thinking of her when he woke up and got ready for work.

He had picked out a tan suit to wear for the day and headed for the door.

When the door slid open he expected to see his new friend waiting outside. He stepped out and looked both ways up and down the hall but to no avail.

"Just like a Sec Guardian. Get what they want and they never call again," he said out loud.

When he walked into the front office at the Lib, Bonnie was nowhere to be seen.

"Bonnie is always here," he thought as he continued on to his office.

Torian saw her bending over, reading something on his desk; she leaned over in such a way that he could see both front and back cleavages at the same time.

"Good morning sleepy head," she said looking up at him.

"Hi, Bonnie," he said with genuine relief.

"This was brought here by one of your Guardian friends. At first I didn't think he wanted to leave it with me, but I leaned up against him and promised that I would give it to you personally. The Guardian blinked a couple of times then gave me the envelope and left. Should I give it to you, *now*?" she whispered with a curt nod of her head holding up the envelope.

"Thanks," he told her. "I always enjoy a quickie in the morning."

She laughed and left the office.

The report inside was from the Med-priest.

He turned on his Comp and activated the voice recognition by drawing the back of his V fingers up his neck and forward under his chin. Then he tapped the fingers of his slightly bent right hand on his forehead a few times so the Comp would interpret the info as he read it out loud and search for any related topics.

Torian's grandmother had been deaf since childhood. She taught her grandson how to use sign language so they could communicate.

Chen had told his student that he should find a unique way of setting passwords on his Comp when he became a Torian, to keep others from accessing confidential files.

When he accepted the position as Torian for Angeles he had inputted visual sign language recognition into his Comp's memory banks.

Torian opened the envelope to look at the autopsy results checking the DNA first.   The report showed that the fetus in the jar had twenty-three pairs of chromosomes normal for humans.   "Subject Male: DNA results: 23 pairs of chromosomes for a total of 46."

There was a notation under the lung contents.

"Lung contents result: Traces of oxygen and carbon dioxide, with a larger than normal concentration of nitrogen, argon and ammonia found in alveoli within the lungs," he said out loud allowing the Comp to register the information.

The Comp started its search and came up with info from a text document stored in the Lib's archives.

The screen showed that the human body was comprised of 23 pairs of chromosomes as part of its deoxyribonucleic acid or DNA. It showed the Double Helix diagram that he had seen in the first file that KJ had opened up on the floppy disk.

The GATC were guanine, adenine, thymine and cytosine.

The S and P were sugar and phosphate.

"The ammonia would have been from the fetus being placed in the jar for preservation, but why nitrogen and argon?" again speaking out loud.

"The organs were basically the same except for one additional organ reminiscent of a smaller version of a placenta or afterbirth located underneath and connected to the heart via an extra artery. Note: This should not be outside of the ovum let alone be present in a male fetus.

Note: Adrenal gland enlarged.

The epidermis contained six to seven layers instead of the normal four to five.

The dermis itself included two kinds of sweat glands, which is usually normal, but it appeared that the fetus had one gland to excrete sweat or excess water and salt. And the second gland, which was larger, could be used to absorb the sweat back in after it has been exposed to the elements. Allowing it to oxygenate and withstand a greater range of temperatures.

Blood Results: Only fetal hemoglobin present in red corpuscles;

acid levels higher than normal."

The Comp's screen changed hearing the new information and now showed that human red blood corpuscles generally have two types of hemoglobin.

A fetal hemoglobin at birth, that changes to an adult type later.

The fetal hemoglobin having a greater relationship with oxygen means lower levels of oxygen are needed to sustain life.

"I imagine that means an adult person could take in less oxygen along with the higher acid levels increasing the blood count and disperse the oxygen more efficiently, but what was the extra organ for?" he wondered out loud.   He thought about the microchips that had been taken from the Kofu Corporation.   Chen had told Torian that the stolen technology had to do with a possible moon base and the type of rockets that were being used on the Metronome.
                    "Traveling into space or other planets was something of a fascination back in the 1960's and 70's."   Mentioning this out loud, the Comp flickered for a moment processing the information about the DNA and space travel together and came up with one word: Mars.

Chapter 25

The unit woke to the sound of an explosion.

Running out the UCV to the back of the hangar where the sound had come from, the Riffs saw huge flames coming from inside the bunker.

"What's going on?" O'Doul yelled at one of the Riffs watching the flames shooting skyward.

"He's what's going on," the Riff said pointing in the direction of the bunker.

Out of the flames walked Sec Guardian 2000, the Guardian that had come with the Riffs the day before. There wasn't a scratch or burn mark on his suit. He walked back to the Med-priest's van and got in.

"Dang it!" O'Doul said to his unit as they turned around and headed back to the UCV.

On their way back to the Riff station they typed up some of their reports but would need more time at the station to finish.

They would be arriving a day earlier than usual, but the clash with the marauders warranted an early end to their time spent in the field.

When the Riffs arrived, O'Doul was directed to follow up with Captain Video.

That was Captain Harding's nickname because of his collection of old video games he kept up on a shelf in his office. Harding didn't seem to mind the name.

The rest of the team went into the briefing room to finish working on their reports, also using the Comps for identifying the marauders that had been shot during the gunfight. They scanned photos that the Med-priest had taken to help with any possible identification.

O'Doul met up with his unit outside next to the truck that had brought the bodies back.

Thompson had totaled the number of toe tags that he had accumulated while Jones went through the personal belongings of the marauders. Their possessions would be sent to family or friends depending on whether they could be located or not.

Mel was talking to the Med-priest who had done the autopsy on whatever it was they had found in the glass jar after he had returned from the city.

"Yes, I handed over the report to the Sec Guardian and L-mailed the info to the Torian once I was done. The Guardian took the report and the fetus that the Torian gave me and told me not to discuss it with anyone else. I'm to stay here," he told Mel as O'Doul approached.

"Somebody wants to keep this thing hush, hush, I think," Mel said.

"Why?" O'Doul pondered out loud.

"I'm not sure, but it has something to do with that thing in the jar," the Med-priest said in a low voice.

Mel and O'Doul walked back to the others in their unit and helped with the task at hand.

A long time ago people convicted of a crime would be sent to a prison where they would get three square meals a day, watch something called television and learn how to commit more heinous crimes from other prisoners. This all paid for by the taxpayers, including the victims of the crimes themselves.

After the Devil's Tail there was a brief period of anarchy in which survival was the law of the land. An eye for an eye became justice and when the Supremes restored order throughout the UCA, they continued with this system. Steal from someone and something would be taken from you. Kill a person intentionally and expect to be terminated on the spot.

It didn't take long before crimes within the cities were almost non-existent.

Outside the city was a different matter.   The Riffs on the other hand would typically detain and bring anyone involved in a crime back to the station for a Sec Guardian to interview. After judgment was determined the person would make up their own mind whether getting shot or arrested in the process was worth it, if they were still around that is.   When the unit was finished with the bodies outside, the Sec Guardian and Captain Harding approached the Riffs.   "You have the rest of the day off then you are to report back here for a special assignment," Harding told them.   "I hope that we're being sent to find out what the marauders are up to?" O'Doul said.

"You got it," Harding replied.

"You have until tomorrow morning and then you will need to head back out and find out what the hell is going on. Oh, and you'll be taking this with you." Harding pointed at the Guardian.   O'Doul frowned as Captain Video walked away.   "Now isn't that special!" Thompson said with a lisp looking at Guardian 2000.

Chapter 26

"Mars?" His Comp was now showing a spinning picture of Mars on the screen.

The Comp started scrolling down through info until it got to where it described the atmosphere of Mars. It was made up of carbon dioxide, oxygen and water in smaller amounts than the Earth, but also contained nitrogen and argon.

The nitrogen and argon along with Torian mentioning space exploration was the association the Comp used to bring up information on Mars.

Torian thought about Area 51 and how the military had supposedly taken a spacecraft with aliens from Mars or some such far away planet to study there.   Of course nothing was ever proven and the government denied any such findings, including appointing a group of investigators to look into the UFO (Unidentified Flying Objects) sightings. It had been named project Blue Book.   "Could the fetus in the jar have been one of the aliens?" The disk they had found seemed to put the human DNA first with the altering of the meiosis taking place after.   Meiosis being a type of cell division resulting in changes in the number of chromosomes, but is re-established when the ovum is fertilized by the sperm. Yet the notations on the disk suggested altering the sperm prior to inception.

The logical order for finding something is to compare it to another known thing of course, but the fact that the Riffs had discovered an area forty eight (this coming before fifty one) made him think something didn't jive.

Sightings of UFO's had been around for a lot longer than the supposed crash in New Mexico.

The government denied any possibility of spaceships flying around but was at this particular crash site very quickly.

Of course there were many such sightings around this particular base so it would make sense that the military would respond quickly.

Torian closed his eyes for a moment then said, "Huh!" out loud.

He thought about Hansen coming to the base to work with Dr. Strode. Hansen worked with engine designs and Dr. Strode researched DNA. He also thought about the sightings near military bases, but the government denying anything.

Even claiming weather balloons as a cause to dissuade the public and eventually closing project Blue Book saying no credible evidence had been discovered.

Bonnie walked in and saw Torian leaning back with his eyes closed.

"Ah! Isn't that sweet. Daydreaming about me again," she said with a smile.

Torian opened his eyes looking up at her.

"The chitchat is that you got the microchips back for the Kofu Corporation without any red tape, so they sent you this hundred-year-old bottle of wine. I scanned it to make sure there wasn't any poison or sedatives added. Just as a precaution," she said turning to walk back out.   "Wait," Torian said staring at her. Bonnie stopped and began to turn around.

                                        "No! Stop right there!" he said quickly.   She was standing sideways and he was looking at her from front to back.

                                Bonnie looked down then back over her shoulder. "That daydream of yours must have worked. See something or *some things* you like?"   "They're real aren't they?" he inquired.

                        "Well of course. You think I make enough working here to get them done. I mean don't get me wrong I love it here but..."   "--That's it!" Torian interrupted, realizing that mankind had been fooling around with genetics and the fertilization of human cells for centuries.

"What's it," Bonnie said looking up and down her front and back as if she had a spider on her.

Also the United States government had been interested in creating rocket ships to travel into outer space, especially after Russia launched Sputnik in the 1960's.

In 1961 the US even sent a chimp in to orbit to see if it was safe enough for a human being.

Finally in 1969 Neil Armstrong walked on the moon. But the human body wasn't designed for long-term space exploration as discovered through long term stays on what was called the International Space Station, let alone surviving on another planet.

Maybe, just maybe, aliens from Mars didn't visit us; maybe *we* were trying to reconstruct humans to visit Mars? Hence the name: Project Metamorphosis.

That evening after they had finished with their reports the unit got some dinner at the Riff mess hall.

O'Doul was going over the reports with Gunner and Ethan from the other Riff unit that had shown up to help with the cleanup and to see if any additional information was needed.

KJ and Mel sat next to each other talking about the Fishbowl nightclub while Thompson was sitting at another table talking with Summer and Ethan.

"It's totally awesome at the club," KJ was saying. "It's up on the eightieth floor. There is a giant sphere like a fishbowl in the middle of the club. That's what they use as the dance floor. When you go in it's like a wind tube only you can float around in the middle of the bowl or dance on the sides. You can go in by yourself or with a dance partner; either way it's a lot of fun. They have tables around the bowl so you can sit and watch the people inside."

"That does sound like fun," Mel said glancing over at Thompson who caught her eye and waved back.   "Are we still getting signals from the tracking devices that we put on Jameson and Number One?" O'Doul asked from across the table.   "We still have Jameson, but Number One must have found the tracking device and deactivated it," Jones replied.   "Well, guess I'm going to get some shut eye. Don't know when we'll get a good night sleep. Good evening," O'Doul said as he got up from the table.

                              "Me too, KJ said standing up.

Mel headed for the report room so she could use one of the Comps to try and reach Trent before going to bed.

She tried the Lib first, but no answer there. Then she tried his dwelling, but he wasn't there either, so she just left a message and headed off to one of the night rooms in the station.

She met Thompson walking down the hall with two female dispatchers.

"Hey Mel, want to join us? We're planning on skinny-dipping in the station hot tub." Thompson asked as he passed by with his arms around the two civilians.

"Not tonight. Maybe next time," Mel replied playfully.

She had let the desk know to relay any incoming calls to her room. She had just walked in when a light next to her bed came on.

"Yes?" Mel said into a speaker.

"The Torian from Angeles is online. Shall I connect you?" the operator asked.

"No, I'll take it in the report room," she replied. That way she could use the Comp to see Trent instead of just hearing his voice. She went back to the report room and retrieved the call.

"Sorry I missed your call. I got your message when I came in and called you right back," he told Melanie.

He could see her smile on his monitor almost as if she were right in front of him.

"After work I went to Sear-mart to get some things for around the dwelling. Hope I didn't interrupt anything?"   "No, I was just getting ready to get some sleep. We have to go back out again in the morning, for how long I'm not sure. I don't know if I'll be off before the weekend or not." "Darn," Trent said. "I received this invitation to a party and was hoping you would go with me." "Who is the invitation from?" she asked. "Believe it or not, it's from the Kofu Corporation." "Sounds like they want to find out how much you know about those microchips we recovered for them," Melanie said. "Yeah I know."

"You all right?" he asked her.

"Of course! Why wouldn't I be? You know this unit has one of the best reputations around."

"Yes I know. I just want to remind you of how proud I am of you and what you do." he could see her face flush with a warm sensation.

"Thanks Trent, you always seem to know how to make me feel good about myself. When we get some time together I plan on making you feel good too," she said with a wink. "Oh, and tell Bonnie to keep her hands to herself or I'm going to put handcuffs on her," Mel said playfully.

"Huh, she might like that," he said with a laugh.

"You're probably right," Melanie said laughing too.

"Night Trent."

"Night Melanie."

Chapter 28

Torian woke up to the sound of roosters "cock a doodle, doing."

"Where does my Comp get this stuff?" Torian wondered.

He got up and dressed telling the Comp to send Bonnie a message that he would be stopping by the Clone Museum today.

As the door opened he stepped outside looking up and down the hall. Still nothing, so he took the lift down to the Transport station listening to typical lift music that reminded him of the old band era.

In the Transport station he stopped by the Info-stand to look for any new net site info that might be interesting to read on the way there, then hopped on board the Tram when it arrived.

When he reached the museum the clerk at the ticket booth said, "Good morning," and let him in without sliding his card.

The Lib supplies a great deal of the information for the exhibits and he usually stops by once a week to check for realism so that the general public gets their wages worth.

The UCA has always been big on entertainment. Old movies, television shows and radio broadcasts from the past had been preserved and shown over the Outernet via the Lib or museum net site.

Torian walked by the morning Info cast booth with Clone-Steve, Clone-Dorothy and Clone-Jillian doing the Info this week.

The museum used clones from the past century and put them on the Info net sites for people who wanted to see today's information presented in an old fashioned way.

These particular anchors were constantly talking over each other trying to get their own viewpoint in and made Torian wonder how anyone could understand what the information was even about. But the polls from L-mails sent to the museum showed that the private sector thought it was entertaining so the museum continued to broadcast it anyway.

He continued through the Info and Radio section to see C-Orson speaking into an old radio microphone and talking about Martians destroying the Earth.

"No wonder they had such a fascination for visiting other planets back then," Torian thought to himself.

He took the museum lift to the Action section to see C-Rocky still sparring with C-Apollo, and C-Harry shooting at a bunch of bad guys. He was shooting blanks of course. The museum wouldn't want any of the clones to really get hurt.

When the UCA legalized cloning toward the beginning of the twenty-first century, people decided it was more exciting to see movie stars from the past for real, rather than wax figures that just stood there posing. So if a person wanted to see a particular star or historical figure all they had to do was send a request into the Museum.

When enough people had asked to see a particular person or event, the museum would contact the Supremes for authorization. The Supremes would then contact any living relatives of the chosen person to get authorization to exhume the body for DNA samples from the corpse.

You would take an egg cell from a donor and replace the nucleolus with the clone DNA then reinsert it, or place it in some type of cylinder filled with biotic fluid to finish the growth cycle. "Kind of like the cylinders they had found at Area 48," Torian thought.

They weren't always able to reproduce an exact replica when done this way.

When Chen had first brought Torian to the museum, he told him about the first sheep that had been cloned in Scotland back in 1997 and how many people of the time feared the prospect of cloning and what it might mean to a person's individuality. So cloning was banned until the obvious lack of people brought renewed interest.

He walked into the Music section and saw the line of girls waiting to get their picture with Clone Michael.

Of course the UCA doesn't allow any cloning of people who are still alive (that would be to confusing) so to be in the museum you had to be dead in order to be immortalized. "Guess that leaves me out," Torian thought happily.

As he left the Music section where different bands from the past were rocking out, he walked into the Comedy section and noticed the Ker from a few days before.

She was wearing a short purple skirt with matching shoes and a yellow blouse with ruffles watching C-Mickey on stage having his head pulled close to C-Marilyn's bosom.

"Hi, enjoying the Museum?" Torian asked her as he approached.

"Why yes. I come here quite often in order to get some tips for my clients."

Torian remembered reading that prostitution used to be banned some centuries ago, even though the profession had been around since before Ra'-hab helped Joshua's spies escape from the Canaanites in the city of Jericho back in 1225 B.C. It had only made sense to legalize it and monitor it for public safety reasons. These days Kers were required to visit a Med-priest every quarter for a check-up. You could visit Under-town or use the Comp to invite a Ker to your dwelling, which ever was more convenient.

"Well, I hope for the sake of realism they don't have you cover your face with a mask or something, I kind of like how you look right now," Torian told her.

She smiled and took more of an interest in him then.

"Say, have you hired me before or been to Madame Wang's in Under-town?" she asked.

"No, sorry I haven't had the pleasure of making your acquaintance. By the way, how is your friend? You know the one who had his attitude readjusted by the Sec Guardian?”

“Oh that’s where I remember you from; it was at the Transport station and in the Tram.”

“That’s right. How is he?”

“Still an idiot! Do you come here often?” she asked him.

“Yes. I’m the Torian here in Angeles and its part of the job.”

“Then you’re the one I should be talking to in case a client asks me for something I’m not familiar with.”

“Well, you can look up information from both the Lib and the Clone Museum’s Outernet sites for past and present events, or you are welcome to come into the Lib and sit down with a good optical disc and a cup of Joe.

Torian liked using old-style colloquialisms in his conversations with people, probably from reading too many books and watching too many old movies. Older generations understood, but most young adults and kids often ignored his slang and continued on acting as if they had understood. Not wanting to feel stupid.

“But if you can’t find what you’re looking for just send me an L-mail and my assistant or I’ll get back to you,” he finished telling her.

“Gee thanks. You’re an all right kind of guy, for a stuffy Torian,” she said with a smile. “My name is Stephanie. If you ever need a little something-extra look me up. It‘s on the house.”

“I’ll try to remember that,” he said as she turned and walked away. “Bye now.”

“Bye,” she replied over her shoulder.

He took the lift to the next floor and walked past C-Walt cutting the tape at the opening of D-land on one stage and walked thru the Presidential section where C-Richard was still professing that he wasn’t a crook.

There was C-George crossing the Delaware and for an extra wage a girl with a blue beret mingling in the crowd of onlookers would hand you a cigar, though Torian couldn’t remember the significance of that.

He went to the next floor and saw a replica of the 2004 Spirit and Opportunity rovers on a set with red clay and dirt and next to that display was C-Neil taking a giant leap and thought about the past day’s events. He thought again about the year 1969 when America took its first step on the moon and with that step; dreams of going to other planets became a reality.

The Orion missions helped us get to Mars, but like landing on the Moon it was viewed as just exploring. Bringing back some rocks and leaving our mechanical litter on another world, including one gravesite.

Was he right in his assumption that they had tried to create humans to visit other planets and if so, whom should he tell? And after all this time did it even matter?

He began to get a bit of a headache, so he decided to go to Under-town and visit a Chinese herb shop there.   On his way out he stopped by the clerk and told her everything looked fine. Last week someone got mixed up and had put C-Arnold in the presidential section by mistake.   He left the museum and walked across the street without looking both ways.

Chapter 29

The Riffs had traveled north of the hangar (where the gun battle with the marauders had taken place) following the signal from the homing device on the buggy.

"I can see why they call this place Death Val," Mel said looking at the barren landscape.

"With little or no food, water or shelter there's not much for someone to do out here. It's certainly the kind of the place to hide if you don't want to be found," O'Doul said.

"There's some sort of structure about a mile further north. Looks like that's where the signals coming from," Jones interrupted.

"What kind of a structure?" O'Doul asked.

"I'm not sure, but it isn't small," Jones replied.

"What's that up ahead?" Mel asked pointing to a pile of stones in the road.

O'Doul stopped the UCV and Mel got out and walked toward the pile. Something took off running from behind it leaving little puffs of dust in the air.

"Must have been some type of rodent," O'Doul said from behind Mel.

"I've got to stop walking up to piles of rocks," she said with a laugh. "Every time I do something keeps jumping out at me."

O'Doul picked up a rusted metal sign with the faded words, "Scott Castle."

"Now, who would build a castle in the desert?" he wondered out loud.

"Who knows, we usually patrol closer to the city and haven't been out this far before," Mel said.

They turned around to see the Sec Guardian standing behind them.

They walked past him as if he wasn't there and got back on board the UCV.

As the Guardian stepped up into the UCV, O'Doul started driving toward the castle.

They were about a quarter of a mile away when O'Doul pulled up behind a hill.

"I think it would be better if we hike in the rest of the way. Jones have they spotted us yet?"

"Nope, I don't think they have anything sophisticated enough to get through our jamming device. The radar shows lots of vehicles around the structure, including the dune buggy and I have quite a few heat signatures coming from the FLIR."

"There aren't a bunch of dogs hanging around the place are there?" Thompson asked with a chuckle elbowing Mel.

"Thanks," Mel said elbowing him back.

"Let's take a look people, and, ah, whatever," O'Doul said as he looked back at the Guardian.

O'Doul, Mel, and Thompson got out and started walking toward the structure.

O'Doul then asked the Guardian to allow them to go in covert style and check it out before the Guardian went in. The Guardian agreed.

O'Doul radioed his unit to spread out as they got closer and come in from different angles.

Jones was giving them Intel on potential positions of marauders over their Mics'.

Mel headed the long way around to the right side of the sandstone castle while Thompson went around to the left side near some hills to come up from the back.

O'Doul followed Thompson for a ways then approached the front of the castle when he saw that Thompson had made his way around back.

Thompson had noticed a huge cross up on the hill as he snuck around to the back of the building. The Sun was directly behind the cross giving off a strange halo.

"I hope that's supposed to be a good omen," Thompson whispered to himself.

He could see the trucks that had been at the hangar and radioed the info to the rest of the unit.

"Take care of the vehicles," O'Doul responded back to Thompson.

Thompson was already heading toward the trucks with his butterfly knife flipped out to disable the tires.

Mel came in from the right side along an outside wall. It was too tall to climb so she went back toward the front to find a way in. Suddenly a man stepped out from around the front of the building with his hands on his zipper, as if he was going to take a leak.

Mel came up with her right boot, aiming at the now exposed target and kicked the guy right where it hurts.

The marauder's knees turned inward and his shoulders squeezed in as if holding his head in place. Mel pivoted on her right foot and did a back round house kick with her left boot hitting the guy square in the head and sending him twisting in the air before he landed. She took out a plastic tie and cuffed the marauder's hands and feet, then went back to the place the guy had come from to find a way in.

Thompson had punctured at least two tires on each of the vehicles and was heading toward some cycles when two marauders came out from around one of the trucks. They each had a bottle of Tequila in their hands and were laughing until one of them spotted Thompson.

Thompson stopped crouching and stood erect, then walked toward the two.

"I see that your trucks have some minor vehicle infractions, may I see your license and registration please?"

The marauder on the right had a shotgun in his right hand and a bottle in his left.

The other marauder on the left started to reach for a handgun in his waistband saying, "Registration? We don't need no stinking registration."

"I hoped you would say something like that," Thompson said throwing his knife at the guy on the left.

The marauder was now holding his throat where the knife was protruding.

The man on the right seeing this dropped the bottle he was holding and raised the shotgun toward Thompson.

"A little late for that now," Thompson said grabbing the barrel of the shotgun with his left hand and spinning around hitting the man in the head with the back of his right hand.

The man let go of the shotgun staggering backward and reached for a machete he had in his belt.

Thompson still had a hold of the shotgun and used the butt of it to hit the man in the face; stunning him for a moment. Then Thompson turned the gun around and hit the guy in the head with the barrel knocking him out cold.

Thompson dragged the two bodies to the rear of the trucks and used plastic ties to cuff the unconscious one, then retrieved his butterfly knife from the dead marauder and wiped the blood off on the marauder's shirt.

O'Doul had climbed through an open window into a room and was standing behind a door that was slightly open, listening to a group of men inside the next room.

Peering in through the opening he could see the guy with the bandana sitting at the end of a big table. O'Doul figured bandana to be the leader and stood listening to them speak for several minutes.

A door opened behind O'Doul and in stepped a guy with a shotgun leveled right at O'Doul. The door that O'Doul had been looking through opened up and another marauder with a handgun walked in. O'Doul put his hands up while the guy with the handgun motioned O'Doul to follow him into the room where bandana was.

O'Doul stepped into the room and two men, one on each side of the doorway, grabbed O'Doul taking his guns, then manhandled him over to the far end of the table furthest from the guy with the bandana.

Bandana raised his bottle, "*Hola gringo*. Glad you could finally join us. We have been waiting to start the *fiesta* in your honor."

Several men came in from the back of the room pushing Mel in front of them and dragging Thompson by his feet.

O'Doul tensed up at the sight of Thompson being dragged by the men, but stopped when he felt the cold end of the shotgun propped against the back of his neck.

"Relax *gringo*. He is not dead. Unlike my men you butchered and the one that was killed outside." Bandana continued. "No, I want you all alive for our *fiesta*."

"You know of course that you are completely surrounded and that there will be other Riffs joining your little *fiesta*," O'Doul mimicked.

"I don't think so, *gringo*."

The double doors in front of the room opened up and Jones was brought in with her hands behind her back and a gag in her mouth.

Chapter 30

After leaving the museum Torian walked across the street to the Saks building so he could use the lift.

The museum was one of the few buildings in the city that didn't have conveyers or tubes connected to other buildings in order to monitor people entering or leaving the museum.

Most of the clothing worn by the clones and other articles used by them were original artifacts. They were very valuable in certain circles and would be a shame to have them stolen. Even the clones had to leave certain items in the museum when leaving for the day.

Inside the Saks building Torian took the lift down to the lower level and from there caught the Tram to Under-town.

After the catastrophe people thought it might be safer to live underground, so extensive work was done in creating a city underneath Angeles.

The problem with living underground for extended periods was that society became susceptible to depression while living in the enclosed environment.

"We needed to be outside and feel the Sun on our face, see the open skies or the stars at night, even if the temperature's during summer ranged on average from 100 F to 115 F," Torian thought.

People continued to live in Under-town even though the majority went back to the surface to rebuild and live in the newly forming cities.

Those that choose to stay in Under-town maintained some type of livelihood even though it became more the seedy side of human nature down there. But many things you couldn't find on the surface or in the city above could be found in Under-town.

A lot of good people still existed in Under-town and worked for companies, maintaining the plumbing, conduits or Trams that were under the city.

From the Tram he walked to the herb shop and stepped inside.

Chang must have hired someone new. She didn't look Chinese, but looks could be deceiving. She was a cute little blonde gal wearing a typical Chinese silk dress the color of turquoise with red dragons printed on it.

"Hello," he said to her.

"Hello to you," she said without an accent.

Torian hadn't recognized the young girl.

"*Wo yao zhi toutong de yao* (I need something for a headache)," he said wondering if she knew the language.

"Would you like some aspirin or do you prefer something a little stronger?" she replied in English.

He could see why she had been hired.

"I'd prefer some of Chang's mix if you don't mind."

"Not at all," she said. "I take it that you have been here before?"

"Yes, Chang is a friend of mine. Is he in?"

"No, he's out for the day. I think it's getting harder for him to work as often as he likes, so he's letting me help out more than before."

"You're not that little girl with pigtails who used to come late in the afternoon and help out around here are you?"

"Yes, I 'm Chang's granddaughter Ling."

"Well I'll be darned. Glad to see you have grown up to be a fine young lady."

"Thank you" she said.

"*Bu keqi* (Your welcome)," he replied.

She handed him a little pouch containing Chang's special mix of herbs and spices that always eased his headaches quickly and kept them from coming back anytime soon.

Chang had told Torian the headaches were from sitting in front of the Comp too long.

Torian gave Ling two coins and told her one was for her and the other for Chang.

She thanked him again and took them promptly to the back room so that no one would see her with them.

Coined money wasn't used anymore but had great collector value to it. Also Chang would know it came from either Chen or Torian and tell his granddaughter to take very good care of his most important customers.

Torian was about to leave when he looked out the window and saw Jameson the dune buggy driver who had been let go by SG. He still had a bandaged arm and was crossing the street with the passenger that had been with him. He wasn't wearing the same outfit he had on in the UCV and Torian wondered if the tracking device had been found.

Torian stepped outside and started to follow them, but stayed on his side of the street keeping a distance between them. He didn't think they would recognize him from the UCV since they hadn't really looked at him when they were let go.

Seeing a tavern coming up on their side, Torian ducked into a doorway just in case they stopped. Sure enough they looked around. When they felt comfortable they went inside.

Torian looked around, but didn't see anyone that was interested in the two he had been following, so he walked across the street and into the tavern.

Jameson and the passenger had gone to the back of the tavern and were sitting at a table with another man whose back was to Torian.

Torian sat down at the bar. The bartender came over and asked, "What'll you have mate?"

"I'll take a light beer on tap," he said placing the pouch of herbs on the counter.

The bartender seeing the pouch knew that Torian had been in one of the local shops and became less tense. "Coming right up," he said.

Torian reached for a bowl of peanuts that was on the bar and started munching on them, again drawing less attention to him by acting like a typical patron.

The bartender brought him his beer and Torian handed him a wage card that was from one of the Under-town factories. The bartender slid it through the reader and the light turned green. "Thanks mate," he said and went back to the end of the bar to watch the Shield game on an overhead Comp.

Without being too noticeable, Torian tried to get a good look at the man sitting with the other two. One thing for sure the man wasn't a local.

He had on a dark blue suit, black polished shoes, a gold ring on his right middle finger and what looked like a gold watch on his left wrist.

You don't flash that kind of stuff around Under-town unless you're packing some heavy heat.

Torian couldn't get a good look at the man's face, but his voice was getting louder and Torian overheard him yell at his two listeners.

"You both should have died trying to get those chips back."

"And how do you suppose I got this bloody arm broken mate," Jameson said holding up his bandaged arm.

The man with the gold ring grabbed Jameson's arm and yanked it down hard onto the table.

Jameson winced in pain and tried pulling his arm back but the man held it down firmly.

Torian couldn't hear what was said after that, as if they realized they had gotten too loud. He looked up at the overhead Comp monitor as if minding his own business and watching the game sensing that the bartender was looking over his way.

Torian using his peripheral vision saw the man with the gold ring get up and leave through a back ally door.

Torian still didn't get a good look at the man's face but saw that he had blond hair.

The other two headed toward the front of the tavern.

As they approached, Torian stuck some peanuts in his mouth to help cover his face and started chewing.

Jameson feigned a look as if he hadn't noticed Torian.

"Should I follow these guys or the one who went out the back?" he wondered. He opted for the new guy and headed toward the rear of the tavern. "Cleansing room is in the back, right?" Torian asked the bartender who was watching him walk by. "Yep, the pisser's in back, but don't use the dungy," he yelled as Torian continued on.

Torian went into the cleansing room and man did it stink. He tried to open a window, but it was nailed shut. He didn't want to walk right out the back door in case the bartender saw him and figured he was following gold ring.

The window was out so he turned to walk back out of the cleansing room when Jameson and the passenger came in.

"Don't I know you from somewhere mate?" Jameson asked Torian.

"Who, me?" was all Torian could think of.

Chapter 31

Thompson opened his eyes to see O'Doul and Mel tied up in chairs across the table from him. He tried to move his hands, but he too had his hands tied up to the arms of the chair he was in. Jones was tied up in the chair next to him.

"Ah! Glad you decided to wake up from your *siesta, gringo*," the guy with the bandana said. "My name is Hernandez, but you can call me *El Jefe*," he said proudly.

"Leader of what?" O'Doul asked.

"Why, me *amigos* here and me are part of the new *revolucion*," Hernandez said as he raised his bottle and took a drink.

A glint of light shined from a gold ring on Hernandez's right hand as he lifted the bottle.

"*Viva la revolucion!*" Several of the marauders chimed in raising their bottles and glasses as well.

"You see we have decided to take back what was once our ancestors and rightfully belongs to us."

"And that is?" Jones asked.

"*Los Angeles* of course," Hernandez replied.

"What if the people of Angeles don't want to join your little revolution?" Mel asked.

"That is easy *senorita,* we will kill anyone that gets in our way," Hernandez replied with a straight face. "But enough talk of dying. We are here to celebrate, right, *amigos*?"   "Right!" the other men yelled.

Music filled the room and some of the marauders were dancing around with some women who had come in bringing more bottles of tequila and wine.

One of the women (much older than the rest) with long gray hair tied in a ponytail, walked over to Thompson and told him, "You will be my *de amor* (love)," and planted a big kiss on Thompson's lips, then laughed out loud showing her missing front teeth.

"That's what you get for being a ladies man," Jones told Thompson, having the gag taken out of her mouth by one of the marauders.

"It's a damn curse always being the best looking guy in town," Thompson said as he tried to wipe his mouth on his shoulder.

One of the marauders walked over and tipped Mel's chair back. "I think you and I shall play house," he said dragging her chair toward one of the other rooms.

O'Doul and Thompson struggled with their ropes but could not pull free.

The toothless woman poured some tequila in Thompson's lap. "I think we shall start a fire to warm things up," she said with a laugh, then lit a match holding it over the front of Thompson's pants.

"Oh shit not that!" Thompson said struggling.

Hernandez sat down on the table in front of Jones pulling out a knife and held it up to her face. "Well now! What have we here?" he said.

O'Doul continued to struggle, but was unable to free himself.

"Where the hell did that Sec Guardian go?" O'Doul wondered.

Chapter 32

"I was just finishing up. It's all yours," Torian said to the two men as he tried to walk past them; but the passenger pushed him backwards.

"You were with those Riffs weren't you mate," Jameson said. "I thought trading the buggy in would keep anyone from following us yet here you are. You know one of those Riffs broke my arm. I need to pay someone back for that and it might as well be you."

Jameson reached behind him with his left hand pulling out a little .22 Caliber handgun and pointed it at Torian's face.   "Can't we all get along?" was all Torian could think of as he raised his hands in the air.

The cleansing room door flew open and in stepped Sec Guardian 5000. His makeshift eyes a steady red as he reached out with both hands grabbing the necks of the two men and slammed their heads together. Both men fell to the floor.

"SG is that you?" Torian asked seeing the 5000 on the Guardian's chest.

"Approved," was displayed across his screen.

"Okay, next time I'll pay for your hotdog too," Torian told him.

"Follow me," was now displayed on SG's screen.

Torian stepped over the two men and followed the Guardian into the tavern.

The bartender was slumped over the bar and a sawed off shotgun was lying on the floor.

The Guardian went out the front door and Torian grabbed some more peanuts and put them in his mouth before going outside.

Torian followed the Guardian to the lift going up to the surface level where the Guardian walked out of the building and out onto the street where he turned toward Torian.

"Return to the Lib;" was displayed and SG turned and walked away.

"Who was that masked man?" Torian said as he headed to the Lib.

When he got there Bonnie was wearing a pretty pink outfit, pink fingernails and pink eyes. "First time anyone *wanted* to have pink eye," Torian thought to himself.

"How did it go at the museum?" Bonnie asked.

"It was just fine. After the museum I went to Chang's place, than I followed two guys to a tavern.

"I didn't know you were a switch hitter?" Bonnie asked. "How long have you had these urges?" she asked, crossing her arms and tapping her foot like a parent waiting for an explanation.

"Well, they did meet me in the cleansing room, but when they tried to kill me the urges stopped immediately."

"Sounds like *you* almost stopped immediately. What changed their minds, your charming personality?"

Torian smiled. "Actually a tall dark stranger appeared out of nowhere and convinced them that an Angeles without a Torian is like a day without sunshine."

"Well, why doesn't some tall dark stranger come and rescue me when I need one?" she huffed, sitting down at her desk.

Torian went into his office and noticed his Comp had a blinking red light on it. He knew that there was an important message that had been sent and pulled up an L-mail from the Supremes requesting he continue to research and locate other possible areas correlating to Area 48.

He sat back in his chair and took out the pouch that he had purchased at Chang's. He was about to call out to Bonnie when she came in with a cup of water for him to mix with the powder.

"What would I do without you, Bonnie?"

"You'd better not try and find out," she replied with a scowl.

Chapter 33

An explosion outside gained the attention of the marauders.

"*Vamos*! (Go on!)," Hernandez ordered the marauders.

Three marauders ran to the front double doors that Jones had been brought in through.

As one of them reached to open one of the doors, both doors came crashing inward knocking him and another marauder to the floor.

Sec Guardian 2000 was standing in the entry way with a glowing red glare.

The marauder still standing near the door raised his shotgun but the Guardian grabbed the barrel and bent it backward 90 degrees while the marauder was still holding it.

The marauder dropped the shotgun reaching for a handgun in his holster but the Guardian grabbed him by the neck with his right hand lifting him completely off the ground. With a downward motion and a sharp upward movement the Guardian snapped the marauder's neck. The Guardian simply let go of the lifeless body dropping it to the floor.

Hernandez yelled at the other marauders to shoot the *"Angel de la Guarda* (Guardian angel)"* as Hernandez ran toward the back of the room.

The toothless old woman sitting on the edge of the table in front of Thompson pulled out a knife to cut Thompson's throat.

The Guardian stepped forward pushing down on the other end of the oak table creating a seesaw effect that sent the old women flying up and over the top of the Guardian. The woman flew out a window above the front entrance. The table was now on its end being riddled with bullets from other marauders.

The Guardian lifted the table and used it as a makeshift shield. He walked several feet forward placing the table down in front of him, still on its end, protecting him from the bullets. He bent over Thompson and Jones and yanked on the ropes tearing them apart easily, then yanked on O'Doul's ropes as well.

The three Riffs quickly got behind the Guardian and the barrier.

The Guardian picked up the table and as he moved forward spun it sideways making a wider shield for the Riffs to hide behind. He continued walking forward driving the marauders back against the wall.

Two of the marauders ran out the back door but three were pinned against the wall as the Guardian pressed the table against them, the legs of the table collapsing against the wall. The Guardian then dropped the table down on top of the marauder's feet.

Three grimacing faces appeared. The Guardian reached for two marauders shoving their heads back into the wall. Their heads left imprints as they slumped forward over the table.

O'Doul used a quick upper cut with his right fist that knocked the third one unconscious as well.

Thompson kicked open the door where the marauder had taken Mel. She was still tied to the chair with it leaning back against the wall. A gunshot sounded and a bullet ricocheted off the doorframe next to Thompson's head.

The marauder hearing the commotion outside the door was trying to climb out a window as he aimed at Thompson.

Thompson winced from the missed shot but went straight for the marauder. Grabbing his ankle with his right hand and tugging on the back of the guy's pants with his left hand pulling him back into the room.

The marauder fired the gun into Thompson's combat vest as he turned around to face Thompson, but Thompson didn't flinch this time. He head butted the man so that the marauder's head made a whiplash motion. He then grabbed the marauder's head by the hair bending the marauder forward. Thompson stepped forward to his left, reaching around the guy's neck with his right arm and spinning himself and the marauder so that they were now back to back. Still holding the marauder's neck with his right arm the marauder's head was now resting on top of Thompson's right shoulder. Thompson leaned forward bending the marauder backwards and up off his feet. Thompson made a quick back and forth motion snapping the marauder's neck. He let go of the marauder that now slid down Thompson's back to the floor and walked over to Mel.

Jones was already untying Mel's right wrist from the chair as Thompson reached over to untie the left.

O'Doul appeared in the doorway with their guns asking if everyone was all right.

Mel stood up from the chair.

O'Doul handed Thompson and Jones their guns.

Mel took her 9mm from O'Doul and walked over to the marauder on the floor.

"Daniel took your life, but your soul belongs to me." She fired one shot into the marauder's lifeless body.

Chapter 34

After relaxing for a bit Torian looked at some of his other L-mails.

One was from the Kofu Electronics Corporation asking for an RSVP for the dinner.

Melanie had said she was on assignment so she wouldn't be able to go. He wanted to go since everything that had been happening seemed to revolve around this company.

"Bonnie?" he called through the open door.

"Yes, dear, what can I do for you?"

"Do you have anything formal to wear to the Kofu Corporation dinner?"

"Do I? You bet your sweet bippy I do."

"Great, I'll meet you at the Kofu tower in Vegas tomorrow night around nineteen hundred. Oh and bring Maggie with you."

Bonnie's smile didn't change, but her eyebrow turned up a bit.

Torian sent a reply that he would be attending the dinner with one guest. He picked up the invitation that was still on top of his Comp and stuck it in his coat pocket then gestured to his Comp as he walked out of the office.

"I'm heading home, Bonnie. See you tomorrow night."

She just waved at him talking to herself and making appointments on the Comp.

"I have to get my nails done, hair done, oh, and a bikini wax, definitely!"

Torian thought he'd grab a bite to eat before going home so he took the wind tube to the Food Theater.

He saw a lady in front of him trying to hold her dress down as she was coming to the end of the tube. The two boys that had been there the other day were at the end pointing up the ladies dress and laughing. Their smiles turned to frowns as he exited the tube. As he was exiting he noticed a women walk over to the two boys and grab each one by an ear, telling them to behave and walked away with the two boys in tow.

Torian looked at the menus available and decided to have some good old-fashioned fish and chips and a Coksi. He got his meal and sat by the window.

He looked up and out, but didn't see any flying nuns the size of a Guardian this time so he took a bite of his fish. He reached for a napkin, but it fell off the end of the table. As he bent down to pick it up he heard a gunshot and the Coksi that was sitting right in front of him exploded. He felt the liquid dripping off the table onto his pants and turned around to see a man with his arm in a sling running toward the wind tube.

Torian grabbed some fries and ran toward the wind tube as well.

Diving in Torian was now horizontal, flying like Superman inside the tube.

The gunman was knocking people down as he pushed off the top and bottom of the tube trying to gain speed. As the gunman reached the end he looked back over his right shoulder to see if anyone was following.

Torian flew out the end of the tube knocking the gunman down. They both went sprawling on the floor as the man's gun went sliding across the floor.

Torian now recognized Jameson who was cursing and holding his bandaged arm.

Torian got up and ran over to pick up the gun while Jameson headed to the lift.

Torian picked up the Glock 9mm realizing that it was made out of a hard plastic, which must be how Jameson was able to get it into the city.

Torian turned around but was too late; the door to the lift was closing.

"Huh," Torian said as he ran to another lift.

The lights outside the lift indicated that Jameson was going up, so Torian pushed the top button inside the second lift.

These particular lifts were located on the outside of the building and had glass windows so that you could see outside as you rode up and down.

Torian could see Jameson in the lift above him looking back down at Torian and flipping him off with his middle finger.

Jameson had reached the top of the seventy-story building and exited the lift he was in.

Torian stepped out when his lift got to the top and heard footsteps fading down the hall, so he ran toward the sound and heard a door slam.

Torian came around a corner slowly and saw a door with the words: "Roof access. Sec Guardians/Maintenance only."

Torian opened the door and peeked in. There were stairs leading upward, so he took them two at a time till he got to another door at the top and opened it up slowly.

He peered out onto the roof with the gun in his right hand and saw several big metal housing units, probably for climate control. He stepped out onto the roof looking left around the door to see if anyone was there. Then he looked right to see if Jameson had gone that way. That's when a pipe came down on Torian's wrist knocking the gun out of his hand.

"Hey that hurt," Torian said.

Jameson picked up the gun and pointed it at Torian.

"G-day mate," Jameson said. "I guess my luck has changed," Jameson said smiling as he pulled the trigger.

Chapter 35

From inside the main room where they had been tied up, the Riffs heard gunfire coming from outside where the trucks were parked in back.

The Riffs ran outside to see the Guardian holding the back end of one of the trucks about three feet off the ground so that the rear-drive wheel just spun in the air.

O'Doul ran to the passenger side and pointed his handgun inside the front window.

"Turn off the engine," he told the driver.   The driver opened his door and jumped out to run away but got kicked in the jaw by Thompson who had gone around to the driver side.

O'Doul climbed into the truck from the passenger side putting the gearshift into park and turned off the engine.

The Sec Guardian let go and the truck dropped to the ground, then walked toward the front of the castle.

"There were still some cycles that I didn't get a chance to disable," Thompson told the unit as they followed the Guardian.

The Guardian was getting on one of the marauders cycles that was parked in front of the castle next to the UCV.

"Must be valet parking," O'Doul said, referring to the presence of the UCV.

The Guardian must have driven it up to the front of the castle.

The unit got on board the UCV and Jones went to her monitors to track the escaping cycles.

O'Doul now in the driver seat took off in the direction the Guardian had gone following the escaping marauders.

"We're not going to catch up to them this way," Mel told O'Doul.

"You're right. You and Thompson get going."

Mel walked back to see that Thompson was already climbing into the left side cycle pod. Mel flipped the switch to open the right pod door panel and climbed down onto her cycle.

The sides of the UCV opened outward like an expanding accordion.

Thompson was sitting on his cycle on the left and Mel sat on hers to the right, putting on her helmet. They started their engines and accelerated so that the rear tires on the cycles were turning as the pods lowered the cycles to the ground.

Once the tires matched the speed of the UCV the two took off from the pods as the sides of the UCV closed back up.

Mel and Thompson could see by the small monitors on each of their instrument panels that they were moving up fast on the targets ahead.

Mel heard music over the speaker in her helmet.

Thompson had turned on his Mic audio and was listening to music as they raced toward the marauders.

Chapter 36

"Click, Click," Jameson looked down at the gun in his hand.

"Oh, I don't really care for guns so I took the liberty of unloading it on my way up here," Torian said to Jameson.

"Shit," Jameson said as he kept pulling the trigger on the empty gun.

A fluttering sound came from above them and Torian looked up to see SG gliding down from the sky. He landed on both feet in a half-kneeling position to ease the impact.   The Guardian stepped between Jameson and Torian grabbing Jameson by the front of his shirt.

The Guardian lifted up his right arm with a jerk letting go of Jameson who was now rocketing skyward; still pulling the trigger and pointing it at Torian as he headed into the sky.

The Guardian walked into the stairway that had led to the roof waiting for Torian to step inside. Torian looked up to see Jameson fading away like a balloon let go on a summer day. The Guardian closed the door and they started down the stairs.

SG seemed in a bit of a hurry and by the time Torian got to the lift the Guardian was gone. He decided he'd had enough excitement for one day and went back to his dwelling.

There were no messages from the Riff station or Melanie, but there was one from Bonnie wanting to know what color suit he would be wearing so they wouldn't clash.

Torian sent a reply saying he would be wearing a typical black Edo and tails and hoped that would suffice.

After cleansing and a bite to eat, without getting shot at this time, he asked the Comp to turn on the Wallavision to the museum's late night channel.   He never could decide whether to watch C- Jay or C- David, so he asked the Comp to split the wall so that both clones were standing next to each other almost as if they were telling each other jokes.

Chapter 37

Thompson and Mel could see three marauders on cycles just ahead of them. One of the marauders started to angle off to the right.

"He's mine," Mel said into her helmet Mic as she veered off to follow him.

Thompson revved his engine to shorten the distance between himself and the other two.

Thompson was coming up fast behind the marauders.

The one on the left looked back over his right shoulder. Seeing that Thompson was behind him, he reached with his left hand for a gun in his waistband. He turned so that he was firing at Thompson from under his right arm.

Thompson swerved his cycle from side to side. After a minute he said, "Enough of this," and pushed a button next to the grip of the left handlebar with his thumb.

A rocket shot out from the front of Thompson's bike and hit the marauders rear tire. The bike flipped forward sending the marauder flying through the air and landing hard about thirty feet from where he had been knocked off the cycle.

Thompson continued on after the other marauder.

Thompson pushed another button on the handlebar giving him a boost of speed catching up to the other marauder so that they were right next to each other.

Thompson turned on his P.A. and told the driver to pull over for failing to yield at a stop sign. With a puzzled look on his face the marauder accelerated his cycle ahead of Thompson.

Thompson slammed on his brakes turning his cycle sideways and sending up a wave of sand.

The marauder looked back at Thompson and thought that he had given up. He faced forward with a big grin, but it lasted only a second as he realized that a Sec Guardian was standing right in front of him.

As the marauder approached the Guardian stuck his right leg behind him for balance extending his right arm out to his side and closed-lined the oncoming marauder.

The cycle kept going underneath the Guardian but the marauder folded over the outstretched arm. The momentum made the Guardian slide backwards for about ten feet before coming to a stop with the marauder still hanging over his arm like a dinner napkin over a waiter's arm.

Thompson rode up to the Guardian got off his cycle, and lifted the helmet's face shield to look at the marauder who had been hung out to dry.

The marauder had stopped, but his eyeballs had popped out and were hanging by strings of nerves from the sockets.   "I've heard of stopping on a dime, but I've never seen it done like that before," Thompson said. He pushed the face shield back down on the marauder's helmet and got back on his cycle. Then he revved his engine taking off in the direction that Mel had gone.

Chapter 38

Torian woke up realizing he had fallen asleep on the couch. The Comp had turned off the wall screen when it determined that he was sleeping.

It was still early evening so he decided to get up and go out. After all, it was a Friday night and usually Melanie and he would be out having dinner or go to the Lib for a movie.

He decided to try the Fish Bowl club that he had read about.

It was on the eightieth of the Union building not too far from his dwelling.

When he arrived he sat down at the bar ordering a drink and checked out his surroundings.

The place was full of people, some sitting in booths or at tables along the circumference of the bowl; others were dancing inside the giant fish bowl in the middle of the club. The people inside the sphere were spinning around dancing on air, literarily.

There was a tap on his shoulder so he turned to see Stephanie standing behind him with a pleasant smile. She was wearing a short red skirt with matching shoes and a see- through pink blouse which advertised it was a little chilly in the room for her.

"Well…well, fancy seeing you here," Torian said.

"Yes, I've been coming here on a regular basis lately. Seems like a lot of my clients have been busy so I haven't had many calls."

"Well, it's their loss and my gain," he told her.

Her smile lit up and she sat down next to him.

"So what brings you out alone on a Friday night?" she asked.

"Couldn't sleep, so I thought I'd come check this place out."

"Yeah, it's kind of nice here. Lots of potentials, if you know what I mean," she said reaching over and put her hand on his knee.

"Yes, I guess you could find a mate if the right person came along."

"Mate," she said with a laugh withdrawing her hand. "Me? Stuck with just one person for the rest of my life? I don't think so."

"Well different strokes for different folks I guess," he said.

She gave him a quizzical look then laughed out loud using her hand to give his knee a gentle push.

He took a sip of his drink and out of the corner of his eye he noticed a man walking toward them. It was the same man that had been wearing the yellow suit in the Transport area. He was wearing a purple suit tonight.

"I've been looking for you," he said grabbing Stephanie by her right arm.

"Hey, you know how to reach me just like everyone else. Let go."

"I'll let go when I'm good and ready."

"I think the lady would prefer that you were good and ready now," Torian said.

"Stay out of this pops," he said with a menacing leer.

Torian could see that there was still some cotton in the man's nostril from the other day so he reached over without getting up and pinched the man's nose between his thumb and forefinger.

"Ouch! Hey, watch the nose. Okay man, I'm letting go," he said releasing Stephanie.

"I believe you owe the lady an apology," Torian said.

"Sorry," he said to both of them with a slight nasal sound and teary eyes.

At this Torian let go.

"That's better," Stephanie said. "You sure I can't talk you into or out of a little something," Stephanie asked Torian, again putting her hand on his knee.

"Sorry. Tonight I just stopped by for a drink, but I enjoyed the pleasant company while it lasted," he told her patting her hand like a friend would.

"Okay," she said with a smile, and then looked at the guy in purple. "I'll go with you, but you'd better behave or I'll plug up the other side of your nose," she said giving Torian a wink.

"Thank you for being such a gentleman and my offer still stands on the freebie." She leaned over and kissed Torian on the cheek.

As the two lovebirds walked off, Torian could see the guy holding his nose trying to see if Torian had done any permanent damage.

Torian chuckled to himself and was finishing his drink when he noticed two men across the room looking in his direction. One of them seemed to be pointing directly at him.

He was about to look over his shoulder to see if there was someone behind him when he realized that the man pointing was the passenger who had been with Jameson--the same man who had pushed him in the cleansing room at the tavern.

He was wearing brown pants and a leather jacket talking to a baldheaded man wearing a dark blue suit. Baldy motioned with his hand to two other men who were sitting at a table behind them.

The two new arrivals stood next to baldy as he pointed in Torian's direction. Then the two men split up, one going to the right, the other to the left. Baldy and the passenger with the leather jacket started walking toward Torian, pushing people out of their way as they approached.

The odds didn't seem to be in Torian's favor and he remembered a saying from an old movie from 1965 with Tony Curtis and Ross Martin called "<u>The Great Race</u>."

Martin played the villain with Curtis playing the hero. The two had been fencing when Martin realized that he was losing said, "he who fights and runs away, may live to fight another day." Then Martin jumped out a window.

Fighting another day seemed pretty reasonable at this point, so Torian got up and headed for the dance bowl.

Several people were coming out from inside the bowl.

Torian looked back over his shoulder to see that the two that had split up were coming up from behind him.

Baldy and leather jacket saw that Torian was heading toward the bowl and tried to cut him off, but the people coming out passed in front of them slowing them down.

Torian went into the sphere and found himself floating up into the center with a few others that where still inside.

Baldy and leather jacket came in after him while the other two stayed down at the entrance.

Baldy was off to the right side and leather jacket was coming up on Torian's left.

Torian pushed off a couple that was spinning next to him so that he had some momentum and headed toward the side of the bowl.

Baldy was doing the breaststroke in midair trying to get up enough speed to catch up with him.

Leather jacket had already reached the side of the bowl and was walking sideways along the inner wall that had suction to it.

As Torian was about to hit the inner wall he did a swimmer's flip turn and pushed off the wall with his feet shooting him back across the middle to the other side.

Leather jacket saw this and pushed off after him.

Baldy had grabbed one of the dancers, who was spinning around in the air, and used him to push off of heading in Torian's direction.

When Torian got to the other side of the bowl, he planted his feet on the inside wall and took off running. Baldy and leather jacket also reached the inner wall and both of them started running after Torian.

It must have looked like a show because Torian could hear clapping coming from the people outside the bowl.

The two men that had been waiting at the entrance came in and started running up the sides of the sphere to cut Torian off.

Torian stopped, seeing that all four of the men were getting close.

Just as they reached out to grab him he squatted down and pushed off with his feet, flying across the middle again. Unable to stop themselves, the four men ran into each other and bounced off into the air in different directions.

When Torian reached the other side, he ran down the sphere to the exit below and stepped outside.

As he walked away he looked back and waved at the four men

scrambling to get to the exit. Torian turned to see where he was going and ran smack dab into the clone from the hangar.

"Huh! Can't a guy get a break around here?" he asked the clone.

Chapter 39

It was getting dark as the chase continued.

Mel could see the glow from the taillight of the cycle in front of her, but it was getting harder to see the road ahead. She could tell there was a hill coming up and the taillight faded around the hill.

She rode up to the point in which she thought she had seen the cycle last and stopped.

She didn't see the light so she looked down at her monitor, but the blinking dot was gone. She turned off the engine and removed her helmet to see if she could hear the sound of the other cycle, but heard nothing.

She felt a presence coming toward her on her right side so she looked that way, but got knocked off her cycle and onto the ground before she knew what hit her.

Mel fell sideways and backward but knew how to roll and got back up on her feet. She reached for her gun but it had fallen out in the dirt.

A light came on from the cycle the marauder had ridden and Hernandez stepped in front of it facing Mel. *"Senorita,* I see that you are not yet done playing house. I, Hernandez, will satisfy your needs." "Your amigo couldn't. What makes you think you can?" Mel replied.

"He was a mere boy. I am a man," he said stepping closer to Mel.

She tried a front kick but Hernandez stepped back and pushed her foot away.

"I like a *senorita* with spirit."

Mel moved forward pretending to throw a punch with her right hand, but spun around using her left arm and hit Hernandez with a backhand. Hernandez's head recoiled from the blow, but he came back with two quick jabs to Mel's chin and hit her in the stomach. She fell to her knees with a trickle of blood coming from her lip.

As she was about to get up Hernandez kicked her from the side in the stomach. Mel grunted from the impact rolling over a cactus on the ground next to her.

Hernandez stood over her as she lay on her back straddling her with his legs on each side.

"Now you will know who El Jefe is."

Mel grabbed some of the cactus that had broken off when she fell over it, sat up, and rammed the cactus into Hernandez's privates. Hernandez yelped like a stuck pig and fell backward onto the ground.

Mel got up and looked for her gun, found it, then walked back over to Hernandez and pointed it at him. He was still in pain and didn't look up as she stood over him.

She heard the sound of a cycle coming toward her and the light was shining in her face.

Thompson pulled up just a few feet from Mel, turning off his cycle engine and taking off his helmet. "I see you have everything under control as usual."

"You didn't expect any less, did you?" Mel replied.

"Say, no matter what happened back there..." Thompson began.

"--Nothing happened," Mel interrupted. "The guy didn't have time to do anything to me but talk about what he was going to do. That privilege is left to whomever I decide to play roughhouse with and nobody else," she paused. "By the way, thanks for ringing his neck."

"No problem. It was only because you were a little tied up at the time," Thompson said reaching down to cuff Hernandez.

While the two Riffs had been talking Hernandez pulled out a concealed gun from his pocket and pointed it at Thompson's face.

Mel's gun went off and Thompson didn't have to worry about cuffing Hernandez any more.

There were footsteps behind them and they turned to see two green eyes coming at them from the dark. The Guardian walked into the lights from the cycles. On his display were the words: "Termination approved."

Chapter 40

Torian looked back over his shoulder and saw the four men exiting the fish bowl, smiling as they came toward him.

Torian turned away from the clone to face the four men.

The clone stepped around and in-between Torian and the oncoming men.

"We have not yet been properly introduced, my name is *Ichi Ban--Torian*-san," the clone said to Torian as he put up his hand to stop the oncoming men.   Baldy reached out and grabbed Ichi Ban's shirt with both hands lifting him up off the ground.

Ichi Ban using the upward momentum kicked the two men standing on each side of baldy on their chins as he was lifted in the air, and then used his hands to clap both sides of baldies head, boxing his eardrums. Baldy let go and Ichi Ban used a karate chop to baldies larynx causing him to move his hands from his ears to his throat.

Leather jacket was still on his feet behind baldy; he grabbed a bottle from one of the tables and smashed it on the top of a stool pointing the sharp end of the bottle toward Ichi Ban.

Ichi Ban made a shame-on-you gesture with his finger then kicked out with his foot knocking the bottle up and out of leather jacket's hand. Leather jacket took off running in the opposite direction, along with the other two men who had gotten up from the floor.

Baldy was still standing there holding his neck, wondering when he would be able to breathe again. Ichi Ban gently moved him to a chair and sat him down. Baldy just sat there with a strange look on his face holding his windpipe taking short gasps of air. Ichi Ban looked over at Torian and said, "My benefactor wishes to see you tomorrow night in good health, *Torian-san*."

"*Domo arigato* (Thank you very much) *Ichi Ban-san*," Torian said with a slight bow.

"*Lie, do itashimashite* (You're welcome)," *Ichi Ban* said as he walked away.

"There goes the Clone Ranger," Torian said to baldy placing his right hand behind baldies neck to release a pressure point so that he could breathe again. He slapped baldy on the shoulder so he could take a gulp of air.

Torian thanked baldy for the dance and left.

When Torian walked in he heard the Comp playing circus music alerting him that Melanie was messaging him. He sat down at the Comp to see an image of Melanie on the monitor with some Riffs in the background.

"Hi Trent, I was afraid you might be sleeping so I was just going to leave a message."

"Hi good-looking," he said, even though Melanie looked as though she was having a bad hair day.

"We got in early this morning. I need to finish my reports then I'm going to get some sleep. If you're not doing anything let me know and I'll come in to Angeles."

Torian told Melanie that he had asked Bonnie to go with him to the Kofu dinner, but if Mel would meet them in Vegas around nineteen hundred then they could all go together.

Melanie said, "That would be great. That way she could keep an eye on the two of them, so that they didn't get into any mischief."

Mel winked and threw him a kiss with her fingers.

He blew a kiss back and told her he would make arrangements for her to be an additional guest.

He checked his L-mail file folder for the RSVP resending it, adding Melanie as an additional guest. He received an immediate response back from the Kofu Corporation advising him that would be just fine.

Torian laid down to get some sleep, but was restless so he got up and left to pick up the Edo he would be wearing for the dinner then headed back home to relax before his big night on the town.

He asked the Comp to turn the wall screen on to the Sec Guardian channel.

You could watch Riffs live when they were accompanied by Guardians via radio frequencies from the cameras mounted on their faceplates.

The familiar opening sound track was being played, "Bad marauders, bad marauders, what you going to do when they terminate you."

Chapter 41

The Riffs were at the station waiting most of the night for the Med-priest and the cleanup crews to come back from Scott Castle with what was left of Hernandez and his marauders.

Not much evidence had been found on Hernandez's revolution, so they had hoped that whatever had started there, ended there as well.

After Mel called Trent, she and KJ went into the wash and dry to clean up before they went into the report room to type their reports.

Thompson had already started when Mel walked into the room.

Mel noticed that he was quiet for a change. "Hey, buddy, what's up?" Mel asked Daniel.

"O'Doul is in the Captain's office getting his butt chewed because we didn't bring the leader back in for questioning. We didn't leave too many suspects around either to verify our stories."

"Since when do we need someone to corroborate our story? The crime scene gives an account of everything that happened."

"I know, but this Guardian hanging around worries me," Thompson said. Jones walked in and sat down. "Why the long faces you two? KJ asked.

Before either could answer, O'Doul walked in with a bewildered expression and sat down. They all looked at him and waited.

O'Doul looked up realizing he was the center of attention.

"The Sec Guardian verified our story."

"All right! That's one for the good guys," Thompson exclaimed.

"So why the puzzled look then, if everything is fine?" Mel asked O'Doul.

"We're going on another assignment. We've all been promoted to senior grade with an additional member assigned to our team," O'Doul replied.

"Yeah baby! That's great. What's her name?" Thompson asked with two raised eyebrows.

"It's not a her," O'Doul replied.

"Who then?" KJ asked.

"Him who, that's who," O'Doul pointed to the doorway where Sec Guardian 2000 was now standing.

Chapter 42

It was eighteen hundred as Torian finished getting dressed in his black Edo, dabbing some cologne on and heading for the door. He had put together an overnight bag with some casual clothes in it.

He took the lift to the Transport station and from there the Bullet Tram to Vegas.

He arrived a few minutes before nineteen hundred and saw that Bonnie was already waiting for him in the Vegas Transport station instead of at the Kofu building.

"I thought you might have stood me up there for a moment," she said.

Bonnie was wearing a black dress with white lace trim around the collar with a pearl necklace and matching earrings. Her eyes had a slight purple tint to them.

"What's the purple go with?" he asked Bonnie looking into her eyes.

"Why, what I have on underneath of course," she replied with a wink.

There was the sound of high-heeled footsteps coming up behind them.

Torian looked over his shoulder and saw Melanie walking toward them.

She was wearing a silk black dress with slightly longer sleeves then Bonnie's.

The V-neck cut of her dress proved that combat vests didn't do her justice.

She grabbed Trent's left arm and said, "Are we all ready?"

He held up his right arm and Bonnie took hold.

"Well aren't we a threesome?" he said as they walked to the lift.

"Don't you wish?" Bonnie answered smiling.

They had to take two conveyors to get to the Kofu building.

Then they took a lift up to the executive floor.

As they entered they were introduced to the CEO of Kofu, Mr. Tanaka, who was standing at the beginning of a procession line.

"*Irasshaimase* (welcome)," Tanaka said as they approached.

Torian bowed politely saying, "Ome ni kakarete, koei desu (I'm honored to meet you). *Taihen, kekko na mono o chodai shite* (Thank you very much for such a wonderful gift)," Torian said referring to the wine Tanaka had sent him.

Tanaka bowed replying, "*Lie, do itashimashite* (you're welcome)."

"This is my future mate, Miss Melanie Jenson, along with my personal assistant Miss Bonnie Kline."

"I have followed some of your exploits Riff Jenson," Tanaka said looking directly at Melanie. Melanie just smiled and shook hands unsure of how to take the comment.

Next to Tanaka was his wife and just behind her was Ichi Ban.

After meeting several other Kofu executives they were taken into the dining area and seated at the end of the table closest to Tanaka signifying their importance.

The dinner conversation was mostly small talk about company products and the climate getting warmer each year.

After dinner the guests were invited into a grand ballroom where a small band was playing music.

Melanie noticed several clones situated around the room keeping an eye on the guests.

One of the clones walked over and invited Torian to accompany him to the CEO's office where he again met with Mr. Tanaka.

Torian stopped in front of Tanaka bowing and said, "*Domo arigato gozaimashita, Tanaka-san.*"

"You are quite welcome, Torian-san. I see that Torian Hara has taught you well."

"*Hai,*" Torian said bowing again.

"I must thank you for the return of the missing microchips. I still would like to know who was stealing them. I don't suppose you or your lady Riff friend would have any knowledge of this?"

"Sadly no, Tanaka-san. The two men that had the microchips were released, believing them to be only transporting them to someone in charge. What I do know of the men is that one is a good dancer and the other, well, let's just say he's up in the air right now."

"I understand that the Riffs may have come into contact with this supposed leader?" Tanaka said with a raised eyebrow.

"That is my understanding as well, Tanaka-san."

"And the information on the microchips-- was not compromised in any way?"

"Not after the Riffs retrieved it," Torian replied. "Before that I cannot say."

"*Mochiron* (Of course). Well, all is well then. We will continue to seek out any loose ends and try to determine how they were able to get the chips out of the city. In the meantime, we should return to the party."

Torian wasn't sure if Tanaka knew about the Supremes contacting him asking to continue researching Area 48 for other possible sites or if this even had anything to do with Kofu's microchips, so he let well enough alone.   They left the office and were heading back to the ballroom when a man approached Mr. Tanaka greeting him with a two-handed handshake.
                                          Torian noticed the man's gold ring on his right middle finger and the gold watch on his left wrist.

"This is Torian Miller from Vegas," Tanaka said introducing the man with blond hair to Torian.

"Hello, a most interesting ring you have there." Torian said looking at the ring.

Miller, with a puzzled expression, held up his right hand and said, "My father gave me this. I was told it had special meaning on my mother's side of the family belonging to her great grandfather John Strode."

"Not *Doctor* John Strode by any chance?" Torian asked.

"Why yes. How did you know?" Miller asked staring intently at Torian.

"It just so happens that I'm also a Torian and very likely came across his name in some old newspaper clippings." Torian said nonchalantly.

"Yes, I guess that's possible. Her great grandfather did have some notoriety in his lifetime."

"Well, nice meeting you," Torian said to Miller with a slight wave then bowed to Tanaka and walked hurriedly back to where the ladies were.

Melanie and Bonnie were listening to the band on stage as Trent came up behind them and pulled them off to the side.

Trent told them about the meeting with Tanaka and being introduced to Miller (whom he believed) was one of the men at the tavern. "What tavern?" Melanie asked. While Trent was explaining his short adventure in Under-town to Melanie he noticed that Miller had met up with two men and all three were looking his way. Trent waved at him with a friendly gesture, but Miller just frowned back as Torian escorted the ladies out onto the balcony.

"Bonnie did you bring Maggie with you?" Trent asked. "Why yes. You asked me too." "Good. We may need her." "What's going on?" Melanie asked.

"Ah, there you are Torian," Miller said as he walked out onto the balcony with the two men he had been talking to.

Baldy from the Fish Bowl and another man also walked out onto the balcony behind Miller, now five against three.

"I believe you know more about John Strode then you are letting on?" Miller said as he walked to the balcony railing peering over the ledge. "If someone was to accidentally fall over the railing it might take a while, but you would eventually hit the ground, isn't that right Torian?"

"I suppose if someone were foolish enough to stand too close and of course *accidentally* fall over then, yes, that could happen," Torian replied.

"I would hate to see what it would do to such lovely faces such as these," Miller said, gesturing toward Melanie and Bonnie.

At that Melanie hiked up her dress and kicked her foot so that her high heeled shoe came off and popped Miller in the face. Miller grimaced putting both hands to his face letting out a "*Meine nase* (My nose). *"*

Miller recovered from the shoe in the face and said, "It's a pity we won't be able to finish our little chat."

Miller walked back into the ballroom still rubbing his nose with his right hand.

Bonnie pulled Maggie out from somewhere under her dress and pointed it at the men in front of her.

Maggie was a snub nosed .38 caliber gun. It had been made with a high polymer plastic to get past metal detectors.

The men moved forward and Bonnie shot the one on the left who was reaching into his coat pocket.

The man on the far right tried to grab a hold of Melanie's arm, but got an elbow to the chin instead. Baldy, who was in front of Bonnie, had a baton that extended out from his sleeve knocking the gun out of Bonnie's hand.

Trent was about to reach out for the man in front of him when Melanie jumped about three feet into the air and did a spinning back roundhouse kick that knocked the remaining three men down to the ground.

At this elevation Melanie kept spinning like a ballerina until she floated back down to the balcony.

"What a woman," Trent said out loud.

"Yeah, but don't ever piss her off," Bonnie chimed in.

"You got that right," he replied.

Baldy recovered first and got up reaching into his pocket pointing some kind of a stun gun toward Trent and Bonnie. He was about to shoot when a shadowy figure suddenly appeared standing on the balcony railing right behind baldy.

Trent recognized SG as he yanked baldy up so hard that he came completely out of his shoes and pulled baldy up and over the rail.

An electrifying shot rang out as baldy shot up toward the balcony as he was falling down.

SG hopped down onto the balcony. With his left hand he grabbed one of the men that Melanie had kicked to the balcony floor by his throat as he was getting up.

"Way to go team," Trent said with his hands up in the air like a boxer, bobbing up and down.   One of the men recovered from the kick he had received getting up quickly and grabbing a hold of Melanie. He had his left arm around Melanie's waist and held a knife in his right hand up to her throat.

"Let him go," the man holding Melanie told the Guardian.

The Guardian didn't budge.

"Let him go or I'll kill her, I swear," the man repeated as he backed up closer to the opening to the ballroom.

SG still holding the man by the neck turned his head toward the man with the knife, but the red eyes had turned to a flashing yellow.

The man holding Melanie lowered the knife at the sight of the Guardian's yellow eyes.

Trent pulled out his Lib card and pushed a small indentation on the card. There was a swooshing sound heard right next to Melanie's ear as she looked up at her captor who now had a shuriken stuck in his right eye.

A shuriken was a six-pointed metal star that when thrown could stick into almost anything. Trent had activated his Lib card turning it into the shuriken.

The man holding Melanie fell to the ground.

Melanie looked over at Trent, as did Bonnie who had her hands up to her mouth.   Bonnie lowered her hands then looked at Melanie and said; "You better never piss him off either."   Melanie stepped toward Trent saying, "Don't worry, I won't," as she looked into his eyes for a moment, then gave him a passionate kiss.

Chapter 43

Torian mentioned to SG that the sooner someone got to the Lib in Vegas to preserve any evidence that Miller may have left there, the better.

Mr. Tanaka displeased with the interruption of his party and that his personal clone protectors hadn't prevented the incident, was in a heated one-way discussion with Ichi Ban as Torian approached.

"I just wanted to thank you Ichi Ban-san for preventing these very men from keeping me away from the party earlier this evening." Torian said.

"If not for Miller's assistance in helping them gain access to the party they wouldn't be here."

"I see that I have misjudged you Ban, *Gomennasai Ichi Ban-san* (I'm sorry)," Tanaka said bowing to his Number One protector.

Ichi Ban returned the bow, and then faced Torian.

"*Domo, moshiwake arimasen Torian-san* (I'm indebted)," he said knowing Torian had just helped him save face.

Torian returned the gesture and went back to where the ladies were waiting.

They had decided that playing the free slot games in Vegas after this evenings events just wouldn't have the same thrill, so they headed down to the lobby to get their suite access cards.

Mr. Tanaka had arranged for them to each stay in executive suites for the night.

"This isn't over is it?" Bonnie asked on the way to the lift.

"No," Trent said. "There's a lot more going on here than meets the eye. I've pieced together some things, but still have questions I'd like answered. Also the Supremes have asked me to continue researching some of the information I found on the hidden bunker that Riff Thompson found as well."

"Maybe that's why they've assigned a Sec Guardian to my unit," Melanie said.

"Huh?" Trent said out loud.

"Yes, we have a new pet," Melanie said.

"Sounds more like a watchdog to me," Bonnie added.

"Good luck going back to the bunker though," Melanie added.

"What do you mean?" Trent asked.

"The Guardian that was with us at the hangar blew it up."

"Huh!"

"Why would a Torian be involved in any of this?" Bonnie asked changing the subject.

"Millers link to this is his mother's great grandfather who was involved in some secret activities at the military base that Melanie and her unit stumbled on.

Area 48, I believe, is but one in a sequence of several facilities that may have been conducting experiments on astronautics and who knows what else.

Miller may have become interested in Strode's work. Of course just how involved he is in this and what he plans to do with the information he's trying to obtain I don't know?"

"Being a Torian would give him access to a great deal of confidential information," Melanie added. "And he wouldn't be scrutinized for his inquiries either."

"That's right," Trent agreed.

"Before the altercation you mentioned seeing Miller at the tavern, but didn't see his face. How did you recognize him?" Mel asked Trent.

"By the gold watch he was wearing and the gold ring he had on his right hand," Trent replied.

"That's funny; now that you mention it Hernandez had a gold ring like the one Miller had."

"Huh," Trent said out loud with his right hand on his chin.

"Well it won't be so easy for him now that he's on the run," Bonnie interjected.

"Maybe?" Trent replied, wondering if Miller had actually done anything wrong at this point.

Coming from the Lobby they arrived at the lift, Melanie whispered something to Bonnie. Bonnie pulled her head back with a surprised look but nodded with a devilish grin and said, "I'll take the next lift up. Good night."

"Good night," Trent told Bonnie.

Trent and Melanie took the lift to the executive dwelling and the door slid open.

Trent saw there was complimentary champagne. He connected the executive Comp with his Comp back in Angeles to monitor and control the suite.

The Comp dimmed the lights and played some romantic music.

Melanie took off her dress and got into bed. Trent handed her the bottle with two glasses and got undressed while she poured.

He slid into bed next to her and she said, "Sweetie, can you get another glass?"

"Another glass? Sure. Who's it for?" he asked with a puzzled look.

The door to the dwelling opened and in walked Bonnie with her shoes in her hand slung over her shoulder and said, "Dessert anyone?"

Chapter 44

Sec Guardian 5000 walked down the steps outside the Kofu tower knowing that the Torian was safe and had plenty of company for the evening.

SG was walking along the street when an internal sensor made him stop for a moment, then he took two steps backward.

Baldy came crashing down onto the top of an Info-stand a few feet in front of the Guardian smashing it to pieces.

The stun gun he had been firing bounced off the pavement next to the Guardian's boot.

"Judgment Applied," flashed on the Guardian's screen as he picked up the gun and continued on his way.

Chapter 45

The next morning Torian stirred to the sound of bugles playing reveille, coming from the Comp in the hotel suite. He moved his right hand along the left side of the bed but didn't feel anyone there, so he rolled onto his back to feel the right side of the bed; empty?

He opened his eyes and was surprised to see his own image looking back, but with glowing green eyes. He opened his eyes wider only to realize that he was looking at his reflection in SG's face monitor. Torian gasped and rolled off the bed.

The Guardian with the glowing green eyes was bending over the bed looking directly at Torian. SG stood erect and what sounded like a short "snort" sound came from the Sec Guardian as if he were holding back a laugh.

Torian covered up and walked into the cleansing room mumbling.

Torian not amused at the Guardian's arrival, leaned back out of the cleansing room and said, "Thanks for the warning Comp." The Comp just giggled as the bugles faded away.

Torian had connected the suite Comp to his own back in Angeles to monitor the room.

SG walked to where Torian was leaning out of the cleansing room.

A message was displayed across SG's screen: "Request your presence at the Vegas Lib to access Torian Miller's Comp; Supremes."

"Wonderful?" Torian thought out loud.

While in the cleansing room Torian noticed two separate lipstick smudges on the mirror, as if someone had kissed it in two places. One was red in color and the other purple.

A smile came to Torian's face remembering last night with Melanie and Bonnie.

He looked in the mirror at his reflection, minus the glowing green eyes this time.

After putting on some casual clothes that he had brought in an overnight bag, Torian asked the Comp to notify the Lib that he would be staying in Vegas a little longer.

He also had the Comp notify a little flower shop in Under-town asking that they deliver some red roses to Riff station ten for Melanie with a note that said, "Thanks for the awesome night." Then he took his suite access card with him and went down to the lobby with SG.

He stopped and asked the front desk if Miss Bonnie Jenkins had checked out yet.

The front desk told him that she was still checked in; so he asked that white roses be sent to her suite.

From there Torian followed SG down to the Transport station wondering if they would be taking the special Guardian Tram they had used before.

SG walked to the regular Tram instead waiting for it to arrive.

Torian walked over to the Info-stand to peruse the info-papers and imaging disks they had on display.

The Tram pulled into the station and SG stepped on board.

Torian walked over and entered the Tram sitting next to one of the small windows that he liked to peer out of.

As the Tram left the station SG was no where to be found, so Torian settled in for the short commute.

After a few minutes Torian lifted his eyes up from the Comp that was embedded in the seat in front of him, to the sound of hydraulic brakes slowing down the Tram. He looked out the window but could only see the wall of the inner tunnel as the Tram slowed down.

Torian got up and stepped out. He looked around for SG, but he was nowhere in sight. "Figures, I open my eyes in bed and there he is; step out into downtown Vegas and he disappears."

Torian had checked for the Vegas Lib's location on the way there. It showed the Lib in an older section of the city but did have Miller's name as the presiding Torian.

Earth's past had changed dramatically with the near destruction of a world but some things never change. Like the quest for knowledge and the desire to learn. The Devil's Tail couldn't take that out of human nature.

"And to think, back in 2027, people were worried about an asteroid dubbed "1999 AN10" passing the Earth's surface at around 19,000 miles away," Torian thought to himself.

The Vegas Lib was not as big as the Angeles Lib that Torian was in charge of. It had several smaller buildings surrounding it. Most seemed to be closed and abandoned.

One, Torian noticed, had the words Pa Star on a faded sign.

Torian wondered if it had been a place that people back in the twentieth century used to take old stuff they didn't use anymore and try and get money for it.

Today paper and coin money was seldom used.

As Torian walked up to the Lib's counter, he asked the young man there if Torian Miller was in. The young man checked his board and told Torian that Miller had not arrived yet. But that his personal assistant might be available. Torian told him that would be fine and the young man called the assistant. Torian was then pointed in the right direction.

Torian took in his surroundings as he walked to the office.

The door to the assistant's office was open and Torian could see a woman sitting at the desk. She was wearing a tan blouse and skirt with long sleeves. She had dark hair rolled up in front with a rat-tail and the back of her hair in a snood.

Torian had seen that kind of hairstyle worn in pictures from the 1940's and 1950's.

If not for the black rimmed glasses she wore she would defiantly stand out in a crowd.

"Good morning. I'm Miss Rawlings," she said with a professional greeting. "The Torian hasn't arrived yet. Is there anything I can help you with?"

"Good morning! I'm the Torian from Angeles."

"Oh, yes. I received an L-mail that you would be arriving and that I was to give you my full cooperation."

"Great, when was the last time you spoke to Torian Miller?"

"It was yesterday around fifteen hundred. He was leaving for the day to go to a dinner party at the Kofu Electronics Corporation tower."

"I see. Did he say when he would be coming back?"

"Yes. He said he would be back today, but when I arrived at work he wasn't here. I did receive an L-mail that you would be coming and to notify a Sec Guardian if I heard from Torian Miller. May I inquire as to what this is all about?" she asked.

"I'm afraid that Miller may be mixed up in some illegal activities. To what extent I cannot say."

"I see. Does that mean I'm a possible suspect in these illegal activities?" she asked with a straight face.

"I'm not here to judge you. Since I too was at the Kofu dinner last night and spent the night in Vegas, the Supremes asked if I could be of some assistance. As a Torian I might have a clearer insight when gathering information. Of course any relevant information would have to be relayed to the Supremes or a Sec Guardian."

Miss Rawlings relaxed her shoulders slightly as a relieved smile came across her face.

"Nice smile you have. Must have been in the file under S," Torian said.

A bigger smile came across her face.

"Sorry. I guess I put myself on the defense."

"It's okay. May I take a look in his office?" Torian asked.

"Of course, right in here." Miss Rawlings opened the door and stepped inside.

Torian looked around then sat down at Miller's desk.

"I don't suppose you know Torian Miller's password do you?" he asked Miss Rawlings.

"What makes you think I know it?" she said in return.

Torian just looked at her with a sincere smile.

"Okay, it's..."

"--UFO," Torian finished for her.

A perplexed look was now on her face, "How did you know?"

"Just a lucky guess," Torian replied.

Chapter 46

Jimmy O'Doul was in the locker room getting ready for work.

Instead of the usual uniform fatigues the Riffs wore, he dressed in outlander attire. Outdated Levi pants a checkered shirt and Shield game hat. He even put on old-fashioned underwear instead of the usual innerwear.

Thompson walked out of the cleansing room over to the lockers with a towel wrapped around his waist.

"So this special assignment that we've been assigned to is going undercover in one of the settlements I take it?" Thompson asked O'Doul.

"Yes, we need to blend in if we are to find out who is behind these corporate thefts. The best place to start is by following the tracking device on the dune buggy the Sec Guardian planted," O'Doul replied. It was the one vehicle that after the altercation at Scott Castle that couldn't be accounted for.

Thompson opened his locker and took off his towel. As he did, Mel and KJ walked by. Mel had a wet towel in her hand twisted up and snapped it at Thompson's butt.

"Hey!" Thompson said reacting from the snap and quickly covering up his front side with his towel.

"Paybacks a bitch," Mel said to Thompson, referring to when Thompson had done the same thing to her.

"You're in a good mood this morning," O'Doul commented.

"She must have got lucky in Vegas," Thompson said putting on his pants.

"You could say that," KJ replied for Mel as they continued on to the briefing room.

After they were both dressed O'Doul and Thompson walked into the briefing room where Captain Harding was giving out section assignments for the next few days.

Mel and Jones were already sitting at a table in the back as O'Doul and Thompson came in and sat next to them.

"Listen up everyone. O'Doul's unit will be going undercover in the outland, so if you see them--you don't know them.

"Does that mean we can shoot Thompson if we need too?" Summer asked.

"No, you can wound him in the leg if you want, but don't kill him," Harding said with a smirk on his face. Gunner and Ethan sitting next to Summer laughed out loud as Thompson's face turned a bit red.

After the briefing Captain Harding dismissed the other Riffs and asked that O'Doul's unit stay behind.

Sec Guardian 2000 came into the briefing room.

"Since the Sec Guardian will be your contact in the field you won't be transmitting anything to the Riff station. The Guardian will be keeping track of you from the UCV. We have an old beat up truck that you will be using to get around in with some modifications of course," Captain Harding told the Riffs. "Any info leading to arrest or capture needs to be done by the Guardian or uniformed Riffs to maintain your cover; any questions?"

"No," O'Doul replied.

"Then get going. And be safe out there," Harding said leaving the room.

Chapter 47

Torian typed in the words: Unidentified Flying Object, into the Comp on Miller's desk.

As Torian had been talking with Miss Rawlings he had been looking around the office. It had several old newspaper clippings of UFO sightings hanging in frames on the walls, including one with the words "Area 51" on it. Torian also noticed a plastic model of a flying saucer on the desk.

"I took a wild guess," he told Miss Rawlings in answer to her question.

"Well then, if you need me for anything please let me know," Miss Rawlings said leaving the office.

Torian looked through Miller's current L-mails. Like the L-mails he himself had received, there was talk of espionage in the making. But to what extent and who was to blame no one seemed to know.

Some L-mails had messages from other Torians', while other L-mails displayed optical pictures of current or past images for the Torian to watch.

Torian thought of Melanie for a moment. He worried about her when she wasn't with him, even though she was more than capable of handling herself. She had proven that time and time again, including the night before at the Kofu Electronics dinner that both Torian and Miller had attended.

This business with microchips and information on rocket engines being stolen from Kofu had Torians' from other cities and continents L-mailing each other.   The Supremes apparently not satisfied that Hernandez was the only one in charge and after the incident with Miller was why Torian was here.

A link to Miller's involvement may have been a Dr. John Strode. Miller's great grandfather.   Torian was here to gather info if he could and relay it to the Supremes.

He hadn't told SG about his theory on the DNA research that had been found at Area 48.

He had come up with his own hypothesis about what scientists may have been doing in the bunker.

Unlike Ilea Ivanov (from Russia) whose concept of altering genetics were geared toward making an army of half man/half gorilla soldiers back in 1925.

Torian believed at one time the US government was involved in creating genetically altered humans to visit other planets like Mars.

Torian returned to the task at hand, but realized that accessing the Comp had been a bit too easy. He wondered what Torian Miller used to open up his personal data files.

Torian used sign language along with passwords to signal his Comp back at the Angeles Lib.

Each Torian had a unique way of accessing confidential information on their Comps'.   Torian's mentor, Chen, had taught Torian this.

"What did Miller use to open up his personal files?" Torian wondered out loud.

Chapter 48

O'Doul and his unit were in the truck provided by Captain Harding.

There was no sense in going back to Scott Castle in Death Val.

The cleanup crew and Riffs sent out there after the altercation with Hernandez hadn't turned up anything O'Doul didn't already know.

The tracking device put on Jameson wasn't showing on KJ's Comp, but the dune buggy's still was. That was the direction the Riffs were now heading.

They were taking a chance that if Jameson was around he might recognize them, but it couldn't be helped. The Riffs knew what Jameson looked and sounded like even if he changed his appearance.

KJ had her portable Comp on her lap tracking the buggy.

"It appears that it's somewhere near Lake Me. Several miles outside the city of Vegas," Jones told O'Doul as he was driving the truck.

"It will be several hours before we get there. Might as well relax till then," O'Doul told his unit.

"Can we stop off at Donald's on the way there?" Thompson asked.

"Since we are undercover it wouldn't be a good idea since they know that we are Riffs," O'Doul replied.

Donald's was a place to stop and get something to eat on the way to Vegas. It had several old style Trams connected to each other to form a large eating and meeting area for outlanders.

Mel in the passenger seat was looking off into the distance reflecting on last night's festivities with Trent when an audible alarm sounded.

Jones said, "Incoming," and O'Doul slowed to a halt.

O'Doul and Mel looked out the front window and up at the sky.

Something gold was falling from the sky and landed a hundred yards ahead of them. It landed with a tremendous crashing sound.

O'Doul started up the truck again and they drove past the old satellite that had smash landed leaving a small crater in the ground. Steam was coming from the top of the scorched satellite.

Jones looked over at the satellite and said, "Good thing Captain Video put an alarm in our truck."

Jones looked over at Thompson who had his headset on turning up the volume to cover up the beeping noise that was interfering with his music.

Chapter 49

Torian had finished looking thru Miller's L-mails and was now going through the desk drawers.

In the top drawer Torian noticed a slightly discolored paper underneath the lining at the bottom of the drawer. He picked up the paper lining at the corner and pulled out an old newspaper from underneath that had been folded to a sideline that read: "New Rocket Booster Will Be Greatest" FORT WORTH (UPI). The article was from the <u>Press=Telegram,</u> Long Beach 12, Calif., Friday, Nov. 22, 1963.

Back when the United States had presidents in control of the country there was a young man named John F. Kennedy. He had been on tour that day in several cities including what was once known as Dallas, Texas. The article in the paper noted one of the president's topics of discussion was the future use of rockets that would take the United States ahead of Russia in the space race. Later that same day

President Kennedy was assassinated, along with a Governor by the name of Connelly.

Torian understood now why it became so important to safeguard information concerning the building of rockets, jet engines and anything else related to astronautics.

Several days before, Torian had met with Jimmy O'Doul and his Riff unit in an old abandoned military base near China Lake.

Riff Thompson had discovered a secret bunker with the words "Area 48" on it. Along with the Riffs, Torian had discovered evidence of Dr. Strode attempting to alter DNA in humans, possibly to survive on Mars.

Torian found an old floppy disk with human chromosomes on it and attempts to alter the Meiosis phase. He also found a fetus left in a jar of ammonia with trace amounts of oxygen, carbon dioxide, nitrogen and argon in the lung tissue.

That particular research was codenamed Project Metamorphosis.

They also found evidence that Dr. John Strode was the leading scientist working there along with a Dennis Hansen who had worked on rocket engines for Wright industries back in the 1940's, like the Cyclone 18. This was one of the engines that helped the B-29 bombers fly past Mt Fuji on its way to Japan later in1945.

This was toward the end of the war between the US and Japan after Japan had bombed Pearl Harbor on December 7, 1941.

"A date which will live in infamy," as put by the president of the time, J. Edgar Hoover.

This article with the idea of space travel was a continuing dream of not just a president, but a nation as well.

After Neil Armstrong had walked on the moon the cost outweighed the return not finding any precious metals on the surface of the moon or Mars when we first landed there.

An agency known as NASA continued to send men into space, but for more practical purposes such as fixing satellites or spending time on the International Space Station conducting experiments.

Instead probes such as "Voyager and Messenger" were sent out into the universe and manned space shuttles were limited to putting up more and more satellites.

"A lot of good that did when they all came crashing down or were swept away," Torian thought.

It was only a few decades ago that the idea of putting another manned space station in orbit around the Earth became a reality.

The Metronome (as it was named) was easy to build and get through the thinning atmosphere now that the gravitational pull wasn't as strong.

"Is this all conjecture or is Kofu supplying the Metronome with microchips designed to control rocket engines on the space station or ships going to the moon?" Torian wondered, thinking about what his mentor Chen had told him.

"And what if anything did altering DNA have to do with it all, or was it a coincidence that [Area 48] had been found?" Torian thought to himself.

"Was Area 48 one of many areas hidden by the US government for testing and research studies like Area 51?"

Torian's train of thought was interrupted as he looked up to see Torian Miller standing with an expression of dismay in the office doorway.

Chapter 50

After a full day of traveling the Riffs pulled into the settlement of Bold. It was on the outskirts of Lake Me several miles from Vegas.

The settlement consisted of travel trailers and mobile homes on wheels like the UCV.   The trailers were placed in ever expanding circles from the center outward.   Trent had told Mel once that the idea came from old western movies people viewed on their dwelling Comps' or from the Lib. It was a way of protecting the people in the inner circles from wild animals. It also made good barricades against attacking marauders.

The blinking dot on KJ's portable Comp showed that the buggy was in the settlement somewhere.

The Riffs drove through a make shift entrance where a couple of armed men were sitting around drinking, not paying much attention to the battered truck the Riffs were driving. Something many of the outlanders used to travel in and around the settlements.

People outside the city lived a different lifestyle than those from within.

Settlements formed by people wanting to live the life of freedom without corporate intervention. Of course this also meant that the strong survived and the meek weren't exactly inheriting the Earth.

The Riffs went to settlements only when summoned by the people there and often ridiculed for their presence.

Sec Guardians visited settlements even less due to poor radio reception in mountainous areas.

There had been some strides in placing Outernet dishes on the tops of mountains to help with transmissions to the Guardians and Riffs, but often these were vandalized.

O'Doul parked the truck next to several other vehicles.

"See if you can spot the dune buggy that Jameson was driving the day we stopped him," O'Doul told Jones and Thompson. "Mel and I will meet you near the center of the settlement," he continued.

Thompson and Jones went in different directions walking in and around the parked vehicles. O'Doul and Mel wound their way between trailers to the middle of the settlement.

The center of the settlement had trailers placed back to back with several on top to form a giant building. Next to it was an old gas station.

Most settlements in the outlands were built around or near gas stations to supply fuel to the older vehicles that were used. Unlike the UCV that the Riffs usually patrolled in that used solar panels on top to recharge batteries stored underneath. It also had vents in front that housed fans that also charged the batteries when in motion. But for old-fashioned get up and go, they could also flip a switch and hit the gas.

Petroleum or gasoline was plentiful and easy to access in the outland. Since only Riffs and outlanders used vehicles of this type.

Also settlements congregated near lakes or rivers for the plentiful food supplies.

O'Doul and Mel walked over to an opening in one of the trailers and saw that inside the trailer the walls had been knocked out to interconnect them. The tops had also been removed so that it had become a giant two-story structure.

There was a bar to their right so they walked over and sat on the stools provided for paying customers.

The bartender sauntered over with a limp and asked, "What'll it be?"

Chapter 51

"You're in my chair," Miller told Torian with a stern look.

Torian stood up moving out from behind the desk.

Miller walked around to sit down at his desk looking at the Comp to see what Torian had been viewing.

Torian had left the newspaper article he had seen in the drawer.

Miller was wearing the same dark blue suit, light blue shirt and black shiny shoes he had worn at the dinner.

"I'm surprised to see you are still in Vegas?" Miller told Torian as he typed on the Comp.

"Yes, I decided to extend my stay a little while longer. I stopped by hoping to learn a little more about your great grandfather," Torian replied noticing the missing gold ring from Miller's right hand.

"Ah! Dr. John Strode was a geneticist with some very advanced ideas that worked for the United States government. I was surprised when you knew his name at the party last night since he was only publicly known for being a simple scientist."

"As I said, I must have come across his name somewhere and became more curious after last night's events."

"I see that one of my associates was found lying on top of what was left of an Info-stand after falling from the Kofu tower this morning," Miller said now looking directly at Torian.

"He must have had a disagreement with a Sec Guardian after you left the party," Torian replied. "You yourself mentioned that accidents might happen when standing to close to the edge of a balcony," Torian said, reminding Miller of his insinuation that Torian, Mel and Bonnie might have the same thing happen to them.

"I see," Miller said reaching under his desk.

Torian saw Miller's movement and started to reach inside his jacket as Miss Rawlings appeared in the doorway.

"Oh! Torian you're here," she said.

"--Yes?"   "--Yes?" Torian and Miller both replied at the same time.

"I believe we will need to continue our conversation another time," Miller told Torian pulling his hand out from under the desk empty-handed.

Miller got up and walked past Miss Rawlings. "I shall be out for the rest of the day. Please respond to any L-mails that need replying to for me," Miller told Miss Rawlings.

"Of course," she replied looking a bit nervous.

"*Ich muss jetzt gehen* (I must go now)," Miller told Torian.

"*Auf Wiedersehen* (Goodbye)," Torian replied.

Torian walked back to where Miller had been sitting at the desk and looked under it, but didn't see anything at first. Then he noticed a small panel on the side and pushed on it. It flipped open but was empty. Whatever was there Miller must have put in his pocket when Miss Rawlings arrived.

"Should I call a Sec Guardian?" Miss Rawlings asked Torian.

"Yes and let him know that I will try and follow Miller if I can."

Torian walked out from behind the desk to see if he could catch up to Miller.

Torian went back to the front desk and asked the young man there if the Torian had just walked by.

"Yes he just left," was the reply.

Torian ran up to the front entrance and looked up and down the street. He saw Miller on a conveyer heading toward the main strip in Vegas. He ran over to the conveyer stepping on the rubber madding and holding onto the moving railing.

There were other people on the conveyer between Torian and Miller, but Miller continued to look straight ahead.

A bit disconcerting to Torian that Miller wasn't the least interested to see if someone was following him.

Fifteen minutes later Miller stepped off the conveyer as it came to the end.

Torian could see him walking up a short flight of stairs that lead to a bridge leading into one of the casinos.

Torian stepped off as well and headed up the stairs behind Miller.

Miller walked through the lobby and into the main casino area. He stopped for a moment to talk to a pretty hentail waitress and walked into the Poker room.

Torian sat down at a Redjack table where he could see Miller sitting down at one of the poker tables.

In Vegas people could play different games of chance. It didn't cost anything to play the old style video games or sit at the Redjack tables.

When you join the players club you are given a set amount of points to play. Once the points are gone you're done for the day.

If you won, the points would accumulate to exchange for meals, suites and merchandise from the company that sponsored that casino. You could even get a Ker if you won enough points.

If you stayed in one of the suites at the hotel your room access card acted like a player's card to wager with.

Torian had looked in to casino gaming over a century ago. It seemed that they were quite affluent throughout the then United States.   Even bands of Indian tribes got in on opening casinos on the federal land given back to them by the US. It was decades before the public outcry to close all but a few casinos occurred.   The Indians received money from the government as well as a share of the profits from people that gambled. People ended up gambling their hard-earned paychecks to the point that their property was repossessed and they lost their homes.   Even though the Indians were cashing in on people losing their money some of the tribes had incidents of Indians shooting at each other over their newfound wealth. Also when the government realized how many senior citizens were losing their social security and welfare money to the casinos, legislation was passed to close those casinos that didn't institute safeguards to protect the public's financial best interest.

Torian was about to lay down his room access card for the dealer when he felt a tap on his left shoulder. He turned to see Stephanie standing there in a red sparkling outfit with tall feathers coming out of a headband around her head and a long feathery boa.

"Fancy meeting you here," Stephanie said to Torian.

Chapter 52

Mel and O'Doul took in their surroundings as they sat at the bar.

They ordered a couple of drinks paying with dried food packets they had brought with them for just this purpose.

Wage cards had no value to the outlanders since they didn't work for any corporation. Food, water and clothing were traded for goods in these parts. If you had actual coins you were considered well off, but subject to being robbed.

There was a group of men on a make shift stage behind the bar playing music.

A heavyset female in blue overalls was singing.

In the center of the room was a square platform raised above the ground.

Two men were in the center of the platform, known as a ring for some reason, fighting each other. There were tables set around the ring for spectators to watch the two men pummeling each other.

Thompson and Jones walked into the place and went across the room to sit next to the ring without looking over at O'Doul and Mel.

Thompson did look up at some of the people standing on the second level peering down at the two men fighting. He noticed one man with no shirt and a black vest sitting on a stool looking down at the people below. The man had a carbine rifle propped up against a pillar and was wearing glasses. The glasses only covered the guy's front set of eyes. The other two eyes on each side of his head stuck out and moved independently of each other.

"I guess when he was younger and the other kids called him four eyes they weren't wrong," Thompson thought to himself.

There seemed to be a lot of mutations that had occurred after the catastrophe that literally shook the Earth, both human and animal. You didn't see as many in the cities as you did when traveling in the outlands.

A gal with cutoff Levi's, brown boots and a red shirt tied up in a knot in front walked over to Thompson and Jones asking if they wanted to wager on the fight.

Thompson said, "Not right now, but can I get some shine for myself, and a brew for the little lady here?"

The gal in shorts held out her hand and Jones took out some sparkplugs she had in a bag she had brought with her. The gal looked at the sparkplugs.

"This will get you the good stuff," she told Thompson and Jones. "May even get you a little something extra," she said to Thompson bending forward for Thompson to see down her shirt.

"Oh brother," Jones said out loud.

"When you got it, you got it;" Thompson said tilting the chair he was in on its back legs.

"That's what I'm afraid of. You got it and it would take a Med-priest to get rid of it," Jones told Thompson with a laugh.

One of the men in the ring was knocked to the ground. A little person with black pants and a black and white striped shirt walked next to the man lying down in the ring. The referee slammed his hand on the platform several times and declared the other man the winner.

Some of the spectators around the ring thru down ticket stubs they had at the defeat of their intended victor. Others held up their stubs while several gals in shorts came out with various clothing items and drinks as winnings for those that had picked the right fighter to win.

The gal in the shorts came back to the table where Thompson and Jones were and sat in Thompson's lap while she handed them their drinks.

O'Doul and Mel were still looking around the room taking sips of their drinks, when a guy in black chaps and an open blue shirt sporting his chest hair walked over to Mel.

"Can I buy you a drink, little lady?" he asked Mel.

"I have one already, thanks," she replied.

"Ok then. Can I just buy you," he said leaning closer to Mel.

"She's with me," O'Doul told him.

"Was I talking to you?" he said now looking at O'Doul.

"If you're talking to her you're talking to me," O'Doul said standing up from the barstool.

The guy in the blue shirt looked over his shoulder at another guy in a white shirt sitting at a table. White shirt got up and walked over to stand next to his friend.

Thompson noticed that the armed man on the second floor was staring over at the bar. Thompson looked over and saw two men facing off with O'Doul.

"Shit," he elbowed Jones and politely eased the gal in shorts up off his lap.

The gal went back to waiting on other people while Thompson and Jones watched the impending standoff.

"We just came in for a drink and don't want any hassle's," O'Doul said to the man in blue.

Mel reached out and grabbed a handful of chest hair then lifted her left knee into blue shirts groin.

While the guy with the white shirt was distracted at his friend falling to his knees, O'Doul grabbed him spinning him around and held him in a full nelson. O'Doul had his arms under the guy's armpits, with his hands up behind the guy's neck bending his head forward in a painful grip.

The bartender leveled a shotgun at the back of O'Doul's head and asked them for a second time, but with a menacing tone, "What'll it be?"

Chapter 53

"What are you doing in Vegas?" Stephanie asked Torian.

"I attended a dinner party last night and decided to extend my stay."

"I see. And have you met our Torian already?" Stephanie asked looking over at Miller seated in the Poker room.

She must have observed Torian watching him.

"Yes, we met at the dinner I spoke about, also earlier this morning at the Lib here in Vegas. But I'm not sure that his motives for being a Torian are what you might say, on the up and up."

"The Torian here does have a bit of a reputation for gambling. And I don't mean for free dinners." Stephanie said.

"What brings you here to Vegas?" Torian asked her.

"Clone-Elvis is performing here this weekend so I'm in the show. I take the Tram on weekends to perform on stage with various clone acts," she replied. "That's why I'm wearing this costume.

"I see that you keep looking over at Torian Miller," Stephanie said.

"Sorry, just wondering what type of conversation takes place over a poker table?"

"Shucks, that's easy," Stephanie said as she walked away from Torian and into the Poker room.

Chapter 54

O'Doul released the control hold he had on the guy in the white shirt.

The woman that had been singing on stage in the overalls was now speaking into the microphone. "It appears that we have a dispute. Settlement ordinance requires that disputes around the ring be settled *in* the ring." The crowd cheered in agreement.

O'Doul stepped forward and said, "No problem."

The woman on stage looked up at the guy in the black vest on the second floor. He was waving a gesture and pointing at Mel and the guy in blue that was now standing next to his friend.

The bartender motioned with his shotgun to Mel and the guy in blue to move over to the ring.

O'Doul started to say something but a few of the band members now had guns in their hands as well, motioning for O'Doul to back off.

Thompson and Jones stayed alert but made no attempt to interfere at this point, waiting for a better opportunity to equal the odds.

The man in the black chaps and blue shirt climbed up into the ring.

The referee motioned for him to go to one of the corners to wait for a signal to begin the fight.

Mel climbed up on another side of the ring and went to another corner.

Each fighter had their weapons taken away from them as they stood looking at each other. The man in blue was starting to limber up by pulling on the ropes around the ring and moving his head so that the bones in his neck cracked. He started to bounce up and down, boxing the air with his fists.

The hentails around the room were taking bets from the customers seated at the tables around the room. The hentail that had sat on Thompson's lap asked if he was ready to make a wager.

"I have a gold watch my mother gave me, that says the old broad takes mister fancy pants there," Thompson said standing up. Several people cheered and some booed.

"I say Rip here is going to knock out her front teeth," the guy in the white shirt said standing below his friend in the ring.

The referee announced; "there are no rules. Whoever is still standing is the winner."

Mel continued to just stand in the corner watching the guy named Rip.

A bell sounded and Rip sauntered out of his corner swaying from side to side, still boxing the air with his fists as he approached Mel. As he got within three feet of Mel she lifted up her left knee as if she was going to kick Rip in the privates again.

Rip already prepared for this having felt it once before dropped his hands down to block the pretend kick.

Mel using the momentum of her knee in the air hopped up with her right knee and using the palm of her right hand hit Rip square in the nose sending him backwards a few steps.

Rip now had tears streaming from his eyes as he held his nose with both hands.

Mel not waiting for Rip to recover jogged toward him and jumped into the air using both of her feet to wrap around Rip's neck. Using her weight and momentum she twisted her body pulling Rip off his feet and flipping him over on to the matt.   Rip had rolled over after landing on his back so that he was lying face down. Mel rolled over from where she had landed and sat on top of Rip's shoulders piggyback style. She placed both feet under the front of Rip's shoulders and slid her butt backwards lifting her feet onto Rip's back pinning his arms together. Mel then put both hands under his chin to lift Rip's head up and backwards causing him to gasp for air. She cupped her hands so that she didn't damage Rip's windpipe but used the palms of her hands to apply pressure to his carotid arteries. Mel's knees, firmly planted on the matt on both sides of Rip's arm's, kept him from rolling to either side and breaking free. After a minute or so Rip stopped struggling and his body went limp.

When Mel felt Rip's body relax she laid his head down on the mat not wanting to kill him.

The referee walked over to the passed out Rip and hit the matt a few times declaring Mel the winner.

Mel climbed out of the ring and walked over to the bar where several people crowded around her offering to buy her drinks.

O'Doul sat back down on his barstool taking a drink.

Thompson was holding up some of his winnings and kissed the hentail waitress standing next to him.

"Oh brother," was all Jones could say again rolling her eyes skyward.

Chapter 55

Torian was playing Redjack while Stephanie paraded around the Poker room.

She sat on some of the player's laps and looked at their cards. Then bet or folded depending on what the cards were.

The players were all laughing and having fun with their new addition to the poker table. She stepped behind Torian Miller peering at his cards and gasped. "You boys better think twice before playing this hand," she said as if Miller had an unbeatable hand.

Stephanie had been in there for twenty minutes or so when one of the casino hosts walked into the room from another door and saw the showgirl interrupting the game. He took her by the arm and escorted her out.

Torian overheard him tell her to find clients somewhere else in the casino.

The host went back into the Poker room and pushed a button next to the doorframe. The clear windows turned opaque preventing onlookers from gazing into the room.

Torian got up from the table and met Stephanie over at the bar.

"Sorry I wasn't in there long enough to get much information on what they were talking about before I arrived," Stephanie told Torian.

"That's okay. I didn't expect you to put yourself out there," Torian replied.

"Hun, I've been putting myself out there for years," she told Torian.

"I did get the names of some of the other players though if that helps any."

"Anything could be of good use," Torian replied.

"There's a guy named Johnson and Johnson he told me as he introduced himself and grabbed his privates. Another man's name was Smith and the older guys name is Hansen. I didn't get the names of the other players before I was asked to leave."

"I don't suppose you noticed if Torian Miller had on any jewelry?" Torian asked Stephanie.

"Why yes, he had a gold watch on his left wrist and a nice gold ring on his right hand," she replied.

"Come to think of it, some of the other men had the same gold ring on too."

"Thanks again Stephanie," Torian kissed her on the cheek and walked away.

"Damn, there goes the man of my dreams and he's only interested in other men wearing gold rings. Oh well!" Stephanie said as she turned and rubbed shoulders with a guy sitting at the bar.

Chapter 56

O'Doul pushed his way through the crowd around Mel to stand next to her at the bar.

"Nice moves," he told her.

"Thanks. It was something that Trent taught me," she replied.

The crowd slowly went back to their tables waiting for the next round of excitement.

O'Doul and Mel continued to have a drink when Rip walked over to them.

The bartender watched intently to insure there wasn't any further altercation between the two fighters.

"I wanted to congratulate you on your victory. Can I buy you both a drink, if that's okay with you?" Rip asked with sincerity this time, rubbing his sore neck.

"Have a seat," Mel told him.

They were here to get any information they could on the thefts that had occurred in and around the city. What better way than to talk to the local bully.

O'Doul told Rip that they had come from a settlement near Frisco.

They had heard that a man by the name of Hernandez was recruiting, but when they arrived in Angeles they found out that a bunch of Riffs had killed him.

Rip told O'Doul and Mel that Hernandez and his marauders was just one of many groups being gathered. Someone was organizing marauders from all around with plans to hijack something of importance. But what it was Rip didn't know.

Rip told them there was another group meeting later that evening and that he would introduce them if they wanted.

"What's in it for us?" Mel replied playing the part.

"How does being a chairman of your own company sound?" Rip asked.

"Chairman?" Mel replied.

"That's what the promise is. Plenty of loot and owning your own company in any city you choose from," Rip told them.

"That's a pretty big order to fill," O'Doul said. "Are you sure they can deliver?"

"Well, I needed food and medical supplies for my family. After one meeting with this group, I was given a truck full of stuff to take home and I got to keep the truck," Rip said.

"You can get any Med-priest to come out and provide moderate care," O'Doul told Rip.

"Used to be that were true," Rip continued. "But in the last year or so the Med-priests have been afraid to come out due to the marauder raids. Even the Vegas Riffs are staying clear. I don't much care for Riffs myself but they *are* supposed to maintain some peace and quiet. Since they aren't even doing that, I figure it's better to join the marauders then be a victim," Rip told them.

"When you put it that way I'm sorry I choked you out," Mel told Rip.

"That's okay, I had it coming. I wasn't always a jerk. Just doing unto others before they do it to me," Rip replied.

Chapter 57

Torian walked away from Stephanie and into the Poker room.

The host walked over and told Torian that this was a live game and that if he wanted to use his player card he would need to find another game in the casino.

Torian pulled out some gold and silver coins from his pants pocket to show the host he had something to gamble with.

The host said, "Ah! Right this way," and led Torian to an empty seat at the table. There were eight players already seated.

Miller looked up at Torian with a smile and didn't seem surprised to see Torian this time.

The player next to Torian said, "Welcome to the game," as Torian sat down at the opposite end of the table from where Miller was sitting.

The dealer told Torian they were playing "Hold-em."

The host came back over with some chips and asked how many he wanted.

Torian again pulled out the gold and silver coins along with a platinum coin inlaid with a big red ruby.

Torian told the host he would use the ruby coin as a card protector.

The eyes of several of the other players widened at the sight of the ruby.

"Shuffle up and deal," the host told the dealer leaving a rack of chips for Torian.

The conversation was casual for the first thirty minutes of play.

Torian did note that each of the men sitting around the table wore the exact same ring that Miller had said was a family heirloom.

"Must be a big family," Torian thought to himself, except for the older man in the gray suit. The one Stephanie said was named Hansen. He had gray hair and was old enough to have retired by now. He had a slight accent like Miller but they didn't look like family.

Hansen didn't quite fit in with the other men at the table. Torian wondered if he was a part of the group or just there to play cards.

A hentail waitress walked around asking if anyone was interested in drinks.

One of Millers associates from the dinner party came into the room.

He was whispering something in Miller's ear when he noticed Torian at the other end of the table. The surprised look on his face disappeared when Miller told him to relax and have a seat. The guy sat down at a small table and chair behind Miller. He unfastened the front of his brown jacket as he sat down.

Torian could see what looked like the butt end of a gun in a holster inside the guy's jacket as the guy smiled at Torian.

After an hour or so of play the other players were getting low on chips that represented their buy in.

Torian and Miller seemed to be the big winners thus far.

Two of the players got up from the table to turn in the few chips they had left to retrieve what valuables they could.

"Well gentleman I believe it is getting late for an old man like me," Hansen said looking at a gold pocket watch he had taken from inside his coat pocket.

"*Gute nacht Herman* (Good night Herman)," Hansen told Miller.

"*Bis bald* (See you soon)," Miller replied.

Hansen left, as did the remaining other players. Torian and Miller were now the only two left.

"Shall we make this the final hand?" Miller asked Torian.

"Sure!" Torian replied.

The dealer pitched two cards each to Torian and Miller.

Torian was already the big blind with a stack of chips out and in front of him.

Miller had a smaller stack out and told the dealer he would just call after looking at his cards.

During the past hour both players were looking for what they call in poker as a "Tell."

A "Tell" was some involuntary gesture that gave a hint as to whether the player had a good hand of cards or not.

Miller was very straight laced with no Tell that Torian could decipher.

Torian himself had left a few phony Tells hoping that it would throw Miller off, but Miller just seemed to be amused by these.

After Miller called the big blind the dealer laid out three cards on to the table face up. A Two of hearts, Ace of spades and King of spades were displayed.

Torian checked his hand allowing Miller to decide if he wanted to bet.

Miller pushed out a stack of chips.

Torian pretending not to know what two cards he had, looked at them again, then placed his cards under his ruby card protector and pushed out a matching stack of chips.

The dealer said called and burned a card in the discard pile.

The next card he took from the deck he turned over and laid it next to the previous three cards.

The Two of spades was exposed as the turn card. Again it was Torian's turn to bet or check. This time Torian pushed out two stacks of chips.

Miller saw that three of the four cards had spades on them, then at Torian.

This time Miller just called Torian by pushing out two stacks of chips matching Torian's bet.

The dealer burned another card and said; "Last card is the river card," as he turned the card face up and next to the other four cards. It was the King of hearts.

It was Torian's turn to bet.

Torian tapped the table checking it over to Miller.

This time Miller lifted his cards as if he wasn't quite sure what he had.

The guy sitting at the table behind Miller squinted to see Miller's cards, and then relaxed with a big smile on his face.

"It appears we are at the OK Corral," Miller said to Torian. "I believe that I shall play the part of the Earp's," Miller said, claiming victory before they showed their cards. Then he pushed in the rest of his chips.

Torian didn't look at his cards.

"I raise." Torian pushed in the remainder of his chips, then picked up the ruby coin and tossed it in as well.

"I'm out of chips and can't match your raise," Miller said to Torian.

For the first time at the table Miller looked worried as he looked down at the ring on his finger.

The guy behind Miller stood up and moved closer to the table.

The host standing near a podium also moved closer.

The dealer just waited for Miller's answer.

Miller took another look at his cards, then took off the ring and placed it on the table next to the stack of chips he had already pushed out; "I call."

"I believe that the Clanton's were shot with a couple of bullets," Miller said laying down two Aces to show that he had a full house. Aces full of Kings.

"I believe that beats your flush," Miller told Torian looking at the three cards with spades on them on the table.

"Flush? No, I was playing my two pairs," Torian said laying down pocket deuces, referring to the other deuces on the table showing that he actually had four of a kind.

"Deuces never lose," Torian said. "Besides, the gunfight at the OK Corral was actually behind the corral in an ally known as Lot 2 on Block 17. But then that doesn't have quite the same *ring* to it, does it?" Torian said with a grin.

Chapter 58

O'Doul asked what time the meeting was.

Rip told him and left with his friend in the white shirt.

O'Doul and Mel finished up their drinks then got up from the bar and left going back to where they had parked the truck.

Thompson and Jones waited about twenty minutes before getting up and exiting the bar as well so that it didn't look suspicious leaving right behind O'Doul and Mel.

The four of them met at the truck and O'Doul went over the information that Rip had given them with Thompson and Jones.

They weren't supposed to contact the Riff station directly, so they decided to get some rest in the truck before the meeting. Besides they didn't have anything of importance to report at this time anyway.

Thompson stood next to Mel.

"I see you've been watching me practice my combat training," Thompson told Mel. "You're getting the hang of some of my moves,"

Thompson said jumping up and down like he was fighting an invisible man.

"Of course I would have taken a little longer to kick his butt, just to raise the stakes a little," Thompson said referring to Mel's fight with Rip.

"I didn't feel the need to embarrass the guy any more than I already had," Mel told Thompson with a smile.

"That's the same reason why I don't spar with you back at the station. I don't want to ruin your image with the other Riffs. You know, by knocking you out and all," Mel said playfully.

They both laughed and got into the truck to get some rest.

Mel and Thompson had a great working relationship. The friendly teasing and banter back and forth helped make them a more cohesive unit.

Thompson knew that Mel had made her pick for a mate when she retired and that was Trent.

Thompson had only met Trent a week ago, but if Mel liked him then he must be okay.

Jones offered to keep watch while the others got some rest.

O'Doul was already closing his eyes in the driver seat.

Chapter 59

As Torian was stacking his chips and admiring the ring he had just won, Miller got up from the table and said, *"Bis morgen* (Till tomorrow)."

Miller left the room but his associate stayed. The man leered at Torian and told him, "Maybe it's okay with him, but it's not okay with me."

The dealer seeing the menacing look on the guy's face got up in a hurry leaving the Poker room through a back door.

The host who was changing the windows back to clear again pushed a button on the wall to call a Sec Guardian, but the guy told the host to "beat it."

The host did as he was told and left the same way the dealer had gone.

The guy walked over and sat on the table in front of Torian with the gun in his jacket clearly visible.

"Shall we talk about my share of the winnings?" the guy asked Torian.

Torian picked up a single chip from one of his many stacks and said, "Sure, here's your cut."

The guy was not amused and leaned closer to Torian.

The front door to the Poker room opened up and in stepped Stephanie with Sec Guardian 5000.

"Him, yeah, that's the guy who stiffed me. And I don't mean in a good way," Stephanie said pointing at Torian.

Miller's associate closed his jacket at the sight of the Sec Guardian and got up from the table.

Stephanie walked over and grabbed Torian by his shirt. "I want what's coming to me yah see, yeah" she said overdramatically.

The Guardian's eyes were blinking yellow and Miller's associate decided it was time for him to leave.

As the guy walked out the door SG's eyes went back to green.

Stephanie seeing the guy leave leaned forward and gave Torian a big wet kiss.

Chapter 60

The meeting was to be held in a cave over a hill on the north side of the settlement near Lake Me.

It had only been a couple of hours when O'Doul, after getting some rest, elbowed Mel next to him.

She had her eyes closed but was completely awake.

Thompson had his headset on and Mel reached back and turned the volume up.

Thompson didn't budge.

She turned the music off and Thompson said, "Are we there yet?"

O'Doul and Mel each carried a revolver in a holster while Thompson and Jones kept their 9mm handguns along with two lever action rifles.

O'Doul expected that their guns might be confiscated before they were allowed in to the meeting.

They wanted to fit in to their surroundings and carrying the revolvers wouldn't stand out.

They didn't need to drive the truck so they left it where they had parked it.

The unit walked up and over the hill and could see a light coming from a cave a short distance away.

"Kind of close to the settlement," Jones commented.

"Must mean some of the people in the settlement know what's going on but aren't notifying the local Riffs," Thompson replied.

"Rip told us that the Riffs are staying away from the area due to the marauders," Mel told Thompson.

"But that's what the Riffs are for," Thompson replied.

"Must be another reason why the Riffs are staying away," O'Doul said.

Thompson and Jones held back a ways to observe since they hadn't been invited.

As O'Doul and Mel approached the cave there were two men outside with rifles.

Off to the right of the cave entrance was a boat dock with several boats tied up and some boats sitting on shore.

"What do you want?" asked one of the armed men.

"Rip asked us to meet him here," O'Doul told him.

The man motioned for the other armed man to go inside the cave to check on the new arrival's story. He came back a minute or two later with Rip behind him.

"Yeah, there okay," Rip told the armed man.

"All right, just leave your guns on one of the tables inside," the armed man told them.

The two went in following Rip and saw two more men sitting next to several tables with various guns on top.

O'Doul and Mel both placed their revolvers on one of the tables nearest the next section of cave and followed Rip further into the cave.

Thompson and Jones went around to the left of the cave entrance away from the lake and climbed to the top of the hill. There was a small hole in the top of the hill and they could see into a giant cavern where lots of men were sitting around.

"I forget which one is the stalactite and which is the stalagmite?" Thompson asked Jones.

"The stalactites are the icicle-shaped lime deposits hanging from the roof of the cave. The stalagmites are the cone-shaped deposits on the ground underneath," Jones replied.

"The way I remember the difference is by thinking of an upside down ice cream cone I *mite* want to eat," Jones told Thompson.

"Hey that's not bad," Thompson said. "An upside down ice cream cone sitting on a hot girl at the beach, melting down the front of her..."

"--Okay, you have your way of remembering and I have mine," Jones said punching Thompson in the arm.

There were benches arranged in several rows with around two dozen men sitting on them. The men were facing a giant flat rock on the ground, about ten feet wide and ten feet long, with a podium on top of it.

O'Doul and Mel followed Rip to one of the benches toward the back and sat down.

They looked around the cavern and saw several men standing along the sides of the cave. Some had machetes in scabbards on their belts. Others had big Bowie knifes in sheaths. There was a mixture of torches and electric lanterns around the cave to light it up.

Mel elbowed O'Doul next to her and looked up at the ceiling only with her eyes.

O'Doul looked up quickly as well and saw the small opening in the top of the cavern. He could see the stars were bright tonight and shining through the hole, as well as two familiar faces looking down.

From the back of the cavern four men walked out of the shadows.

Three of the men went and stood in front of the giant rock below the podium.

The fourth man stepped up onto the rock and walked over to the podium.

The four Riffs were each in their tan uniforms and wearing their weapons harnesses.

The Riff now standing behind the podium said," You're all under arrest."

Chapter 61

"Thanks," Torian said as Stephanie sat down on his lap.

"I saw Torian Miller leave the Poker room. Then when the window cleared I saw the guy sitting in front of you and he didn't look like he was asking you for your dwelling Comp number," Stephanie told Torian.

"So I was coming in to see if you needed any assistance. As I got to the front door this Sec Guardian showed up and well, I just figured you could use a hand," Stephanie said rubbing Torian's chest and straightening out his shirt where she had grabbed him.

"Looks like you came to my rescue," Torian told her.

"Yeah well, you stood up for me at the Fish Bowl nightclub last week. It was the least I could do," Stephanie told him.

SG was standing with his arms folded across his chest as if waiting for them to finish their little chat.

"Oh, and I guess I owe you a thank you too," Torian said to SG, seeing the Sec Guardian waiting impatiently.

At that the Sec Guardian dropped his arms to his side and turned sideways waiting for Torian to get up so they could leave.

"I think he wants me to go now," Torian told Stephanie.

"Just because he's bigger doesn't mean he's better," Stephanie said getting up off Torian's lap and looking at the Guardian with a smirk.

Torian told Stephanie thanks again and left the casino with SG.

On the way to the Lib Torian told SG what had occurred prior to the end of the poker game.

When they reached the Lib they both went inside to Miller's office.

"Ah, I see you found him," Miss Rawlings said to Sec Guardian 5000.

SG had responded to the call that Miss Rawlings had made requesting a Guardian come to the Lib.

When SG arrived she had told him that Torian Miller had been there and left with the Angeles Torian following him.

"Yes, it seems like we're attached at the hip sometimes," Torian told Miss Rawlings as he swayed his hip toward SG.

SG just stood there with no reaction as Torian frowned. "Guess you had to be there," he said and walked into Millers office again.

Torian sat down at Millers desk in front of the Comp.

Torian took out Millers ring that he had won in poker and put it on his right middle finger.

He typed in, "Unidentified Flying Object," again but had a different result come from the Comp.

The Comp's screen turned a bright blue and the bookshelf to Torian's left slid backwards and to the side making an entrance through the wall.

Miss Rawlings standing in the doorway slightly behind SG gasped.

"What's that for," she said with a surprised look.

"Shall we find out?" Torian asked as he got up from the desk and walked over to the opening.

When Miller had come to his office that morning he sat down typing, but didn't have the ring on his finger. After he left the Lib and Torian looked under the desk and found the empty compartment. Torian wondered what Miller had taken from it. When Torian followed Miller to the Poker room, Stephanie had told Torian that Miller was now wearing a gold ring, along with some of the other players.

Torian figured that Miller's ring had more than just a sentimental significance, which meant that it could also be used to signal the Comp to open Millers personal files.   Of course Torian hadn't expected the wall to move when he put on the ring and used the Comp.

Torian asked Miss Rawlings to wait while he and SG took a look inside the hidden passage.

Torian walked down a short corridor to a small room in back. It had another desk there with another Comp sitting on it and several pictures of Miller on the wall.

One picture Miller was shaking hands with Mr. Tanaka, the CEO of Kofu Electronics.

Another picture was with Miller standing next to Hansen. Hansen was holding the gold pocket watch that Torian had seen him with earlier that evening.

There was a smaller picture with Miller standing with eight other men in a group photo.

Torian had seen seven of these men earlier at the Poker room. They all had the same gold ring that Miller had, except for Hansen.

There was an article in a frame below the picture of Miller dedicating a ceremony to Hansen for his grand design of the Metronome.

The article was dated in the year 2141, around the time that the Metronome had been publicly announced throughout the UCA.

At the time, many people wondered why they needed another space station orbiting the Earth. But as time went by people just went about their own business hoping the damn thing didn't fall down on top of someone.

Torian sat down at the desk and tried typing on the Comp. He still had the ring on but nothing happened.

Torian sat back in the chair and put both feet up on the desk. He put his hands behind his head while he continued to look at the pictures.

There was a picture of a younger Hansen with a small boy with blond hair.

Torian wondered if the boy was Miller and if Hansen had been his mentor. The boy had an uncanny resemblance to Miller that made Torian believe it was indeed Miller.

There was a picture of Miller with a woman. She was standing to the left of Miller resting her head on Miller's shoulder like a sweetheart would do. Miller had his usual stern look on his face, the same as the boy in the picture with Hansen.

Torian looked under the desk for a minute, tapping on the sides underneath.

"Nothing," he said, hoping it would have been that easy.

Torian closed his eyes for a moment. Then it hit him. "Hansen."

Dennis Hansen had been the name of the man that worked on the Cyclone 18 engines that powered the B-29 bombers that flew to Japan during 1945.

Hara, the Torian from Toyo, had sent him some old footage of the bombers flying past Mt. Fuji.

Torian typed in, Mt. Fuji: "Invalid Password."

Torian typed in, Cyclone 18: "Invalid Password."

He looked at the article below the picture of Miller and Hansen again.

The article discussed the lineage of Engineer Don Hansen's father, Danny Hansen working on the Titan Four rocket engine in the 1990's and the J2-X rocket engine in the year 2012.

Danny Hansen's father, Engineer Dennis Hansen had worked on the B-29 jet engine during World War II and later on the A-12 Blackbird.

Danny Hansen in his earlier days had helped with Ramjet and Scramjet technology before the Devil's Tail.

Torian looked at the Comp and noticed the microreader just above the keyboard.

Torian fumbled in his shirt pocket for a moment hoping that he hadn't forgotten it in his Edo at the hotel. He pulled out the access card that O'Doul had given him the week before.

The access card was recovered along with the microchips that had been given back to the Kofu Corporation. But O'Doul had kept the card and given it to Torian.

Torian slid the access card in the microreader and typed in: "Ingenieur (Engineer)."

"*Bitte, Herr Miller,*" was displayed on the screen.

Torian turned to give SG a smile and a big thumbs up, but SG was no where to be seen.

"Dawg gone him. I need to find an old cowbell and hang it around his neck," Torian said to the empty room.

Chapter 62

Rip and the men seated in the cave all laughed as the Riffs in front started shaking hands with some of the men on the front benches.

O'Doul and Mel just looked at each other for a moment then back at the Riff up front.

"Quiet down; quiet down. I thought that would get your attention," the lead Riff yelled out.

"As you know my name is Douglas. For over a year now we've been recruiting more and more marauders and gathering supplies. Recently we had a slight setback with one of our brother marauders. Some Angeles Riffs shot Hernandez in the back."

The group of men started yelling out obscenities about the dirty Riffs from Angeles.

Mel looked at O'Doul as if she wanted to stand up and yell out it was a lie.

Mel had shot Hernandez when he tried to kill Thompson.

"Keep it down," Douglas yelled out again. "I know how you feel. My unit and I have been working with our leaders from the beginning and have done the best we can to keep the Sec Guardians and other Riffs out of our hair. The Angeles Riffs just showed up out of nowhere and started shooting up the castle," Douglas said referring to Scott Castle.

"Luckily those Riffs didn't find the hidden supply camp we had just a short distance away at Ubehebe Crater," Douglas continued. "Don't worry we are in the process of moving the supplies to a secondary crater further south."

O'Doul noticed a man come from the back of the cave where the Riff unit had come from. He walked along the side of the cave behind the lanterns that were placed so that the light focused on the men seated on the benches.

O'Doul couldn't see the man's face only the lower part of his body as he walked.

The man would stop for a minute as if he were peering at the faces in the crowd then moved further along the wall.

O'Doul could see that the man was dressed much nicer than the group of marauders. He could even see a reflection of light off the shiny black shoes the man was wearing.

As the man walked further along the wall he stopped again parallel with the row that O'Doul and Mel were in. The man stepped out into the light walking toward O'Doul.

O'Doul didn't recognize the man but was preparing for whatever might come his way.

O'Doul used his right foot to tap Mel's foot to the right of him.

Mel looked over at O'Doul and then at Torian Miller from Vegas.

"Oh shit!" was all she could say.

Chapter 63

Torian had originally assumed that Miller had been interested in his grandfather's work, which is why Don Hansen may have been Miller's mentor.

The screen on the Comp displayed a map of the surrounding area around Vegas. It had several red highlighted spots on the map.

One of the spots highlighted was Scott Castle where Mel and the Riffs had a run in with marauders. Mel didn't go into any great details about the incident, just that it had dire consequences for the marauders.

Another spot east of the castle had been highlighted but had a line through it. It was called Ubehebe Crater. Further south, near an old abandoned military training center, Amboy Crater was highlighted as well.

Torian noticed that the settlement of Bold, near Lake Me, had been highlighted.

"That's not too far from Vegas. I wonder if Herr Miller might seek some shelter there." Torian wondered.

As Torian was about to see if he could print the map it began fading away.

"What the heck?" Torian tried typing on the Comp but couldn't get anything to come up.

Torian heard what sounded like a crackling sound coming from the Comp. He could see what looked like sparks coming out the sides. The crackling became louder and Torian realized it was time to leave.

He got up and ran quickly back out of the hidden room. As he reached Miller's office he dropped down to the floor opening his mouth and covering his ears.

An explosion was heard from the hidden room as smoke and dust shot out of the room onto Torian.

Torian sat up patting the dust and debris off his jacket realizing that the explosion was confined to the hidden room. A program in the Comp was probably designed to destroy the information if certain continuing passwords weren't entered in a timely sequence.

He started to relax but was startled when Miss Rawlings suddenly ran in with an extinguisher and pointed it at Torian. She squeezed the nozzle so that a blast of white foam sprayed all over him.

"Are you all right?" she asked him as she stopped spraying.

Torian got up wiping off some of the foam from his clothes.

"Thank you, Miss Rawlings. I believe that will be all for today."

Chapter 64

Miller snapped his fingers and pointed at Mel. Two men grabbed Mel lifting her to her feet. Rip stood up and so did O'Doul.

"Who is this woman with?" Miller asked out loud.

"Me," O'Doul answered.

"And who are you?" Miller asked.

"I came here for the meeting. I'm here to offer my services if the price is right," O'Doul told Miller.

"And who invited you?" Miller asked.

"They told me that they came from Frisco to join Hernandez," Rip offered up.

"How convenient that Hernandez is not around to validate your claims," Miller said to O'Doul. "I don't know who this young lady is but I owe her something."

Miller lifted up his right foot and took off his right shoe holding it by the heel. He then slapped Mel across her face with the toe of the shoe.

Mel recoiled from the slap then starred back at Miller. Before O'Doul could retaliate two men grabbed him as well.

"I believe even a Sec Guardian would admit that we are now even. Would you agree?" Miller asked Mel.

The night before at the dinner party, Miller had implied that Mel and Bonnie were going to be thrown over the edge of the balcony by Miller's associates. Although Miller had left before the real fight began, Mel had slipped her foot out of her high-heeled shoe and kicked it into Miller's face.

"Yes, I guess that would make us even," Mel replied.

"I don't know who you are. I only know that you were with that mettlesome Torian from Angeles that keeps following me around. As for you, Hernandez is not around to speak for himself, but I'm sure that he would not have had a gringo, as he would put it, join his particular band of marauders.

Douglas the head Riff now joined Miller.

"What's the trouble?'

"Do they look familiar to you?" Miller asked Douglas.

"No," he replied.

"Well then we have our selves a bit of a mystery?" Miller said putting his hand to his chin wondering what to do to with the two interlopers.

"I invited them; I'll take care of them," Rip said.

"Yes, good idea. Douglas if you and your men would be so good as to assist Rip in removing the trash." Miller said as he turned and walked back to the back part of the cave.

Chapter 65

“I’m so sorry. I saw what looked like smoke coming from your clothes and thought you were on fire,” Miss Rawlings told Torian.

Torian continued to wipe off some of the foam and told Miss Rawlings that everything was fine.

“I just need to get cleaned up a bit,” he told her.

“Do you have a change of clothes with you?” she asked.

“No this was my only change of clothes, except for an Edo that I wore to the party last night. I hadn’t planned on being here this long or taking a foam bath for that matter,” Torian told her.

“Well! Next time I think you’re on fire maybe I’ll just let you smolder a while,” Miss Rawlings told Torian with her hands on her hips.

Torian looked down at his dripping pants and began to laugh.

Miss Rawlings laughed too.

“Torian Miller has some extra clothes he keeps in his closet,” Miss

Rawlings said. She walked over to a closet and opened up a door pulling out a dark suit.

"He always wears dark clothes for some reason," she said taking the pants off the hanger and holding them up in front of Torian.

"I believe these will just fit you," she said laying them down on the desk.

She left the office and closed the door behind her while Torian took off his wet clothes.

Torian realizing that his skin was a little damp looked for something to dry off with when Miss Rawlings opened the door ajar and put her arm through the opening with a towel in her hand.

Torian walked over and took the towel thanking her as she shut the door. He dried off and put on Miller's suit.

Torian was taking his things from his clothes and putting them in his new suit when he came across a folded up paper in Miller's pants pocket. On it was a meeting time and place outside of Vegas somewhere near the settlement of Bold.

"Shoot, the meeting started an hour ago," Torian realized looking at the time.

He opened up the door to speak to Miss Rawlings when low and behold there was SG standing there waiting for him.

"We need to get somewhere fast. I don't suppose you can arrange for us to get out to the settlement of Bold in a hurry?" Torian asked SG.

"Follow me," was displayed across the Sec Guardians screen.

As SG turned to walk away Torian made another motion with his hip as if he had a rope tied around his waist and was being pulled along as SG was leaving.

"Got to go," he said waving goodbye to Miss Rawlings.

Chapter 66

Rip led the way out of the cave.

Mel and O'Doul had been bound with some rope and were being pushed from behind by Douglas and his Riffs.

"It might be in your best interest to tell us why you're really here?" Douglas asked O'Doul.

"We told you. Some guy told us that a man named Hernandez was hiring for some raids on the city of Angeles. That's why we came down here. When we got here we heard Hernandez was dead and we didn't know who to talk to, so we came here," O'Doul told Douglas.

"Hernandez did hire a couple of Australian fellows to help him with some things, but they didn't work out so well," Douglas told O'Doul.

"I'd like to ask them a few questions as well. Seeing that the raid on the castle happened after they came into contact with those Angeles Riffs I spoke about earlier in the meeting. I don't suppose you'd know anything about that now would you?" Douglas asked looking at Mel.

"*No comprender*," Mel replied.

"Cute. Will see how cute you are when we take you for a little swim," Douglas said pointing at one of the boats tied up to the dock.

O'Doul and Mel were taken aboard a large boat with the name <u>Pelican</u> written on the stern. It was thirty feet in length and had a cabin that Rip went into to start the engine.

As they began to pull away from the dock they herd several shots coming from the front of the cave entrance.

Douglas looked back but yelled at Rip to keep going.

Thompson and Jones had observed everything from the opening in the top of the cave. When they saw O'Doul and Mel being tied up they went down the side of the hill closest to the lake to try and stop the Riffs from taking O'Doul and Mel away.

As Thompson rounded a big rock he came face to face with a marauder taking a leek.

The marauder surprised by Thompson, tried to button up the front of his pants but Thompson hit the marauder with an upper cut fist that knocked the marauder to the ground.

"Are you done yet?" another marauder said coming from the front of the cave.

He saw the marauder on the ground and Thompson standing over him. The marauder turned and ran back to the front of the cave entrance yelling an alarm.

Thompson and Jones headed for the boat dock but before they could get ten feet shots hit the ground around them.

They both dove for cover behind an upside down boat left on shore.

Thompson and Jones both returned fire in the direction of the cave.

Men were yelling out, "over there, over there," as they scrambled for cover.

Thompson continued to shoot back with his lever action rifle wishing they had brought more ammo with them. He turned to ask Jones how many rounds she had and saw that she was gone.

"Jones, where are you?" Thompson whispered out loud.

The start of an engine behind him made Thompson look over at the dock.

Jones was in a small speedboat starting it up and signaling for him to hurry up.

Thompson took a couple more shots in the direction of the cave and scrambled over to the boat. He hopped inside and Jones pushed the throttle to full as the boat sped away from the shore.

Jones headed in the direction of the larger boat that O'Doul and Mel were on.

The speedboat was smaller and faster and they were gaining on it.

O'Doul and Mel were looking over the stern of the <u>Pelican</u> wondering if the shots being fired were coming from Thompson and Jones.

"Seems you have friends coming this way," Douglas said out loud. "I think now would be a good time for a swim, don't you?" Douglas said as he pushed Mel over the back of the boat.

Thompson seeing Mel go over stepped up on the railing and jumped in after her.

"Well that was easy," Douglas commenting on O'Doul's departure.

Douglas yelled at Rip to turn the boat around and run over the two swimmers.

Rip did as he was told and took a long wide turn in the <u>Pelican</u> and headed for the two bobbing heads on the surface of the lake.

Jones saw that Mel had been pushed over the back of the boat and that O'Doul had jumped in after. She also saw the boat arcing in a semicircle back toward the two members of her unit treading water. Jones pushed on the throttle as hard as she could heading straight for O'Doul and Mel.

"What are you doing?" Thompson yelled out at Jones, realizing she was heading straight for the Mel and O'Doul.

"Praying," Jones yelled back.

The two boats were converging on O'Doul and Mel as they tried to keep their heads above water.

"I hope you can hold your breath," Mel yelled at O'Doul. They both took a gulp of air and sank beneath the surface.

"What do they think they're doing?" Rip yelled at Douglas as the oncoming speedboat headed straight for Rip and the other Riffs.

"Keep going straight," Douglas yelled back at Rip.

The two boats kept getting closer and closer until at the last moment Rip veered to the right, just missing Jones and Thompson who had stayed their course.

Jones after passing the <u>Pelican</u> pulled back on the throttle and swung around back toward where O'Doul and Mel had been last seen.

The Pelican couldn't turn as quickly and had to take a wider semicircle to head back in the direction they had come.

Jones pulled up and stopped the boat where she estimated O'Doul should be.

O'Doul's head popped up above the surface of the water as he took another gulp of air. He saw the hand of Thompson reaching for him and dragging him up and into the boat.

Jones started to untie O'Doul's hands as Thompson looked into the water yelling for Mel.

Mel's head popped up just a few feet from where O'Doul had surfaced and she yelled, "I'd hold my thumb up in the air but I'm a little tied up at the moment."

Thompson reached out and pulled Mel into the boat as well. He untied her hands as the Pelican slowly cruised around and to the starboard side of the speedboat.

"One big happy family," Douglas said, as his Riffs pointed M-16's at O'Doul and his unit.

Thompson started to reach for the gun he had laid down before helping O'Doul and Mel into the boat, but O'Doul quietly said, "No Daniel."

"Take his advice," Douglas said pointing his 9mm at Thompson.

"I think this is where we will say are final goodbye's," Douglas said lifting the handgun.

The Riffs on the Pelican pulled back the actions of their M-16's in preparation of shooting O'Doul and his unit.

A loud humming sound was coming from the middle of the lake. There was a mild fog covering the center of the lake and Douglas looked to his left over the stern of the Pelican and saw some kind of a craft coming out of the fog. It looked as if it were hovering above the water and heading straight for them.

It was about sixty feet in length and thirty feet in width. It had blue flashing lights as it approached the two boats.

Standing on the front of the boat behind a railing was a Sec Guardian with red glowing eyes that pierced the darkness of the night air.

Rip not wanting any part of that gunned the engine of the Pelican and headed back to shore.

"Next time!" Douglas said waving goodbye. "Next time!"

The hovercraft pulled alongside of the speedboat.

A hatch on the port side of the Hovercrafts Bridge opened up and a familiar face in a dark suit looked out and waved.

"I always wanted to pilot one of these things!" Torian yelled out.

"Trent!" Melanie yelled back.

Chapter 67

O'Doul and his Riffs climbed out of the speedboat and onto the hovercraft.

A member of the hovercraft's crew got on board the speedboat to take it back to shore.

Trent went back onto the bridge to pursue the <u>Pelican</u>.

"How come you two aren't wearing water wings this far out from shore?" Trent asked; noticing Jimmy and Melanie were all wet.

"This is getting to be a habit of yours, showing up when least expected," O'Doul replied.

"Let's just say I was in the neighborhood and decided to go for a three-hour tour. A three-hour tour," Torian repeated, singing it this time.

The Riffs not really sure what Torian was humming just looked out the bridge windows at the fleeing boat.

The hovercraft was catching up quickly to the <u>Pelican</u>, but not before it reached the dock.

O'Doul could see the Vegas Riffs getting off the boat quickly and running for the cave.

The hovercraft went passed the dock and up onto shore. It stopped and began to settle to the ground.

O'Doul and Thompson jumped to the ground and ran toward the cave. They stopped at the front entrance and peered inside. They could see that the tables, where the guns had been, were empty. Even the guns that O'Doul and Mel had brought were missing.

Sec Guardian 5000 just walked past the Riffs and into the cave.

O'Doul and Thompson looked at each other then followed the Guardian inside.

The cave was empty and O'Doul looked toward the back where Douglas and the man with the shiny shoes had come from. He walked along the side of the cave and into another part of the cavern. There was a back exit and O'Doul could hear the sounds of engines fading away.

The Guardian and O'Doul walked out the back exit and could see several trucks in the distance.

Thompson came out the exit as well, "damn," he said seeing the trucks in the distance.

Jones, who had also jumped from the hovercraft, had run to get the truck they had parked in the settlement. She drove it around to the back of the hill and pulled up next to the Riffs. "Need a lift?" she yelled.

O'Doul and Thompson got in the truck. "We're going to lose them in those mountains and hills," O'Doul said.

Mel came running up to the truck and climbed in.

"Where you been? Playing nice, nice, with your Torian friend?" Thompson asked Mel.

"I know where they're going," Mel replied.

Just before reaching shore, Trent had told Melanie about the secret room at the Vegas Lib and the map he had seen on Miller's hidden Comp.

Trent told Melanie that there were several highlighted areas on the map including Ubehebe crater and Amboy Crater.

Melanie told Trent that Douglas had mentioned that their supplies had been moved from Ubehebe Crater near Scott Castle to another crater further south.

After getting the information from Trent, Melanie gave him a quick kiss and jumped off the hovercraft heading for the cave as well.

Trent had climbed down from the hovercraft and started to walk along the beach.

Melanie and the Riffs were doing their jobs and he didn't want to interfere if not invited.

It was dawn and the sunrise was coming up to burn off the fog that was moving slowly across the lake.

He stopped to pick up a flat rock and threw it so that it skipped along the surface of the water. He hadn't even gotten a chance to thank Melanie for last night and he had sent the red roses to the Riff station thinking that she had returned there.

"Damn, I need to get a hold of Bonnie and tell her what's going on, as well as thank her for the night before," Trent thought to himself. Flowers are a nice gesture but he needed to tell her in person.

"That's why there was an empty seat!" Trent said, remembering what Melanie told him about Hernandez being at Scott Castle and that he also had worn a gold ring.

At the poker game there were nine chairs at the table. One chair was empty so Trent was able to sit down and play. There were nine people in the picture that Trent had seen in Miller's hidden room.

His thoughts were interrupted by the sound of footsteps on the sand behind him. He turned to see who it was.

This time Trent had the surprised look on his face when he saw Miller and two of his associates walking toward him. One of the associates was the one from the poker game.

"I want my ring back," Miller told Torian with a straight face.

The associate from the poker room had a big smile on his face as he pulled out the gun from his brown jacket.

"I'm sorry, did you gentleman have an appointment? Torian asked.

Chapter 68

Mel told the Riffs about the brief encounters that Trent had with Miller while in Vegas and about the map he had seen.

Jones had switched places with O'Doul so that he could drive while she pulled up the GPO coordinates for Amboy Crater.

Jones told O'Doul he was headed in the right direction. But that her palm Comp wasn't as reliable as the Comp in the UCV.

They also didn't have radar in the older truck and weren't sure that Douglas and his band of marauders were actually heading in that direction.

They had traveled southwest for a couple of hours and were eating some food rations when they heard a honking sound behind them.

O'Doul looked in the rearview mirror as the others looked back over their shoulders.

A UCV was coming toward them and as it got closer they could see a Sec Guardian driving it.

O'Doul slowed down and stopped the truck and the Riffs got out.

The Urban Command Vehicle came to a stop just behind them and out stepped Sec Guardian 2000.

"Now how did he do that?" Jones said wondering how the Guardian was able to find them in the middle of nowhere.

"I don't know and don't care," O'Doul said.

The Sec Guardian stood outside the door of the UCV as the Riffs gathered up a few things from the truck. They all stepped up into the UCV and O'Doul got behind the driver's seat.

"Well this should even things up a little," O'Doul said as he put the UCV in drive.

Mel sat in the front passenger seat as Jones sat at her Comp to continue monitoring the GPO.

The Sec Guardian stood near the back while Thompson sat on the bench behind O'Doul and asked, "Are we there yet?"

Chapter 69

"Is that one of my suits you're wearing?" Miller asked Torian with a quizzical look on his face, staring at the dark suit Torian had on.

"This old thing, why yes, I believe it is. You wouldn't want to put any holes it now would you?" Torian asked Miller.

"Shoot him in *der kopf* (the head)," Miller told his associate with the gun.

The associate in the brown jacket raised the gun a little higher now pointing it at Torian's head.

Torian started to smile.

"Now why would you be smiling at a time like this?" the guy with the gun asked Torian.

"Because I know something you don't," he replied.

"And what is that?" Miller asked.

The associate in the brown jacket was lifted up off the ground and turned completely upside down in a one-eighty, then driven back down into the sand headfirst. His head was buried up to his shoulders like an ostrich hiding its head in a hole. His legs were moving in the air as if he was trying to run away.

The other associate reached into his jacket but SG grabbed the associate by the arm and the leg. SG spun around a couple of times and let go of the associate flinging him out across the lake skipping him like Torian had skipped the flat rock.

SG's eyes were red as he now faced Miller.

A message displayed across SG's face monitor: "Treason against the UCA consists in levying war against it, adhering to its enemies or giving them aid, and can be committed by persons owing allegiance to the UCA. The penalty shall be death."

When becoming a Torian a person makes a promise to always act with integrity when gathering or giving information to the public or representatives of the United Corporations of America.

"Miller finished reading the Sec Guardian's monitor and turned toward Torian.

"*Konnen Sie mir bitte helfen*? (Can you help me please?). I fear my days are numbered. My choices were made generations ago by my ancestors and left me little choice but to follow in their footsteps. I'm a product of discontent that started with the rise and fall of Nazi Germany. I was raised believing in something that no longer existed and was told it was my destiny to reconstruct a notion by a mad man that history has shown can't be won by force," Miller told Torian.

"The German people were misled by a dictator of Austrian descent who surrounded himself with advisors only interested in power. Ultimately they paid the price for their egotism, but at the cost of millions of lives including their own," Torian told Miller.

"History often repeats itself with only a few to realize that the future is what we make of it, not what it makes of us. It has been and shall always be that way, until we as a human race find content in our own lives, without the need to disrupt others," Torian continued.

"*Ich habe mich verlaufen* (I'm lost), Miller told Torian.

"*Viel Gluck Herman* (Good luck Herman), Torian told Miller remembering Hansen calling Miller by his first name at the poker table when he left.

Torian turned and walked away leaving Miller to his own fate.

Chapter 70

They had traveled several more hours through the rough terrain and were getting closer to the crater.

"I think we are almost there," Jones told the Riffs. "I'm picking up a lot of radio transmissions but I can't decipher what is being broadcast.

Jones had contacted Riff station ten for reinforcements asking them to meet at the crater just in case they were right.

An approval for dismantling the band of marauders and their supply camp was given by any means necessary by Sec Guardian 2000 riding in the UCA with them.

An hour passed by and they hadn't received any messages from the station.

Even the Guardian's eyes were blinking yellow.

"Any word from Captain Harding on their ETA? (Estimated Time of Arrival)," O'Doul asked Jones.

"No. We are experiencing radio interference now that we are getting closer to the crater. The marauders may have tampered with the Outernet in this area," Jones replied.

"I think that's it," Mel said seeing what looked like a mountain in front of them.

O'Doul drove the UCV within five hundred yards from what looked like an entrance to the crater and stopped.

The crater had an opening on one side that allowed vehicles to drive in without having to go up the side of the crater and down into it. There were several tire tracks that could be seen on a dirt road leading to the entrance.

"How do you suggest we approach them, quietly or straight up?" Thompson asked.

Several shots interrupted his question as bullets ricochet off the front window of the UCV.

The Urban Command Vehicle was built to withstand any penetration from normal arms fire.

"I guess that means straight up!" Thompson said answering his own question.

O'Doul put the UCV back into drive and headed for the opening of the crater.

Jones got up from where she was sitting and walked to the back.

A sound of hydraulics came from the top of the UCV as a platform raised up with Jones sitting behind a pair of M-60 machine guns mounted on the swivel turret. She drew back the lever and pivoted it toward the men on top of the crater.

She took aim and began firing the machine guns.

Bullets riddled the top of the crater as marauders fell backward and down the sides of the crater.

A truck came from the entrance with two men in front and another one in back standing in the rear firing a machine gun at the UCV. A barrage of bullets was now hitting the command vehicle.

Jones swiveled her guns toward the oncoming truck and fired a salvo of bullets of her own, hitting the truck, and sending it off in another direction.

The truck hit an embankment and skipped up into the air landing on its front bumper, then flipped upside down.

O'Doul drove into the entrance of the crater and stopped just inside.

"Oh crap!" Mel said looking out the front window.

In front of them were about a dozen trucks with marauders running from tents that had been set up in and around the inside of the crater.

Bullets were hitting the front of the command vehicle again as marauders fired from various positions.

O'Doul drove over to the right where there was an outcropping of boulders big enough to give them some cover.

He pulled up and stopped, pushing the button to open the door and out went Mel and Thompson.

On top, Jones was still firing the M-60's at various marauders as they scrambled for cover.

Thompson already had his favorite toy out and jogged up and around one of the boulders to fire his M-249 machine gun.

Thompson was ripping the tents to shreds making sure there weren't any marauders in them.

O'Doul came out and climbed on top of one of the boulders and began to fire his CAR-15. It was a more accurate firearm and he was shooting marauders in stationary positions.

The light on one of the bigger trucks turned on and was now heading toward the Riffs position. The top of it had a tarp on it and was pulled down exposing several marauders with AK-47's and one guy with a bazooka. The guy with the bazooka lifted it onto his shoulder, but before he could get off a shot, the truck was hit in front and it exploded driving off to the right and crashing into another truck.

O'Doul looked down and to his left and could see Mel standing in front of the boulders with a M32A1 40mm Grenade launcher. She fired five more grenades from her position then ducked down to reload.

"That's my kind of woman," Thompson yelled up at O'Doul looking over at Mel.

Mel reloaded then waived at Thompson to let him know she was ready to fire again.

Thompson laid down some suppressing fire as Mel stood up and aimed for other trucks still parked.

Explosions rocked the trucks as they bounced into the air and twisted in to hot metal.

Bullets were ricocheting off the rocks around the Riffs and keeping them from leaving their positions.

A hail of bullets coming from a stationary machine gun nest on the inside of the crater to their left made Mel and Thompson duck behind the rocks for cover.

The firing stopped and O'Doul looked over to see if the gunmen were reloading.

Instead he saw marauders being flung out of the nest and then the machine gun being held up in the air by Sec Guardian 2000 who bent the barrel of the gun into a U shape.

A rumbling sound came from the back of the encampment and Jones yelled down at the Riffs. "Is that what I think it is?" she yelled.

A tank was rumbling toward them with the barrel of a cannon turning in their direction.

"Do you think the Guardian could bend that barrel the same way he did the machine gun?" Jones yelled down at O'Doul.

"If he can he better do it quick," O'Doul yelled back.

The tank came to within twenty yards of the Riffs and stopped. A door hatch on top of the tank turret opened up and Douglas from the Vegas Riffs stood up.

"I told you there would be a next time," Douglas yelled.

Chapter 71

Torian was on his way back to the Vegas Lib to see if he could salvage the picture of the men in the group shot with Miller.

After changing into Miller's suit and finding the meeting time he wanted to get there in a hurry. Now that he had time to think about the possible connection with Hernandez, Miller and the other men from the poker game, he realized how important the photo was.

SG had taken Torian back to Vegas. Torian didn't ask SG about Miller thinking it best not to dwell on it.

Life is a precious thing and not to be taken lightly.

In the past history of the then United States, putting people in prison was an acceptable consequence to someone's criminal actions. The sad thing was that it didn't discourage people that committed crimes against society. Even the threat of a death penalty wasn't enough to stop someone from driving by in a vehicle and shooting children as they played in their own front yards a century ago.

After the catastrophe struck the Earth, survival consisted of the strong of mind and will over the lesser minded, let's hope everything turns out okay; mindset. Even though the Earth's population had diminished considerably, allowing others to roam around freely killing indiscriminately for whatever purpose could not be tolerated.

The UCA giving the Supremes the authority to make life and death decisions had become a necessary evil. The death of one life could save countless other lives in the process.

"And I wasn't going to dwell on it," Torian thought to himself.

At the Vegas Lib, Torian walked into Miss Rawlings office to find Bonnie sitting on the desk facing Miss Rawlings.

Bonnie was wearing a light green pantsuit with a low cut blouse.

Bonnie turned around showing her now green eyes.

"Oh there you are. We were just talking about you," Bonnie said.

"I went for a boat ride and took a stroll along the shore of Lake Me," Torian replied.

"With anyone I know?" Bonnie asked.

"Well yes, I did see Melanie briefly, but you know her, always chasing other men," Torian said with a smile.

They both laughed a little with Miss Rawlings not quite sure what they were laughing about.

"I took the liberty of salvaging some of the photos that were in Torian Millers hidden room. The Comp was completely destroyed however and anything else that might have been in his desk," Miss Rawlings told Torian.

"That's great!" Torian said with vigor.

"I don't suppose you know if Torian Miller will be returning anytime soon?"

"I'm sorry to tell you that Miller has reluctantly resigned his posting," Torian said delicately.

"I see," Miss Rawlings said looking down at her desk.

Bonnie got up from where she was sitting looking at Torian and walked over to one of the walls with several pictures on it pretending to be interested in them.

Torian walked over and sat on the desk where Bonnie had been sitting and reached out to lift Miss Rawlings chin up.

"Those pictures you saved from Miller's hidden office may help us in finding others that are trying to create anarchy. I believe there is a movement to destroy all that we have come to know and take us backwards to a time of war amongst ourselves," Torian told her.

"We survived two civil wars. I'm not sure we can survive another," he continued.

"Thank you," he said looking into Miss Rawlings eyes.

Miss Rawlings blushed looking down again but with a smile on her face this time.

"May I take this picture with Miller and the other men with me?" Torian asked.

"Of course," Miss Rawlings replied handing him the frame.

Torian took the picture out of the frame. As he did Miss Rawlings took a hold of the picture gently.

"I don't know all of the men but I have met these three," she said pointing at the picture.

"This is Don Hansen, creator of the Metronome. This man's name is Smith and the other one is a brutish man by the name of Johnson," she said.

"Hansen is retired and living here in Vegas. The other two are from Den City. They work in the command center that communicates with the Metronome," she continued.

"They would come here to the Lib and wait for Torian Miller, I mean Mr. Miller, until he arrived and then they would all leave together."

"That's great information," Torian told Miss Rawlings.

"There was one other man that always waited outside the Lib. I think his name was, Her, Hern..."   "--Hernandez?" Torian finished for her.

"Yes, that was his name," she said.

Torian got up from the desk and walked over to Bonnie. "Are you ready to go?" he asked her.

"Yes," Bonnie replied.

"By the way, my name is Judy. Judy Rawlings if you ever need any more help," she said modestly to Torian.

"If it has to do with Vegas you're the first one I'll call on," Torian replied.

"Thank you again, Judy."

Judy's smile got bigger in the hopes of seeing Torian again.

Torian and Bonnie walked out of the office.

"I always knew I liked you, but now I know why," Bonnie told Torian.

"You're a good man Trent. I mean Torian."

"By the way, thank you for the white roses you sent me," Bonnie continued.

"They are a thank you for the other night," Torian told her.

"Other night?" Bonnie looked at Torian as if she didn't know what he was talking about.

"You know, when you, Melanie and I spent the night..."

Bonnie held up her finger to Torian's lips to shush him gently.

"Of all people you should know that what happens in a Vegas suite; stays in a Vegas suite," Bonnie said and walked out of the Lib.

Chapter 72

"I suggest that you lay down your firearms and come out with your hands in the air," Douglas told the Angeles Riffs.

O'Doul stood up on the boulder and laid down his CAR-15.

Thompson looked up with a disappointed look and laid down his M-249 after seeing O'Doul lay down his rifle.

Jones stood up on the UCV and put her hands up.

Mel put down her weapon but stayed slightly behind the rock she had used for cover.

Sec Guardian 2000 walked over and stood in front of the tank. About fifteen yards to the left of O'Doul and his unit. The Guardian's eyes were glowing red.

The tank turret turned the cannon to the right and was now pointing directly at the Sec Guardian.

Several marauders were forming a semicircle behind the tank and facing toward the Riffs and Sec Guardian.

"Stand down Guardian," Douglas told Sec Guardian 2000.

The Guardian's eyes blinked red a few times then turned to yellow. The Guardian began stepping backwards.

Douglas seeing the Guardians eyes change to yellow, smiled.

Mel stepped out from behind the rock with her G-club in hand and dropped a Mag-ball on the ground.

The G-club was not a standard issued weapon and Douglas seeing Mel with the club and the little white ball started to laugh.

Mel took a stance with her feet slightly apart looking down at the Mag-ball and used the G-club to hit the ball toward the tank.

The ball rolled underneath the tank and Mel pushed a button on her belt activating the magnetic ball so that it bounced up and attached itself to the tank.

Douglas finished laughing and said, "even if that *is* some type of an explosive, it's too small and won't penetrate the steel armor under this tank."

Mel stepped back a little ways behind the rock she had been behind and said, "It's a homing device for specially designed anti-tank piercing RPG rockets."

"And who is supposed to home in on it, if I may ask?" Douglas said.

"Them," Mel said pointing up toward the rim of the crater.

Captain Harding standing at the top of the hill yelled out, "Riffs!"

"Riffs!" Was the roaring response from a hundred other Riffs standing all around the top of the crater. They were pointing weapons of all kinds including portable rocket launchers down into the crater at Douglas.

"You have the right to remain silent. Anything you say can and will be used against you before a Sec Guardian. You have the right to die. If you can't afford to die we will gladly appoint someone to shoot you," Thompson said out loud, now standing on top of the boulder next to O'Doul.

Chapter 73

Torian walked out of the Vegas Lib behind Bonnie. They stopped to talk awhile outside the Lib.

Torian told Bonnie about the past day's events.

As he walked down some steps he saw two men stepping off the conveyer and walking hurriedly toward the Lib.

They passed Bonnie and Torian as if they weren't even there.

The two men walked as if they had a specific agenda in mind.

Torian finished telling Bonnie about the poker game and his brief encounter with Melanie and Miller.

They started to walk toward the conveyer when Torian said, "Bonnie wait a moment."

He stopped and started walking back to the Lib.

Torian walked in and looked around to see if he could see the two men.

They both had been wearing tan pants and brown jackets.

Something about the brown jackets and their demeanor disturbed Torian.

Torian walked toward the Info desk but the young man that had been there before was not around. He started to walk back to Judy's office and noticed that the door was closed.

He went to the office and opened the door and stepped in.

Judy was sitting at her desk with a frightful look on her face with one of the men standing over her.

The guy turned to look at Torian as he entered the office.

"Pardon me but is the Torian available?" Torian asked Judy.

The guy standing over Judy turned toward Torian and said, "He's busy right now. Come back later."

"Huh, well then maybe you could help me. I've been looking for some information on dwelling decorating and..."

"--I said we are busy," the guy interrupted Torian taking a step toward him.

The other guy came out of Millers office and asked, "What's the problem Skip."

"No problem Brad. Mr. Fancy Pants here wants to make his dwelling look pretty," Skip said with a smile mocking Torian.

"Did he say your name was Skippy?" Torian said mocking him back.

Skip stopped smiling and took another step toward Torian.

Bonnie walked in and said, "Oh there you are. Did you find what you were looking for?"

"Let's go!" Brad told Skip.

Brad led the way out and Skip followed behind leering at Torian as he left.

Judy got up quickly from her desk chair and hugged Torian.

Torian said, "Everything's fine now."

Bonnie peeking out the door watched to see if the men had gone, then looked back into the office crossing her arms seeing Judy embracing Torian. "Huh!"

Torian could only stand there and pat Judy on the back with a-- what do I do now-- look on his face looking back at Bonnie.

Chapter 74

Douglas seeing his predicament dropped back down into the tank closing the hatch.

Marauders standing around the tank were dropping their weapons to the ground but when they saw Douglas disappear in the tank they scrambled for cover.

The tank turret started to turn back toward the Riffs.

"Take cover," O'Doul yelled out as he and Thompson jumped down behind the rocks.

Seeing the turret move on the tank, the Riffs on top of the crater fired their rocket launchers bombarding the tank with missile's that homed in on Mel's Mag-ball.

Explosions rocked the top of the tank before it could fire.

Some of the marauders were firing up the hill from their positions but were being mowed down by the incoming hail of bullets coming down from the Riffs.

After twenty minutes or so Captain Harding sent up a cease fire flare.

The Riffs stopped shooting and about half started coming down the inside of the crater. The other half stayed in their positions on top to protect the ones climbing down.

O'Doul and Mel met with Harding as he reached the bottom of the crater.

"Glad you could join us," O'Doul told the Captain.

"You'd think I was getting to old for this crap," Harding replied.

As the clouds of smoke cleared Sec Guardian 2000 walked over to the tank and climbed up and began pulling apart the twisted metal hatch peering inside.

Thompson followed the Guardian but the tank was too hot for him to climb up on it.

Jones remained on top of the UCV with her M-60's providing cover.

The Guardian climbed down and stood in front of Thompson.

Thompson looked at the Guardian's face monitor watching a digital replay of what the Guardian had seen inside the tank. He then walked over to where O'Doul, Mel and the Captain were. He had a disgusted look on his face.

"Three men are dead in the tank. Only one of them is one of the Vegas Riffs we saw. Douglas isn't among them," Thompson told O'Doul.

"What?" Mel said.

"There is an escape hatch under the tank and it's open."

"Vegas Riff? And who is Douglas?" Harding inquired.

Chapter 75

Miss Rawlings regained her composure and stepped back from Torian.

"Sorry, I--They--I was frightened for a moment, but I'm fine now," Judy said.

Bonnie relaxed her arms and walked over to Judy. "What did they want?"

"They told me that Herman, Mr. Miller was dead and they were here to take some of his things.

"I didn't see anything in their hands as they left," Torian said.

"No, Brad yelled out to Skip that the room had been compromised, but the data had self-destructed. They thought I was the one that opened the hidden room," Judy told Torian.

"If they think she opened it then she won't be safe here," Bonnie told Torian.

"Bonnie, would you mind accompanying Judy to her dwelling

until I can notify a Sec Guardian to keep an eye on her?" Torian asked.

"Not at all," she replied.

Judy gathered some of her personal belongings from the desk and walked out of the office looking at Torian as if she wished he were the one escorting her home.

Bonnie seeing the look from Judy rolled her eyes at Torian and said, "Women!"

Torian with a bashful look on his face sat down and used Miss Rawlings Comp to contact the Guardians.

A few minutes later he got up and left the Lib.

He took the conveyer that would take him back to his hotel.

As he reached the end of the conveyer he took some stairs into the hotel and walked through a corner of the casino.

Torian stopped for a moment to take in one of the lounge acts where clone Frank was singing that it was his kind of town.

Stephanie walked over in a bright yellow costume with feathers sticking out behind her.

"You're still here?" she said.

"Yes, still in one piece I might add," Torian replied.

"But for how long?" Stephanie asked.

Puzzled; Torian looked at Stephanie. She put on some fancy mirrored glasses that must have been part of her costume.

"Look into my eyes darling," she said.

Torian looked into the mirror and saw Skippy about twenty feet behind him with another man watching Torian.

Stephanie tilted the glasses down a bit on her nose looking over the top of them, "Is it just me?" Stephanie asked.

"Huh?" Torian said.

"Well either you are following guys with rings on or their following you."

Torian reached up and pushed the glasses gently back up on Stephanie's nose. He leaned a little closer to Stephanie and could see the glint of a gold ring on the man standing next to Skippy. Torian looked at the man's face and it was one of the men from the poker game by the name of Johnson. He had also been in the photograph with Miller.

"I don't suppose you could take me to your dressing room could you?" Torian asked Stephanie.

"Now you're talking. Do you think I can convince you to come back over to my side of the fence?" Stephanie said playfully.

"I think you could convince clone Simmons to stop doing jumping jacks.

"What?" Stephanie said.

"Never mind," Torian said taking Stephanie by the hand and leading her away.

Stephanie stopped, tugging on Torian's hand and said, "You aren't kind of kinky and planning on trying some of my outfits on are you?"

"Actually that's not a bad idea," Torian replied pulling on Stephanie's hand again.

Chapter 76

A Captain from Diego had overheard the emergency message sent out by Captain Harding and brought several Diego Riff units with him, including Sec Guardian 1000.

Sec Guardian 2000 was walking around the marauder encampment administering judgments while O'Doul told the Captains' about the meeting in the cave near the settlement of Bold and the incident with Miller and Douglas. He explained about the Sec Guardian showing up on the hovercraft but left out the part with Torian being present.

Captain Harding told O'Doul that Sec Guardian 2000 had been notified of their situation and had requisitioned the UCV after receiving the message from Jones.

Harding had provided the Guardian with a tracking code to locate the truck O'Doul and his unit was driving. He also sent out an emergency signal to all Riffs patrolling the outer eastside of the Angeles area to meet and converge on the crater.

The Diego Captain heard the broadcast and sent his northeast Diego Riffs up to meet at them the crater.

It wasn't until both the Angeles and Diego Riffs met around the outside of the crater that Captain Harding realized the other Captain had responded as well.

Captain Howard told Harding that he tried to notify him of their willingness to help out but there was interference with their radio signals.

Harding had told Howard, "the more the merrier."

While O'Doul was briefing the Captains', Mel and Thompson were helping Guardian 2000 locate any marauders that were still in hiding. They were also looking for Douglas.

Jones had stayed up on the UCV keeping an eye on her unit and the other Riffs that were gathering up wounded marauders.

A Med-priest had accompanied both sets of Riffs and was tending to the wounded marauders just in case the Guardians gave leniency.

Near the back of the crater one of the marauders that had been hiding came out from behind some crates with a rifle in both hands and pointed it at some uniformed Riffs walking toward him.

The marauder started to raise the rifle to his shoulder then hesitated recognizing the approaching Riffs. The marauder's expression turned to a quizzical look as the leading Riff shot the marauder twice in the chest.

A Riff about twenty yards away heard the gunfire and jogged over to the three Riffs that had just shot the marauder and asked if they were okay?

"We're just fine," Douglas replied.

Chapter 77

Bonnie and Judy had left the Lib heading to Judy's dwelling.

They took the conveyer to a section of Vegas that was predominantly for residents.

While on the conveyer Bonnie took out a compact from her pants pocket to powder her nose. She looked in the little mirror in the compact and saw the man named Brad following them.

He had an Info paper up in front of him peering over the top of it watching them.

At the end of the conveyer Bonnie took hold of Judy's arm and told her she had a better idea.

Bonnie stepped onto a conveyer that headed back toward the casinos.

The two conveyers ran parallel to each other but in opposite directions.

Judy, wondering why they were heading back toward the casino's spotted the passing Brad trying to hide behind the Info paper.

"Oh my!" she said to Bonnie.

"Maybe we are better off at one of the casinos until we can find a Guardian," Bonnie told Judy.

At the end of the conveyer Brad stepped off and back onto the other conveyer Bonnie and Judy had taken.

About ten minutes later Bonnie and Judy stepped off the conveyer and headed to the hotel that Bonnie and Torian were staying at.

They walked into the casino area and over to one of the lounges.

Bonnie didn't see Brad yet so they walked into the lounge.

There was a crowd of people there waiting for the next act and Bonnie thought this would be a good place to blend in.

Bonnie and Judy went to the right side of the lounge and sat down in one of the booths facing the stage.

They saw Brad at the entrance to the lounge looking inside trying to locate them so they ducked down in the booth.

Two men came up behind Brad and started talking to him. One of them was the guy named Skip.

"That's Johnson. The one I told you and Torian about," Judy told Bonnie referring to the third man with Brad and Skip.

Johnson was taller than the other two men and was wearing a dark business suit.

The three men were talking and looking around the inside of the lounge.

The booth had a high backing on it and Bonnie and Judy were able to sit back so that they weren't seen from the sides and behind.

Brad and Johnson left to go check the rest of the casino area for the girls.

The lights in the lounge dimmed and a spotlight focused on the stage.

"Oh good," Bonnie said, referring to the lights going down.

An announcer's voice was heard in the lounge.

"And now; live on stage; brought to you by Kofu Electronics Corporation; the King himself," the voice stopped and out walked two pretty showgirls, one in pink and the other in yellow. Both had feathery costumes with big fluffy fans and stood on either side of a microphone stand in the front of the stage.

A man in a white costume and cape walked out onto the stage. His shirt collar was a couple of inches tall and he had a huge belt buckle.

You could see the big sideburns under the sunglasses as he walked up to the microphone. He put one foot out in front of the other and took the microphone as the music began to play.

A host near the front entrance asked Skip to please sit down and not block the entrance to the lounge.

Skip walked to his left and sat on a barstool in front of the bar still looking around the lounge.

Bonnie and Judy kept peeking over the side of the booth keeping an eye on the Skip when Bonnie heard a familiar voice. She looked up at the entertainer on stage and squinted trying to see past the sunglasses. Her eyes widened as she recognized Torian singing, "Viva--Viva--Vegas!"

Chapter 78

Mel and Thompson met up with O'Doul and told him that there was no sign of Douglas and the other two Vegas Riffs.

One of the Med-priests jogged up to O'Doul and asked him to follow him.

They followed the Med-priest to the back of the crater where a Riff was kneeling next to a wounded marauder.

"This guy says he has some information on some Vegas Riffs," the kneeling Riff said to O'Doul as he approached.

O'Doul kneeled down next to the marauder who had been shot in the chest.

The marauder had a steel flask inside his jacket pocket that had stopped one of the bullets to his chest. But a second shot had hit the marauder in the shoulder and was bleeding.

"Douglas, Douglas is the one who shot me," the marauder said. "I know where he's going to hide," he continued.

"Where, where did Douglas go?" O'Doul asked him.

"There is an old abandoned military center near hear. Douglas will go there first," the marauder replied.

O'Doul looked up at the Med-priest. "The bullet passed through cleanly. He will be fine as soon as I can patch him up and stop the bleeding," the Med-priest told O'Doul. "But not sure what will happen after the Sec Guardian talks to him," the Med-priest continued.

"I won't say thank you for what you've done here, but I'm glad you spoke up. Even if it is for revenge against the guy that shot you," O'Doul told the marauder.

"Back to the UCV," O'Doul told Mel and Thompson.

The three Riffs jogged back to the command vehicle.

O'Doul held up his right hand and made a swirling motion so that Jones could see him as they approached.

Seeing the signal Jones pushed the button so that the turret on top of the UCV descended back down inside. She then joined the other Riffs up in front as they stepped in.

Sec Guardian 2000 was already inside as O'Doul sat down in the driver's seat.

O'Doul told Jones what they had learned from the wounded marauder and she sat down at her Comp to try and locate the old military center. It was west of them heading back toward Angeles.

Mel sat in the front seat as Thompson paced back and forth inside. He was still keyed up from the excitement and his adrenalin was flowing.

"Sit down, your making me nervous," Jones told Thompson looking over her shoulder.

"If Mel and I take the cycles we might be able to catch up to Douglas?" Thompson said to O'Doul.

"Fine, but only for reconnaissance," O'Doul said.

Mel walked back to see that Thompson was already climbing into the left side cycle pod. She flipped the switch to open the right pod door panel and climbed down onto her cycle.

Both sides of the UCV opened outward, Thompson on his cycle on the left and Mel on hers to the right.

They started their engines preparing to ride off from the UCV.

Once the tires matched the speed of the UCV the two took off from the pods as the sides closed back up.

Jones looked up from her monitor and saw a message displayed on the Guardian's display screen.

They were given the okay to terminate if necessary or capture the Vegas Riffs and bring them before Sec Guardian 2000.

Jones told O'Doul about the message then relayed the info over the Mic to Mel and Thompson.

Thompson was all for the termination part.

Chapter 79

As Torian continued to shake his hips, he spoke to each of the showgirls on stage sending them out into the audience.

The showgirl in yellow walked down some stairs on the right side of the stage waving the big fluffy fan around.

The showgirl in pink did the same thing on the left side. She stopped in front of Skip at the bar holding the fan up behind her as if she were in the center of a feathery frame.

Skip distracted by the showgirl took a good look up and down the pretty gal.

The showgirl in yellow stopped in front of Bonnie and Judy and said, "My name is Stephanie. Torian would like you to come with me."

Stephanie walked back to the stage with the fan on the left side of her with Bonnie and Judy walking on Stephanie's right.

The audience clapped seeing the two lucky girls that got picked to go up on stage.

Stephanie led the two girls up the stairs and then back behind the curtains.

The showgirl in pink looked in the mirror on the wall behind the bar where Skip was sitting. She fluttered the fan behind her giving Skip a wink then turned to go back on stage as well.

Torian was finishing his song when the showgirl in pink stopped to stand next to him again.

The music stopped and Torian took a bow. The spotlight went out leaving the stage in darkness as the announcer came back on the speaker.

The King has *left* the building.

Chapter 80

It only took them about twenty-five minutes from the crater to the outskirts of the old center.

There were lots of dirt roads going in different directions but Jones had picked up something on her Radar and told O'Doul to keep heading west. She also relayed the info to Mel and Thompson.

Mel and Thompson passed several torn down shacks and passed some obstacle courses like the ones the Riffs used near station ten.

They were fanning out looking for any signs that Douglas had come that way when they received the communication from Jones to keep heading west.

It had been an hour now and they were approaching several bungalows in the distance.

Mel was watching her monitor in-between the handlebars in front of her that connected with a zoom lens on the front of the cycle. She thought she saw movement and pointed in that direction. Thompson looked over and saw the signal from Mel and slowed up to follow her lead.

Mel contacted Jones using her helmet Mic and told her about some bungalows up ahead.

Jones relayed the info to O'Doul and to head toward one of the bungalows near the rear of what appeared to be a compound.

O'Doul drove up about two hundred feet from the structure Jones had indicated and said, "End of the line."

Jones went up to the front of the UCV to monitor the Riffs as O'Doul went outside.

Thompson had waited for O'Doul to arrive and walked over to meet him.

"Mel is already around the back of the bungalow," he told O'Doul. "She is on radio silence due to the thin walls of the buildings."

The Sec Guardian now standing outside started to follow O'Doul and Thompson, but O'Doul asked the Guardian to wait so he and his unit could scout it out first.

Thompson simply said, "Stay," holding up the palm of his hand toward the Guardian.

The Guardian's eyes blinked a couple of times then he went back into the UCV and stood behind Jones.

Jones used the FLIR (Field Laser Infrared) to detect any heat signatures being emitted from the surrounding bungalows.

O'Doul motioned for Thompson to go around to the left side.

O'Doul jogged straight up to the front of the bungalow and over to a door. He turned the handle on the door and it opened up. He waited a few minutes for Thompson to make his way around then stepped inside.

There was a long hallway that went all the way to the back of the building with a backdoor.

There were several doors on each side of the hallway and he took turns opening them up and peering inside.

There was a small office near the front full of dust and an old desk.

The other rooms seemed to be meeting rooms with long tables and chairs scattered everywhere. There were long greenish boards hanging from the walls in each room. He looked at the floors in each one and didn't see any footprints on the dusty floors so he continued along the hall. As he got halfway down the hall the door at the end of the hallway opened up and Mel poked her head in and out of the door.

When she saw O'Doul she took a longer look then came inside.

O'Doul motioned for her to check the doors on the left and he would continue checking the ones on his right.

Each room was the same as the others, empty.

Mel came to the last door on her right and to O'Doul's left.

O'Doul motioned that he would go in high and she should go in low.

He opened the door slowly then shoved it open with a bang pointing his 9mm at Thompson sitting in a chair facing O'Doul with his hands up in the air.

There was an open window behind him and standing next to the window to the left was Douglas pointing his 9mm at Thompson.

Chapter 81

"I didn't know you could sing?" Bonnie said to Torian.

"I usually only sing in the wash and dry, but I always wanted to try karaoke," Torian replied.

After going back stage with Stephanie, Bonnie and Judy waited for Torian to meet them.

Torian said thank you to the showgirl in pink and gave Stephanie a kiss on the cheek and told her, "Thanks you're a doll."

They took a hallway that led to the casino floor.

"Great, I finally convince him to start liking girls and he takes off with two. And I'm not even one of them!" Stephanie said as Torian walked away.

Torian walked out into the casino with Bonnie and Judy following behind him.

Several people started clapping for the entertainer and his entourage as they walked.

They were halfway to a lift when Torian heard a shout.

"There they are," Brad said to Johnson.

The two men walked hurriedly toward Torian and the girls, pushing people out of the way as they tried to catch up to them.

Torian reached the lift and got in with the girls behind him. He pushed the button and the door closed as the two men approached.

Torian had pushed the button for the fifth; tenth and fiftieth floor hoping that it would confuse the men following them.

Near the front of each lift at the hotel there was an indicator panel signaling which floor the lift was on so Torian and the girls got out on the fifth floor and went to another lift going back down to the first floor.

The door opened up and he and the girls stepped back into the casino.

Torian stepped out with confidence thinking his trick had worked until he heard a familiar voice say, "There they are."

"Dang it," Torian said as he took both girls by their hands and walked hurriedly back through the casino.

Brad and Johnson didn't have time to get on a lift before the second lift came down and Torian stepped out.

The two men were gaining on Torian and the girls.

Torian was heading back to the entrance of the casino by the lounge.

Skip had waited in the lounge until all the people left. Then he walked out of the lounge as well. He saw Torian and the girls coming toward him with Brad and Johnson right behind them. He walked toward Torian with a smile thinking they had nowhere else to go.

Brad and Johnson were right behind Torian when someone stopped in front of Torian and said, "May I have your autograph?" Ichi Ban asked.

Chapter 82

"Here we are again. Me pointing my gun at you and you ready to die for all the wrong reasons," Douglas said to O'Doul still pointing his gun at Thompson.

Two men stood up from behind tables on either side of the room pointing their M-16's at O'Doul and Mel.

O'Doul lowered his gun and so did Mel.   The Vegas Riff on Mel's side walked over and took the guns from Mel and O'Doul while the other Vegas Riff covered him.

"How does sitting behind a nice big desk with a couple of busty personal assistants answering your phone and sitting on your lap sound?" Douglas asked.

"Sounds good to me," Thompson said raising his left hand a little higher.

"Why not just quit the Riffs and work in the city if that's what you want?" O'Doul asked Douglas.

"That could take years of waiting for a promotion or someone to retire. This way I can have it sooner than later and pick the corporation I want to run," Douglas said.

"Who is filling your head with this nonsense about owning your own company overnight?" Mel asked.

"No, Corporation. Others will have their pick of companies, but I get a city all to myself," Douglas replied.

"Again, same question?" Mel asked.

"Men with a vision, to lead us out of our humdrum lives and give us the power that we deserve," Douglas replied.

"Well if you and the other marauders are running the companies and corporations, where does that leave these men with visions you're talking about?" O'Doul asked.

"They won't even be around to see what they're missing," Douglas said.

"But now I think it's time to say our final goodbyes," Douglas said looking down the barrel of his gun pointing at Thompson.

"Any last requests?" he asked Thompson.

"Yes, I *mite* want an upside down ice cream on one of those busty assistants you were talking about," he replied.

Chapter 83

Ichi Ban had helped Torian with some unseemly characters back in Angeles at the Fish Bowl nightclub.

"Why yes, you can have an autograph, but you'll have to wait your turn. You see these men were in line first," Torian said turning and looking at the three men now standing next to him.

"Beat it or will make your face flatter than it already is," Skip told Ichi Ban.

Ichi Ban looked at Skip. "May I ask what your name is?"

"His name is Skippy," Torian said with a lisp.

Skip not amused at Torian's making fun of his name took a step in his direction.

Ichi Ban sidestepped in-between Torian and Skip.

"As a representative of Kofu I must ask that you go back to having a good time in our casino," Ichi Ban said.

"And if we want to have a good time with one of the girls?" Brad asked referring to Judy.

"Apparently she is already occupied with our entertainer here, but I can arrange for some other entertainment if you would like," Ichi Ban said raising his left hand and snapping his fingers.

Four clones identical to Ichi Ban walked over and surrounded the three men.

Johnson finally spoke up, "I think we shall amuse ourselves at a later date," and walked away. Brad and Skip followed behind him.

"Wearing that cape won't save you next time," Skip told Torian as he walked away.

Two of the clones followed some distance behind the three men to ensure there was no more trouble.

"*Domo, arigato* (Thank you), *Ichi Ban-san*, Torian said.

"*Lie, do itashimashite* (Your welcome), Ichi Ban replied.

"But I merely wanted to prevent any damage to the costume that you borrowed," Ichi Ban told Torian with a smile.

Chapter 84

As Douglas pulled back the hammer on the handgun, two black hands with reddish arms came crashing through the wall behind him. The two hands grabbed Douglas pinning his arms to his side as the gun went off and the bullet hit the floor next to Thompson's chair.

Douglas was then pulled backward making a human silhouette in the wall next to the window.

The Vegas Riffs were distracted by Douglas being yanked through the wall, and gave O'Doul a chance to grab the rifle of the guy in front of him with his left hand and move in close enough to use his right elbow to hit the guy on the chin. O'Doul then spun his body still pulling the rifle with his left hand and grabbed the guy's right arm and bent forward, flipping the guy over O'Doul's back. The guy landed with a thud on the floor.

When Mel saw the Riff in front of her look to his right at where Douglas had been; she used her left hand to extend her G-club out then grabbed it with both hands and swung at the Riff hitting him in the face. A cracking sound came from the guy's jaw.

The Riff recoiled from the hit to the jaw, but recovered by bringing the M-16 up and pointing it at Mel.

Thompson got up and grabbed the barrel of the rifle with his right hand pointing it up in the air as it went off. He then kicked the Riff in the midsection making him lean forward.

As the Riff was bending over, Mel followed up with a right knee to the Riff's face knocking him backwards and unconscious.

O'Doul was in the process of cuffing the Riff that he had knocked down when Sec Guardian 2000 looked in through the outside window.

His eyes were red, but turned to green seeing that the Angeles Riffs were safe.

Thompson saw the Guardian turn and walk away. He went over and leaned out the window; "Okay, you can come."

Chapter 85

Ichi Ban escorted Torian and the girl's back to the dressing room so Torian could change back into the suit he had been wearing.

"I sent your clothes out to be cleaned, but I wasn't sure where to send them at the time so they should be back at the Lib by now," Judy told Torian. "Bonnie told me you are both staying here, *in separate suites,* so I will have them brought here," she continued.

"That would be fine. Maybe you and Bonnie can wait in *her* suite until a Guardian comes to escort you home," Torian said noticing Judy's emphasis on the separate suites part.

Bonnie had also noticed the inference to the separate suites remark and said, "Yes Judy, why don't we hang out upstairs for a while. I'm sure all this running around has you all *hot* and *bothered.* Maybe you should take a cold wash and lay down for a bit.

Bonnie stared at Torian as she took Judy by the hand.

Torian looked back at Bonnie with a--what did I do--look.

"Remind me later to ask you who Stephanie is?" Bonnie said walking away.

Ichi Ban had the other two clones accompany the girls upstairs.

Ichi Ban asked some questions about the three men and wanted to know their intentions toward Judy.

Torian told Ban that Judy was Miller's assistant and that Miller had been judged by the Supremes. But that Judy may have been put in a compromising situation by Torian's presence at the Vegas Lib.

The three men thought that Judy had something to do with Miller being caught.

Torian didn't give Ichi Ban anymore information then he needed to know. He just wanted Ichi Ban to help until a Guardian arrived.

As Torian mentioned the need for a Guardian one showed up to listen to the information that Torian was giving Ban. The Guardian then went upstairs to Bonnie's suite.

It had been over a day since Torian had slept and he thought it was time to get some rest.

The clones that had followed Johnson and the other two came back to report that they had left the building.

"Would you like us to accompany you to your suite?" Ichi Ban asked.

"No, I think I can make it from here," Torian replied.

Ichi Ban left with the other two clones.

"There goes Ban with two clones, count them, two clones in one," Torian said out loud. "I must really be tired," he thought to himself.

Chapter 86

"Does Torian have a mate?" Judy asked Bonnie after arriving in Bonnie's suite.

"No, but I believe he is spoken for. He has a future mate picked out and the attraction is mutual between the two of them," Bonnie replied carefully answering the question. "And she's not the type you would want to piss off if you know what I mean."

"Oh I see," Judy said using the Comp to contact the Vegas Lib.

"Hum!" Bonnie wondered if she *did* see.

They had only been in the suite for about ten minutes after the clones left when the Comp beeped showing Bonnie and Judy that there was a Sec Guardian at the door.

Bonnie told the Comp to open the door and it slid open.

The Guardian displayed a message on his monitor letting Bonnie know that he was here to escort Miss Rawlings to her dwelling.

Judy told Bonnie how much she appreciated Torian and her

helping and she left with the Guardian.

After the door closed, Bonnie sat down on the bed and took off her shoes so she could lie down sideways on the bed and pulled the pillow snuggly under her head.

She closed her eyes and thought about her night with Trent and Melanie.

She hoped they were both okay as she drifted off to sleep.

Chapter 87

Thompson was telling O'Doul and Mel how he had come through the open window and got caught off guard by Douglas.

The three were walking back to the UCV with the Guardian guiding the two Vegas Riffs in front of him.

The Guardian had indicated that Douglas didn't survive his exit from the room they had been in. The Guardian was taking the other two to be held in the holding cells in the UCV until they could be questioned.

Jones came out of the command vehicle and asked if they had caught all four of them.

"Yep, the Guardian's going to talk to those two and Douglas? Well, let's just say he's on a permanent vacation," Thompson told Jones.

"That's only three?" Jones said.

"The forth Vegas Riff was one of the men found dead inside the tank back at the crater," O'Doul told Jones.

"Guess we forgot to mention that to you since you were stuck up on the UCV back at the marauder encampment," Thompson said.

"Yes, you did forget to mention that, but I'm talking about the four people here," Jones said.

"Four people?" O'Doul asked.

"Yes, there were three heat signatures I saw in the bungalow you went into but you didn't answer your radio. The Guardian saw it too and since you weren't answering he took off around the left side of the bungalow nearest the heat signatures," Jones clarified.

"So that's how he knew where we were," Mel chimed in.

"You said four people?" O'Doul asked again.

"Yes, when we first got here I checked the surrounding buildings with FLIR. There were three signatures in there and one in that small building over there," Jones said pointing at another building to the right of the bungalow.

The Riffs looked over at the other building then faced O'Doul.

"Mel, right flank, Thompson you take left."

Jones back inside and everybody use their Mics this time.

The three headed toward the building.

Jones went back into the UCV to inform the Guardian that they weren't done yet and sat down at the monitor to see if she could locate the forth heat signature again.

The building was smaller than the other bungalow and it didn't take Mel and Thompson long to go along the sides of it and meet in back.

There weren't any doors or windows along the sides or in back so they went back to the front.

O'Doul tried the door handle but it was locked.

Mel and Thompson had jogged back around to the front door next to O'Doul.

"Mel let me borrow one of your Mag-balls," O'Doul said.

Mel took one of her explosive Mag-balls from her harness and held it in her hand in front of her near the door. She pushed a button on her belt and the ball hopped out of her hand and attached itself to the metal door handle.

The three Riffs stepped back around the sides of the building and Mel pushed another button that caused the ball to explode.

It left a hole in the door where the handle had been and the Riffs went back over to the entrance.

O'Doul pushed on the door and it opened up.

It was dark inside and O'Doul took out his flashlight and turned it on holding it up underneath his 9mm as he entered.

Mel and Thompson did the same with their lights.

O'Doul stepped inside to his left while Mel went in to her right. Thompson came in behind the two and walked straight in the middle.

The room was completely empty.

Chapter 88

As Torian reached his suite there was a bellman with Torian's casual clothes waiting for him.

Judy must have contacted the Vegas Lib and had them brought over.

Torian thanked the bellman and took his clothes and went inside.

He took off the dark suit of Miller's that he had been wearing and was glad to be out of it.

Thinking about wearing Miller's suit now that he was gone was kind of morbid.

He walked to the cleansing room and turned on the wash and dry manually. The warm water gave him a slight shivering sensation as he stepped in. The water changed to a soapy liquid after a minute or so, just long enough for him to scrub up and shampoo his hair then back to water. When he was ready he pushed the drying sequence that sent down a blast of warm air to dry him off.

He stepped out to dry his hair just a little bit more with a towel. The suite wash and dry wasn't as efficient as his was at his dwelling.

He moseyed over to the bed and saw that it had clean sheets.

He laid his head down on the pillow and closed his eyes.

If only Melanie was here to keep him company.

Chapter 89

O'Doul and Mel walked back outside of the building.

O'Doul shrugged his shoulders while Mel used her Mic to ask KJ if they were at the right building.

Jones told her "yes" but that she could only detect the three of them now.

Thompson got on the Mic and asked Jones if there was a broom in the UCV.

"Did you say broom?" Jones asked, wondering if she had heard him correctly.

"Yes, broom," Thompson said again.

O'Doul hearing the request went back into the building.

Mel followed him inside.

Thompson was walking around the empty room with his flashlight shining on the floor and trying to swipe the dust on the floor with the toe of his boot.

O'Doul pointed his flashlight down and could see what looked like large letters painted on the floor.

Mel started to swipe the floor with her boot as well when all of a sudden the room was filled with light.

The three looked over by the door and Jones was standing there with a small whiskbroom in her left hand and her right hand on a light switch next to the door.

"We have to start remembering to check for light switch's when we do this kind of stuff," O'Doul said, referring to when Jones had turned the light switch on at the bunker near China Lake.

Jones laughed a little. She had grown up in Under-town and was used to turning things on manually. In the city when you walk into a room the lights came on automatically.

Thompson took the broom from Jones and started sweeping the floor.

"When you're done can you stop by my dwelling. I haven't been there in over a week and it could use a little dusting," Jones told Thompson with a smile.

Thompson continued sweeping the floor then walked over and stood next to Jones.

"Oh no, not again," Mel said.

On the floor "Area 49" was printed in big letters.

Chapter 90

Torian woke up to what sounded like an organ playing. He opened one eye moving it from side to side half expecting to see his reflection again.

He opened both eyes. No reflection and no green eyes. "That's a relief," he said out loud.

The Comp was blinking and Torian knew that there was an important message waiting for him.

He sat up slowly in bed and walked over to the Comp.

He pulled up an L-mail that was waiting for him.

The L-mail was from Melanie. She had sent him text message that required him entering in his CIN. He put in his Corporate Identification Number realizing that the message was confidential and since he was still in Vegas the Comp he was using could be compromised without his identification number.

The L-mail opened up with GPO coordinates and one phrase,

“Area 49.”

“Here we go again,” Torian said out loud.

Chapter 91

Thompson was searching the room for any hidden switches.

He had discovered a hidden bunker last week with the words “Area 48” written on the outside door. They had discovered hidden rooms with scientific laboratory equipment and specimens in jars filled with ammonia.

The Angeles Torian had even been flown out in a helicopter by a Sec Guardian to inspect the bunker at the request of the Supremes.

Since Sec Guardians were the only ones allowed using aircraft of any type, the Riffs knew that it was an important find.

Since Trent had been sent to investigate Area 48, Mel had gone back to the UCV to send a message to the Riff station and asked that it be relayed to him marked confidential.

She knew that he would understand the short message and decide if it was important enough to want to come here himself. She was hoping that he would.

Jones had accompanied Mel back to the UCV to check the FLIR again to see if she could pick up any other heat signatures in the area.

O'Doul was on the outside of the building talking to Sec Guardian 2000.

He was concerned about how the Guardian would take the news that they had discovered Area 49.

The Guardian had blown up the bunker that Thompson found last week and O'Doul was worried the Guardian might do the same thing here before the Riffs were able to uncover the significance of Area 49, if any.

Mel checked on the prisoners in the holding cells then asked KJ if there was anyone else in the area.

KJ told her no and they both walked back to the building.

They walked past O'Doul and the Guardian and stepped inside the room.

Thompson was standing in the middle of the room with his arms folded and mumbling to himself. "I know it's here somewhere?"

"What?" Jones asked.

"Another button, lever, switch, something's here I can feel it," Thompson replied.

O'Doul walked into the room with his unit. "Jones you're sure you saw someone in this building?"

"Don't make me second-guess myself," she replied.

"You're right," I'm sorry KJ," O'Doul said sincerely.

Sec Guardian 2000 appeared in the doorway. His green eyes got brighter and brighter to the point that the Riffs had to turn and look away.

The room filled with a green glow all around the Riffs.

The eyes dimmed back to their normal color and the Guardian walked to the center of the room. He reached up with his right hand and pushed an indentation next to the florescent ceiling lights.

There was a sound of hydraulics and the entire floor beneath them started to descend.

"Like I said, not again," Mel said watching the ceiling get further and further away.

Chapter 92

Torian had only been asleep for a few hours before the Comp woke him up.

He got dressed in his own clothes and went to Bonnie's suite to check on her.

The door slid open allowing him to enter.

Bonnie was lying in bed with her eyes slightly open.

"Just checking on you," he replied.

He walked over and sat on the bed next to Bonnie.

"Did Judy leave with the Guardian?" he asked.

"Yes, he showed up about ten minutes after we came to the suite. After they left I must have fallen asleep. What time is it?" she asked.

"Time for you to go back to sleep," he replied.

Torian pulled a blanket at the foot of the bed up over Bonnie and tucked it down under her chin.

He brushed some of the hair from her eyes and started to get up.

"So who is Stephanie?" Bonnie asked with a slight frown.

"Just a Ker I know from Angeles," Torian answered casually.

"Oh, that's nice," Bonnie said closing her eyes. "Are you planning on going *or* coming to bed?" she asked.

Torian leaned over and put his finger gently to her lips.

"What happens in a Vegas suite stays in a Vegas suite."

Bonnie laughed a little, but kept her eyes closed.

Torian got up and left.

The other night with Mel and Bonnie was fun, but he would never betray Melanie's trust in him. Or Bonnie's for that matter.

"But it had been totally awesome!" Torian thought to himself with a smile as he walked out.

He took the lift down to the casino floor and left the casino.

He planned on going to the Transport station and hoped that SG would appear out of nowhere and give him a ride to Melanie's location.

Torian took the conveyer to the station but SG hadn't shown up.

So he went to a wall Comp to contact the Guardians. He slid his Lib card through the microreader.

The face of a Guardian came on the screen and Torian asked to be connected with Sec Guardian 5000.

He felt a tap on his shoulder and turned to see SG standing there.

"Oh, you're good," he said turning off the wall Comp.

Chapter 93

The floor was like a huge lift lowering the Riffs downward.

After a few minutes an opening appeared toward the back of the lift as they descended.

The lift stopped and the Guardian walked into the darkness. His now yellow eyes got brighter to light up the area in front of him.

A row of lights came on, then another, then another and so on until they could see that they were in a giant warehouse of sorts.

The Guardian's eyes dimmed as the warehouse got brighter inside.

O'Doul was standing just outside the lift to the right with his hand on a light switch. "I guess you *can* teach old dogs new tricks," he said to Jones.

There was a ladder next to the wall switch that O'Doul had used to turn on the lights with. Sitting on the ladder was a small metal box with some buttons that had "up" and "down" written next to them.

"Whoever is down here must have used this remote control for the lift," O'Doul said looking at the device.

The warehouse was twice the size of the old military hanger they had been in the week before.

On the left side of the warehouse there were several crates lined up along the wall.

In front of the crates were sections of exercise equipment.

There were treadmills, stationary bicycles and benches with weights stacked on shelves by them.

On the right side of the warehouse was an empty cement swimming pool.

Around the pool were racks of cylinder shaped tanks with hoses sticking out the tops.

The exercise equipment was old fashioned but recognizable.

At the Riff station they had the same type of equipment, but they hooked up to machines that could raise or lower the desired resistance per the operator's request.

Only Thompson liked using the free weights he had found in an old abandoned building one time and brought them back to the station.

"Yeah baby?" Thompson said looking around the warehouse.

"Everybody spread out, don't forget that we're not alone," O'Doul said, reminding them that Jones had seen someone in the building.

Mel walked along the right side of the warehouse with Thompson taking the left side.

O'Doul walked down the middle with Jones standing near the lift watching both sides of the warehouse.

The Guardian followed a short distance behind O'Doul.

There was a noise that came from behind some crates in front of Thompson. He held up his left fist and withdrew his 9mm from his holster and pointed it in that direction.

O'Doul angled to his left with his gun up as well.

Mel had stopped at Thompson's signal and waited covering the other two.

Another sound came from behind the crates and Thompson walked cautiously up and peered over the top of the crates.

A two-headed cat jumped up on one of the crates and hissed at Thompson.

Thompson reared back-startled, then said, "Darn cat!"

A sound of laughter came from a doorway about ten feet to Mel's right.

She had walked past the empty pool when Thompson had signaled to hold still. She had been looking at Thompson and O'Doul when she heard the laughter.

She walked closer to the wall and held up her left hand so that O'Doul and Thompson would know to come over to her location.

O'Doul jogged over to the opposite side of the door that was slightly ajar.

Mel signaled to O'Doul that she was about to go in when just below the height of the doorknob a small hand protruded out with a little bell. The small hand rang the little bell and the two-headed cat ran across the room and through the door where the hand had come from.

O'Doul looked at Mel and shrugged his shoulders. Mel opened up the door with her boot and stepped inside. O'Doul followed her in.

Inside the room was a very little man, the size of a child sitting in a chair petting his two-headed cat.

Thompson came in the room with his gun held up then pointed it down at the ground.

The cat was purring in harmony with both heads looking at the Riffs.

The little man didn't even look up at the three Riffs standing in his dwelling until Sec Guardian 2000 walked in.

The little man looked up and got out of his chair and ran over to the Guardian. He grabbed a hold of the Guardians leg hugging him and said, "Where have you been?"

Chapter 94

The chairs in the room were too small to sit in.

Thompson was sitting on a small cot petting the cat.

Mel and O'Doul were kneeling down by the doorway as Jones peeked inside.

The little man picked up a ladder that was just behind the door and opened it up and climbed up so that he was eye level with the Guardian. He had on a small utility belt and took out a small tool of some kind and reached up next to the Guardian's face monitor poking around behind the monitor.

O'Doul was shocked that the Guardian didn't even react to the possible threat from the little man.

The Guardian's yellow eyes turned to green as the little man said, "There that's better. They always did have poor reception underground."

"My name is Jimmy O'Doul. We are from the Angeles Riffs and

we're wondering who you are?"

"My name is Tinker. My cat is called Twiddle Dee and Twiddle Dum," Tinker replied.

"How long have you been down here?" O'Doul asked.

"What year is it?" Tinker asked.

"2151," Mel replied.

"Then that means I have been here three."

"Three years?" Jones asked.

"Three decades," Tinker replied.

"That's thirty years," Thompson said.

"Give or take," Tinker said climbing down the ladder.

Tinker walked over to a small appliance and opened it up. "Would any of you like something to drink? I so rarely have visitors," he said pulling out some aluminum cans with logos on it that the unit had never seen before.

"Got any beer?" Thompson asked.

"Sure! Follow me," Tinker said putting down the cans and walked out of the room.

The unit, not sure what to make of Tinker, just followed behind him.

He walked to another door about ten feet further on the right and reached up and opened it up. He walked inside and the unit followed him, along with the Guardian.

Inside the next room was a giant kitchen with several old fashioned refrigerators.

The Riffs had seen these in houses that had been ransacked by outlanders and marauders alike.

There was a stepstool in front of one and Tinker stepped up and opened the door to the large refrigerator.

"What kind of beer do you like?" Tinker asked Thompson.

Thompson walked over and looked in. The fridge was stocked full of different brands of beer. Some that Thompson knew and others he had never seen before.

"I think we need to stay here for a long time and investigate this place thoroughly," Thompson told O'Doul.

"The last time you took a siesta with alcohol involved a Spanish girl poured it in your lap," Jones reminded Thompson of when they had been captured by Hernandez and his marauders.

"Don't spoil the moment. I'm thinking about beer and upside

down ice cream," Thompson replied.

"I got plenty of that too!" Tinker said climbing down the stepladder and went over to a walk in cooler. He opened the large metal door and a burst of cold air came out.

Inside were rows of frozen foods on shelves.

"Who was all this for?" O'Doul asked looking inside.

"Them!" Tinker said pointing at the two Guardians now standing just inside the doorway. Sec Guardian 2000 stood there with green eyes and next to him now stood Sec Guardian 5000 with yellow eyes.

"Did I hear someone say ice cream," Trent said trying to squeeze past the two Guardians.

Chapter 95

Trent was eating some Neapolitan ice cream while Daniel had Rocky Road.

Jimmy and Melanie were drinking some sodas and Katelin was looking at the other appliances.

"It's been a long time since I've seen some of this stuff in working order," KJ said. "In Under-town we still use some of these things but the rest belongs in a museum," she continued.

"Does anyone else live here beside you?" Jimmy O'Doul asked Tinker.

"You mean besides Dee and Dum?" Tinker said standing on a ladder next to SG as he was probing around SG's face monitor like he had the other Guardian. "No, just us," he replied.

"There, that's better," Tinker said seeing SG's eyes turn green.

"How do you know so much about the Guardians?" Trent asked.

"I helped make them," Tinker replied climbing down the ladder.

"The Guardians?" Jimmy asked surprised.

"No, the face monitors silly," Tinker said to Jimmy putting the ladder back against the wall.

"Funny," Tinker said.

"What is?" Melanie asked.

"You called them Guardians," Tinker replied with a giggle.

"What do you call them?" Trent asked.

Before Tinker could answer SG kneeled down and leaned forward so that Tinker could read something on SG's monitor.

The others couldn't see what the Guardian had on his screen.

"Oh, I see," Tinker said reading the words displayed on SG's monitor.

"I get to ride in a helicopter!" Tinker said with excitement. He thought for a moment then looked up at SG with a sad face and said, "Can Dee and Dum come too?"

SG turned toward the other Guardian for a moment then leaned back down toward Tinker. Trent could see the big "Yes!" printed on SG's screen.

"I'm sorry. I have to pack some things for my trip. You're all welcome to stay here while I'm gone," Tinker said walking toward the door in a hurry. He stopped for a moment looking down at the ground as if contemplating something and walked back over to where Trent was standing.

Trent kneeled down and Tinker started whispering in his ear.

After a minute or two Tinker left the kitchen with SG following behind him.

Sec Guardian 2000 stayed in the kitchen with his eyes blinking in Torian's direction as Melanie asked, "What did Tinker say to you?"

"He wants me to ask Daniel not to eat all the Rocky Road while he's gone."

Chapter 96

O'Doul, Mel and Thompson were checking out the rest of the warehouse.

Jones and Guardian 2000 had gone back up to ground level to check on the prisoners in the UCV.

Guardian 5000 had come up with Jones and escorted Tinker and his cat over to the helicopter that Trent and the Guardian had arrived in.

Jones watched as the helicopter lifted off the ground with Tinker in the front passenger seat-waving goodbye.

After an hour of searching the inside of the warehouse O'Doul met up with Thompson.

Thompson told O'Doul that there were about ten rooms with bunks in them down a hallway toward the back of the warehouse.

Mel walked up to both of them and said she had found some offices in the back but that nothing had been left behind.

Thompson asked if Mel had checked under the desks for any hidden floppy disks like they had found in the bunker at Area 48.

Mel told him she had checked but there wasn't anything hidden that she could see.

"By the way, where is Trent?" Mel asked.

"I thought he was with you?" O'Doul said.

"No, after Tinker left with the Guardian we all walked out to check the rest of the warehouse. I didn't see him come out of the kitchen," Mel replied.

"Maybe he's in there eating Tinker's Rocky Road?" Thompson said. "And he's going to blame me."

Mel laughed and walked back to the kitchen.

"Trent?" Melanie said out loud. She looked around the kitchen but Trent wasn't in there.

She came back out and told O'Doul she didn't see him.

"How long has it been since we saw him?" O'Doul asked.

"At least an hour while we've been looking around," Mel said.

"You don't suppose he went back up to the surface?" Thompson asked.

The three Riffs walked toward the front of the warehouse where the lift was.

The lift was in the process of descending and the Riffs could see a pair of long red legs coming down.

Guardian 2000 appeared in front of the Riffs with Jones standing next to him as the lift leveled off.

"Did Trent go up with you?" Mel asked KJ.

"No, just the Guardians and Tinker, I only saw Tinker and one of the Guardians leave in the copter," she replied.

"He must have gone up. We've searched the entire warehouse and you checked back in the kitchen," Thompson said to Mel.

"Maybe he came up while I was checking on the prisoners," Jones said. "But I had the remote for the lift with me," Jones continued.

"Okay, let's all go up and see if he is in one of the bungalows above ground," O'Doul said.

The Riffs stepped onto the lift but the Guardian stayed behind.

"I don't like the looks of that," O'Doul said as he and his unit ascended without the Guardian.

Chapter 97

Jones went into the UCV to check the FLIR. She didn't see any heat signatures in any of the surrounding bungalows.

O'Doul and Thompson were standing outside waiting for Jones to notify them if she saw anything.

Mel went into the UCV a minute after KJ did to look at the FLIR with her.

They were both looking at the monitor when Mel said, "What's that?"

Mel was pointing at a reddish glow on the monitor that was getting brighter back in the building they had come from.

Mel looked out the window and saw Trent walking out with Guardian 2000.

Trent looked over at the command vehicle as Melanie stepped out and he waved at her as if nothing was wrong.

O'Doul looked over at Torian and just shook his head.

"You all look a little tired," Trent said as he approached Jimmy and the others.

"What would you say to a little vacation in Vegas?" Trent continued.

"You're pulling my chain?" Daniel said.

"No really. Guardian 2000 here has been in contact with Captain Harding and he is giving you all two days to get some R & R (Rest and Relaxation).

"Are you coming with us?" Melanie asked.

"Well it's either that or I have to hitchhike," Trent said pulling up his left pants leg showing off his bare leg and holding up his right thumb.

"What about Area 49?" Jimmy asked.

"The Guardian says it will be taken care of," Trent replied.

Thompson had already hopped up into the UCV and was waving at the others to hurry up.

They all joined Thompson as O'Doul headed toward Vegas.

About fifteen minutes after they left the old military center there was an audible alarm that sounded.

It was the signal that something was falling from the sky.

O'Doul slowed to a halt and he and Mel both looked out the window.

"That's funny, my radar shows that whatever it is, isn't falling like normal debris would," Jones said.

"What do you mean?" O'Doul asked.

"It's almost as if they are coming in horizontally rather than vertically," Jones said.

"They?" Mel inquired.

Two fighter planes came into view flying at a low altitude leaving a thunderous roar as the planes flew over the top of the UCV.

"Wonder where they're going? Jones asked.

"I think I know," O'Doul said turning and looking at Sec Guardian 2000.

The Guardians eyes were blinking yellow then turned back to green as the Riffs heard several explosions coming from the military center they had just left.

"So much for Area 49," O'Doul said.

Chapter 98

Jimmy O'Doul and Katelin Jones were sitting by the pool in their bathing suits sipping drinks with little umbrellas in them.

"So what became of the two Vegas Riffs?" KJ asked O'Doul.

"They were found guilty of treason?" he replied.

Daniel Thompson was in the pool with a girl sitting on top of his shoulders trying to push another girl off the shoulders of the guy in front of them.

Trent was in his suit laying in a lounge chair with Melanie in a lounge chair on his right side and Bonnie sitting in a chair to his left.

Melanie had on a black bikini and Bonnie was wearing a one-piece bathing suit that matched her now blue eyes.

There was a band playing on a small stage on the other side of the pool.

A woman stepped up on the stage wearing a pink blouse and short red skirt taking the microphone from a stand on the stage.

"This next song is dedicated to a very special Torian I know."
The band began to play and the girl singing had a very nice voice.
Melanie sat up and looked over at Torian.

"A very special Torian? Is there something you need to tell me?"
Melanie asked Trent.

"Oh, that's just Stephanie. She's a Ker from Angeles that Torian
knows," Bonnie said to Melanie nonchalantly sipping her drink.

Chapter 99

Sec Guardian 5000 stood on a balcony overlooking Torian and the
Riffs.

The Torian once again seemed to be in good hands.

There was a lounge chair on the balcony behind the Guardian with
an umbrella over it and two little feet sticking out with the toes
wiggling.

A two-headed cat jumped up on the chair and began to purr.

On SG's screen were the words: "Viva Vegas."

Chapter 100

Torian woke up to the sound of music coming from his Comp. It was good to be back in his own bed at his dwelling in Angeles.

The lights in the room were getting brighter as he opened his eyes and saw a picture of the ocean on the Wallavision. There were seagulls diving into the water trying to catch fish that got too close to the surface.

The Wallavision was an extension of his Comp's monitor screen only it covered an entire wall. That way instead of sitting in front of his Comp he could lie back in bed to watch programs from the Lib or scenes from the Clone Museum.

Torian was glad to be back in Angeles and ready to get back to the Lib.

The only good part of being in Vegas was the nights he spent with Melanie and Bonnie.

He had always trusted Bonnie and after spending the last few days with her he had come to know her intimately as well.

Melanie had made a playful suggestion to Bonnie when they were all in Vegas that turned out to be awesome as far as Torian was concerned. He hoped that it wouldn't ruin his and Bonnie's working relationship.

Torian got out of bed and walked into the cleansing room. The wash and dry turned on automatically so he stepped in and felt the warm water spraying down his body.

He stepped out and looked in the mirror as he combed his brown hair. He liked his mustache, but decided to shave off his goatee.

"A little change every now and again doesn't hurt," he thought to himself.

He got dressed in a light blue suit.

Torian let the Comp know he was on his way to the Lib. The Comp turned down the music and the lights went off as he exited.

He took the lift down and instead of taking the Tram he decided to use the conveyers that traversed the sidewalks taking people from block to block.

For some reason Torian looked up at the sky thinking about the past day's events and wondering if he could see the Metronome circling the Earth.

Chapter 101

Mel was dressed in her tan uniform and putting on her weapons harness as KJ walked over to the locker next to Mel's.

Jones was wiping off some of the water still streaming down her body as Daniel Thompson walked by and snapped a wet towel at KJ's butt.

KJ had seen Thompson out of the corner of her eye and pulled back reaching into her locker; she pulled out an old toy water pistol and fired it at Thompson.

Mel reached into her locker as well and was spraying water at Daniel too.

"Hey that's not fair, two against one," Thompson yelled as he ran in the opposite direction.

Mel and KJ laughed as Mel walked out of the locker room and headed to the mourning briefing with the other Riffs.

Mel's unit had been given a couple days off in Vegas and she had a great time while she was there, mainly because of Trent.

O'Doul was sitting at one of the tables in the briefing room going over some info-papers.

Mel sat down next to O'Doul and Jones came in a few minutes later.

Captain Harding was at the podium tapping his finger on it as some of the other Riffs came in and sat down.

Thompson finally came in patting down the wet spots on his uniform with a towel.

"Well now, is everyone cozy?" Harding asked looking at Thompson.

"I want to commend O'Doul and his unit for disbanding the marauder encampment at Amboy Crater. I have been in touch with Captain Nelson from Vegas, who assures me that he had no knowledge of Douglas and his Riff unit's involvement with the marauders," Harding told the Riffs.

"Sec Guardian 2000 has also done some extensive interviewing of the wounded marauders that were left alive after we kicked their... you know whats'," Harding continued.

"Ho-rah," was the resounding cheer from the Riffs in the room.

"And we didn't even have to shoot Thompson in the leg," Summer said from another table.

Laughter came from the Riffs now looking in Thompson's direction.

Thompson stood up and took a bow.

Chapter 102

Torian was getting closer to the Lib in downtown Angeles.

People often used slang or partial letters on old faded signs to rename something found that wasn't familiar to them. Torians' generally knew the correct names for places based on their knowledge and only corrected people when needed.

It took Torian longer than normal to reach the Lib since he decided to walk rather than take the Tram at the Transport station.

Back in the year 2141 the UCA had announced they were putting up a space station called the Metronome.

Miller had been involved with marauders and a Vegas Riff named Douglas. Both were found guilty of treason against the UCA and terminated by the Sec Guardians.

But Torian didn't believe that was the end of it. He had found a photo of nine men including Miller and another man by the name of Hernandez.

The link between Hernandez, Miller and seven of the other men in the photo with Miller was that they all wore gold rings on their right middle fingers.

The one man in the photo that didn't wear a ring was a man named Dan Hansen.

He was an engineer from a long line of engineers dating back to 1945 when his grandfather worked on B-29 bombers that flew to Japan during World War II.

Hansen didn't strike Torian as having any involvement with the thefts, but Hansen had been at the poker game with the possible conspirators and was the man that had designed the Metronome.

Taking the conveyers and walking to the Lib had given Torian time to think.

He even laughed when he remembered meeting Tinker at an old military center near Amboy Crater. It was under the center that they had discovered Area 49, possibly linked with several secret government centers like Area 48 and Area 51.

He finally arrived at the Lib and walked inside to where his office was.

Bonnie was sitting on her desk with her back to Torian. She had on a dark blue skirt with matching shoes and a light blue shirt. She turned around and said, "It's about time."

Torian wasn't surprised to see that Bonnie's eyes were now light blue.

Somehow she was able to change the color of her eyes to match her outfits.

"Sorry, I decided to walk to work this morning," Torian replied.

"Well you know that's fine with me, but your appointment has been waiting for a half-hour."

"Appointment?" Torian said puzzled. "I didn't know I had an appointment with anyone this morning."

"*Guten Morgen* (Good Morning). You must forgive me, I took the liberty of inviting myself to meet with you," Don Hansen said sitting in Bonnie's chair.

Chapter 103

After the briefing Captain Harding asked O'Doul and his unit to stick around.

"I've been going over your reports along with information I have from Sec Guardian 2000. Seems as though the thefts of microchips from Kofu Electronics and the marauders stockpiling heavy artillery at the crater is only the tip of the iceberg," Harding said.

"I have a copy of a photo here that our Torian came across, with pictures of other possible suspects. If there is a conspiracy to disrupt the UCA and Angeles is on the list; then it is our duty to help locate these men and bring them before a Guardian. I know this is outside our normal responsibilities, but the Supremes seem to think that your unit has been very successful in eliminating this potential threat," Harding continued. "You're going to Den City."

"What's in Den?" O'Doul asked.

"A man named Johnson works at the Metronome command center

there. This is him in the photo," Harding said pointing to a large man in the photo.

"If you find him then you're to bring him before a Guardian to try and locate the other men in the photo for the same purpose," Harding said. "And yes you're going as Riffs."

"Won't the local Riffs feel like we are invading their territory?" Jones asked.

"Probably, but you have the backing from the Supremes and your favorite escort will be accompanying you."

Sec Guardian 2000 walked into the briefing room.

"I see. When do we leave?" O'Doul asked.

"Ten minutes ago," Harding said looking at his watch.

O'Doul got up from the table and walked out of the room with his unit and the Guardian following behind.

The Sec Guardian was going to provide them with transportation to Den City.

The Riffs walked out to where the UCV's were parked and sitting on the heliport was a twin rotor helicopter.

They hopped aboard the copter and sat on bench seats behind the cockpit.

Sec Guardian 2000 stepped into the pilot's seat next to another Guardian.

"I hope this isn't a one way flight?" Mel said to Thompson.

Chapter 104

"If you care to step into my office I would be happy to chat with you," Torian told Hansen.

The two men went into Torian's office.

Torian pulled out the empty chair from next to the desk and offered it to Hansen. Then he moved his chair out from behind his desk and sat across from Hansen.

"I must say you are quite the poker player," Hansen said referring to the poker game in Vegas where they had first met.

"Yes, well I must apologize, my motives for being at the game were strictly to gain information on Torian Miller," Torian said. "In fact I would like to reimburse you for any losses you suffered during the game," Torian continued.

"*Nein, Nein* (No, No)," Hansen said. "What's done is done. Maybe we can play again someday, but for fun this time," Hansen said playfully noticing the ring on Torian's finger.

Torian laughed a bit looking down at the gold ring he had won from Miller.

"I was talking with Supreme Justice Milton yesterday and he bared the bad news about Torian Miller. He was a student of mine you know?" Hansen said wondering how much Torian knew about his relationship with Miller.

"Yes, I believed that might be the case," Torian replied.

"It came as a great shock that Herman would be connected with such trivial pursuits knowing the importance of my work," Hansen said.

"The Metronome," Torian said already knowing the answer.

"*Ja* (Yes)," Hansen replied. "Would you like to see it?"

"Yes, do you have a picture?" Torian asked.

"*Nein* (No), I mean would you like to see it?" Hansen said with a stoic look.

Chapter 105

They had been in the air for several hours.

Thompson was up pacing the aisle way asking, "Are we there yet, are we there yet?"

A light came on inside the helicopter advising everyone to fasten their seat belts for the landing.

O'Doul had been looking out a small window watching the green mountains passing by for the last hour.

The ground beneath them had leveled out for the last part of their trip as they flew over Den City. From there they had flown northwest for about another hour before a light came on indicating they were going to land.

The Riffs had never been to this area of the country before. It was a striking contrast to the dryer desert region around Angeles. The mountains had white snow at the peaks and beautiful giant green trees.

Thompson finally sat down and Jones had been too busy on her palm Comp to look out the window.

They were landing in a restricted area known as the Rocky Mountain Center.

The copter landed and Thompson said, "It's about time."

They hopped out onto the helipad and walked toward a waiting truck.

Standing next to the truck was a woman in a black dress and white lab coat. She had a clipboard in her left hand and a pen in her right.

"Names?" the woman asked as O'Doul approached her.

"My name is O'Doul. This is Mel Jensen, Daniel Thompson and Katelin Jones."

The woman checked off the names on her clipboard then said, "If you will please get into the truck, we will be on our way."

The woman was very attractive and Thompson stepped up and said, "I'm Daniel and it's a pleasure to meet you," he said sticking out his hand.

"Yes, It's *your* pleasure," the woman said ignoring Daniel's hand.

She walked around to the passenger side of the truck and got in.

A man in a green uniform was behind the truck waiting for the Riffs to climb in.

"Don't mind her, I hear she sleeps on an icebox to keep from defrosting," the man in uniform whispered.

"My name is Chuck. If you need anything just give me a holler."

The Riffs climbed into the back of the truck along with Guardian 2000.

Chuck closed the canopy on the back of the truck so that the Riffs couldn't see out the back end.

They were in the truck for about twenty minutes when the inside of the truck got dark, as if the Sun was gone. An overhead light came on and they traveled for another five minutes before stopping.

Chuck opened up the canopy and lowered the hitch on the back of the truck for the Riffs to get out.

"Follow me please," the woman directed them and walked to a nearby lift.

They were in a huge cavern with several vehicles parked inside. They followed the woman and stepped into the lift.

The door closed and the lift moved sideways instead of up or down.

After a few minutes the lift stopped and the door opened.

The woman stepped out into a wide area that had several hallways leading in different directions.

She took the hallway to the right several feet and opened a door on the right side and one on the left.

"You can leave your weapons in here. There are two bunks in each room and a cleansing room next door," the woman said.

"Where do you sleep?" Thompson asked the woman with a smile.

"I sleep alone," she replied.

"What a shame," Thompson said as the woman walked away with the Guardian.

The Riffs went into the rooms and took off their weapons.

They had been on the trip for almost five hours and each took turns in the cleansing room.

Chuck knocked on the doorjamb asking if they were ready.

The Riffs followed Chuck back to the center hallway and down to the end of the hall.

Chuck slid an access card in a microreader outside a door and it slid open.

The room inside was huge with long tables with several Comps' on them.

On the front wall was a giant monitor with several smaller monitors on each side.

There were about a dozen people sitting in front of the Comps' typing and talking into microphones hanging from headsets sitting on their heads.

The woman that had greeted them was standing near the front table with a headset on as well.

Sec Guardian 2000 was standing near the back of the room on the right side observing.

The main monitor on the front wall came on and an image of a woman appeared on the screen. "Den, we have a problem!"

Chapter 106

	Torian let Bonnie know that he was leaving with Hansen and didn't know when he would return.
	Hansen and Torian went to the Transport station and SG was waiting for them.
	They took the special Tram that Torian had taken before with SG.
	This Tram was smaller than a normal Tram and got up to three times the speed.
	They sat quietly for about a half-hour before it stopped. As they exited Torian noticed a sign next to a lift in front of them. It had, "Wards Air Base" written on it. They took the lift up to a hanger where several different types of aircraft were located.
	SG led Torian and Hansen to a jet plane that was already waiting with its engines on as they walked up the stairs inside.
	Giant doors opened up allowing the plane to exit and begin to taxi down a runway.

After they were in the air, Hansen told Torian how he had come up with the idea of the Metronome.

"About eleven years ago I dropped my gold pocket watch and it stopped working. So I went to a clock maker to see if it could be fixed. It was my father's watch and I was worried that I had ruined it. I was here in Angeles at the time and was told about a man in Under-town that could fix the old-style watch. So I went there and he took a look at it and told me that a spring had come loose and he could fix it at no charge. He told me it would be a few minutes and while waiting I looked at some of the other clocks and timepieces he had in his shop.

I looked at an unusual device and asked the maker what it was. He told me that it was a metronome. A clockwork device, with an inverted pendulum, that beats time on a desired note.

I found it so interesting and since the maker didn't charge me for fixing my watch, I bought it from him.

I took it home and each night I would sit in front of it listening to it keep a constant beat.

I held my father's watch in my hand and came up with an idea," Hansen said.

"I took out my drafting paper and began to draw a giant circle. I then drew another smaller circle within the giant circle until I had five circles like an archery target.

My plan was to make a sphere with a pendulum hanging down, like a grandfather clock instead of the inverted pendulum on the metronome, inside the smaller circle. Also instead of the pendulum swinging I wanted it to turn like a drive shaft on an old car.   A giant magneto drove it at the top and had a magnetic iron ball (comprised of black iron oxide) attached at the bottom of the shaft with fins on it.

As the shaft turned, the fins would churn the protoplasm made with Liquid Sodium and magnesium in the desired direction. On the inside of the core were vertical ridges. Once the protoplasm was set into motion it would flow against the ridges spinning the outer sphere like the Earth does. The inner core would be made out of Steel and Platinum.

In space there isn't any friction to prevent the sphere from turning, thus it would create a magnetic field around the central core, creating a gravitational pull inside the sphere along with the heat needed to maintain warmth in space.

Designed after Mother Earth you might say," Hansen told Torian.

Also excess Protoplasm would be piped to different areas of the sphere, pressurized with Argon gas and bombarded with radio waves, this became the propellant to move and stabilize the ship.

"Did it work?" Torian asked.

"A small prototype was made and sent into orbit and yes, it worked. The bigger version was called the Metronome where my idea originated from," Hansen replied.

A light came on in the cabin letting them know they were landing.

The jet touched down about two hours after they had left and as Torian and Hansen exited the plane Hansen asked again, "Would you like to see it?"

Torian looked across the landing runway and about five hundred yards from where they landed Torian saw a space shuttle on a launch pad being prepared for lift off.

"I wonder if I'll see Jameson on the way to the Metronome." Torian thought to himself.

Chapter 107

"Den this is Commander Mills asking about an unscheduled shuttle requesting docking procedures?"

The woman in the white lab coat looked up at the screen. "Commander this is Director Woods at Den Center advising you to implement docking procedures for space shuttle <u>Greyhound</u>. It has been authorized by the Supremes and is carrying needed cargo and one passenger."

"Den Center this is Commander Mills acknowledging your transmission. A little more notice would be nice in the future," Mills said.

"Understood," Woods replied.

The screen turned off and Woods turned and noticed the Riffs standing at the back of the room.

Woods walked over to O'Doul and the others.

"As you may have surmised I'm not at all happy with your

presence here," Woods told O'Doul.

"If it makes you feel any better neither am I," O'Doul replied.

Woods took out some access cards from her lab coat and handed them to O'Doul.

"You will need these while you are here. Hopefully your visit will cause as little disruption as possible," Woods continued.

"Chuck will be your liaison here. Please contact him for any requests. He will keep me informed of your activities," Woods said.

"What about nocturnal activities?" Thompson asked Woods with a wink.

Woods ignored the comment and left the center.

O'Doul asked Chuck about a man named Johnson that supposedly worked here at the center.

Chuck told them that Johnson did work there and that he had been on leave for the last couple of days. Johnson was supposed to return to the center later that evening.

O'Doul asked if Johnson had sleeping quarters here at the center.

Chuck said yes and took them back down the same hallway they were staying in.

Chuck tried to open a door that was two doors past the cleansing room, but it was locked.

Chuck pulled out his access card and tried in in a reader next to the door. It still didn't open.

"Let me try," Jones said as she pulled out her palm Comp and slid an access card with wires connected to it and her Comp.

The door opened and inside the room was a man lying face down on the floor with a pool of blood next to his head.

O'Doul went in and turned the body so that he could see the face.

"Is this Johnson?" O'Doul asked Chuck.

"Yeah, that's him," Chuck replied.

"Will you please advise Director Woods that the nocturnal activates here at the center include murder," O'Doul said.

Chapter 108

Torian looked out a small porthole from the shuttle at the giant sphere spinning slowly like a top coming into view.

The shuttle commander told Torian that the station was 1,609.7561 meters around.

Torian asked the Commander if he could put that into laymen's terms.

"It is 5,280 feet in circumference or one mile around," the Commander told him.

It had taken seven years on Earth to build and three years in space to put the twenty six pieces together to form the sphere.

Each piece had been designed on Earth to interlock with a corresponding piece.

Welding torches with oxygen tanks (like the ones used underwater) were used to weld the seams of the piece's that would remain intact on the sphere while in space.

The shuttle commander maneuvered around the station so that Torian could get a good look at it as they passed the sphere on the right and the moon to their left.

Torian could see that the top section of the sphere protruded like the top edge of a cork on a bottle and stayed in one position as the sphere turned.

The Commander told Torian that was where central control was located. It still had gravity in central but when looking out the windows you needed to be able to focus in one direction or you could end up with motion sickness.

As they approached the lower part of the sphere a large platform descended for the shuttle to land inverted (inside the makeshift docking bay) as if they had landed upside down on the bottom of a ball.

The bottom of the sphere became the top of the shuttle bay as it ascended back inside to form a circle again.

Torian could hear hydraulics sounds as the platform lowered them into the station and he began to feel a gravitational pull on his body.

The spinning of the Metronome created artificial gravity, but rather than being pushed against the outside of the sphere, the spinning of the inner core produced the proper gravitational pull toward the center. This coupled with the magnetic field generated by the inner core and the thin metal threads sewn into the flight suits and clothing worn, provided extra magnetic attraction on your body. This also helped prevent bone and muscle loss due to the weightlessness of space for prolonged periods of time.

The shuttle commander told Torian it would be a few minutes for the shuttle bay to pressurize.

"You mentioned that some of the pieces would remain intact?" Torian asked the Commander.

"There are sections of the sphere that are designed to separate. Those sections can be used as housing and work areas individually apart from the sphere," the Commander replied.

A rolling staircase was moved into position alongside of the shuttle and the door hatch was opened.

The Commander was the first one out to inspect the outside of the shuttle.

Torian climbed out next and walked down the stairs to the deck.

He jumped up and down a few times and landed in the same spot each time.

"Just like home," he said out loud.

Two women and one man approached Torian with a steady gait.

The woman leading the trio was tall with brown hair and light skinned, wearing a white outfit.

The other woman had black hair with dark skin and wearing the Red Cross symbol on her neck collar.

The man was taller than the other two with brown hair and wearing a white outfit as well.

"You must carry some weight back on Earth for you to just hitch a ride on a twenty million-wage space shuttle!" the woman said.

Torian looked down at his feet. "Well I guess I could lose a pound or two, but as long as I can see my toes and everything in between I'd say I'm about average for my height," Torian replied.

"He's funny," the second woman said smiling.

"I'm Commander Mills. I am in charge of everyone and everything aboard this spaceship and run a very tight ship," she said.

"If I were in your shoes, besides our toes being cramped, I would completely understand. By the way did you say *spaceship*?" Torian asked.

The woman next to Mills tried holding back a laugh at Torian's humor.

"I can see I'm going to have trouble with you," Mills said taking Torian's right hand and looking at the ring he was wearing. "And yes, I said spaceship," Mills replied.

Chapter 109

Jones and Thompson checked Johnson's quarters for evidence.

Chuck called for a Med-priest to declare Johnson officially dead then took Mel to the surveillance room to watch the past thirty hours of optical images to see if they could see when Johnson had returned to the center.

O'Doul went to have a word with Director Woods.

"Oh my," Woods said as O'Doul informed her of Johnson's demise.

"I didn't believe they could get this close to us," Woods said.

"They?" O'Doul asked.

"I had received information from the Guardians that the integrity of the base and the Metronome was in danger of being infiltrated, but I didn't want to believe it was possible. And now because of my lack of due diligence someone is dead," Woods said.

"That someone is the person we came here to talk too," O'Doul told her. "We were under the impression that he was one of the conspirators in league with marauders that are trying to overthrow the UCA," O'Doul continued.

"I'm sorry I wasn't very hospitable when you arrived. My name is Carol Woods," she said holding out her hand.

"I'm only here to help," he said shaking Carol's hand.

They walked back to Johnson's quarters together.

The Med-priest was finishing his crime scene investigation and had already bagged Johnson's hands. He was ready to take the body back to the medical facility for a complete autopsy.

"Find anything?" O'Doul asked Jones.

"Nothing unusual on his Comp," she replied.

"His little desk in the corner looks like it has been gone through," Thompson said. "Guess we are at a dead end," Thompson said turning around and seeing Woods standing next to O'Doul. "Sorry," Thompson said looking at the director.

"No, I'm sorry. Daniel is it?" Woods said extending her hand out.

Thompson shook her hand gently.

"Well one big happy family," Jones said.

"Where is Mel?" O'Doul asked.

"With Chuck in surveillance," Thompson replied.

"I will take you there," Woods told O'Doul.

Chapter 110

"This is our Med-assistant Jill Jones," Commander Mills said introducing the woman with the black hair.

"What's up Doc?" Torian replied.

Jill laughed out loud this time.

"And this is my first officer..."

"--Wait, let me guess, Spock right?" Torian said laughing uncontrollably.

"My name is Williams and I think you may have too much oxygen in your system. Jill would you please take our new arrival to the Med-bay until he gets acclimated to the O2 levels here on the ship," Williams said.

Jill took Torian by the arm as they both laughed leaving the shuttle platform.

After about ten minutes of resting and breathing into a brown paper bag Torian felt better.

"I see that the UCA went all out on medical supplies," Torian said referring to the paper bag.

"Sometimes the old-fashioned remedies are the best," Jill told him.

"Commander Mills said your name was Jill Jones?" Torian said noticing the gold ring she had on her right middle finger.

"Yes, but you can call me Jill or JJ."

"I don't suppose you have a sister?"

"Yes, I had one sister and two brothers."

"Her name wouldn't happen to be KJ would it?" he said seeing a slight resemblance.

Jill's smile went away and she walked over to Torian.

"You knew my sister?"

"No, but I *know* your sister if her name is Katelin Jones," Torian said.

"She's alive?" Jill said grabbing a hold of Torian's arms.

"Yes!"

Jill reached around Torian hugging him tightly.

"Is this some new radical type of treatment?" Commander Mills said walking into the Med-bay.

Chapter 111

Mel and Chuck were reviewing the footage from the surveillance cameras.

They saw that Johnson arrived at the center early that morning around four in the morning. They used the multiplexer to change camera views following Johnson from the entrance to the lift until he entered his quarters. After a minute the image of the hallway where Johnson had entered his room went blank.

Chuck tried other camera locations in the surrounding hallways and they were blank too.

"Who has access to this room?" Mel asked Chuck.

"Director Woods, Med-priest Smith and I. The equipment is automated and I only need to check it once a week," Chuck responded.

Director Woods opened the surveillance door with her access card and walked in with O'Doul and the other Riffs right behind her.

"Find anything Mel?" O'Doul asked.

"Johnson arrived at four this morning. He went to his room and then the images stopped a minute later," Mel replied.

"Who has access to this room?" O'Doul asked Chuck.

"I do, Med-priest Smith does and..."

"--I do," Director Woods continued for Chuck.

"Chuck, can you track who and when Johnson's room and the surveillance room were entered?" O'Doul asked.

"Not from here. We need to use the security Comp in the main control center," Chuck said.

O'Doul and the Riffs followed Woods and Chuck into the control center.

Chuck sat down in front of the security Comp and Jones sat next to him.

Chuck pulled up the time stamps from one hour before Johnson arrived until O'Doul and the Riffs had entered the center.

It took a few minutes then the screen showed that there were three time stamps for Johnson's quarters and three entries on the time stamp for the surveillance room starting with the most recent entries first.

Johnson's quarters had two entries not recognized and one for Johnson at 0400.

One of the unrecognized entries must have been when Jones used her palm Comp when they found the door locked.

The next screen showed the time stamps for the surveillance room.

The last time was when Director Woods entered with O'Doul.

The time before that was when Chuck and Mel entered to review the optical images and the first time stamp had been five minutes before Johnson entered his quarters. The holder of that access card matched the last time stamp belonging to Director Carol Woods.

Chapter 112

"I was told my sister was dead," Jill told Torian and Commander Mills. "We haven't spoken in years. Ever since I was recruited to work on the Metronome," Jill continued.

"When did you last see KJ?" Jill asked Torian.

"It was a couple of days ago in Vegas. She was sipping a martini and throwing water balloons at a Riff named Daniel Thompson," Torian told her with a smile on his face.

"I knew KJ was trying to get on with the Angeles Riffs, but why was she in Vegas.

"Well it all started with..."

"--Just hold on a minute. Who are you?" Commander Mills interrupted Torian.

"I guess I had better introduce myself. I am the Torian from Angeles."

"I see, and have you been assigned as the Torian for the

Metronome?" Mills asked.

"Assigned?" Torian asked.

"Yes, assigned to the Metronome for our journey?" Mills asked again.

"Journey?" Torian asked with a worried look.

"Yes, our journey to Mars."

"Mars--Spaceship--Journey to Mars in a spaceship," Torian said chuckling to himself.

"Jill, I think the Torian is still breathing in too much oxygen," Mills said.

"Here is the paper bag," Jill said holding up the bag for Torian to breathe into again.

"I'm fine really. I guess I have been sent here to find out if I would be the right Torian for the job."

"Well then, in that case--Jones can you show Torian the Lib.

"Of course!" she replied.

"Wait, there is something we need to do first," Torian said as he took Jill by the hand.

Chapter 113

"That can't be correct. I haven't been in the surveillance room at all this week," Woods told O'Doul.

"Chuck you said Johnson entered his room at 0400 correct?" O'Doul asked.

"Right," Chuck replied.

"And that the director's access card was used five minutes before that at 0355 in the surveillance room correct?" O'Doul asked.

"Correct."

"Where were you at 0355?" O'Doul asked Woods.

"I was in bed, as I said before. I sleep alone," she replied.

"And what did you wear to bed last night?" O'Doul asked her.

"I beg your pardon?" she replied.

"What I mean to say is that you didn't wear your clothes or lab coat with your access card in it correct?"

"No," Woods replied.

"Chuck, pull up the access time stamps for the Director's quarters."

Chuck started to type on the security Comp when the main monitor screen came on.

"Den Center; this is Commander Mills aboard the Metronome requesting a relay transmission to Riff station ten in Angeles."

"That's where we are from," Thompson said.

"Woods walked over to the front table and picked up a headset and said, "Commander Mills I have representatives from Riff station ten here at Den Center. What is your transmission?"

Commander Mills pulled back out of the picture and a familiar face appeared on the screen.

"--Trent!" Melanie said.

"--Torian?" O'Doul and Thompson said at the same time.

"How in the world did he get up there?" Jones asked.

"Melanie I can see you but I can't hear you," Trent said.

Mel picked up a loose headset sitting on one of the tables.

"Can you hear me now?" Melanie asked.

Torian laughed at Melanie's question.

"Melanie, is KJ there with you?"

KJ stood up from where she was sitting next to Chuck. He handed her a headset and she put it on.

"I'm here Trent," KJ answered.

"Happy Birthday Katelin!" Torian said.

"How did you know it was my birthday?" KJ asked Trent with a puzzled look on her face.

Torian smiled and moved out of the picture the same way that Mills had.

A new face appeared on the giant screen, one that KJ hadn't seen in several years.

"Happy birthday sis, I love you!" Jill Jones said with tears in her eyes.

Chapter 114

KJ and Jill talked for a few minutes then Jill told KJ she would talk to her again later.

Trent appeared back on the main screen. "So how's the weather down there?" Trent asked.

"You shaved your goatee," Melanie noticed.

O'Doul took the headset from Jones interrupting the conversation and told Torian about finding Johnson dead in his quarters.

"Was there anything on his Comp?" Trent asked Jimmy.

"No, Jones checked it but didn't find anything unusual," Jimmy replied.

"Was Johnson wearing a gold ring on his right hand?" Trent asked.

"The Med-priest bagged his hands and took the body to the medical facility," Thompson said now that Chuck had turned on the overhead speakers in the control center. "We didn't collect any of his belongings at that point," Thompson continued.

"Speaking of which," Chuck said. "You asked me to pull up the time stamps for Director Woods's quarters. The only access time stamp for today's date is at 0300 this morning by Med-priest Smith," Chuck said to O'Doul.

"What?" Woods said with surprise.

"After you left your quarters this morning I take it you haven't gone back to your room. Is that right?" O'Doul asked Woods.

"Correct," she replied.

"Apparently Smith was in your room this morning and if you were asleep alone then he took and used your access card," O'Doul said looking at her.

"I assure you I was asleep," Woods told O'Doul.

"I didn't hear all of it but did you say Smith?" Torian asked over the speaker.

They all looked up at the main screen forgetting that Torian was still there.

"Yes," O'Doul replied.

"Med-priest Smith is the one that told Jill that KJ was dead. Also Hernandez, Miller, Johnson and a man by the name of Smith are connected to the marauders," Torian told them.

"We were only told about Johnson," Jimmy said to Torian.

"Do you have a copy of a photo I gave the Guardians to give to you?" Torian asked Jimmy.

"I have it," KJ replied.

She took it out of her pocket and held it up for them to see.

In the photo next to Johnson was a picture of Smith, but in the photo he was clean-shaven.

That was why the Riffs hadn't recognized Smith when he reported to Johnson's quarters. Smith now had a mustache and full beard.

"We need to have a word with Smith," O'Doul said.

"Melanie, do you remember telling me that Hernandez wore a gold ring?" Trent asked over the speaker.

"Yes, I remember," Melanie replied, realizing Trent was providing her with a possible connection between the men.

Chapter 115

O'Doul and the Riffs followed Director Woods to the medical facility to talk to Med-priest Smith.

When they got there Johnson's body was laying on a table covered up.

Mel put some latex gloves on and removed the bag from Johnson's left hand seeing that the bag on his right hand was already off. "No ring."

"Smith must be here somewhere," Thompson said.

"Carol can you lock down this facility so that no one leaves?" O'Doul asked.

Director Woods went to the wall Comp and asked Chuck to secure the facility.

Chuck reported that after the Riffs left he went back to surveillance and saw Smith on the camera's taking the lift to the entrance to the cavern where the vehicles where parked. He was in the process of notifying the Director when she called him.

The wall Comp began to blink a red light on it as a beeping sound came from a speaker overhead.

Director Woods pushed a button on the Comp and asked what the alarm was for.   A voice came back asking if Med-priest Smith had clearance to take off from the hanger deck.

Director Woods told the voice no and to secure the hanger doors.

The voice came back and told her that it was too late and that Smith had already left the hanger and was taxing down the runway.

"Taxing in what?" O'Doul asked Carol.

"We have two F-16's left over from the days when this base housed military weapons and supplies," she replied.

"And Smith knows how to fly one?" Thompson asked.

"Apparently," O'Doul said.

"Okay, who here knows how to fly an F-16?" Jones asked.

Sec Guardian 2000 walked into the medical center. "I do!" scrolled across his face monitor.

Chapter 116

After the transmission ended Torian walked with Jill to the Lib.

When they reached the Lib she told him how grateful she was and that she would leave him to get acquainted with his potential new office.

Torian walked in and saw three rows of tables with Comp's on them.

They were spread out so that one or two people could sit in front of each one.

The walls in the Lib had shelves full of optical disks like the Lib in Angeles, only on a smaller scale.

He looked at the different sections on the shelves and saw that it was quite an extensive collection from A through Z.

He walked to the back of the Lib where the word "Office" was on a sliding door. It opened up as he approached.

"Hey!" Judy Rawlings said picking up a shirt off the desk to cover her bare breasts.

"Oops!" Torian said stepping backwards so that the sliding door would close.

"Judy is that you?" he asked through the closed door realizing who it was.

The door opened up again and Judy walked out and gave Torian a hug now that she had her shirt on.

She adjusted her black rimmed glasses on her nose after hugging Torian.

"Yes, it's me. What are you doing here?" she asked him.

"I'm not really sure, but here I am never the less."

"How did you get here?" Torian asked Judy.

"After the incident in Vegas, I was asked not to go back to the Lib, and since I was already in the process of transferring to the Metronome the Supremes hurried up the process and here I am."

"I didn't know that you were planning on transferring here," Torian said.

"Torian Miller and I were both supposed to transfer, but, well, you know why he's not here," Judy replied.

"Yes, I guess I do," he said, noticing Judy now wore a gold ring on her right middle finger.

"Sorry, I spilled some coffee on my other shirt and was changing into this one when you opened the door. I wasn't expecting anyone obviously," she said.

"Obviously," he replied.

"Are you going to be our Torian?" she asked with a hopeful gleam in her eye.

"I'll have to get back to you on that one," he said.

"In the meantime maybe you can take me for a tour of the rest of the ship?" Torian asked Judy.

"Of course!" she replied.

They left the Lib and Judy took hold of Torian's arm and started pointing out the different sections within the ship.

There are eight levels from the top of the ship to the bottom.

The top half of the sphere held twelve tiers and so did the bottom half consisting of sixty-eight bays altogether.

Central command took up most of level one.

Some of the top half bays contained galley-one, scientific and research bays, training and fitness bay one, Med-bay one, and four residential tiers. The Lib was in the same tier as the Med-bay and Laboratory.

There were agricultural tiers in both halves.

Engineering completely encircled the inner core.

The top half of the engineering housed the magneto or generator that drove the shaft churning the liquid protoplasm within the inner shell, which helped maintain the perpetual motion causing the outer shell to spin. It also generated a heat source due to the composition of the protoplasm moving inside the core that was used to provide warmth throughout the sphere.

The shuttle platform was on level eight where Torian had first arrived.

Other bays in the bottom half consisted of galley-two, Med-bay two, maintenance/cargo bays, fitness bay two and four more residential tiers.

Other bays contained the Arts, Meditation, Creative and Storage bays.

Cleansing rooms were shared between every two staterooms in the residential tiers.

"This is quite an accomplishment," Torian said.

"Yes, I was excited when Uncle Don--I mean Mr. Hansen showed me his original design," Judy said biting her lower lip.

"So that would mean that your mother is Hansen's sister?" Torian asked.

"Please don't tell anyone! Uncle Don asked that I keep it to myself, so that it didn't look like he had influence in me getting the position here," Judy said.

"*Did he* influence anyone in order for you to be here?" Torian asked Judy.

"No! I am here on my own merits, but he didn't want the possibility of impropriety to prevent my desire to be here," she said.

"Well in that case, enough said about the matter," Torian told her.

Judy stopped biting her lip and smiled at Torian.

"Thank you. Oh and this is where my stateroom is. Right across from the Torian's stateroom," Judy said smiling at Torian.

Chapter 117

Sec Guardian 2000 was in the cockpit of the jet fighter preparing for takeoff.

Jones was in the seat behind the Guardian.

With her knowledge in Comp technology she was the logical choice to go with the Guardian.

They were given clearance and the Guardian accelerated the fighter to take off speed.

The Guardian connected a wire from the instrument panel to the bottom of his face monitor so that communication would be displayed on one of the monitors in front of Jones.

They were leveling off at twenty thousand feet and the Guardian, via the monitor, asked that she turn on the radar.

Jones saw the fleeing fighter approximately ten miles ahead of them at an altitude of thirty thousand feet.

Smith apparently wasn't worried about being followed.

The Guardian maintained his altitude not wanting to show up on Smith's radar and hoping he hadn't bothered turning it on since he was flying the plane on his own.

They had been flying due west for approximately forty minutes then Smith changed his course-heading due south.

After another twenty minutes flying south Smith began to descend.

The Guardian descended as well trying to stay below Smith as much as possible.

Jones looking out the canopy window told the Guardian it looked like they were crossing the Grand Canyon below.

Smith continued his descent until he went off radar.

"I think he is landing somewhere near the canyon," Jones said.

The Guardian asked that Jones mark the area on the onboard GPO and turned the fighter around heading back to Den Center.

They headed in a northeasterly direction using a straighter line to get back to the center.

They didn't want to use the radio on the way back in case Smith was monitoring radio frequencies.

It took them less time to get back to Den Center and after landing Jones transferred the GPO coordinates into her palm Comp.

O'Doul and the other Riffs were waiting for her return and Jones told them that Smith had landed somewhere in the Grand Canyon.

"We have an installation there," Director Woods told O'Doul.

"What type of installation?" O'Doul asked.

"It is where we pre-assembled the Metronome," she replied. "We wanted to be sure everything fit properly before we re-assembled it in space."

"That makes sense, but why a canyon?" Thompson asked.

"We needed an area of seclusion and big enough to assemble it in," Woods said.

"After construction the pieces were moved at night using zeppelins back and forth from the shipyards where they were made.

"Why would Smith go there I wonder," Mel interjected.

"I imagine the installation is primarily vacant now that the Metronome is in orbit," Woods replied. "There may be only a handful of workers left to help maintain the installation."

They heard the sound of the twin rotor helicopter landing on the heliport.

"Looks like our ride is here," Mel said.

Chapter 118

"You know quite a bit about the <u>Metronome</u>," Torian said to Judy.

"I've been preparing for my transfer for a year now," she replied.

"I'm still learning, but now that I'm on board it has been easier."

First officer Williams joined the two as they were walking toward the agriculture tier.

"I see you have met your assistant," Williams said to Torian.

"She has been giving me a tour of the ship," Torian replied.

"Wonderful. If you have any questions I'm sure you will be able to find the answer. If not I'm at your disposal," Williams said and walked away.

"Thanks," Torian replied.

Judy took Torian into agriculture tier one.

They had to pass through two pressurized doors and wore oxygen masks while inside so that they didn't contaminate the plants or air.

The tier, comprised of three bays within, had catwalks from floor to ceiling with plants secured on many different levels.

Ventilation ducts passed through the bay from all over the ship.

The carbon dioxide that humans breathed out was filtered and circulated into the bay and the oxygen from the plants was dispersed back throughout the ship.

They were using photosynthesis to grow and maintain most of the plant life.

At the top of the tier there was a huge window that also allowed sunlight to shine in as the sphere rotated.

There were all kinds of vegetable plants, dwarf fruit trees and one section had different types of flowers. That section was sealed off separately due to the bees that were able to pollinate the flowers inside.

Byproducts of bees include honey of course and wax.

Silkworms were also brought along so the silk could be used in making clothing.

In tier two was where the livestock was housed. There were chickens, goats, sheep etc.

They looked funny wearing the makeshift outfits providing them with the additional magnetic pull keeping them firmly on the floor.

Like the silkworms or caterpillars, the sheep's wool could be used in making clothing as well.

A lot of thought had gone into selecting the right animals and plants to take along with them.

Judy told Torian that agriculture tier three contained more plants and that A-4 is where the aquarium and fisheries are located.

"I guess fish don't need to wear sweaters," Torian said amusingly. "I'm starting to feel like I'm on an ark," he continued.

"Now that you mention it, it's sort of reminiscent of Noah's Ark," Judy replied.

"Besides the animals there will be one male for every female," Judy said.

"Two by two," Commander Mills said walking in to the room.

"But can humans really live on the surface? I know that man has dreamed of living on other planets, but the last time we were on Mars we didn't bring back a lot to show for the trip," Torian said to Mills.

"In answer to your question, can humans live on the surface--no-- not yet, but if you care to follow me," she said walking out of the bay.

As Torian followed along with Mills he mentioned that he hadn't seen any Guardians onboard. She told him that Sec Guardians weren't needed.

Commander Mills walked to one of the residential tiers in the lower half of the ship.

It wasn't like the residential tiers in the top half.   The walkways to the staterooms had sliding pressurized doors.

"You will need to put this back on," Mills said referring to the oxygen mask. "Here you might want these as well," she said handing him a coat and gloves.

Judy was asked to wait outside while Mills and Torian entered the residential tier.

There was a lounge off to the right and Mills and Torian walked in.

Torian came to an abrupt halt looking at some of the residents sitting in the lounge.

Some were typing on Comps'; others were reading Info papers and one resident waved at Commander Mills and Torian.

The resident that waved was looking over the shoulder of one of the others sitting at a Comp. He stood about six-ten, wearing a green suit and short black hair. His skin complexion reminded Torian of the American Indians, except his lips were blue.

"Torian, I'd like to introduce you to Pontus, he will be one of the first Martians to inhabit Mars on a permanent basis," Mills said.

Pontus walked over and shook Torian's gloved hand.

"I'd like you to meet my companion, Gaia!" Pontus said.

Gaia wore a green suit as well, but the top of the suit was unbuttoned enough to know that she was a female. She was about six foot one with long black hair down to her waist.

"Hello!" Gaia said.

"You're stunning!" Torian said. "Both of you," he said looking at Pontus too.

"Commander, I don't know who this man is but I like him already," Gaia told Mills.

"I must apologize for staring. You're the first Martians I've ever met," Torian said with a smile.

"We aren't Martians yet, but we look forward to occupying our New World. Oh and the green suits are kind of an inside joke. You know, little green men and all," Pontus told Torian.

Then it dawned on him, "Project Metamorphosis," Torian said out loud.

Chapter 119

It took the helicopter longer to fly to the Grand Canyon then it had taken Jones to fly there and back in the jet fighter.

The copter landed about a three miles south of where the installation was located.

Director Woods had shown the Guardian how to get to the installation without having to land directly on the airfield.

The copter landed and they jumped to the ground wearing backpacks and bending forward, running off to the side of a small meadow they had landed in.

The copter took off leaving O'Doul and his Riffs there. Along with the Guardian who was carrying three large duffel bags. One slung over his shoulder and he carried the other two in his hands.

They hiked for a mile or so before coming to the edge of the canyon.

"It's beautiful," Mel said.

"It's a big hole in the ground," Thompson said shaking his head.

"Which direction do we go?" Jones asked.

"The installation is approximately five miles west of here," was displayed on the Guardian's face monitor.

"You mean we have to hoof it?" Thompson asked.

"Only part of the way," was displayed on the Guardian's screen.

The Guardian walked about a hundred feet along the rim of the canyon until he found a trail leading down. The Guardian then started to hike down the mountain.

The unit followed the Guardian down into the canyon for about an hour and a half.

When they reached the bottom there was a large river in front of them.

"Okay, now what?" Thompson said.

The Guardian dropped the duffel bags on the ground and took the one over his shoulder off and unzipped it. As he did he pulled a cord on the side and a loud hissing sound came from the inflatable raft.

"That's what," O'Doul said answering Thompson's question.

The Riffs opened up the other two bags and inflated the other two rafts.

Inside the bags were small paddles that they would need to make their way down the river.

O'Doul and Mel were in one raft.

Thompson and Jones were in the second raft and the Guardian had one to himself.

They paddled down the river heading in the direction of the installation.

They river helped push them along so that they had covered a mile in about twenty minutes.

The river began to flow faster as they noticed small rapids up ahead.

Their rafts started bobbing up and down as they maneuvered themselves in and around huge underwater rocks that created the rapids.

Thompson and Jones went over a large rapid and went sliding down the other side.

"Yeah baby, this is awesome," Thompson yelled.

This time it was Jones that said, "Are we there yet," feeling a little seasick from rolling over the rapids.

The river smoothed out as they paddled further down.

They came around a bend in the river and ahead of them was a giant steel frame that looked like the bottom of a huge bowl.

"That must be the installation," O'Doul yelled out.

The river flowed under the bowl and the unit paddled over to the riverbank on the right side.

They pulled the rafts out of the water and hid them behind some bushes.

There was a trail under the bowl that led up the side of the mountain.

They followed the trail about half way when they came across an outside lift that would take them to the summit.

Once at the top there were several buildings along the crest of the mountain.

As they walked toward one of the buildings Mel pointed at a hanger about a hundred yards away with the F-16 inside.

"Guess that means Smith is still here," O'Doul said quietly.

O'Doul pointed at Thompson and Jones holding up one finger for them to search the first building. He and Mel went to the second building and the Guardian went to the third.

Thompson and Jones went inside to clear the rooms. There was some noise coming from down the hall and they both creped down the hallway. The door was open and they could see that is was a cleansing room.

O'Doul stepped in first and heard some laughing coming from one of the stalls.

He walked over to the stall while Jones covered him from the doorway. He pushed on the metal door and caught Smith literally with his pants down.

Smith was sitting on the toilet looking at a copy of Playman's Hunnies.

Chapter 120

"Apparently Mr. Hansen has chosen the right Torian for our voyage," Mills said as she left the lounge.

"If I may, can I ask you several thousand questions?" Torian asked Pontus and Gaia.

"Maybe it would be easier for you to view some information located in the Lib. It also may be more comfortable for you," Pontus said noticing Torian rubbing the arms of his coat.

The temperature in the tier was about twenty degrees colder than the rest of the ship.

"Project Metamorphosis is listed there. After you have had some time, please come back and visit with us," Gaia told Torian.

"You wouldn't happen to be the Torian from Angeles would you?" Pontus asked.

"That's me," Torian replied.

Pontus just smiled a knowing smile at Torian.

Torian took their advice and went back to the Lib. Before he left he noticed that the Martians weren't wearing any rings.

When he arrived at the Lib, Judy wasn't there so he looked at the shelves that were listed alphabetically.

He found it under M and pushed the button directly under the disk. It slid back into the shelf and one of the Comp's on the table beeped.

He sat down in front of the Comp and it prompted him for his personal CIN.   He typed in his CIN and on the screen Project Metamorphosis was displayed.

Metamorphosis is a change in form, structure or function, specifically the physical change undergone by animals.

Scientific genetic research was rediscovered by Doctor John Strode Jr. and given to his daughter Professor Marcia Strode.

Professor Strode, one of many scientists and researchers at Lang Center was part of the team that discovered the new threat.

When living on the surface of the Earth began again, astronomers discovered the frightening truth that life on Earth was in danger of extinction once more.

Earth's climate was constantly changing and was attributed to the change in the Earth's axis tilting from twenty-three and half degrees to twenty-five and the Earth's moon moving further away.

The reality was that with the new source of fuel the Sun had received not only was it getting hotter but the habitable zone that the Earth was in was moving further outward. Mars was now in the outer part of the green zone making it a viable place to live.

After Lang Center was able to reestablish contact with one of the old robotic rovers left near Olympus Mons on Mars, it collected data on the changes Mars was undergoing.

They discovered that the edges of the frozen ice caps were melting.

Other space probes were launched and craters and valleys were becoming lakes and rivers due to the melting ice and water rising from the surface.

The CMRT (Corporate Mars Relocation Taskforce) was instituted and plans to relocate to Mars went into effect.

The taskforce launched unmanned rockets to Mars that carried robotic blimps that deployed after landing on the surface. When deployed they weren't constrained to having to maneuver around obstacles on the ground and easier to control than drones, that needed constant communication to remain active.

They were made from flexible graphite that after being filled with helium expanded to make the blimp.

The container housing used to transport and land the blimp, held extra helium for the blimp to refill if needed. It also contained various seeds for planting by the robotic arms on the blimp. They carried specially selected microorganisms and enriched organic materials to seed various locations; especially along the equator in order to jump-start the terra formation process.

They even dropped varying sea plants in the rivers that were forming to induce the melting ice water to oxygenate as the frozen carbon dioxide was released.

CMRT worked with only a few corporations in order to prevent mass panic by the population.

The CEO's that contributed to the taskforce were promised safe passage when the time came to begin the relocation process.

Increased temperature changes, water and newly formed plant life that flourished from the seeding of the planet, have increased the oxygen levels to support life on an ever increasing scale.

As part of the terra forming process CMRT coupled with an innovative concept from Don Hansen will allow us to send the Metronome to orbit Mars and send down genetically altered beings that can withstand the colder climate and lower oxygen levels until the terra forming process is complete, allowing human beings to invade the planet when it becomes more hospitable.

This was where Professor Strode's work came into play.

The continuation of Project Metamorphosis became a process inundated with a sense of urgency.

Continued development of the pre-existing mutations coupled with innovative ideas from Professor Strode allowed a fully functioning alien to form over sixty years ago.

The original idea of creating a man that could explore other planets comfortably already existed, but was put on hold after the catastrophe.

The genetically engineered aliens were housed in underground bunkers designed to emulate conditions on other planets in the hopes that the natural selection process would provide future offspring without having to continue creating artificial mutations.

Their services have been in place for the past generation, but their intended use is now at hand.

The Metronome will provide needed support and communication

to the Martians that will develop the planet for habitation.

The Greek goddess Gaia was known as mother Earth, a bit ironic seeing that Gaia and Pontus were on their way to Mars, Torian thought to himself.

"Wow!" Torian then said out loud.

Chapter 121

"What do you want with me? I haven't done anything," Smith told O'Doul.

O'Doul and the others rejoined Thompson in the first building.

Smith was denying any wrong doing and saying he had nothing to do with Johnson's death.

"Where is Johnson's gold ring?" Mel asked Smith.

"Okay, I did take it, but since Johnson won't be using it I thought I could give it to someone else."

Smith took the ring off his right index finger, next to the gold ring on his middle finger and handed it to Mel.

The Guardian took a hold of Smith's right hand and yanked off the other ring.

"Hey, that hurt. Please, don't take my ring. I want to go, please I want to go," Smith kept repeating.

"Go, go where?" Jones asked.

The sound of a gunshot was heard and Smith felt something

strange trickling down his face. He wiped his face with his hand and then looked at the blood on his hand. His eyes rolled up into his eyelids as he fell to the floor.

The Riffs had already dropped to the floor and scrambled close to the walls.

O'Doul closest to the window where the bullet came through peered out looking to see if he could see where the shooter was.

Another shot came through the window hitting the windowpane near O'Doul.

Thompson used the back of his M-16 to shatter the window that the shot had come from and began to shoot back.

O'Doul also fired a few rounds out the window.

The Guardian walked down a long hallway and went out a back door.

"Where's he going," Jones yelled out.

"When you gotta go, you gotta go," Thompson yelled back.

A few more shots were fired into the building and then it stopped.

"Are they reloading or did our friendly neighborhood Sec Guardian pay them a visit?" Mel asked.

O'Doul peered out his window again and so did Thompson.

A few more minutes passed by without any more shots being fired.

"What do you think?" Jones said.

The door to the front of the building opened up and the Guardian walked in carrying two men, one on his left shoulder and the other one under his right arm.

The Guardian dropped both men to the floor

Jones and Mel checked the men. "This one's still alive," Mel said.

"This one too," Jones said.

Thompson took his canteen from his backpack and poured the water on top of the two men's faces.

They both woke up spitting out water and looking up at the Riffs.

"What are you trying to do, drown us," one of them said.

"Not quite, but the day isn't over yet," Thompson told them.

Chapter 122

"Wow is right," a woman behind Torian said as she entered the Lib.

"My name is Professor Marcia Strode."

She was an attractive older woman with gray hair, glasses and wearing a white lab coat.

"Howdy, I'm the Torian from Angeles," Torian replied.

"Yes, Pontus told me you were on board. Seems you have been very busy down below," Marcia said.

"Huh! I feel like I'm always playing catch up," Torian replied.

"Understandably we can't allow the whole world in on our current situation. There is always the possibility of reprisals and upheaval occurring when fear sets in," she said.

"Even the travelers destined to make the journey with us have little knowledge of the true nature of our mission. Don Hansen has elected to stay behind to help with the engineering of other ships that will follow at a later date," Marcia told Torian.

"How much longer does the Earth have?" he asked.

"Who knows, a hundred--three hundred years? Before the Devil's Tail the Sun would increase its temperature ten degrees every billion years," she replied. "With the sun knocking on our doorstep, making plans to escape to the next habitable planet is a must," she continued.

"How long would we have on Mars?" Torian asked.

"Granted if the planets continue to maintain their current orbits we may have several thousand years or more available to us there. But if the orbits decay we will continue to move from planet to planet until we reach another solar system where human life can exist and thrive once more."

Chen had been right when he told Torian that "The moon was but a stepping stone to the universe."

"I see," Torian said crossing his left arm across his chest and holding his chin with his right hand.

"Two things come to mind. One is that an uprising of sorts has already begun. Lives are being lost and promises to people believing that they will be in charge of their own company, unknowingly on a doomed planet, is already happening.

Secondly when you talk about fear are you talking about the people of Earth, that when confronted with a holocaust, have time and time again rallied together to overcome their differences in support of each other—their ever resilient transition working together to conquer whomever or whatever their oppressor may be, or are you talking about your fear or the fear of this relocation taskforce that is only interested in self-preservation?" Torian asked Marcia.

She looked at Torian with a very satisfied look and said, "I see why the Supremes have chosen to protect you. You're Father and Chen would be very proud of you Trent," she told him as she turned and walked out of the Lib.

Chapter 123

"What are your names?" O'Doul asked the two men.

"I'm Brad and he's Skip," Brad replied. "We were told that if Smith was to show up here without Johnson that we were supposed to eliminate him," he continued.

"Who told you that?" Mel asked Brad.

"Johnson! He was worried that Smith and Miller were planning on hijacking the Metronome and cutting out some of the others including him," Brad replied.

"He even had us go to Vegas to keep an eye on Miller while he watched Smith. When we heard that Miller was dead, Johnson wanted us to destroy any information he had. When we went to the Vegas Lib, his assistant had discovered Miller's secret room. We wanted to find out from her what she knew, but some Torian from Angeles showed up before we could talk to her," Brad said.

"She didn't know anything to begin with," O'Doul told Brad.

"What were you promised?" Thompson asked.

"Same as everyone else, a company of our own," Skip replied. "Who cares if they want to live in a giant steel ball floating around the Earth," he continued.

"Who fired the shots?" Jones asked.

Neither of the two men answered. They knew what the consequences of killing Smith meant with the Sec Guardian present.

The Guardian grabbed a hold of the two men by the front of their shirts and lifted them up to their feet.

"He did it!" Skip said pointing at Brad.

"Shut up!" Brad said trying to hit Skip.

The Guardian left the room with Brad and Skip both trying to hit each other.

"It sucks to be you," Thompson said to the two departing men.

Chapter 124

Torian sat down in the office in front of a Comp on the desk.

He tried to contact the Lib in Angeles to let Bonnie know he was all right.

The communications officer from the command platform told Torian he would connect him, but that he was not to disclose his location or information about the ship to any non-travelers.

Bonnie appeared on the Comp's screen. "I was wondering when you were going to call. I'm running out of candles," Bonnie said referring to the time she told Torian that she would keep a candle burning in the window for him.

"You know you don't have to worry about me. Apparently I've had a guardian angel looking over my shoulder for longer then I realized," Torian said. "And if anything did happen to me just remember I will always be looking down at you Bonnie," he continued with a look of sincerity.

Bonnie's face changed from worry to a forlorn look of sadness.

"Is there something you're not telling me?" Bonnie asked.

A light blinked on the Comp. Probably letting Torian know that his conversation was being monitored and not to divulge his whereabouts.

"Everything is just fine," Torian told her. "I'm not sure when I'll be home again? In the meantime keep lighting those candles."

Judy walked into the office and saw Torian on the Comp.

She motioned to Torian asking if he wanted her to leave.

He motioned back for her to come over next to him.

She moved a chair by him and sat down looking into the screen.

"Bonnie! It's only been a couple of days and I miss you already," Judy said.

"So that's where you are, back in Vegas," Bonnie said to Torian seeing Judy.

Judy looked at Torian then back at Bonnie. "Well, I just wanted to say hi and thanks for your help in Vegas--I mean here in Vegas," Judy told Bonnie.

Judy got up and touched Torian on the shoulder and left the office.

"You wouldn't be moving to Vegas and taking over the Lib there would you?" Bonnie asked.

"Not without you," Torian replied with a smile.

Bonnie smiled back. "Melanie hasn't sent any L-mails here in the last couple of days. Do you know if she is all right?" she asked.

"I talked with her earlier today and she was just fine. Melanie is with her unit and they have a strong bond that holds them together. I almost think they have a guardian angel that looks out for them as well," Torian replied.

The light on the Comp was blinking again. "I have to let you go for now," Torian told Bonnie.

"Okay, as long as you don't mean literally," Bonnie said with her usual playful manner.

The screen went blank and Torian felt a little homesick.

Chapter 125

The Riffs walked out of the building they had been in and walked over to the rim of the canyon to look down at the giant structure that was used to assemble the Metronome.

Thompson looked up into the sky and said, "It must be one big son of a..."

Thompson was interrupted by the sound of twin rotors from the helicopter that had dropped them off. It was landing near the hanger where the F-16 was located.

Guardian 2000 was walking toward the copter with Skip.

"I guess Brad was the one that shot Smith after all," Mel said realizing that Brad wouldn't be riding back with the rest of them.

Another Guardian from the copter met with Guardian 2000 and escorted Skip into the copter.

Guardian 2000 was on his way toward the Riffs when there was an explosion that rocked the copter.

Skip and the Guardian jumped from the copter and ran toward the hanger as another explosion ripped up what was left of it.

The Riffs headed toward the building they had come from and it too exploded.

Smoke filled the air as remnants of the building cascaded down around the Riffs and Guardian 2000.

Trucks with marauders where speeding across the tarmac heading toward the Riffs.

"Run for cover behind the other building," O'Doul yelled.

The Riffs ran toward the remaining building.

Bullets were now hitting the ground around their feet as they ran.

Thompson fired some rounds from his M-16 toward the oncoming trucks.

They reached the back of the second building each taking up a position to begin firing at the marauders.

"What happened to the Guardian?" O'Doul yelled out.

"I was too busy shooting and running to see," Thompson shouted back.

"Over there!" Mel yelled.

The Guardian was standing in front of an oncoming truck.

The marauder driving the truck saw the Guardian with the red glowing eyes but kept driving toward him.

As the truck got closer the Guardian took a giant side step to his right as the truck passed by him just missing him.

As the truck went by the Guardian reached out and grabbed a handlebar on the side of the truck and hopped on to the foot railing along the side of it.

The Guardian smashed the window on the driver's side and yanked the driver out of the window. The driver hit the ground and rolled for about twenty feet.

The Guardian hopped back off the truck as it headed for the rim of the canyon.

The truck drove itself over the edge as marauders in the back of the truck tried jumping out flailing in mid-air as they followed the truck down into the canyon.

The Guardian was still facing the canyon as another truck was speeding toward him from behind.

Thompson ran out from behind the building and aimed the M203 grenade launcher on his M-16 at the truck.

The truck was hit by the grenade and careened to the left of the

Guardian and drove off the edge of the canyon as well.

Thompson smiled then realized he was exposed to a jeep that was coming toward him with marauders standing up in it and shooting at him.

"Shit," he said and fired back.

Thompson heard gunfire from just behind him as O'Doul, Mel and Jones were all running toward Thompson firing at the jeep.

Two of the marauders that were standing in the jeep were hit and fell backwards and out of the jeep. The windshield in the jeep imploded and the driver's head snapped backwards as the jeep turned right and headed toward what was left of the first building.

A ball of flames shot up into the sky as the jeep hit the building.

There was only one vehicle left. A car that was following the jeep made a sharp right turn and headed back the way it had come.

As it passed near the hanger the other Guardian came out from the side of the hanger.

He was carrying a long steel pole and as the car sped toward him he drove the pole into the ground in front of him at an angle holding the back of the pole up in the air. It formed a ramp that the car drove up and flipped as the left side went up the make shift ramp. The car landed on its top smashing the marauders inside.

"Now that's what I'm talking about!" Thompson yelled out seeing the car flip over.

"Ho-rah," O'Doul said quietly to himself.

Sec Guardian 2000 walked over to the Riffs and stood in front of Thompson.

The makeshift eyes were green and the monitor screen was blank.

"Don't mention it big guy. Just returning the favor," he told the Guardian.

Chapter 126

Torian sat and thought about taking the journey to Mars.

How exciting it would be to watch Mars revived and be one of the first pilgrims to step foot on a new Plymouth Rock.

How exciting indeed, but he had spent his life learning about a planet he would have to leave, along with people that he loved and may never see again; namely Melanie.

Torian contacted central control, to see if they would patch him through, to speak with his mentor Chen.

Central control gave the okay with the same admonishment he had received earlier.

A few minutes later the face of his mentor Chen came on the Comp's screen, smiling at his favorite student.

"*Ni hao* (Hello)," Chen said.

"*Ni hao*," Torian replied. "*Mayfan ni*? (May I trouble you?)," Torian asked.

"You are never a trouble to me my *xuesheng* (student)."

"I'm not at liberty to speak openly through this communication link," Torian said, letting Chen know that their conversation was being monitored.

Torian could see Chen looking down at the keyboard in front of his Comp and typing on it. The light on Torian's Comp blinked a couple of times then faded out.

"That will give us a few minutes of privacy," Chen told Torian, letting him know that he was able to hack into central control and make a direct connection with Torian's Comp without control being able to hear what was being said.

"I'm on the <u>Metronome</u> with a one-way ticket to Mars," Torian told Chen. "Am I fulfilling my destiny by choice or accident?" Torian asked his mentor.

Chen amused at the question said, "The inevitable successions of events that have surrounded your life have always been aimed at your ability to think for yourself. As a small boy I learned to look both ways before crossing the street, yet it was always clear to me that when the time was right I would need to walk straight ahead to get to where I was going. Knowing when to step forward is a decision you are now faced with," Chen told Torian.

"So if I decided not to step forward, but to take a different path?" Torian asked.

"Ultimately you will reach the other side, even if it takes a little longer to get there my *xuesheng* (student)," Chen replied.

"*Xiexie* (Thank you)," Torian said.

"*Bu keqi* (You're welcome)."

The sliding door to the office opened up and in walked First Officer Williams with another man who had a frustrated look on his face.

Torian turned off the Comp and stood up from the desk.

"Ni hao--I mean welcome to the Lib Mr. Williams, and this must be the communications officer that has been so kind in helping me with my Comp calls," Torian said looking at the man with the red face.

Chapter 127

It had been about two hours or so before another helicopter landed at the airfield.

A cleanup crew and a Med-priest were on board wearing blindfolds and had to take them off before hopping to the ground.

O'Doul and the Guardian met with the Med-priest and advised him to gather all belongings from the marauders before placing them in body bags. He also asked that any Info papers be kept for the Riffs to inspect before leaving with the bodies.

The Med-priest agreed and walked toward the overturned car.

Thompson jogged up to O'Doul and one of the Guardians.

"No sign of Skip," Thompson told them.

After the copter blew up, Skip took off running from inside the hanger.

The Guardian obviously stayed to help the Riffs rather than chase after Skip.

The Med-priest yelled over at O'Doul that he had one still alive.

O'Doul, Thompson and the Guardian went over to the car.

There appeared to be two men inside, one dead and the other moaning.

"I can't get the door open," the Med-priest said as he was pulling on the half-open car door.

The Guardian stepped over and grabbed a hold of the door and pulled it completely off the car.

"He's better than a crowbar," Thompson said.

The Med-priest pulled the man the rest of the way out.

O'Doul recognized Rip from Lake Me.

"Is running your own company worth all this?" O'Doul asked Rip.

"No," Rip replied.

"He should be okay, I just need to get him bandaged up," the Med-priest told O'Doul.

Mel and KJ were searching what was left of the trucks down in the canyon below with Guardian 2000.

"Not much left down here. This truck must have been the one Thompson hit," Mel yelled over to KJ who was searching what was left of the marauder's bodies that had jumped out of the falling truck.

"Yeah, not much left down here," KJ yelled back.

Guardian 2000 was standing next to the truck that he had pulled the driver out of. It wasn't damaged as bad as the one hit with Thompson's grenade.

He opened the truck door and reached inside opening up the glove box. Inside was a map with highlights on it.

The Guardian walked over next to Mel and handed it to her. They both looked at the map.

It was torn in several places leaving only part of the map legible.

Mel recognized several of the highlighted areas.   The Grand Canyon where the installation was located was highlighted along with the settlement of Bold, near Lake Me.   Next was Ubehebe Crater near Scott Castle where they had a run in with Hernandez and Amboy Crater was where the Riffs had a firefight with Douglas and chased him to an old abandoned military center.

Mel was aware of all the highlighted areas except one north of where they were called Ion Park.

Mel showed the map to KJ as she walked over by Mel and the Guardian.

Part of the cleanup crew was coming down the mountain and told

Mel they would take care of the bodies.

Mel, KJ and the Guardian went back up to the rim of the canyon.

O'Doul told them about Rip and Mel showed O'Doul and Thompson the map.

"This group of marauders must have come from the settlement of Bold if Rip was with them," Mel said.

"Most likely," O'Doul replied.

O'Doul asked Guardian 2000 to contact Captain Nelson from the Vegas Riffs to send a unit to Bold.

"Ion Park. That's in what they used to call Utah right?" Thompson said, still looking at the map.

"I believe so," Mel replied.

"That's where that guy had sister wives," Thompson said with a smile on his face.

"Guy?" O'Doul asked.

"Yeah Brigham Young, right?" Thompson said.

"Daniel you would know that," Jones replied.

Chapter 128

After assuring First Officer Williams that he didn't know why the communications officer's Comp stopped working during his call, Torian went to talk to Pontus.

On his way there he thought about Area 49 and meeting Tinker.

Tinker had been living in the secret area for thirty years. He had worked on the face monitors that the Guardians wore. Eventually the area was no longer needed and it was abandoned. Tinker had stayed behind living and maintaining the area in case the Guardians ever returned.

SG had offered to take Tinker away from there and Tinker jumped at the chance, but not before whispering a secret to Torian.

Torian didn't tell the Guardians or the Riffs about it and while they were busy, Torian went into a secret room concealed in the back of one of the walk in freezers.

In the room were files kept on the training of the Guardians.

At the end of the Guardians training outlanders were brought in and charged with crimes in order for the Guardians to apply judgments against them.

The final test was a termination order to ensure that the Guardians would obey the judgment.

Torian knew that soldiers from Earth's history had learned how to kill the enemy as part of their training. Even predecessors of the Riffs were trained in a paramilitary fashion and learned how to kill for self-preservation or to protect others, but no one could predict for certain how they would actually react during a life and death situation until it happened.

Even during Roman times when the gladiators fought in the coliseum their opponents were armed, except for a few Christians here and there.

Torian wondered what effect those tests might eventually have on the Guardians, even if they passed.

He walked to the lower residential tier and put on the O2 mask.

He put on a coat and gloves that were left in a locker outside the tier and went through the pressurized doors.

He went in and found Gaia still in the lounge. "Do you still have a thousand questions?" she asked Torian as he entered.

"No, just one?" he said looking around the room at the other Martians and one officer from the crew sitting in front of one of the Comp's.

Gaia looked over her shoulder slightly and said, "Come with me," realizing Torian needed a more private audience.

She walked out of the tier allowing Torian to take off the mask and coat and leave them in the locker.

They took a lift to level one where there was an observation deck.

It was like the lounge, but bigger and had a giant window that you could see the stars slowly going by as the Metronome rotated.

There was only one person in there reading an info-paper and Gaia asked the person if Torian and she could have a few minutes to themselves. The person got up with a smile on his face and waved at Torian as he exited.

After leaving the Martian's tier, Torian noticed that Gaia's lips changed from blue to a normal red color that most people had.

Gaia stood next to the window and said, "We should be able to see Mars pass by in just a minute. It will be just a small speck of light passing by, but soon we can all see it like we see the Earth below us," she said looking out the window with a smile on her face.

"All of us?" Torian asked her.

Gaia's smile faded away as she looked down then turned to Torian with a saddened look on her face.

"I see," Torian said looking into Gaia's eyes.

"I knew I liked you from the moment we met," she said.

Chapter 129

The Riffs waited for a second helicopter to land. This one brought equipment that O'Doul wanted to take with them. He had asked the Guardian to relay the request into Riff station ten after talking with the others and looking at the map they had discovered.

When the copter arrived the Riffs climbed aboard.

They had brought a few rations with them originally, but O'Doul wanted more for their trip to Ion.

Thompson was already eating something before the copter left the ground.

Guardian 2000 accompanied them and sat next to Thompson who held out half of a fish sandwich for the Guardian.

The Guardian didn't move and Thompson said, "More for me then."

The flight lasted a little over a half-hour before they were hovering over white capped mountains.

"Is that snow?" KJ asked looking out the window.

"Yes, I take it you've never seen snow before?" Mel said.

"On the Comp at the Lib I have, but never in person. I was born in Under-town and only went to the city of Angeles on weekends," KJ replied.

"Seems like it's been a long time since I've seen snow myself," O'Doul added. "It's almost as if the winter seasons get shorter and shorter," he continued looking out the window of the copter.

The Guardian flying the copter signaled for Guardian 2000 to come up front.

The Guardian stood near the cockpit for a few minutes then came back to where the Riffs were.

"We have been scanned by radar. Helicopters fly over this region from time to time so if it keeps going it won't look unusual," was printed on the Guardians display screen.

"But if we keep going how are we supposed to search the area?" Jones asked.

The Guardian went to the back of the copter and started handing out parachutes to the Riffs.

"Awesome!" Thompson said putting on the chute.

"Oh no, you're not shoving me out a perfectly good helicopter," Jones said dropping the chute on the ground.

"You got seasick in the raft but not in the speed boat at Lake Me. You got to fly in an F-16, which I hate you for by the way, and now that we get to really enjoy ourselves you're complaining," Thompson told Jones.

"First of all I was driving the speedboat and in control. You can't control a giant rubber band with a thin piece of material going over rapids. Secondly, in the jet fighter I was busy watching the monitors and didn't have to jump out in order to land," Jones said.

The Guardian had his parachute on and unbuckled a harness that was attached to the front of it.

A green light next to the door began to blink and the Guardian opened the copter door. The light turned to a steady green and the Guardian pushed out several large duffle bags with chutes attached. Then he lifted Jones up and pulled her backward toward him, reaching around her and in-between her legs clipping harness buckles together to prepare for the tandem jump.

Jones just stood there with her eyes closed tightly gritting her teeth. "Just tell me when it's over," she said as the Guardian lifted Jones up and jumped out of the helicopter.

"Last one down is a rotten fish egg," Thompson said leaping out the door.

Mel went next and O'Doul went last.

"I hate caviar," O'Doul said as he crossed his arms and jumped out the door.

Chapter 130

Judy was in the Lib sitting in the office typing on the Comp when Williams walked in.

"Have you seen the Torian recently?" he asked.

"Why no, not since Commander Mills took him to the residential tiers," she replied.

"Well if you see him please let him know that he has been invited to the commander's dinner later this evening. I need to get back to central control. The shuttle <u>Greyhound</u> will be leaving shortly heading back to Earth," he told Judy.

"If I see him I will definitely let him know," she assured Williams.

After Williams left, Judy continued typing on the Comp when the screen blinked a few times and the words: "Left bottom drawer," were displayed on the screen.

Judy opened the drawer and inside was a beautiful yellow rose.

Judy looked at how pretty it was then it dawned on her. She stood up as if to run out the door, but sat down gently instead and smiled as she smelled her flower.

When Williams reached control the shuttle commander was announcing his final check off list over the communications Comp.

Williams looked over the shoulder of one of the crew at the monitor screen showing all green lights.

"Shuttle platform; begin your descent," Williams said into the Mic.

The bottom of the sphere opened up and the upside down shuttle slowly moved out from the shuttle bay and into space.

The shuttle maneuvered its way up along the spinning Metronome to the top where central control was and Williams was standing looking out the windows.

Commander Mills walked into control and asked Williams if he had invited Torian to the dinner party she was having later.

Williams told her that he left a message with Judy, but hadn't seen the Torian for some time.

"Well, I'm sure he will want to eat with us eventually," Mills told Williams.

"I don't think the Torian will be attending dinner," Williams told Mills.

"No?" she replied.

"No!" Williams said looking out the control window and watching Torian waving goodbye from the shuttle window on its way back to Earth.

Chapter 131

O'Doul had lost sight of the rest of the Riffs as he glided down on top of the mountain. It was starting to get dark so he wrapped up his chute and stuck it behind a bush and used his flashlight to signal into the trees hoping the others would see the light.

Another light flashed back and Jones walked toward him.

"Where is the Guardian?" O'Doul asked Jones.

"He went to get the duffle bags with the supplies in them," she replied.

Mel walked out from behind some trees with her flashlight pointing on the ground.

"Anyone seen Thompson?" she asked.

"I'm right here!" Thompson said above them.

The three Riffs pointed their lights up into a tree and there was Thompson swinging from the ropes of his parachute.

Jones took out her palm Comp and took a flash picture of Thompson in the tree.

"That's not right," Thompson said covering his face.

O'Doul climbed up the tree and out onto a branch and told Thompson to get ready.

He took out a knife and cut the ropes.

Thompson fell but landed on his feet with his knees slightly bent.

A pair of green glowing eyes came out of the darkness and Guardian 2000 was carrying the large bags.

O'Doul opened up one and took out a pair skis and some poles.

"We need to ski down that side of the mountain to get to where the area on the map was highlighted," O'Doul said.

They all took out some skis and put them on. They followed O'Doul who turned on the mini lights on the tips of his skis.

They had to go up a side of the mountain for a little ways before skiing down the other side.

Going up was fairly easy due to the spring-activated louvers on the bottom of the skis directly under the bindings. When skiing, the louvers would lay flat inside, but when going uphill the louvers would spring out from underneath giving the skis a ridged grip in the snow.

They only went up for about ten minutes before they could see down into a valley below.

"I've never done this for real you know," Jones said out loud.

The Guardian came up behind her and lifted her up on his shoulders and away they went down the mountain.

Hey, that looks like fun," Thompson said leaning forward and following behind them.

Mel went next and O'Doul brought up the rear.

They skied down the mountain for a mile or so and slowed up at the bottom.

The Guardian put Jones back down on the ground. His green eyes got brighter as he scanned the area up ahead. He pointed ahead and took off his skis.

The Riffs took off their skis as well and stacked them near a tree.

As they followed the Guardian they began to hear music.

They walked a little further ahead and could see lights flickering through the trees.

There was a small two-story cabin in a clearing where the music was coming from.

The lights were on inside the cabin.

O'Doul motioned for Mel to go right and Thompson to go left. He and Jones walked straight up to the front with the Guardian standing about twenty feet behind them.

O'Doul was next to the front door on the left and Jones on the right. He pulled down on the door handle and pushed the door open. As he did he stepped inside but was knocked backwards by a gray and white dog.

O'Doul was laying on his back in the snow with the Husky standing over him growling.

Jones moved over toward the dog with her 9mm handgun out and pointed it at the dog.

O'Doul was also slowly reaching for his gun.

"I wouldn't do that if I was you," a voice came from behind Jones. She could feel the cold ring of the barrel of a gun on the back of her neck.

"You better make a snow angel while you're down there mister if you plan on using that BB gun," the man said seeing O'Doul with his hand on his gun.

Mel and Thompson came from around each side of the cabin and stopped, seeing the standoff.

The Guardian walked into the light coming from the open cabin door.

"I'll be damned, Bigfoot?" the man said looking at the Guardian with the yellow eyes.

Chapter 132

It had been about eight hours after the shuttle left the <u>Metronome</u> before it landed on a runway back on Earth.

This time Torian was the first to disembark the shuttle walking down a rolling staircase that had been pushed against the door.

He stopped at the bottom of the stairs and jumped up and down a couple of times like he had on the <u>Metronome.</u>

"Much better," he said out loud and taking a breath of fresh air.

A Med-priest walked up to him and asked how he felt.

He told the Med-priest he was fine, but the Med-priest insisted that he have a thorough exam just to be sure.

Torian went to the medical facility and waited patiently why he was examined.

Afterwards the Med-priest gave him a thumb's up.

Hansen had shown up toward the end of the exam and waited for it to be over before speaking with Torian.

"I asked you if you would like to see it. I was hoping that once you had, you might consider staying on board," Hansen said after the Med-priest left the exam room.

"Well I love to travel and Mars would be the ultimate travel destination."

"But?" Hansen asked.

"But I've learned that we each must choose our own path before we end up at our final destination. I believe I am still needed here for the time being," Torian replied.

Hansen just looked at Torian wondering what Torian's path might entail.

"Oh and Judy is just fine," Torian said.

Hansen's eyes widened a bit realizing Torian knew Judy was his niece.

Chapter 133

The man lowered his shotgun looking at the Guardian.

Jones stepped back so that she was facing the man. He was older with long white hair and white whiskers, wearing a big furry brown coat.

"Excuse me but would you mind calling off your dog?" O'Doul said to the man.

"Tioga heel!" the man said.

The dog walked over and sat down next to the man.

"Thanks," O'Doul said getting up.

"What you doing sneaking up on an old man in the middle of the night?" he said.

"We are looking for a band of marauders that might be in this area," O'Doul said. "My name is Jimmy O'Doul and we are from the Riffs."

"Where's he from, outer space?" the man said nodding toward the Guardian.

"He's a Sec Guardian," Mel said walking over next to O'Doul.

"Never heard of it," the man said. "They call me Boone, Erik Boone and I are a mountain man. Lived here nearly twenty yearlong years, I have. But enough of this jawing in the cold, come in and wipe your boots off," Boone said walking back into the cabin.

The Riffs followed Boone inside.

O'Doul introduced the rest of the Riffs while Boone took some cups out of a cupboard and started pouring coffee into each cup.

He handed the cups to each of the Riffs and offered one to Bigfoot, but the Guardian just stood there. "Just as you like," Boone said and kept the cup for himself.

Boone sat down next to the fireplace that had a warm fire burning inside.

Tioga lay on the floor at Boone's feet.

"Marauders yah say. I don't know who the folks are that are making all that racket downstream, but they been scaring the game away for months now," Boone told O'Doul.   "They've been using old highway number nine, bringing stuff in and out heading toward the settlement at Saint George," he continued.

"Saint George, that anywhere near Vegas?" Thompson asked.

"North of Vegas, about two hours in the UCV," O'Doul told Thompson.

"Maybe the marauders at the installation were there to meet up with Smith," Mel said.

"If Rip was with them then they came from the settlement of Bold, just outside Vegas," Thompson added.

"Can you show us where the people are?" O'Doul asked Boone.

"Course I can, but it's too late to go fretting around the woods at night. Have to wait till mourning," he replied. "You women folk can sleep upstairs. And they'll be no hanky-panky," Boone said looking at Thompson.

"What did I do?" Thompson said shrugging his shoulders.

Chapter 134

Torian hadn't slept in the last thirty hours. He was glad to be on a Tram back to Angeles.

He sent Bonnie an L-mail from the Tram letting her know he was on his way to his dwelling. He figured she wouldn't get it till the next day but wanted to let her know he was headed home.

When he finally reached his dwelling the sliding door opened allowing him to enter.

The Comp turned on the lights automatically as he entered and turned on the Wallavision with a live giant picture of the moon in the night sky with the moonlight shimmering off of a tranquil lake in the mountains. There was the sound of a night owl hooting in the distance.

"Right where it ought to be," Torian thought to himself looking at the Moon on the screen.

Chapter 135

The Riffs woke up the next morning to smelling something they had never smelt before. Each one of them had slept for over eight hours and O'Doul was surprised at how well rested he felt.

Mel and Jones came down stairs and sat at the table in the kitchen area.

O'Doul and Thompson were already sitting there sipping coffee and looking at the plates of food in front of them.

"What kind of meat is this?" Thompson asked Boone.

"Venison, deer meat that is, with eggs, bacon and hash browns. Just like momma used to make," he replied.

"Smells wonderful," Jones said having never seen food like that before.

They all ate wholeheartedly and Thompson had a second helping of the hash browns.

He also snuck some pieces of bacon for Tioga who sat staring up at Thompson.

"When will you be able to point us in the right direction?" O'Doul asked Boone.

"Point, hell I'll take you there," he replied.

"I can't ask you to endanger yourself," O'Doul said.

"Dangers my middle name," Boone said as he took his fur coat of a hook next to the door.

He led the Riffs out to an old two-story barn behind the cabin.

The Guardian had been outside the cabin waiting for them.

"I shouldn't have had seconds if I knew we were going to be riding donkeys," Thompson said as they walked to the barn.

Boone stopped and looked at Thompson. He laughed to himself then opened up the two big barn doors.

Inside was a very long black truck. Something O'Doul remembered the military using at one point a long time ago.

"What kind of truck is that," Jones asked.

"It's what they call a Hummer Limo," Boone told her. "I are a mountain man, but momma didn't raise no fool," he said opening the driver's door and letting Tioga get in first.

Chapter 136

Torian had slept for over ten hours. He woke up without his Comp having to wake him. He asked the Comp if there were any messages.

The light on the Comp's screen lit up and showed the most current L-mail from Bonnie.

She had received Torian's message that he was coming home and reminded him of his need to visit to the Clone Museum sometime this week.

He L-mailed her back and let her know that he would stop by there on his way to the Lib.   He walked into the Music section after arriving at the museum and saw the line of boys waiting to get their picture with Clone Britney.   "I wonder who will be famous in the Clone Museum on Mars." Torian thought to himself.

As he left the Music section where C-Cole Porter was playing the piano, he walked into the Comedy section.

Torian was half hoping to run into Stephanie like he had the week before. She had helped him and Bonnie in Vegas and he wanted to thank her once again.

Torian knew what Stephanie did for a living and didn't judge her because of it.

He continued to stroll through the Comedy section and laughed at the four men sitting on stools talking about being a redneck if you thought Mars was a candy bar.

He walked into the Action section and saw a girl standing in front of Clone Steven with his Samurai sword slicing up some bad guys.

She was wearing a short purple skirt with matching shoes and a yellow blouse with ruffles on it.

Torian walked up behind her and tapped her on the shoulder.

"Yes," the woman said turning around

Torian could clearly see that it wasn't Stephanie, but a much older woman.

"Sorry, my bad--I thought you were someone else," Torian said and walked away in a hurry.

He left the museum by telling the front clerk that everything looked fine today and not to let C-Steven and C-Jean Claude get into an argument again. Each time they did the museum had to replace the furniture in those sections.

Chapter 137

Boone drove for about thirty minutes. The sky was slightly overcast with small snowflakes falling down around the limo.

Tioga had his head out the front passenger window with his tongue hanging out.

Near the rear of the limo Thompson was standing up sticking his head out the sunroof with his tongue out trying to catch snowflakes like Tioga.

The Guardian sat along the inside of the limo on a long leather bench seat.

Jones was pushing buttons in an armrest that kept turning on strobe lights within the limo.

O'Doul was sitting near the front looking through a sliding glass panel and out the front window.

Mel was looking out her window and up into the sky, wondering when she might see Trent again.

Boone came to a stop. He told O'Doul to look out his right side window and across the canyon along the side of the mountain.

O'Doul could see what appeared to be holes cut out in the side of the mountain.

The holes allowed light to filter into the tunnels that had been cut through the mountain allowing an old highway to run through it.

The highway ran for several miles like that.

Boone told O'Doul he had seen the lights of several trucks going through the tunnels at night. He could also hear the sound of explosions thundering from the canyon all the way back to the cabin.

Boone backed up and turned the limo around heading down the side of the mountain. He stopped about fifteen minutes later and told O'Doul they were within a twenty yards of the highway.

It didn't take long before a covered military truck drove passed them on the road. They had parked sitting back in the tree line.

O'Doul thanked Boone for his hospitality and told the Riffs to check their equipment.

The Guardian and Riffs got out and started walking in the direction the truck had gone.

They walked for about ten minutes before seeing the cave entrance to one of the tunnels.

The Guardian stopped and pointed up to a spot on the side of the hill.

O'Doul took out a pair of binoculars and could see a marauder sitting on the ground with his back up against a tree.

O'Doul waved at Mel and pointed up the right side of the hill.

She waved back and took off in that direction.

Mel climbed higher up the hill so that she was at a higher level than the marauder. She made her way stopping behind several trees then slowly walked down keeping the tree the marauder was leaning against between them.

O'Doul had his CAR-15 out and was watching the marauder through the scope on his rifle.

Mel kneeled down behind the tree and took out some rope with a weight at each end. She looked around the right side of the tree to see the marauder still sitting there. Judging the height of the marauder's head leaning against the tree she swung the rope with her right hand around the tree so that it went across the marauder's neck. She grabbed the rope with her left hand as it came around the other side and pulled on both ends.

The marauder was caught off guard and grabbed at the rope

pulling his neck back against the tree.

Mel held firmly until the marauder stopped struggling. She let go of the rope and came around the tree and hit the marauder in the head with her G-club just to be sure he was unconscious.

She waved in O'Doul's direction and he motioned for the Riffs to follow him.

When O'Doul reached the entrance to the cave, Mel was already waiting for them standing on the right side of the cave motioning for them to come ahead.

They jogged across the highway and walked along the tree line along the side of the hill.

When they reached Mel she indicated that there was movement inside the tunnel.

O'Doul went in first with Mel behind him.

Once inside Thompson and Jones jogged back across the highway to the left side of the tunnel so that they could cover both sides as they continued in.

The Guardian walked about twenty feet to the rear of O'Doul.

The Guardian dimmed his green eyes so that they were barely discernable.

About thirty yards inside, near one of the holes on the left side of the tunnel that allowed the light to shine in, was a table with several men sitting and talking.

Along the both sides of the tunnel were several vehicles, including the truck that had passed by them earlier.

The Riffs were able to use the vehicles as concealment as they approached the men sitting at the table.

Thompson was closest and heard the men complaining about having to keep moving supplies from place to place.

"First we had the supplies at Ubehebe. Then we had to move half of it to Amboy and the other half to the Salt Desert," one of the men was saying.

"We should have just left it at Ubehebe. Just because the Riffs were at the castle didn't mean they would find it at the crater," another man said.

"Look, we do what were told and there is something in it for all of us. In the meantime we use these old tunnels to hide the trucks during the day when the Guardians could spot us on the road," a third man said.

"Jake, I just heard that the Riffs attacked the group that was supposed to pick up Smith," another man said approaching the three men at the table.

"What, any survivors? Jake asked the man standing.

"Yeah, Rip. But he was pretty banged up. The Med-priest took him away in a helicopter. We're trying to find out where they took him," the man said.

"How did we get the info?" Jake asked.

"From me," Skip said walking up behind the man.

Chapter 138

When Torian finally reached the Lib he walked into the outer office and saw Bonnie inside sitting at her desk reading the Info on her Comp.

She had on a long sleeved white blouse with black trim on it. Her eyes had a reddish hue to them and Torian wondered if they matched something Bonnie had on underneath.

"I'm sorry the Torian isn't here, may I help you?" Bonnie said making fun of the fact that Torian hadn't been there for several days.

"Why yes, I was wondering if you had an opening for a Torian," he said playing along.

"I have several openings, but they're reserved for one Torian in particular," she said winking at Torian.

"And on that note, I think I'd better go read my L-mail's," he said walking into his office with a smile.

The screen on Torian's Comp lit up as if aware of his presence.

He entered in his password, "Melanie," and as he hit the enter key with his left hand he placed the fingertips of his right hand at his chin and opened his hand as he made a counterclockwise circle around his face.

The Comp accepted the password.

One of the L-mails was from Torian Mariah.

Mariah wondered if Torian had seen the most recent Shield game and wondered when Torian was coming down to collect his prize.

Torian L-mailed Mariah back that he had been busy, but would try and get away in the next day or two.

The next L-mail was from Torian Hara in Toyo.

Hara let Torian know that Mr. Tanaka had spoken highly of Torian and looked forward to his next visit in Vegas.

Torian responded back to Hara letting him know that he had enjoyed the dinner with Mr. Tanaka and his wife and looked forward to future communications with Mr. Tanaka.

Torian opened up another L-mail that was a thank you from Judy for the yellow rose.

She also let Torian know how mad Commander Mills was after he left the _Metronome_, but for some reason both Pontus and Gaia were able to calm Mills down, reassuring her that he was the Torian they wanted to accompany them to Mars.

Torian's Comp blinked letting him know that there was an incoming call.

He had to enter in his CIN to accept the private call.

"Greetings Earthling," Gaia said with a smile.

Chapter 139

Skip told Jake and the others that Brad had shot Smith while in the custody of the Riffs and how he had barely escaped after the dumb marauders fired rockets at the helicopter he was in.

Skip told them how he had to fight off the Sec Guardian with his bare hands, but was able to knock the Guardian down and get away.

Thompson hearing the lie that Skip was telling the marauders about knocking down the Guardian stood up from behind the truck and said, "You chicken shit," then realized he had just blown his cover.

Skip looked over at Thompson and yelled, "Riffs!"

The other marauders jumped from the table and pulled out their guns from their holsters and started firing in Thompson's direction.

Thompson dove back behind the truck as Jones pointed her M-16 around the corner of the truck and fired back.

Skip and Jake ran in the opposite direction heading for a truck to escape in.

The other three marauders kept shooting at where Thompson and Jones were.

O'Doul and Mel ran to the front of the truck they had been behind and were able to fire across the hood at the three marauders near the table.

Two of the men were caught in the crossfire and fell backward. The third man standing next to the hole in the side of the tunnel was hit by one of O'Doul's bullets and fell backwards out the hole and down a hundred yards to the canyon below.

Thompson and Jones jogged up to the other two men to make sure they wouldn't be getting up anytime soon.

"One of these times you're going to get your butt shot off jumping out like that," O'Doul said to Thompson.

"Sorry, Skip ticked me off when he said he knocked the Guardian down back at the hanger," Thompson replied.

"No harm, no foul," O'Doul said.

The Riffs heard the sound of an engine further up the tunnel and started running in that direction.

About twenty yards further in; gunfire erupted hitting the ground around the Riffs feet.

Several more marauders were firing at the Riffs.

O'Doul and Mel were still on the right side of the cave and began shooting back.

Thompson and Jones also jumped behind another truck and returned fire.

O'Doul shot one of the marauders in the head with his CAR-15. Jones hit another with her M-16.

Mel had climbed up on top of the truck they were next to and was able to take out a marauder standing behind a jeep.

Thompson moved up behind a truck but before he could position himself a marauder jumped from the back of the truck and knocked Thompson down to the ground.

The marauder got to his feet before Thompson and stood to the left of him pointing his revolver at Thompson.

Before the marauder could shoot a growling sound came from where Thompson had come from.

Tioga jumped into the air biting down on the marauder's right arm in midair so that as the gun went off it missed Thompson.

The man struggled with the clinging dog and pulled out a knife with his left hand intending on stabbing the dog.

Thompson pulled his 9mm out and shot the marauder from his

position on the ground.

The marauder fell down and after tugging on the fallen marauder's arm a few times Tioga let go and walked over to Thompson to lick his face.

'Okay, okay, we're even," Thompson told Tioga pushing him back so that he could get up.

O'Doul yelled at Thompson to "Quit playing with the dog" and to "Hurry up" as he and Mel continued up the tunnel.

Jones was already several yards ahead of the other Riffs toward the end of the tunnel.

She yelled back at the Riffs that it looked clear, but that Skip must have taken off with Jake.

The sound of another engine was heard behind them and as they looked back they saw the limo pulling up alongside of them.

"Get in," Boone said.

The Riffs jogged over to the waiting limo and got in.

O'Doul standing outside holding the door open saw the Guardian walking over with two marauders under each arm. The Guardian dropped them to the ground and got in as well.

O'Doul started to get in and Thompson yelled, "Wait."

Boone whistled and Tioga jumped into the limo as O'Doul got in and closed the door behind him.

Boone hit the gas and the limo was speeding through the tunnels. It didn't take long for the limo to catch up to the slower truck.

O'Doul was sitting near the front looking out the front window.

"There they are," Boone said as he came up behind the truck.

"Now what?" Boone asked.

There was the sound of footsteps coming from the top of the limo and both O'Doul and Boone looked up.

A pair of black boots stepped down on the hood of the limo as the Guardian motioned for Boone to speed up behind the truck.

Boone pulled up right behind the truck almost bumper to bumper as the Guardian leaped from the hood of the limo onto the back of the truck.

The Guardian grabbed a hold of a railing on the back of the truck and stepped into the back.

A few moments later the truck began to slow down and pulled off to the side of the highway.

Boone slowed down as well and stopped several feet behind.

The Riffs jumped out and ran up to the truck.

O'Doul ran up to the back of the truck and looked in.

Mel took the right side and Thompson took the left side.

Jones stayed near the limo covering them.

Thompson and Mel opened up the front doors about the same time and saw the Guardian sitting in the driver's seat with Jake and Skip slumped over next to him.

"If they wake up I want to see their license and registration," Thompson told the Guardian.

Chapter 140

"Salutations," Torian replied.

"<u>Greyhound</u> docked an hour ago. Pontus and I were there, but to our surprise there weren't any Sec Guardians' on board?" Gaia told Torian as Pontus sat behind her looking over her shoulder into the screen.

"Were you expecting some?" Torian asked.

"After you left the ship I spoke with Pontus. He was concerned that you would prevent us from continuing our voyage," Gaia said.

"After speaking with my mentor I decided to return home where I can do the most good. I've spent a lifetime learning and teaching Earth's history. Where you're going you will need a Torian who will do the same thing, only it will be about the history of Mars," Torian told them.

"Earth has a violent history. Some would call it a means to an end. Others would call it unavoidable. What will a Martian Torian call it a century from now when they are speaking to *your* grandkids?" Torian asked Gaia and Pontus.

"Will it be filled with the senseless need for possessions including slavery, or one of diversity and the inalienable right of all to coexist peaceably?" Torian continued.

Gaia looked over her shoulder at Pontus with concern.

Pontus continued to look at the Torian's face on the screen wondering how Torian could have possibly known that once on Mars his race planned on becoming the sole inhabitants and humans would eventually become obsolete.

"We are derived from emotional beings as you well know. Even if I believed that humans and Martians could stand next to each other as the forefathers of Mars, how can One make a difference against so many of my kind with plans of rebellion against their human creators?" Pontus asked Torian.

"Two!" Gaia said still looking at Pontus.

"Three!" Torian replied.

Chapter 141

After Jake and Skip woke up, the Guardian interrogated them.

Skip had been in Vegas and didn't know about the supplies that Jake had mentioned in the tunnel. Jake told the Guardian that there were marauders with supplies located in some caves just outside the Salt Desert near the settlement of Dover.

O'Doul told Boone that they would be heading to the settlement in Saint George and thanked him for his help.

Thompson was petting Tioga and letting Tioga lick his face.

"He's a good boy, yes he is," Thompson was saying to Tioga.

"Now if Tioga were a girl you would have found your future mate," Jones told Thompson with a laugh. "Maybe you still have," she continued.

"Ha! Ha!" Thompson groaned.

Boone whistled to Tioga as he got into the limo. He told the Riffs they were welcome to come back anytime and that it had been the most fun he had in years.

The Riffs left for the settlement of Saint George.

When they were about a half-hour from Saint George the Guardian was able to re-establish communications.

Captain Harding was also informed and he called Captain Nelson in Vegas to send a UCV to Saint George for the Riffs to drive back to Vegas.

Captain Harding also notified the Salt City Riffs to meet O'Doul somewhere outside Dover. The Salt Riffs would know the area better and be able to help O'Doul.

O'Doul didn't like the idea of the Salt Riffs joining in.

Douglas from the Vegas Riffs had been working with the marauders and O'Doul didn't know who else might be involved.

O'Doul also asked if they could transport their Angeles UCV north so that they would be familiar with it.

When they reached Saint George they only had to wait for about twenty minutes or so before a UCV pulled up with a unit from Vegas.

"We were the closest to you when we got the message to meet you here," one of the Riffs said walking over to O'Doul.

"Thanks," O'Doul said as he walked past the Riff and stepped into the UCV.

"Wait a minute. Where do you think you're going?" the Vegas Riff asked as Mel, Jones and Thompson climbed aboard the UCV behind O'Doul.

Sec Guardian 2000 stepped in-between the Vegas Riff and the UCV, holding up the palm of his right hand and printed on the monitor screen was the word: "Stay!"

Thompson leaned out the door of the UCV and said, "Now you're getting the hang of it," as the Guardian turned and joined them on board.

Chapter 142

After saying goodbye to Pontus and Gaia he told them he would be in touch. Torian had surmised on board the <u>Metronome</u> that project Metamorphosis had not only crated a new race but a race that had been in a semi-slavery position on Earth. Given the opportunity to finally go to Mars, being their original intended purpose, might open Martians eyes to the possibility of a new found freedom. It wouldn't be the first time a people seeking freedom wouldn't hesitate to kill any and all that might stand in their way. That was why he insinuated his thoughts to Gaia and received the answer he didn't really want to hear.

Torian could only hope that he gotten through to Pontus and Gaia.

Torian then sent an L-mail to Torian Mariah that he would like to come down for a visit this evening.

A few minutes later he received a response from Mariah letting him know that would be fine.

Torian faced his Comp and placing the palm of the right open hand in front of his face he moved it down to chin level bringing the fingers together. This signaled his Comp to go into sleep mode.

Torian stepped outside his office to let Bonnie know he would be heading to Diego after lunch.

"Would you care to join me?" he asked Bonnie.

"I thought I already did," Bonnie said referring to the night in Vegas.   "Unfortunately I'll have to take a rain check," she continued. "While you were gone I made arrangements for a group of children to visit the Lib today. They will be here in about twenty minutes."

"Would you like me to stay and help?" Torian asked.

"No, I'll be fine. If they give me any trouble I'll introduce them to Maggie," Bonnie said with a smile, referring to her .38 handgun.

Torian knew that she was only joking and told her to make sure it was loaded as he left for lunch.

He left the Lib and went to the building next door.

He took the lift up to the fiftieth floor so he could take the wind tube to the building where the Modern Food Theater was located.

As Torian exited the lift he walked over to the wind tube.

He stepped inside and felt weightless as a strong cushion of air swept under him in the direction of the building he was going too.

As he reached the end of the tube he felt the cushion of air subside as he gently stepped out of the tube and onto the floor.

He was able to see the menus for each of the different food stations from a Comp in the center of the seating area.

He ordered a grilled fish sandwich and Coksi and swiped his Lib card through the reader.

When his sandwich was ready he went and sat in his usual place near the window so that he could look out at the Ocean.

Chapter 143

O'Doul drove the UCV south on old highway fifteen.

There was a Tram that ran from Vegas to Salt City.

The Guardian had informed them that there was a storm north of them and that using the copter would be unsafe.

It took them about ninety minutes before they arrived in Vegas.

"Seems like we were just here," Thompson said.

"We were, but for different reasons," Jones replied.

O'Doul stopped just outside the Vegas Transport station. Vehicles weren't allowed within city limits.

O'Doul asked Jones to send a message to the Vegas Riffs letting them know where their UCV was and then they headed to the Transport station.

They boarded the Tram that went to Salt City.

The ride lasted only an hour and a half, but if they had taken the UCV it would have been a five-hour trip one way from the settlement at Saint George.

Once there, a Captain from the Salt Riffs met them.

"You're a little far from Angeles aren't you?" Captain Craiger asked O'Doul.

"You're right we are, but at the request of the Supremes," O'Doul replied.

"Yes, so I've been told. Your UCV from Angeles was transported in a cargo Tram earlier and is waiting for you outside the station. Riff Stone will be accompanying you to Dover," Captain Craiger told O'Doul.

"I take it he is familiar with the area around Dover?" O'Doul asked.

"Yes, *she* is," the Captain replied.

"I'm Stone, Kris Stone," a woman about five feet seven with brown medium length hair said.

"Stone Fox!" Thompson said under his breath.

Jones standing next to Thompson elbowed him in the ribs. "Hey!" he said.

"Fine," was all O'Doul said and walked to where the Captain told them their UCV was.

"Don't mind him. It's been a long day and we could use a little rest before we get to Dover," Mel said.

"I'm Mel and this is Jones. The guy with his tongue hanging down to his boots is Thompson," Mel continued.

"Daniel Thompson?" Stone asked.

"Why yes, I see my reputation precedes me," Thompson replied.

Stone looked at Thompson up and down then said, "Funny; I only see two hands. I heard you had three or four," Stone said then turned and followed O'Doul.

"She's got your number Daniel," Mel said taking him by the arm following Stone.

"She likes me--I can tell!" Daniel said to Mel, referring to Stone.

Chapter 144

Torian was sitting on the Tram on his way to Diego.

Once he arrived, he stepped out and saw a Guardian in the Transport station.

He wondered where SG had been keeping himself.

He walked upstairs to a conveyer and headed to downtown Diego where the Lib was.

It only took about twenty minutes to get there.

He walked in and asked the clerk if the Torian was in.

The clerk said yes and asked if he needed directions.

Torian told him no and that he had been here several times before.

Torian went to the back office and walked in.

There was a young man sitting at a desk.

"May I help you?" He asked.

Yes, is the Torian available? I'm the Torian from Angeles," Torian told him.

"Oh yes! She is expecting you," he said and pushed a button on his Comp.

The door opened up and out walked Torian Mariah.

She was wearing a black skirt that covered her knees, black shoes and a white blouse. She had blond hair that was tied back in a ponytail and wore gold rimmed glasses.

She walked out and gave Torian a brief hug and welcomed him to Diego.

They went in and sat down in her office.

"Rumor has it that you've been busy?" Mariah said looking inquisitively at Trent.

Oh! And what rumors are those?" he replied.

"You've been out playing cops and robbers again, haven't you?" she said.

"More like a spaceman," he replied.

Mariah laughed. They had played together as children. Games like cops and robbers, spacemen and superheroes.

Mariah had actually got the idea of being a Torian from Trent when he had invited her to go to a Shield game with him and Chen.

She had listened to Chen tell his stories to Trent and became fascinated like Trent had.

Torian was a couple years older than she was, but not old enough to be her mentor.

"So how is Chen?" she asked.

"His body is slowing down, but the mind is as sharp as a tack," he said.

"So why are you here? I know it's not because your team won and we had a bet. You know you could collect anytime," she said.

"Diego used to be further south, right?"

"Yes, luckily the Magnasonics rebuilt Diego along the cliffs above what used to be old Diego. The change in the Earth's axis is causing the Polar Regions to melt increasing water levels. Luckily Angeles was already inland and wasn't effected by the rise in seawater," she told him.

"There used to be a bay that was a tourist attraction and Boa Island that you could drive too. Now it's all underwater," she continued. Even Cat Island was getting smaller, like Hawaii it's only about half the size that it was."

"Do you think the cause is strictly the change in the Earth's axis?" Trent asked Mariah.

"A century ago the Moon was moving an inch or so away from

Earth's orbit every year. After the shock wave from the Devil's Tail happened the Moon began moving several inches away each year. That, along with the change in axis, is why Earth's weather has been increasingly more dramatic,' she replied. "Why, is there something else that may be causing the harsher climate changes?" she asked him.

"How well versed on astronomy are you?" Trent asked her.

I know the basics. There are eight planets plus Pluto being more the size of a large moon and that the positions of planets vary from day to day. The planets have a steady light or glow and the stars glitter or twinkle. You know, twinkle, twinkle little star, how I wonder what you are?" she said humming the song.

Although the Devil's Tail was eventually seen by the <u>Kepler II</u> space telescope we didn't realize the dramatic effect it was going to have. It was already traveling with such velocity that we weren't able to predict exactly where it was going until it was too late," she said.

"Some of the probes monitoring the Sun like <u>ACE II</u> and <u>SOHO II</u> might have recorded the impact, but there wasn't enough time for them to transmit the information before they were swept away by the radioactive shock wave," she continued.

"Since that time we have sent other probes to monitor the Sun, but they keep failing, possibly due to radiation. We knew that the neutron star provided a new source of fuel and that the radiation levels had increased directly afterwards, but expected the radiation to eventually subside."

"Huh!" Trent said, as if he were looking off in the distance.

"Okay, I've told you what I know. It's your turn? Mariah asked staring at Trent.

"So I can pick out any artifact I want as my winnings right?"

"Yessss!" Mariah said slowly, recognizing Trent was avoiding her question.

"I had my eye on something the last time I was here. Can we have a look downstairs?"

"Hum! Follow me," Mariah said.

They went down to the basement where the Lib stored many artifacts.

The old things found and kept there weren't as popular as the belongings of someone famous like at the Clone Museum and mostly just gathered dust.

Mariah opened a door near the rear of the Lib and turned on a light switch so they could walk down a flight of stairs.

At the bottom of the stairs she turned on another switch to light up the basement that was the size of the first floor of the Lib.

The basement hadn't been automated like other buildings that turned on the lights as you entered a room.

Torian started looking around, "Now where was it that I thought I saw, oh yeah, there it is," he said walking over to a shelf near the basement wall.

He picked up a long black and brown box with red writing on it.

He took it over and placed it on a table and opened it up taking out the telescope.

Inside the box were all the parts necessary to put the telescope on a tripod, along with several different lenses.

There was also a black and white square piece of metal that could be affixed to the telescope to observe the Sun without burning the retina of your eye.

"Just wanted to make sure that it was all here," he said.

He put the pieces that he had taken out back into the box then said, "Here!"

"I thought your team won?" Mariah asked a bit perplexed.

"They did. Now that I've selected my prize it's mine to do with as I please correct?"

"Yessss!" Mariah said again.

"Then I would like you to set it up on the roof of your dwelling and invite me over for dinner a week from now to show me how to use my prize," Trent told her.

"So let it be written, so let it be done," she said as she saluted Trent with a playful gesture.

Chapter 145

"Hey big guy, you're starting to freak me out with those eyes of yours," Thompson told Sec Guardian 2000.

They had been driving in the UCV for over an hour and were driving in a storm on their way to Dover.

The storm was effecting the Guardian's communications with the Supremes and his eyes were alternating from green to yellow.

The Guardian moved his head slightly toward Thompson then back. The eyes blinked a couple of times then remained yellow.

"Thanks!" Thompson said.

O'Doul was driving with Stone sitting in the front passenger's seat.

Jones was in her seat behind Stone watching her monitors, but the screen kept flickering like the Guardians eyes had.

"He's not the only one who's having an issue with communications," Jones said looking over at the Guardian. "Also I'm not receiving any GPO dishes in the area," she continued.

"I know where I'm going," Stone said looking back over her

shoulder at Jones.

Jones looked at Mel and mimicked Stone's "I know where I'm going" under her breath.

Mel held back a laugh.

O'Doul could see lights shimmering in the distance.

"That's the settlement at Dover," Stone told O'Doul. "I have a contact there that can provide us with accommodations and maybe some information."

O'Doul parked just outside the city where Stone directed him to park.

The Riffs put on black rain gear and went outside into the pouring rain.

The Guardian stayed with the UCV.

The sound of thunder was loud as they ran toward a small group of trailers just outside the settlement.

Stone knocked on the trailer door and a big guy with an eye patch opened up the door and said, "What do you want?"

The guy saw Stone and backed up letting them inside.

The guy wasn't very tall but had broad shoulders wearing a green cutoff shirt with Levi pants on.

They took off their rain gear and hung them on a hook next to the door.

Stone walked toward the back of the trailer with the guy with the eye patch for a few minutes then came back up and told the Riffs that they would need to wait until the storm cleared before they went toward the caves.

She told them that two of the trailers next-door were vacant and that they could stay in them for the night.

O'Doul said he would go back and stay in the UCV with the Guardian.

Mel and Jones said they would stay in one of the trailers.

The guy with the eye patch said, "They call me Greg," and took Mel and Jones to the trailer.

"I guess that leaves the other one for you and me?" Thompson said to Stone.

She looked at Thompson and said, "I think I can handle just two hands," she replied.

Chapter 146

Torian left Diego and headed back to Angeles.

He hadn't come right out and told Mariah anything that the Supremes might not want him to say. If she did some research on her own and asked questions based on the premise of showing Torian how to use the telescope she may get answers to questions without Torian telling her.

Mariah knew Torian well enough to know that he wasn't at liberty to just tell her without putting her at some risk.

Even so, if she discovered what Torian was hoping she would, she would wait and discuss her findings with him first.

By looking at the reflection of the Sun through the scope Torian hoped that Mariah would do a little research and realize the Sun was increasing in heat and radiation.

While on the Tram he pulled down the Comp in the headrest of the seat in front of him. He looked at the weather forecast for the city of Angeles.

It would be slightly cooler in Angeles tomorrow due to a storm coming in from the northeast.

Torian wondered if the storm had passed Den Center where he last spoke to Melanie.

"I hope she is staying warm and dry."

When he arrived in Angeles he thought he would stop by the Fish Bowl nightclub, not too far from his dwelling.

When he arrived he noticed that it wasn't as busy as it was the first time he went there. The place only had a few people sitting in booths or at tables along the circumference of the bowl.

There was a young couple dancing inside spinning around literarily dancing on air.

Lacking the excitement from his first visit to the club Torian decided to just head home to his dwelling.

He hadn't heard from Melanie since he left the <u>Metronome</u>. She probably thought he was still there.

He didn't plan on sending her an L-mail until he knew that she was back in Angeles.

Chapter 147

The next morning O'Doul knocked on the trailer that Mel and Jones had spent the night in.

The weather was still overcast but the rain had stopped.

Mel and Jones both came out fully dressed.

Jones walked over to the second trailer and knocked.

Stone opened the door and stepped outside.

"Thompson will be out in a minute," she told Jones.

"I'm coming," Thompson yelled from inside the trailer, hurrying to zip up his jacket and stepping outside.

KJ put her right hand on Daniel's chin and turned his head left and right.

"Hum! No bruises from being slapped. I guess you were good last night," KJ said playfully.

"I'm always good, you might even say, very good," he replied teasing her back.

"So you keep telling me," KJ said.

Stone standing behind Jones said, "He kept telling me the same thing."

"And you didn't believe him either, right?" Jones said.

"Nope, not until he proved it that is," Stone said turning and walking toward the UCV.

Thompson had a big grin on his face.

"Proved it? What does she mean proved it?" KJ asked Daniel.

O'Doul yelled at the two Riffs to hurry up.

"Better hurry up or we'll miss our bus," Daniel said as he headed for the UCV.

KJ stood there for a moment, shook her head, and then said, "Nah!"

Chapter 148

Torian woke up to the sound of dogs barking. He opened his eyes and looked at the Comp with the blinking light.

He got up and walked to the Comp to see what the message was.

The Comp turned off the barking dog sound track now that Torian was awake.

Torian saw that there was an L-mail from the Supremes.

He wondered how long it would be before he heard from them.

He was a little surprised that SG or someone hadn't been at the shuttle landing to haul him off to some secluded place and put him in isolation after he landed.

Torian had gathered a great deal of information in the last few days, most of which Professor Strode may or may not want him to share. That was why he was so careful when he spoke with Mariah.

The L-mail had today's date and a time to meet with Supreme Justice Milton.

Milton was the person that Hansen had spoken with before Torian went into orbit.

The L-mail indicated that a Sec Guardian would be arriving soon to escort him to the destination.

Torian hurried up and got dressed. He told the Comp to let Bonnie know he wouldn't be in this morning and if she didn't hear from him by this afternoon to call out the marines.

Of course there wasn't any such thing as marines anymore, but Bonnie would know he might be in trouble if she didn't hear from him.

He approached his dwelling door and as it slid open, standing in the doorway, there was SG.

"Have I told you lately what a lovely shade of green your eyes are," Torian said slightly relieved.

Chapter 149

The Riffs headed north from the settlement at Dover.

Stone told O'Doul that it wouldn't be very far to the caves.

O'Doul asked her if there was a way of approaching the caves without being seen.

She told him there was a dirt road that came in from the eastside of the caves that she had explored when she was little.

Once on the dirt road Stone told O'Doul that they were getting very close.

O'Doul stopped within about a hundred yards of the caves near a rocky outcropping that concealed them from the mouth of the cave.

Stone pushed the button for the door to open and the Riffs stepped out.

"Mel, you and I will take right flank. Thompson, you and Stone the left flank," O'Doul said.

Jones and the Guardian stayed on board the UCV.

Jones used the FLIR to detect any heat signatures being emitted from the surrounding cave. The FLIR wasn't able to penetrate the rock walls inside the cave so she radioed the Riffs and let them know.

O'Doul asked Jones if she could see the four of them and she told him yes.

O'Doul and Mel made their way to the right side of the cave, while Thompson and Stone went to the left.

Stone told Thompson that there was a small opening where they could look inside.

"How do you know so much about this place?

"My parents used to bring me here when I was little. They liked spelunking and would take me with them," she replied.

Thompson looked a little puzzled not knowing the fancy word, but tried not to show it.

Jones was able to hear the Riffs over the open Mic. "Spelunking means to explore caves," she added.

"I knew that!" Thompson whispered into his Mic.

They climbed up several large rocks and Stone peered in through a small opening.

She could see inside the large cavern and the light coming from the mouth of the cave.

"The stalactites are the icicle-shaped lime deposits hanging from the roof of the cave. The stalagmites are the cone-shaped deposits on the ground underneath," Daniel told Kris looking into the cave.

"The way I remember the difference is by thinking of an upside down ice cream cone I *mite* want to share with a good looking gal like you," he told her.

"O Brother!" was heard over the radio.

"Can the chatter," O'Doul said into his radio.

Stone held up her finger to her lips and pointed inside the cave.

Two marauders were walking from the back of the cave toward the front.

Thompson clicked on his Mic three times without saying anything.

O'Doul and Mel hearing the signal stopped in their tracks as they approached the front.

The two marauders stepped out from the cave both puffing on an e-cigarette.

O'Doul heard one of the marauders tell the other about the lousy conditions of having to sleep in sleeping bags on the hard rocks inside the cave.

"How much longer before the rest of the men come back?" the

marauder asked his partner.

"Not till later. Until then it's just you and me," the other replied.

"Glad to hear that," O'Doul said stepping out from behind a rock.

The two marauders started to reach for their guns, but Thompson jumped from the top of the cave knocking both of the men down.

Thompson rolled on the ground to his feet and walked over to handcuff one of the men.

O'Doul walked over to cuff the other.

Mel turned on her flashlight and went inside the cave.

Further back in the darkness she could see large shapes covered with dark green tarps.

She walked over and lifted up one of the tarps revealing a truck underneath.

Stone had followed Mel inside and used her flashlight to lift a tarp up on some hidden crates.

She pulled out her sheath knife and pried open one of the crates.

Inside was a cache of small arms and ammunitions.

O'Doul and Thompson walked in with the prisoners.

"Planning a little get together?" Thompson asked one of the marauders.

The marauder didn't say anything.

"When will your friends arrive?" O'Doul asked the other man.

From inside the cave the deafening sound of motorcycles approaching was heard.

"Oh, I'd say about now," the marauder replied.

Chapter 150

Torian followed SG to the lift and they went down to the first floor.

From there they took the conveyer to a small park with trees and a small manmade pond with a fountain shooting water up in the air.

SG stopped and pointed to an older man sitting on a park bench who was tossing seeds to the pigeons.

Torian walked over and sat down next to the man.

"Hello Trent, my name is Supreme Justice Milton."

"Hello! Mr. Hansen informed me that the two of you spoke about Torian Miller's demise," Trent answered.

"Yes, it was difficult for Don to hear the news that Herman had been plotting to take over the <u>Metronome</u> to try and revive a newly formed faction of old Nazi Germany," Milton said. "It seems that some ideas never fade away," Milton continued shaking his head.

"My understanding from the Riffs was that a man named Hernandez wanted to take control of the city of Angeles, all in the name of his ancestors," Trent said.

"Yes, Guardian 2000 relayed that information to us. There seems to be a recurring theme happening," Milton replied.

"Unfortunately Douglas, the leader of the Vegas Riff unit that was involved, passed away before we could determine what drove him to participating in this universal plot."

Universal?" Trent asked.

"It seems that other continents are seeing a rise in insurrections against major cities as well as the UCA," Milton replied.

"Maybe Professor Strode is right?" Trent said looking at the fountain in the lake.

Justice Milton looked at Trent for a minute then continued feeding the pigeons.

"Deciding a man's fate is a difficult one, deciding mankind's fate is almost impossible, but we must start somewhere," Milton said.

"Man--kind?" Trent said looking at Milton.

Justice Milton looked at Trent again. "I have heard rumors of dissention amongst our created saviors, but as of yet they have not been substantiated. My understanding is that you have made quite an impression with two of them on board the Metronome?" Milton said with an inquisitive look. "Even Sec Guardian 5000 has asked to be assigned to you on a fulltime basis, in the guise of your wellbeing of course. You do have a tendency to be involved in, let's say, unhealthy adventures," Milton said with a smirk.

Trent laughed.

"Now about your visit with Mariah," Milton said feeding the pigeons again.

Trent looked at Milton with a concerned look.

"Oh don't worry; she and Bonnie are just fine. Melanie on the other hand we cannot predict due to her chosen profession of course, but you must realize the significance of your actions. If indeed besides the uprising within the human factor any possible rebellion from the Martians then any or all of you could be deemed a threat," Milton said with genuine concern.

"Is this the part where you tell me that in my best interest I should be put in a safe place?" Trent asked.

Justice Milton looked at Trent and smiled. "Now where's the fun in that," he said handing Trent some seeds.

Chapter 151

Jones was on the Mic telling the Riffs that there were four men on motorcycles and two jeeps with four men each out front.

They had come from behind several hills and Jones hadn't picked them up on radar until it was too late.

Thompson grabbed a hold of the two marauders in the cave with them and pulled them behind one of the hidden trucks.

Mel jumped behind some crates along with O'Doul.

Stone climbed up on some rocks to a higher vantage point.

The cycles came into the cave first then the jeeps.

One of the marauders hopped off his cycle and walked over by the side of the cave.

He started a generator that turned on several lights within the cave.

"Where are those knuckleheads?" one of the marauders said.

"They better not be playing around with that dynamite," another marauder said.

Thompson had used some quick ties to secure the prisoners to the hand railing on one of the trucks. He had also taped their mouths shut with some duct tape.

O'Doul heard the man say dynamite and tried to get Mel's attention.

She was hiding behind some crates and for all he knew the dynamite could be in one of them.

Mel also heard the marauder and was already on her belly crawling underneath one of the other trucks.

A scuffling sound came from her harness scrapping against the rocks she was crawling over.

"Ted! That you over there?" one of the marauders asked hearing the sound.

The marauder walked in Mel's direction slowly pulling out his handgun.

Another marauder followed the first man.

The other marauders where taking some crates from the back of the jeeps and stacking them against the inside of the cave.

Stone made a scrapping sound with her knife on a rock making the two marauders look to their left.

The first marauder pointed in Stone's direction for the other guy to check out. Then he continued in Mel's direction.

"Ted you better not be messing with me?" the first guy said.

As he got closer he lifted up the tarp pointing his gun up at the truck cab.

Mel rolled out on the other side and quietly stepped up onto the running board of the truck as the guy dropped the tarp and looked underneath the truck.

The guy stood up and looked back toward the second marauder shrugging his shoulders wondering what the noise had been.

As he walked around to the front of the truck to look on the other side he heard a swooshing sound as Mel's G-club hit the guy knocking him to the ground.

The guy went down with a thud.

The second guy that had been walking toward Stone stopped and turned around seeing the first marauder fall down.

Stone jumped down from the top of the rock and knocked the second guy to the ground.

The other marauders not paying much attention at the time seeing Stone getting up from her jump pulled their guns out and started walking toward her.

The sound of the UCV was heard outside the cave entrance and Jones was on the P.A. telling the marauders to drop their guns and come out with their hands in the air.

The marauders turned facing the entrance to the cave and Thompson stood up on the hood of one of the trucks.

"We're from the Angeles Riffs department and you're all under arrest," Thompson said pointing his 9mm at the marauders.

O'Doul stood up next to the truck and pointed his gun at them as well.

Mel stepped out and said, "You heard the man, drop your guns."

One of the marauders asked, "Did you say Angeles Riffs?"

"That's right," Thompson said.

The marauder looked over his shoulder at the others and dropped his gun to the ground.

The other marauders did the same.

"Well that was easy," Thompson said with a disappointed expression on his face.

Sec Guardian 2000 walked into the front of the cave and saw the Mel and Stone were picking up the guns that the marauders dropped to the ground.

Thompson brought the first two men out from behind the truck while O'Doul motioned for the other marauders to have a seat against the side of the cave.

The Guardian began interrogating the marauders.

Stone stepped over and asked one of the marauders why they didn't try and fight.

"We heard you Angeles Riffs are bad asses," the guy replied.

"You got that right," Thompson said standing behind Stone.

Chapter 152

Torian sat and pondered what Supreme Justice Milton had discussed with him after SG and Milton left.

Torian took a conveyer to the Lib and stepped into the outer office.

Bonnie was there waiting tapping her fingernails on her desk and looking at the clock on the wall.

"I was going to give you just one more hour before all hell broke loose in the city of Angeles," Bonnie told Torian.

"Thanks Bonnie. I just had a one on one conversation with one of the Supremes," Torian told her.

"Oh I love their music, so you were at the Clone Museum then?" Bonnie asked.

"No, I mean one of *the* Supremes," Torian replied.

"You're kidding. What did she look like?"

Torian laughed for a moment. "Is God a man or a woman?" he asked her.

"A woman of course! Who else would have the sense of humor to create man," she replied playfully. "But I'm awfully glad she did, especially in your case."

"So much for women's lib," Torian said walking into his office.

He turned on his Comp and there was an L-mail from Melanie.

She would be coming back to Angeles in a day or so and wanted to know if she needed reservations on the next space shuttle to the Metronome in order to see him.

He sent a reply that he was back in Angeles and looked forward to seeing her.

He spent the rest of the day reading other L-mails and responding as needed.

The Comp blinked at him letting him know there was a live message from Mariah.

Torian pushed a button and Mariah said, "Hello."

"Hello," he replied.

"Are you busy this evening?" she asked.

"Not tonight, what's up?" he replied.

"I've been looking through the telescope you asked me too and doing a little research. I know you said to call you next week but I was wondering if you wouldn't mind dropping by my dwelling tonight for a little homework."

"No problem. I was just about to leave for the day anyway," he told her. "I'll see you in an hour or so," Torian told her.

As he walked out of his office, Bonnie was getting ready to leave as well.

He walked over and kissed Bonnie on the cheek without saying a word and walked out whistling "<u>Someday We'll Be Together</u>," a song from 1969 by "Diana Ross & The Supremes."

Bonnie blushed slightly, picked up her purse and left humming the same song.

Chapter 153

Another Riff unit from Salt City showed up to confiscate the marauder's supplies.

Sec Guardian 2000 had applied judgments against the marauders, most of who were let go with a warning that there would not be a second chance.

KJ told Mel that she had an L-mail from Torian.

Mel had a big smile on her face knowing that Trent was back in Angeles waiting for her.

O'Doul came into the UCV and saw Jones inside.

"Where's Thompson this time?" O'Doul asked.

"I believe he is keeping up with inner lateral relations between cities," Jones said pointing out the window.

Daniel was kissing Kris near the front of the cave.

He turned and jogged toward the UCV waving at the Angeles Riffs.

"Every dog must have his day," KJ said with a smile.

"Okay, now where is Mel? O'Doul asked.

"Looks like she is hitch hiking it back to Angeles," Jones said looking out the front window of the UCV and pointing up in the air.

Mel was looking down and waving goodbye as the helicopter with a Sec Guardian flying it lifted off.

Epilogue

Torian was on the roof above Mariah's dwelling.

The telescope was pointing at the setting Sun as the reflection faded away on the white metal square that kept them from hurting their eyes.

Mariah walked over to a small table and poured some chocolate milk into some cups. As she did she looked up and saw someone step out onto the roof from the access door. Mariah smiled and left the two cups on the table as she walked over and gave the person a hug and then left the way the newcomer had arrived.

Torian removed the square and the straight lens now that the Sun had set, putting on a ninety-degree lens, and then pointed the scope into the night sky.

He pulled up a chair and sat down, looking directly into the lens.

He put his right hand up in the air and waved as if someone was looking down at him.

Melanie walked over with the cups that Mariah had poured wondering who the heck Trent was waving at and looked up into the night sky.

On the rooftop of the building next to Mariah's there was a hooded figure peering down at the Angeles Torian. The hooded figure also looked up briefly but then back down at the two figures on the roof below, lifted a rifle to his shoulder and looked through the scope on top of the rifle. The figure aligned the crosshairs onto the back of the Torian's neck.

Torian suddenly slapped the back of his neck with his right hand startling Melanie as she was standing behind him.

"Darn Mosquito!" Torian said, wiping the back of his neck and looking at his hand.

The hooded figure that had been looking through the scope was now slumped over the edge of the top of the roof with his neck broken. SG standing behind the now deceased looked up into the night sky as well. The Moon and a small round shiny object could be seen on the face monitor of the Sec Guardian, and the word: "Four!" was displayed underneath.